Eternal Threads of Time

Book 1

By

Alice Matthews

Copyright © 2025 by
Alice Matthews

ALL RIGHTS RESERVED.

NO part of this book may be reproduced or transmitted in any form by any means, electronic or mechanical, including photocopying and recording, or by any information storage and retrieval system, except as may be expressly permitted in writing from the author.

ISBN: 978-1-965875-28-5

For the dreamers who know love defies time, that fate is meant to be rewritten, and that even in the darkest moments, magic and warmth can be found in the most unexpected places. This story is dedicated to those who dream of love, redemption, and hope for a better future.

Sally,

Thank you so much for supporting my book! I hope you enjoy stepping into the world of Virelith! Alice

Trigger Warnings

This book contains the following themes that readers might find distressing, please make a note of these if any of the following may trigger you into emotional distress. Violence and gore: physical fights, torture, blood, and injury. Death and loss: grieving, and trauma. Abduction and imprisonment: kidnapping, imprisonment, and interrogation. War and rebellion: themes of war, resistance, and destruction. Psychological manipulation: gaslighting and possession. Slavery and enslavement: mentioned of forced servitude and oppression. Abuse and trauma: emotional, physical, and implied sexual abuse. Dark magic and curses: possession, supernatural manipulation, and evil forces. Betrayal and political intrigue: deception, conspiracies, and trust issues. Fire and destruction: large-scale fires, arson, and destruction. Loss of Agency: characters being controlled or manipulated beyond their will.

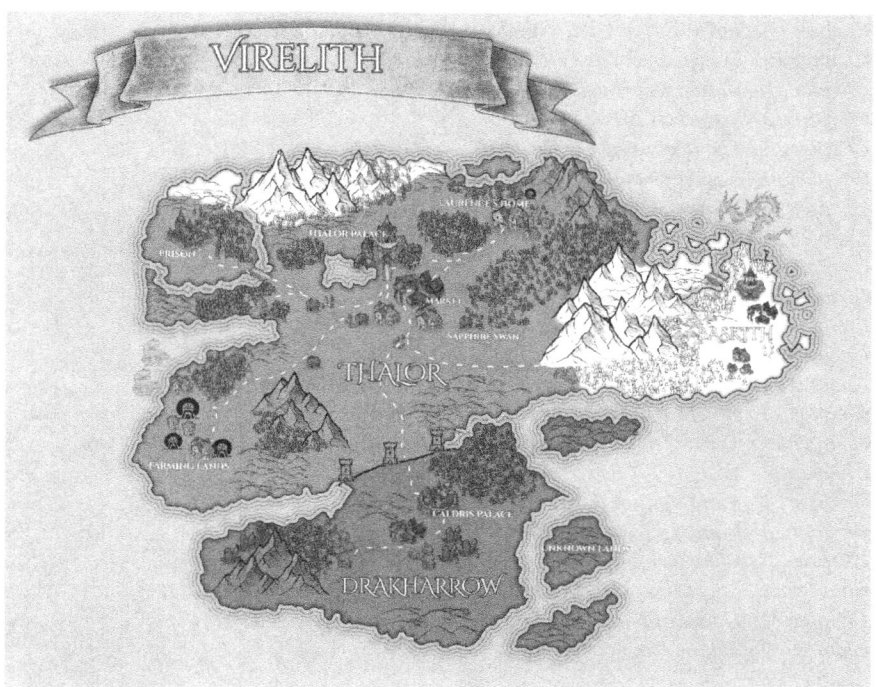

Spotify Playlist

Step into the world of Eternal Threads novel with a curated playlist by the author that mirrors the love, beauty, and chaos of the scenes with how the characters are feeling in that chapter. Simply open the Spotify app, click on the camera icon, and scan the code above to begin your experience. For those on an ebook, the link can be found below. Enjoy!

Eternal Threads of Time Spotify Playlist Link

Prologue - Runaway & Space Song
Chapter 1 - Overcome
Chapter 2 - State Lines
Chapter 3 - Horns
Chapter 4 - Fireflies
Chapter 5 - My Blood & The Greatest Show
Chapter 6 - All For Us & The Chain – 2004 Remaster
Chapter 7 - Who Is She? & Gimme Gimme - Club Mix
Chapter 8 - Solitude & Medusa

Eternal Threads of Time

Chapter 9 - The Power Of Love & Welcome Home, Son
Chapter 10 - Evergreen & Die With A Smile
Chapter 11 - Slipping Through My Fingers & Fade Into You
Chapter 12 - Breath Of A Life
Chapter 13 - The Beginning Of The End
Chapter 14 - Happier Than Ever
Chapter 15 - Willow
Chapter 16 - Work Song
Chapter 17 - Game Of Survival
Chapter 18 - Home & Into The Open Air
Chapter 19 - My Tears Ricochet & Ribs
Chapter 20 - Fire In The Water
Chapter 21 - Lights Are On & Love You In The Dark
Chapter 22 - Where Are They Now???
Chapter 23 - Touch The Sky & Black Out Days
Chapter 24 - Wouldn't It Be Nice
Chapter 25 - Run Boy Run & We Have It All
Chapter 26 - Running Up The Hill & Try
Chapter 27 - Sailor Song
Chapter 28 - I Bet On Losing Dogs & A Million Dreams
Chapter 29 - Home - Edith
Chapter 30 - Take A Chance On Me
Chapter 31 - Lion
Chapter 32 - I Was Made For Lovin' You & Electric Love
Chapter 33 - Army Dreamers - 2018 Remaster
Chapter 34 - Dreams
Chapter 35 - Bitter Sweet Symphony - Remaster

PROLOGUE
Clea

"I'm glad someone is drinking the red wine" Laurence teases across the table from me. The wine swirls in my glass, dark and velvety, staining my lips a deep crimson. Notes of cherry and clove linger on my tongue, the warmth pooling in my stomach and steadying my nerves. Two large glasses in, and even then, it's not enough to dull my senses, but enough to leave a telltale stain on my lips. I stick out my tongue in response, teasing a chuckle from him in amusement, though his own fingers tighten around his glass. We both needed courage. This was the palace after all.

Laurence and Bonnie were the main guests invited, and me by extension. I had never liked the large stone palace, something about it put me on edge. Maybe it's the tall windows and golden chandeliers or that every surface is polished with an inch of its life, no dust bunnies in sight. Perfection always hides cracks beneath the surface. Laurence feels it too by his constant shuffling in his seat. He had visited before for trade, but tonight, they had received the royal invitation. They had insisted I accompany them, one Thalor deemed the *Winter Meal*, it was a grand occasion for the royalty here but was clearly a pretence to showcase their wealth and prosperity, even though those who reside in the land lack enough money to feed themselves and rely on thieving. I cannot deny that the leaders haven't tried, it is vastly better than the previous rulers, but I can't shake the feeling of unease of being in here. Soft footsteps descend into the room as servers of all ages glide in holding trays of steamed vegetables, roasted turkey, and a heavenly aroma of pumpkin soup. The rich scents intensify as the gleaming dishes are gently placed in front of me and all around the table, flashes of soft grey material flicker about as they hurry to fit each dish perfectly on the large space, leaving little room for anything else. The amount of food causes my eyes to widen as my stomach grumbles in protest, saliva pooling in my mouth at the sight. A groan slips out of me as I reach for the lumps of turkey, piercing it with my fork, but just before I can stuff the juicy meat into my mouth, Bonnie coughs opposite me shaking her head with her lips between her teeth. Ah yes, we must wait for the leaders.

I sigh and drop the turkey back to my plate and reach for more of the wine to dull my hunger. She had told me on our journey here that it was tradition to wait for the leaders before tucking into any food. An absurd rule of theirs. But one we must follow if we wish to stay, so I keep my mouth shut - only for Laurence's sake, who wishes to solidify his business deal tonight. My mood is dulled even further as a winged male takes his seat beside me, the scent of charcoal attacking my senses. Flicking my eyes to the name card beside me, a huffed breath escapes me at the writing neatly scrawled in dark grey ink, Evreux.

You've got to be kidding me.

Now seated completely, black feathers graze against the side of my arm as the muscles of his wings push against me, leaving little room to move freely. My arms now squished and pinned at my sides, any attempts to free myself fail from his strength. I had the misfortune of meeting Evreux at Laurence and Bonnie's wedding, he had attended as a representative of the palace, the head guard accomplishing his duties by being an arrogant asshole. The Fae in question had infiltrated my plans in refilling my power reserves, it was a sloppy move made to lure a party guest who spoke improper filth towards Bonnie and had to be promptly removed, their blood drained from their body had been a great solution in my eyes. Evreux had caught on to my actions and thrown me to the ground, chastising me with his hand around my throat and scaring away the fool, his face leaning dangerously close to mine, invading my personal space with a wicked smile shadowed by the moonlight and swaying trees in the breeze. But once his face shifted into the light, his jaw painted in shadows, I barked out a laugh that shattered his timid mood. It was known by many that he was a ruthless enforcer, judging me on my actions was hypocrisy at its finest. Before I could tell him as such, he stalked out of the woods, the opposite direction of the party.

Unfortunately for me, I bumped into him a few times after the event in which he swiftly avoided me each damn time. Not that I care, even if his wicked dark eyes tempted me at first, begging me to uncover his secrets. Out of spite I had stayed away too, not that he noticed.

His wings continue to spread further, gaining more space for himself, and the smirk on his beautiful face grows in place only succeeding to agitate me further. My retaliation was small, but he will find out soon enough. Each time he turned to speak with another guest, I took the opportunity to sprinkle yet another layer of salt onto his food. My eyes kept flickering to the door moments before my attack, hoping to not get caught in the act by the leaders who hadn't graced us with their magnificent presence yet. I couldn't complain, not really, as we were plied with alcohol and gifts to keep us satiated while they pressed their already non-creased clothes. The gift sat on the table before me, the chunky golden bracelet was a sweet gesture, but it was too much for an outsider like me, and the noise of my wrist movements would catch his attention.

Just as my hand releases the salty white dust for the fourth time, a child with dark brown curls watches my movements, his toothy grin widening in mischief. My hand stills, my breath caught in my throat until he leaps off of his chair to patter his feet towards the space in between Evreux and the woman he's talking with. Wedging himself into their conversation, the woman coos and awe's at the boy, and at that my breath releases finding myself with an ally in this dining hall for the mission to cure my boredom and seek revenge on my growing lack of space at the table. His head peaks out behind Evreux and I nod my head in thanks, turning my attention back to the main doors as the leaders finally enter for the evening.

Once everyone is seated, the hunger that gnaws inside my stomach is quickly replaced with joy as Evreux pierces some turkey with his fork, bringing the salty meat to his mouth, my eyes greedily watch his face as he is blissfully unaware of the sodium bomb that awaits him. With a confident bite, his once glorious face transforms immediately, eyebrows vaulting upward, lips puckering as his eyes start to water and his entire body convulses forward, coughs escaping him as his arm reaches for the crisp water needed to rinse down the vile taste. Before I can claim my victory, Evreux grapples the young Fae beside him with a lighter touch than I would expect as the boy releases tiny giggles of laughter, a second saltshaker in his small hands. The movement causes salt to fly onto the table, the golden bracelet turning a darker hue now not under candlelight and a chuckle escapes Evreux too, the deep voice rumbling through his chest causing an unexpected flutter in mine, my cheeks heating without my permission as I lift my gaze towards his lazy smile. Something within me grows at the sound, the resentment I had earlier drifts away out of my body as something warmer takes route. I cough to expel the feeling, trying not to put a label to the emotion that bubbled inside of my heart. It's probably just the common sense leaving my body.

The room descends into darkness so quickly that I miss the cause for the mood to shift, guests around me slump in their chairs, some of their perfect faces smashing into the piled-up plates of food, their hair seeping into the delightful meal untouched by their hands. The grand doors burst open, the hinges creaking as the wood slams against the walls, accompanied with large soldiers tearing into the room with swords raised ahead. Footsteps smash along the clean floors as orders are thrown around, the pounding in my heart growing faster the closer they reach us and my head spins while I endlessly search for anyone conscious. I grab the dinner knife from the table, my instincts screaming at me to stab and slice my way out, hands fumbling from the adrenaline coursing through my veins. To my left, a male Fae's head lulls against the back of his chair, a sickening black stain crawling up his bare arm - attached to the now charcoal bracelet that seeps of an inky substance, the same bracelet

I had taken off mere minutes ago that rests next to my name card. Without thinking, my arms latch onto those closest to me and I grip their arms with as much strength as I can muster, my head pounding in my skull to pull at the power within me lying dormant. I rip through space and time and *pull*.

Wet leaves push into my knees, crashing into the soft grass landing me in a field outside of the palace, my hands stick to the rotting leaves with the force as my head slowly lifts to the once grand palace now leaking thick puffs of smoke. Fire licks up the side of the building as chunks of stone crumble and fall in sickening thuds against smaller outbuildings to reveal three winged beasts the size of houses beating their wings as their claws sink deeper into the palace walls. A soundless scream rips from my throat, my vision blurring as I feel within myself for that power again, I need to transport myself back into the dining hall. But there's nothing I can grasp onto, I push myself further causing pinpricks of pain to bite into my palms.

Bonnie and Laurence.

Arms trembling, I push further and further, ignoring the pounding in my head and crescent shaped puncture marks piercing into my hands.

A hand grasps along my ankle tugging me back gently as my hands sink into the ground in defeat, I push my head to find the arm attached to me belongs to the Fae I had sat next to - his mouth agape, blinking up at me unseeing with his arm outstretched. We stare at each other for what feels like an eternity as stone crashes against stone. A muffled groan catches our attention as we both turn to see the second Fae I had saved, a bundle of feathers wrapped tightly against the front of his body. Evreux blinks awake, his arms tightly bound to his chest as his wings unfurl to reveal a small body curled up in his embrace sleeping soundly. Small arms tinged with cold that causes him to tuck his body in tighter, just as the grey skies crackle and scream for us. As the other two Fae look up at the palace, I can't help but stare at the boy, familiarity piercing through my memory as it all clicks in my head. That face, I had seen it in the paintings around the castle of a young boy standing proud with his parents. Rainwater drips onto my face and arms, mixing with my salty tears as I unknowingly saved the only heir from the attack at the palace.

CHAPTER 1
Clea

Five years later…

The dead tree I'm using for a seat crumbles as I shift my body. It's not the most comfortable of choices, the bark digging into my sore thigh, but it's better than the floor in the barren wasteland we have called home for many years. I watch the flames of our fire flicker and glow in an amber hue, the tips of the flames dancing into the soulless night. The wood spits and cracks, seeping into the dried dirt, drowning out the howling wind and the faint sounds of monsters lurking nearby.

It scared me half to death at first, but we slowly adapted, we *had* to, we have been without a home and on the run for far longer than we anticipated. Fabian, quiet but always scheming, sits beside me. He's talking to me, but I can't hear him over the sound of my heart thumping in my chest.

What if this goes wrong?

What if we change too much by going back?

I focus on his face, the concern in his deep green eyes, as his words finally reach me. "This will work, Clea. This plan will work."

his voice grits out "I'm certain of it" and yet his reassuring voice does nothing to stop my mind from spiralling, this could go *so so wrong*.

"Look at me." he says more urgently now, commanding me to lift my head and face his concerned one "We have gone through each possibility, I can see you're clearly not okay. Do you want to talk about it?"

I shake my head softly, my matted hair swaying gently in the breeze as I fiddle with the golden band around my thumb. The metal, adorned with cracks and rust glides along my skin, instantly calming my mind. I knew Fabian had double-checked, heck, triple-checked the plan, we spent countless hours staring over the tattered map discussing each scenario. Meanwhile, my mind spiralled through every possible failure, unable to settle the unease in my gut. I tend to overthink the worst-case scenarios in my head. The way I see it, if I could visualise the outcome it would make it less terrifying, imagining alternative routes and expectations from others before it actually happens. A bad habit I picked up a long time ago.

"No. My only concern is being trapped in the past reliving that all again, what we are trying to achieve… theft and gods-damned murder of a royal" I blink away the memories that try to resurface, we had exhausted every resource and tried breaking into the palace multiple times. But each time we would never be fast enough, never well prepared, or we'd lose more innocent lives to the rebellion.

Fabian purses his lips, tilting his head to weave confidence in his words, confidence that I do not have "It will not come to that. I can't spend another second without her…" he grips the dirt, knuckles turning pale. I swallow hard, pushing down the memory of

Sophie. We have no idea what condition she's in and if she's still alive at all. On the last day our lives seemed normal, trivial even, was the first and last time I had seen her. Her lifeless face comes into view, a painful reminder of the night that shattered all of our lives. A darkness swept through, ripping away the people we loved, leaving behind only grief and echoes of what once was. Although he disagrees with me, he was lucky to be beside me that night. His mate, however, was not so fortunate. And now, all he has left of her is fading memories and whispered stories over the roaring flames.

The sharp bite of cold metal against my thumb grounds me, a tether to the past - back to the warmth of happier days, before that night stole everything. Before that night, life was simple. We had warm beds, late-night card games, and nothing to fear. Now, all we have are memories, and worrying when our next meal would come, or if we were raided by guards.

The beasts I could handle, their ghastly movements could be heard for miles and they didn't wear the face of someone you once knew, who had a family, forever enslaved by an ancient being. They were stripped of their consciousness, everything that made them *Fae*, now lifeless husks with one sole purpose of destroying the peace Thalor once had. Waking up to our tent on fire was one of my least favourable memories, wearing nothing but Evreux's shirt and grabbing the closest sword near me to defend our makeshift home. It was a close fight, I still bore deep scars in the soles of my feet when there was little time to adorn shoes, if it weren't for Fabian's handmade alarm system of bottles tied up with string, the knocking of glass wouldn't have woken us. It was an oversight on our part to stay there for longer than necessary, we chose it due to the delicious fish that frequented the nearby river. The boys would throw makeshift wooden spears into murky water and Ev would stride out of the river, droplets cascading down his torso to joyfully present me with his latest catch. Even now my mouth tilts up just thinking about it. Later that evening the prized salmon would roast atop a fire, and we would sit side-by-side feasting on its flesh, picking apart the meat from the bones savouring every last bite. I cling to those nights while I spent tonight without him, my anchor to this world and beyond.

"Are you going to be alright, seeing Sophie again?" I ask softly, his eyes shudder for a moment, then harden, almost as if he had forced the vulnerability back inside himself "I can't guarantee I will be my charming self, but…" he winces "This is the best plan we have come up with, going back to retrieve those pages before Eva is taken over completely, it gives us a chance to save her too. She wasn't always this way, she was kind, and she truly cared for her family" he finishes with a nod and swiftly returns his gaze to the fire, adding more driftwood.

Pushing out my hands to the newly roaring flames to warm them, my mind drifts to Evreux and his judgement with his task to rescue those lost to us. He should be halfway towards the prison by now, it was a few days' horse ride, and he took with him most of our soldiers. The prison was a hard place to crack, we had worked tirelessly to find a way to break the wards, well Laurence did, the only Fae who managed to break from the prison during the capture. He had kicked and screamed at us the moment I held him in my arms once freed, pulling at our bodies to free himself to save Bonnie, but he was weak, and the magic potion still ran through his blood enough to dull the senses within himself. Once he healed himself weeks later, he released the tale of his escape and told us of the horrific conditions within the prison walls. I held onto Evreux tighter that night, both of us needing the comfort only the other could give to dispel the knowledge that our loved ones were under such mental and physical suffering. After that night, Laurence shifted into his tiger form and insisted he be left alone, deep claw marks could be found shredded into the trees that still stood tall and never failed to tear me up inside.

It took Fabian, Evreux and I exactly two different library raids, scouring through abandoned homes, and losing a few of our own soldiers to discover the evil that plagued Thalor. This led to our current and only plan, our last hope to salvaging our lives back and restoring the land. First, we would break out those lost to us at the prison, and then we would travel back before everything turned to shit. We couldn't afford more time to wait, all of us tirelessly impatient to do *something.*

This evil, had festered deep into Eva, a sweet and innocent Fae enthralled by the madness of an ancient being. *Eva,* the second in line for the throne, had been manipulated to succeed in lowering the defences of her family. On the *Winter Meal* she had taken over the palace by bestowing all guests with a golden bracelet, then continued to slaughter whoever stood in her way by throwing her beloved sibling and friends in prison. Not only was Eva related to the most powerful leaders in the Kingdom, but she suffered with a hearing disability, and we had guessed that she became invisible to her family over time. Morvath used that desperate need to be *seen,* to be *heard.* And that night, the evil won as the palace was slowly taken over by sickness and decay.

The book with the information on Morvath sits beside me now, the pages frayed and burnt on the edges. It was the missing piece to give us all the answers to what befell on Thalor. It told stories of long-forgotten lands, and a forgotten evil defeated by our ancestors called Morvath that if strong enough - they can possess Fae, controlling their movements to their will. The more victims under their thrall, the more power they gain. The 'hero' in the story was able to defeat them, locking Morvath away rendering them powerless. My fingers lightly touch the frayed pages, and once again nausea hits my stomach reading the description.

'This being is not a demon or ghost but a sentient, primordial darkness- a remnant of an ancient calamity that craves destruction and chaos. Morvath is a patient and insidious entity that can bide its time, whispering dark thoughts until its host is ripe for possession. Once it fully controls someone, it becomes clear that an unnatural evil has taken root. Morvath likes to seduce its victims, whispering sweet nothings into their ears. Fire is the only way to kill the sickness and it can be impossible to completely remove it all from the host. It is wise to be cautious, and the only way to rid Morvath from the world is to...'

Unfortunately for us, a chunk of the book had been ripped out, by who, we do not know.

Typical.

I remember the day we had found the book, hot anger rippled through my body "This asshole had to put the solution to all of our problems in another chapter, but no, the author wanted to keep us in suspense to find out how to trap them" spitting out my words, I contemplate throwing the useless book at the wall - it was damaged anyway, and would relieve me of some of my frustration.

"I wonder who wanted to remove the pages?" Fabian had theorised "If only we could go back and see exactly how this *great hero* trapped Morvath". At that, Ev wrapped his arm around my waist, a comforting weight around my hip as he slowly chilled my temper.

"What, you want a tutorial Fabian? Step 1, Grab the object of choice. Step 2…".

"Well, we know where this book *used* to be." Fabian states, cutting Evreux off.

According to his memory, it was pulled off of the shelf a few days after the annual *Spring Ball*. He had gone there with Sophie for his birthday. Once our destination was confirmed, this led to countless nights discussing time travel, of all things. As a warlock by birth, Fabian practised of course, travelling back a few minutes; an hour, a few days. Each time, assessing the risks and potential outcomes.

On one of the experiments, going back eight days, he accidentally killed a butterfly, Ev and I were cosying up by the fire and looking up at the stars on a rare night we had alone - when Fabian came rushing in like a mad man thinking he might have caused us harm by the aftereffects. Evreux had collapsed to the ground when he appeared, moaning, and clutching his throat. Only for him to burst out laughing seconds later, and gaining a bruised arm I had tended to later that night. "Asshole" Fabian had called him the entire time he whacked him, "Hey, don't hit me, there could be a butterfly on me". I laughed so hard my stomach ached, laced with an unsettling feeling deep in my gut. It was the reminder that although we were cautious, we could never let the unknown scare us, and if we kept trying... kept our people alive, we could find a better alternative for the future of Virelith. Which is exactly what we were fighting for, since we were scattered into the woods, finding refuge anywhere that was not being watched by Eva.

Staring at my hands, I reach within me and find the Sang-like cat purring under the surface of my skin begging to be released. Teasing it to the surface, a small cat materialises in the palm of my hand, purring softly as it curls up comfortably. Watching their tiny lungs expand in a deep sleep, breathing in long waves takes away the bitter edge of the anxious emotions digging into me as I hold onto the book.

"I think I prefer those to the swords... less terrifying. Do you need to refill your *ability* before we leave in the morning?" Fabian asks, now on the other side of the fire.

I blink at him, now realising he had moved during my inner rambling and started setting up his bedding for the long night ahead.

By birth I was forced with an unnatural ability to form large, glass-like substances materialised by blood. A gift I know as Sanguinara, born from the unique mineral grown in my homeland of Drakharrow. This powerful crystal requires blood to form larger and better structured objects, using my own blood has helped me escape tight situations, but drawing blood from others allows me to create even larger and stronger forms depending on the magic flowing through their veins. The power alone is unstable, uncontrolled and disastrous if used without proper training. It is all I have known, fighting the urge within me to tamper down the strength takes more courage than I possess sometimes, and on my darkest nights I wish the power were gone entirely. But I have grown to accept it, a part of me that I can use to my advantage if maintained and kept hidden. Swords are my favourite due to their strength in combat, but gazing down at the small cat sleeping soundly in my palm calms me in ways only a feline ever could. I haven't seen an actual cat prowling the streets in years, a fact I try hard not to dwell on. Even if I could control this power, if *he* found out where I was, the Fae responsible for this gift, Virelith could fall into his awaiting hands. I have managed to remain hidden these last eleven years since I escaped Drakharrow, and I intend to keep it that way.

Brushing my thumb over the soft fur, I drift my eyes over to Fabian lying somewhat comfortably on the ground "I should be alright, thanks, I drank from Hale earlier" I flash my teeth at him for emphasis "He wanted me to make a bird for him".

His head tilts forward, clearly not believing me "A bird? Not a sword, or a rock to smash someone's head in?" he replies, and I chuckle "Yes, a bird, I think he was hoping for a distraction before tomorrow".

I continue to brush their fur in smooth patterns, focusing on making its whiskers next. "How is he?" Fabian asks, looking over to Hale propped up against a tree that withstood the scorches of fire the area had battled against, his chest rising and falling in a steady rhythm and I pause, he was the third Fae I managed to get out of the palace before it went to hell. He has grown up to be one grumpy asshole, constantly avoiding our gazes and focusing on rebuilding our defences.

"As you'd expect, though he doesn't share your optimism about tomorrow."

Fabian's eyebrows tighten, then relax, but he doesn't respond and simply turns over in his bedroll for the night, pulling his tattered green jacket over his torso. Flexing my hand, I dissolve the Sang-cat and lower myself to the ground, feeling small rocks and debris digging into my back, with the fire as a comforting heat beside me.

For the sake of love and friendship, I will fight. And this time, we will not lose.

CHAPTER 2
Clea

The practice runs were nothing compared to this. The pressure pounds into my skull as we move through time, a crushing sensation that reminds me of being deep underwater. As quickly as it started, the sensation stops as my vision clears. Cracked marble stone shifts slightly under my boots, I press my feet into the floor as Fabian follows me through. With a final pulse of pink light, our old life drifts away, leaving us standing alone in a small room wrapped in flickering candles dripping wax. I lift my hand to lean along the walls, the sting of the cold seeping through as the wind batters against the side. Old brooms filled with cobwebs lay across the room, along with stacked handwoven books and draped aprons. I approach the wooden door, the latch closed shut as light flickers outside, clipped footsteps descend the halls outside and my eyes close allowing me a moment to catch my breath. All I can do is hope that once we step outside, our last resort would manifest and we would be standing in the Thalor palace on the eve of the *Spring Ball,* before the evil had taken route. Fabian's hand grazes my shoulder, a featherlight touch to urge me to continue, the calm shadows in his eyes betray the rising panic I can feel underneath and with a final breath, I pull the latch open.

"Right away miss!" the sharp melody of a woman's voice pierces the hallway, followed by hurried steps that sweep past the door, she greets us for a moment before rushing towards the winding staircase to the far right, disappearing entirely.

I snap my gaze to Fabian, his wide smile growing evermore as we timidly press into the hallway to more women floating by holding baskets full of linens, candlesticks, and chunky bars of soap. Lavender and thyme drifts around us accompanied by the crisp scent of freshly washed bedsheets, and inhaling deeply, I return his smile. There are no cracks in the stone walls, light spills in from the windows, and more importantly- no one is screaming.

It worked.

The white fabric of my gloves cools my cheeks as I press my hands firmly along my face, a shocked expression growing on my smile set in place. We had done it.

"Careful with the ink" Fabian whispers beside me, my hands instantly removing the pressure and I attempt to form a quick apology as words stick in my throat. Right. Just before vaulting into the swirly pink mass of my gift, Fabian and I woke at the crack of dawn to paint witch markings along our arms. From his experiments, by doing so would allow our minds to stay intact, otherwise time could rip us apart, not only was that dangerous in itself, but touching another soul within this timeline could have devastating effects. One Fabian found out the hard way. The black ink swirled up and around to my elbow, gloves would stop any lingering stares or questions. I hadn't had tattoos up my arms like he did. If anything, the paintings on his forearm enhanced the beauty of his existing ink, the art unlike anything I had seen before. The cold wet brush lined with the thick ink was a strange sensation, paired with the tingling up my arm as the warmth spread through my bones from Fabian chanting the right words needed, Hale studying close by.

Fabian pulls a grey cloak from the broom closet, tossing it towards me. My fingers tremble as I fumble with the rough buttons, every moment stretching far longer than I'd like. A few moments later, we both descend into the kitchens following the soft voices of other women working and the sweet aroma of pies cooking. Fabian had informed us that the path to the library was directly across from the kitchen along a long corridor. I trusted him of course, he had lived here for many years and knew the place inside out. Our noses carry us into the large open space as Fae wearing similar outfits to mine, prepare sweet cakes, tarts, and uncork fizzy wine. Their bodies moving in a blur, rapidly rolling soft dough and boiling fruit in sugar.

"Fabian!" a woman cries, her legs propelling her forward towards us as her sun-kissed cheeks crinkle with warmth. She stands tall as her hands dust away the flour patches adorning her apron "We made your favourite, apple pie!" her melodic voice drifts through the room, her arms clutching together against her soft body that look like she would give the most extraordinary hugs, squeezing you tight to greet you after a long day whilst wrapping you in a soft blanket. "What are you doing in this part of the palace? You should be enjoying your evening and getting ready to spin that lovely mate of yours around the dancefloor at the ball". Fabian's grin slips a fraction, turning into something sugary sweet that is so unlike the man I know today "Yes, I am on my way now Miera, I strolled down here to grab this" he says, lifting a lemongrass soap bar in the air, and with a wink to Miera he stalks off with his back turned to me.

When did he grab that? Sly asshole.

She beams, turning her body sharply back to the counter to squeeze the lumps of dough into the powdered white flour. "What a thoughtful man! I bet Sophie ran out again" she chuckles to herself, muscles pushing the dough in rhythm with her humming. The kitchen is truly a warm haven, pots and pans dot the walls as the afternoon sun trickles in. Jars of spices lay neatly along shelves with drying herbs tied up in string, bunched up ready for picking.

"Lucy, dear, don't forget to send up those clean sheets to Miss Eva" Miera says behind me, I brush my fingers along the counter as flour clings to my fingers and I bask in the calm of the moment.

"Lucy?" she pushes again, and I turn at her stern expression pinned directly at me. "Oh! Sorry ma'am, are you new at the palace?"

"Uh.. yes! I can take those sheets for you" I blurt out, and for a moment, her eyes narrow as she studies me. Then, as if shaking off a thought, her hair shifts from the gentlest of head shakes as a warm smile spreads across her face.

"Thanks dear, I don't think I have seen your face before?" she asks, carefully handing the linen to me with instructions on where to find Eva's room. My grin quickly dissolves as her hand grazes mine ever so slightly, causing me to pull back sharply.

"Only been here a week, ma'am, my name's Clea"

"Now that's a name I would remember" a voice says behind me.

I know that voice.

His voice.

I could sense him behind me, impatient and restless. The air between us impossibly thick. I would know him anywhere, my body yearns to turn and close the distance. But he... he doesn't know me yet - I knew I would have to face him, and yet, my feet do not move. Clutching the linen tight, I begin to count the scratch marks on the used wooden chair sitting by the fireplace, urging my body to stay still.

"Mr Evreux, it's lovely to see you down here. So many visitors today!" she dusts off her apron, a small red tint to her cheeks. "It's alright, Miera, I just saw Fabian and wondered where he came from, he's acting rather peculiar".

Observant as always, Ev.

Using their conversation as a distraction, I slowly bow and walk towards the exit not moving my head an inch. Once I reach the hallway, I break into a full sprint around the corner, regretting my decision to linger about after Fabian to get information. I thought my mind was stronger, more refined, if a run-in with Evreux could cause me to be a bumbling mess, then Fabian overestimated my mental stability in coming here. Pressing my palms to my face, I shake my head back and forth '*I can do this*' I chant to myself. With those words I hold the sheets tight to my chest, the fabric bunching up into a tight ball from the pressure, and with slow purposeful movements, I make my way towards the library.

Nudging open the grand library doors, I soak in the smell of the leatherbound books and the glow of the candlelight in the room carefully placed and most likely enchanted to not knock over. If Hale were here, I have a feeling he would burn down every book here with a flick of his wrist to find the one we needed. But he knew books had knowledge, and knowledge was power in this Kingdom. The land he would one day inherit.

I run my gloved finger along the bookshelves, gold and silver writing edged along the spines of dark browns and reds. My eyes bounce between books, fingers picking up dust as I go along searching for the specific gold writing I had seen a thousand times, the very book I had in my satchel for so long. That book was imprinted in my brain, staring at it for days on end hoping to unlock its secrets.

My sigh is audible, I had promised them all I would find it without a doubt, but looking up at the *thousands* of books in the collection I fear I may use up all of our time here trying to find it. If only we found a locator spell, but no, Fabian used his spare time figuring out how to change the colour of his hair - saying it would help him against his former self. He had claimed that he could 'sneak attack' his former self if he had bright green hair.

Rubbing my hands along my face, the fabric soaking up my relentless energy buzzing through my veins, I contemplate finding Sophie and asking her where it may be *'Hey Sophie, you don't know me yet, but we need to steal a book so the future doesn't end up like a wasteland, saving you in the future from being enslaved to an old ancient being'*. She would call for the guards so quickly, I wouldn't get a chance to ask her all of the questions I longed to know. Especially why Fabian sleeps with his socks on at night, like a crazy person.

As sly as a fox, I hear him approach, softly closing the library doors, "Found it yet?" he asks hopefully, "Did the green hair work?" I respond, raising my eyebrow, noticing he is now wearing a grey woolen hat, green hair just peeking out. He smirks at me, "Like a charm, he didn't notice me at first. But it was weird… he's knocked out for a few hours, enough time for us to find the pages and get out of here." I nod, continuing my search - I grab the ladder, granting me access to the higher shelves, and it's then I spot it. "Yes!" I cry, grabbing the book against my chest.

I place it on the oak desk in the centre of the room, holding my breath, I open the book and greedily flip through the pages seeking the answers we need. My stomach drops, a leaden weight plunging into an endless pool of despair as dread overwhelms me. This book… it is the exact same as mine.

There are no burn marks, yes, or frayed edges from years of it being outside of a library. But the pages look freshly ripped out, clawed out by the seams as chunks of pages bunch in the corners with dried tears dotting the page. Stealing another glance along the bookshelves, each title is neatly in its own place – every single book neat and organised, just like Grus liked it from Evreux's stories.

Crashing realisation hits me.

"This is in the wrong place" Or rather put back in the wrong place, whoever took it was careless and in a rush.

Fabians eyes meet mine, wide and blinking, the frantic drumbeat of my pulse echoes the devastation etched across his face. We stand frozen, helpless, staring at the book - our salvation to all of this ripped from our awaiting hands. My fingers pull at my hair, a small sob escapes my lips as the telltale pin pricks seep their way across my skull travelling all the way through my arms. The sharp pain does nothing to calm me, nothing to dull the ache inside my heart at the complete failure of our task.

"Someone took it before we arrived" he says, no emotion lacing his words. "How? Who would have taken this book, if not for Eva?" shaking his head and staring down at the book, "She started acting strange *after* the *Spring Ball*, I vividly remember her forgetting Hale's name later in the year."

"We stay until the end of the ball then, it looks freshly ripped, so if we blend into the crowd, we could gain some information from any servants or guards who might know something." Tucking the useless book in the bedsheets from Miera, I steel my gaze, ready to switch to our next task. *I will not fail this time*. "I'm going to find a better dress to blend in, want me to look for some black paint for your hair?" I smack my hand against my mouth hiding my laugh that threatens to spill, Fabian cracking and joining me as a ray of hope splits its way into this moment. "It should wear off in a few minutes, I just wish it wasn't such a *bright* shade."

My head peaks through the first large bedroom on the second floor as time ticks along, the clock against the wall mocking me in our time wasted. In my favour, the majority of the guards and kitchen staff were too busy with the preparation of the ball to notice me wondering around trying to find the direction of the main bedrooms. This place was *huge*. With the book discarded on the large double bed, I make swift work of tucking the sheets along the mattress to hide the tattered book. Only fifteen minutes until the ball officially begins. Running my hands along the bedside tables, the soft dark wood creaks ever so slightly as I shift it open, tiny bedroom objects glimmer in the candlelight – a golden hairbrush, hair bands of all sizes and bookmarks haphazardly thrown in. I push them aside, leaving no trace of a sound behind while snooping about the occupant's room. Moving to the bed next, I smooth my hand along the soft fabric and lower my body to peek under the bed. With no luck, I creep over to the armoire. The wooden structure takes up the entire wall, dark wood polished and gleaming, with small brass knobs just waiting to be opened. Wrapping my fingers around the handles, I pull with little effort to gaze upon the neatly hung gowns in cascades of gold and yellow, the sequins catching in the warmth of the afternoon setting sun – light spilling across the room in hundreds of glowing lights. Something warm and fuzzy creeps up into my gut, a grin seeping its way across my face.

Sophie supposedly loved this colour, for its vibrance and radiance. Just looking at these gowns pushes the visions of her waking up early and adorning these gowns into my mind, smile lazy and wide as she prepares for the day. Maybe with her nose in a book too. Fabian had said she loves to read as I do, to shut out the world. And in these visions of her, I see myself there too, sharing a pot of tea and swapping stories of the heroines in our books. Bonnie is there too of course, laughing in the way I long to hear, and even the thought of her name continues to spear through my soul. But

Sophie... the stories Fabian would share of Sophie late at night over the campfire would feel so *real*, the depth of love between them like waves lapping up on the ocean after a storm.

"Can I help you?" A stern, yet calm voice says to me.

Fuck. I'm caught. Again.

I slowly turn to see the most beautiful woman I have seen in years, well five years to be exact. "Hello" I replied nervously and instantly drop the gown I was holding.

Her gown.

"I'm sorry," ringing my hands together and attempting to swipe the shock, and excitement from my face.

"I was tasked to bring these sheets up to Eva... uh, Miss Eva." I glance down, feeling the blood rushing to my cheeks, and hoping the woman in front of me might just see me as a woman indulging in a little dress-up fantasy in a beautiful, elegant palace. If we pull this off everything would go back to normal, Hale would have his parents back and I would see Fabian smile again, a real smile, hand in hand with Sophie. *Sophie,* the woman I'm just standing here staring at.

"That's alright," she says in a soft voice, like I'm about to bolt any moment. "Her room is just a little further down the hall. I haven't seen you around before. That gown is my favourite, I've used it many times, clothes hold memories, you know? Do you want to try one on?" she raises a manicured eyebrow in question, "I bet you'd look stunning in a lilac gown. It goes nicely with your eyes." She claps her hands once, making me startle, and calls for her handmaidens to come in.

"Thanks, that's very kind, but I must be leaving now." I bow and fold my hands over my gown, pressing onto the fabric to hide my shaking hands. With her back turned, and realising I would be a terrible spy - I brush the cobwebs from my dress, picked up from crawling underneath her bed searching for the missing pages like a creep. It's like Caldris would say, *'If at first you don't succeed, destroy all evidence that you tried.'*

Three women come bustling in blocking my exit. Their arms bursting with an assortment of colourful pots, hairbrushes, and honey-drenched cakes. I look in awe as they push Sophie to the mirror, with eagerness and delight in their eyes. They gush at her, and Sophie smiles back tenderly, "Ann, oh is this the new lipstick I saw in that market?" she takes the small shiny metal tin in her hand and studies it, bringing it closer for inspection, her thick black hair swaying with the motion. "Yes it is, ma'am, it's a thank you for taking such care of my boy this summer by giving him a job in the stables, he has saved up lots of coins and plans to own his own ranch one day," Ann replies with such love in her eyes, the motion warming me inside as my heart is flooded with such warmth and belonging. I don't think I have ever had such a feeling from my elders, nor women who would aid in my dressing, my heart aches to step into the bubble they form around Sophie – but this is and will never be my life. Not if we fail our task, or even worse get trapped here reliving all of the torment again. Would we speak up and warn folk? We'd be locked away to rot, never able to see the light of day again.

Growing up in the neighbouring land of Drakharrow, ruled by a tyrant, my bedroom did not have clothes, maids, or even a bed. I would sleep most nights with the stars keeping me company, the floor slick with my sweat and tears. The older I got, the more *accommodating* the place became, my fate was sealed when I was born for one sole purpose. Those nights his men would call for me would be the ones I dreaded most, when he wanted company only my small body gave him. Caldris would stroke my hair and tell me tales of what I would become by his side, the power I would gain from his touch. Back then I had thought it was love, but now I understand it was possession, he owned me mind, body and soul. And he took it. There were no soft words, bright yellow dresses, or cozy blankets.

I'll wrap him in blankets one day, buried six feet underground.

While the women continue to talk animatedly, I peel my eyes away from the lovely scene and slowly make my way out of the room. If I remember correctly, Eva's room is not far, I need to be more careful while up here, someone will see right through this charade.

"You better not be slipping out," Sophie says, piercing me with a look stronger than a rolling tide, and I'm mesmerised once again by her presence. She rises, and reaches to take my hands, I pull away at the last moment adjusting my hair, "I'm sure we have a dress lying about, we all deserve the night off once in a while. And you look dreadfully overworked."

"That is so kind, thank you," I say, trying to hide the relief in my voice. Without realising it, Sophie has become my biggest ally, at least I didn't have to steal a dress.

"I knew you'd cave. Ladies, I need your help…" she stops and pins me with sharp eyes, "I'm sorry I didn't catch your name, although you look awfully familiar," with her gaze lingering on my face I jump in with the only truth I can tell, "Clea." With so many lies already whispered today, the truth feels right somehow.

A woman I now recognise as Ann holds up a gorgeous lilac gown adorned with sequins, my face brightening as my feet pull me towards it. Beautiful fabric, thick and inviting with small gems catching the light, the corset looked impossibly tight. For an agonising second I almost stop, wanting to hide away in the shadows, this isn't my life – this isn't *me*. I don't deserve any of this finery, or to be with Sophie, I had failed her and the legacy that was built here. Ann steps forward, face dripping with delight as she lifts her concerned eyes upon me and tilts her head in warmth, the single act washing away the bad thoughts that had crept up into me. With her arms outstretched, I step towards her warm eyes with a deep breath.

I undress, feeling my cheeks growing red from being exposed, and step into the gown with Ann behind me, my scarred back bare for her to see.

"I was right about the colour, it definitely suits you. When did you start at the palace?" Sophie asks from her dressing table, holding the golden hairbrush I had spotted earlier.

Ann moves to peel off my gloves, and I quickly shake my head stopping her movements, her hand pauses and she takes a step backwards, a small smile gracing her lips with a knowing glint sparkling in her grey eyes. Now fully dressed, I finally lift my eyes to the large mirror against the wall, my eyes scour along the cascading lilac gown as tears threaten to spill down my cheeks. I had once imagined I would wear such a gown at my own wedding, but ours had been quick and without the full celebration I longed for us to have, our family by our sides. But now, trousers and long tunics were essential for our survival, the clothing was necessary for us to fight, and we needed to wear material that could be soaked in a river, a sweeping gown would probably cause me to drown with the weight of it.

Stealing one more look at the bundle of sheets containing the book for a moment, making sure it is still there. I reply tentatively, "Just this week, I'm saving up money to get back home."

A lie, but in truth all of this is to go *home.* I finally snap my gaze up to my bird nest of hair and grimace at the plaits fraying with little twigs sticking out. Unfortunately, there are no tools of beauty out in the woods, not much of anything really. Sophie gives me an electric smile in the mirror, clutching her gown in one hand and the other with her golden brush and sparkling silver hairpins. Before I can protest, her hand angles up towards my hair as the soothing feeling washes over me like a tide, my eyes close as Sophie continues to make me look normal again. A feeling I cannot recall before the invasion of Morvath. With mumbled words, the smell of lavender and honey filling my nostrils, I decide to savor this moment, because if what we are about to do goes wrong in any capacity… at least I have a story to tell Fabian this time.

CHAPTER 3
Evreux

Earlier that day in the palace...

My fist connects with his face, bone breaking under my fist as the gold ring on my index finger splits open his cheek. This pathetic excuse for a man crumples so easily, the sour stink of fear and the metallic taste of blood thick in air. I think his hair used to be brown, sweat and blood have matted it to his head so I couldn't recall entirely what he looked like before. Sweat is pouring down my face too, soaking my shirt, and dripping onto the floor. My muscles are burning, my lungs working overtime as I try to catch my breath. But I'm locked in, focused on cracking this motherfucker.

"Tell me where it is, and this will become so much easier for you," I command, asking him the same question for the third time - once again he does not respond, only gritting his teeth. I wonder how many severed fingers it'll take before he pisses himself. My guess is two, he looks easy to crack, and I've had a long day.

He is the third person I have interrogated, the others were partially innocent and now lie in our underground jail until the trial tomorrow with Amazu. The air is thick, suffocating me from the relentless questioning, and my new friend here like many others before him spotted the stains up the wall. This special room of mine never gets cleaned, not to Athena's standards, anyway, the small drain in the floor working overtime to allow the bodily fluid to flow out of here and into the sewers. When I started using this room, for the *chats* I would have with people, Fabian joined me and slipped - falling backwards in a pile of vomit and was one of my favourite, yet grotesque memories. It took him weeks to wash the smell out of his trousers, Sophie shoved him into the bath afterwards - pinching her nose the entire time and using up all of her favourite soap.

The smell never leaves the room, it was suggested we paint over the walls, but I have come to enjoy the look on their faces when they wake up, eyes blurry, sockets bruised from the beating - they would know, looking around, that they would die in this room. That's what happens when you steal from the palace, and as Thalors enforcer and head guard, I will do whatever it takes to have justice and rid the land of thieves.

The man's jaw pulses as he straightens his spine again, awaiting my next punch. I pull and tighten the leather restraints on the chair he is half sitting, half falling out of - and grab his jaw, forcing him to look in my eyes. His eyes widen at the sight I am sure he sees, lifeless and ready to continue.

"I will ask one more time, if your answer isn't exactly what I need, I'm going to start cutting off fingers. I doubt you'll be able to steal or have anyone warm your bed without those." He spits on my face in response.

"It's your funeral…" I walk over to the metal tray and inspect the assortment of tools I need to break him. The metal coated with dark red dried splotches - I did drench them in strong chemicals once, when an innocent man walked out and got a nasty infection days later that the healers had a hard job of clearing. But after that I gave up, there's no chance of them leaving this room alive anyway.

I pick up a nasty tool designed to cut through bone, weighing it in my hand, toying with the equipment. His eyes shift to look at the weapon in my hand, raising his eyebrows as his eyes bounced across the room.

Finally, I get a reaction out of this asshole.

"You want to know where I got this lovely tool? I bartered for it, it cost little to nothing, but the seller was a butcher and wanted to get rid of it - said it didn't cut all the way through, not as sharp as it used to be," I stretch my smile, eyes not moving, showing him exactly how much I would enjoy this. "Sometimes it takes one or two slices to cut through, the screams I have teased out of pieces of shit like you are always worth it."

"I didn't take what you're accusing me of" he pleads, eyes widening at my approaching footsteps. The light casts a shadow on my face, leaning forward I throw all of my malice and intent into my face, speaking with lethal calm. "Talk. Now." I roughly grab his thumb, holding it up to the light, assessing the veins in his filthy hands and slam it onto the table next to us.

"If this doesn't jog your memory, maybe my words will. Six nights ago, Sophie - a woman who is highly regarded in the palace, visited the market, and wore a very precious bracelet that was very sentimental to her. One of my guards has an eyewitness report matching your description. Even better, the bracelet was enchanted last year..." His eyes widened for a moment, in fear or panic - I couldn't care less.

For her birthday last year, Athena and I visited an underground witch within the town, they had used the heliotrope flower commonly known to grow in the palace, enchanting the jewelerry with dark magic. Sophie had admitted it was once worn by her brother who was brutally murdered on the street because of who he was, and who he loved. It was a hate crime so heartbreaking, she wore it as a reminder of him, to keep fighting for the right side of history. She never took it off, but being of high value in price it has been stolen once before. I'll never forget the sense of loss her body emitted when being parted with it, without her control. So, we decided to make sure whoever stole from her again, would pay the price.

"...and you see, the spell bound to it leaves a potent cherry scent and once stolen from the owner, it will bring upon the worst nightmares. Tell me Andreas, have you been having nightmares?"

He swallows audibly at my statement and use of his name, tightening his fists, recognition in his gaze.

"I can tell by the deep shadows under your eyes, you haven't slept a wink these past nights, and from my sources - you have been waking up screaming, so you waste all of your money on liquor, and women, trying to rid yourself of these visions. I'd say you're having trouble sleeping." Chuckling, I line up the tool to his thumb, tightly positioning the metal to the skin. I continue my interrogation, "Now, what's funny, is if you had told me earlier where it went, I may have been sympathetic - you have clearly had a shitty life, and I am in no position to judge where we come from and know first-hand the hardships we get in this life."

"Please, man, I didn't do anything…you're crazy!"

At that, I squeeze *hard*. Sophie hates that word.

His screams pierce the room, his thumb half hanging onto his hand as his blood stains the wood. He stares intently at my hand still attached to the weapon. Veins protruding, he thrashes against my grip moaning and cursing words I will not be repeating to Athena in our debrief later.

I squeeze again as his bone cracks and splinters, until his thumb rolls onto the table. He leans forward, face going pale, and vomits all over the floor, and it *reeks*. Whipping his head upright, he began staring at it like it wasn't his own – like it belonged to someone else. His head bobbed, leaning forward assessing the wound and then lazily back to the weapon still tight in my grip. Then the scream came, high-pitched and raw. Using my back muscles, I lift up my wings not touching the floor, that would be a bitch to clean. And Athena would be pissed at me if I turned up to her ball this evening dragging vomit onto the polished dance floor.

"What a filthy mouth. Talk and your nightmares will cease to exist."

I lie effortlessly, the smell of heliotrope no longer sticks to his skin in suffocating potency, it lingers softly and I can see he clearly is still plagued with the darkness of the night. From what I have heard, stealing anything with this spell never goes away, the heliotrope flower was the obvious choice to use as we would recognise it anywhere from growing in own gardens. The sweet cherry scent was sickly sweet and would stick to your clothes when trimming the surrounding bushes. From what we had done to the bracelet, it's a potent spell, one the owner agrees to knowing the aftereffects. After a few moments, his body slumps forward, looking defeated.

"Do you really know how to stop it… Please, you must help me." He whispers, pleading with his voice.

He looks to me like I would stop this, like being here isn't my favourite place in the world, even though I'm loving every second of this.

So, he is as stupid as he seems.

Still holding his hand, I grab the index finger this time, "Tell me where it is." I bark at him, no emotion in my voice. If this takes any longer, Sophie will not be pleased and may even intervene. Her wrath is like a powerful storm through your veins, one I do not wish to experience ever again.

"I… I don't have it anymore, I promise, please don't!" I line up the tool and look at him for a long moment. I raise my eyebrows and tighten my lips, impatience clearly visible.

"I sold it! Stop, *please*. I sold it, okay?" Shaking my head at his response, "That's not a location, Andreas." I say, the index finger now finding its way next to the detached thumb, warm blood now pulsing out of the wound. It truly looks grotesque, two stumps on his hand, not a clean cut by any means, the skin hanging off at an odd angle.

He dry heaves, a dark stain now spreading his crotch, seeing him close to passing out - I slap his face, hard, with the back of my hand. His eyes roll in his head, mouth dripping saliva and vomit still sticks to his chin.

"I sold it to the owner of the Swan." He finally admits, head bowing as his breathing slows, "I told you what you wanted to know, now tell me how to get rid of these demons!" his eyes now tired and defeated, lifting to mine taking all of his remaining energy as the spark of hope lights behind the dullness of his gaze.

"The Sapphire Swan? The owner is a woman with red hair, correct?" he nods excitedly, "Yes! The whore needed payment, she has a nasty temper so I thought she would deserve these wretched nightmares too. That'll teach her for saying no to me." He laughs, looking at me like it's a shared joke between men.

It wasn't.

I decide at that moment to prolong his suffering, anyone who degrades women, especially those who wish harm on them after being denied something they claim is their right.

"Thanks" I say, neatly stacking the tools together as my arms relax in a peaceful gesture. Relief floods his face, and I step around and untie him, avoiding the pooling bodily fluids on the floor. He motions to stand, legs buckling as he sways upright, giving him a moment to adjust – I swing the wooden door wide, and breathing heavily, I enjoy the feel of the clean air hitting my face.

Holding the door for him, he shifts his feet looking unsure. But after a moment he stands tall, clutching his mangled hand to his blood-stained grey shirt.

He stops at the door, head tilting towards me, "Will it end? Will those *things* not appear in my mind at night?"

Slapping his back, I lean close to his ear and whisper.

"No."

Using his shoulder as leverage, I snap his neck and let his body slump to the ground. Blood still dripping from his hand as his head pounds on the stone, his face now leaning in a sickening angle. I'm nothing but efficient, and I have somewhere to be after all.

Sophie steps into the room, hearing the encounter, "So, The Sapphire Swan?"

"Yes. Fancy a drink?" She smiles at me in response, and nods her head, looking down at the piss-stained man on the floor. "Guess he didn't know death or exorcism is the only cure, hopefully we can make it back in time for the ball this evening."

"Don't worry, you will have at least five hours to sort your hair, if we go now," I wink at her, she shoves my shoulder playfully in response. "Asshole."

Chapter 4
Evreux

Standing in the grand hall, I watch as the guests glide and whirl across the dance floor, moving in time with the rhythm of the music.

I decided to dress up for the occasion, Athena insisting I wear my finest armour. I had cleaned the blood off of it a few hours ago, after Sophie and I visited the woman who supposedly had her bracelet. She had it, but unlike the asshole from earlier - she gave it willingly. The owner had wanted to rid the bar from Andreas who had a very high bar tab, she claimed he was notoriously known for never paying the full number of coins for his liquor, and thought the gleaming bracelet in his pocket would have covered it. There were no nightmares or pleadings from her, a thief's treasure passed to someone else as the curse had gone silent, sticking to Andreas like a bad cold.

Sophie and I stayed for a few drinks, catching up on her plans to implement better safety in the areas where there were less guards, where the law can bend and slip unnoticed. She also spoke of her work volunteering at the local schools too - teaching sword safety and self-defence. She is truly inspiring, a warrior by trade but kind in her heart. Her presence within a room of toddlers commanded attention, a blend of elegance and determination that left no room for doubt about her strength. Yet, despite her inspiring aura, she didn't hesitate to push us both out of the crowded tavern with an exasperated sign, her hands firmly pushing me toward the street and back to the palace, back to where our duties lie.

"You smell like a pig that just rolled in shit," she declared bluntly, though her tone carried that teasing edge beneath her words I had known for years. The sharpness of her observation was never cruel, but gut-wrenchingly honest. A trait that is needed in and out of the palace walls, to help shape younger minds into expressing emotions in a healthier way. She had gestured to the grime and stains on my hands, urging me to thoroughly clean up before the ball.

The melodic song of Athena's laugh washes over the room pulling me from my thoughts. She's stood beside Amazu with arms outstretched, long fabric sleeves drape and sway with her movements, weaving her mastery of storytelling. Her charm spilling from her as guests listen intently to each word, leaning forwards and buzzing with enough energy to burn a hundred candles. But that was the charm of the leaders, and somehow, through all of the busy events and long nights – they always have time to speak with each guest that wishes to. As always, the royals are layered with intricately woven designs of black and gold, their hair nestled with golden pins and swirls that catch the light with each turn of their head. The empty throne chairs on the other hand seem to sink into the darkness, collecting metaphorical spider webs from the misuse of them. The last time a royal had used these powerful ornaments, was just before Amazu's father's death, and for reasons I don't completely understand, Amazu and Athena had decided to not use them at their events. You would expect from their position this would be the case, but at each event you would spot them dancing and laughing the night away. Even now, the spark in Amazu's eyes are evident as he watches her with a draped arm around her hip. Their marriage was one of convenience, bringing two lands together to unite Thalor, an easy alliance if war was ever declared by Drakharrow.

A warm, familiar feeling swells up in my chest. Something like happiness for them, but just beneath it, jealousy simmered, sharp and unavoidable. I longed to have someone look at me the way she looked at him, like I was all that mattered in the world. I knew it wasn't right to feel this way, to want what they had, but there I was, rooted in place, my heart tightening with a mix of admiration and bitterness. I stand alone, with nothing but this hollow ache, each time I picture meeting my mate I see her running away screaming. I'm always covered in blood from my position in the palace, not an attractive quality for sure. Don't get me wrong, I've had many men and women warm my bed. But looking into their eyes, I can almost picture someone loving me like that, running with me *into* the fight, leaping into the madness and chaos of this world hand clutched tightly with mine.

I was just a young Fae when Amazu found me, starved half to death and sweeping the floors of cobwebs and rat droppings in the palace prison. He had looked at me in confusion, dressed head to toe in his signature golden outfit. One of the finest outfits I had ever seen someone wear. He was clutching his father's hand so tight as his body trembled with the emotion I couldn't place at the time, "Father, why is there a boy here?" His face would deflate when peering in my direction, but it was the pity in his eyes that made me drop mine back to the floor. It was his family that left me there to rot after all. I had kept my gaze trained on the floor, seeming uninterested at the new guests, his father ignored him and ushering him into the next room towards the largest cell of all down there. Where my mother would cry each night, waking me from any semblance of rest I could gain. My arms ached, but my punishment would be worse if I didn't do my chores.

As a witch, my mother bartered and tricked villagers into bad deals and was thrown into jail, some of my earlier memories were plagued with strange visitors frequenting her cell – eliciting awful screams that would haunt my nights all alone in my lockless cell. Even now, the sound of a metal grate groaning reminds me of stale bread and rat droppings. I had stayed for her, and did not wish to leave the confides of the prison without her. Even now I avoid the cell she once occupied, the memories too raw and unyielding, the echoes of her muffled screams would bounce off of the wall seeming to last forever. Being born and raised in the prison by guards and a mother I could not embrace left me with nothing and no title. Not knowing who my father was, and not interested in the slightest to find out. When Amazu's mother became pregnant too, a bad one at that, he exhausted all of the healers and ended up in a bad bargain with my mother. She spun tales of a wondrous power she could bestow on their son and heal her sickness that befell the mother, promising their son with special powers that would make the strongest men tremble to their knees. Being desperate he believed her, and my mother gave their new born son, Amazu, advanced hearing. He could hear a bird chirping a mile away, and the beating heart of any living creature nearby. They had promised my mother her freedom. Alas, she remained in those same four walls. Once their second was born, a baby girl, my mother sought her revenge in the most gut-wrenching way possible. She ripped the child of her hearing, claiming the magic used for Amazu required a higher price, that it was their fault their daughter could not embrace the world as she wished, that the leaders were responsible for making such a reckless decision in toying with magic and fate. All a lie of course. A ploy to conceal her wicked act, her heart stained with betrayal.

Amazu's father was outraged, he ignored the tutors and his wife years later when they pleaded with him to help Eva learn a different type of communication. Since then, I refuse to train in the magic my mother gave me through birthright, steel is better to cut a man's throat anyway. It's more satisfying watching the blood drain from their eyes from my blade than tricking minds into bargains.

Thankfully, Amazu and Eva never held me accountable for my mothers misdeeds, and Amazu visited me each day in my cell. It slowly became the best part of my day. He even snuck me bread and wine the day I became an adult Fae. A few years later, I was drafted into the Thalor army along with Amazu, the army he would one day inherit. With Sophie by our side, it was just the three of us for many years training and eating together, not knowing what tomorrow would bring.

Sometime later, when my mother fell ill, I left the camp to see her one last time. Her withered hands grabbed mine, and she said those final words that I would never forget, "My son, before I die, I shall grant one final wish. A wish to allow you to fly high away from here, to be who you were born to be." She was half mad at the time from sickness and years spent imprisoned, she passed away a few days later. I didn't hear of the news but *felt* it. Large black feathered wings burst from my back, knocking Sophie to the floor who was reading her book next to me in the gardens, her bewildered expression painted on her face, while I screamed and clawed at my back. The pain was beyond anything I had felt before, stripping me of sleep and the shred of sanity I managed to keep from her death. If it wasn't for my family, I fear I would have fallen into the madness of it all.

Eva, now fully grown, silently observes the crowd from beside the throne, unable to move into the crowd as always. I catch her gaze and sign, "How are you?", she chews on her lower lip, "I'm okay, it's a little loud in here though," a small chuckle leaves me at her sense of humour, giving me a shy smile in response. I never understood how her father or any man could be so cruel by casting aside his only daughter, if the man wasn't already dead I would have hunted him down with Amazu as we had once fantasised about. As luck would have it, they were killed in an accident on a trip to Drakharrow last spring. The difference within a year has been so vast with the work Amazu has managed to do, unravelling all of his father's savagery and setting Thalor right. The final piece is the land of Drakharrow, a dark and untouched land by Thalor. It has been claimed to be the home of an enchanted crystal. Now destroyed, there are rumours of its power whispered over the borders of his land. Caldris has ancient ties to his land, and people. From the stories I have heard, he's a brute Fae who imprisoned women and children. He hasn't shown his face in years, but from Amazu's stories he had graced his presence in the palace before.

    I look out to the dancers again, and promise to do right by them, not caring how much traitorous blood would need to be spilled. Intricately woven dresses and pressed suits shift and move as Fae continue to dance, and just on the edge of the dancefloor, a woman enters by herself in a sweeping purple gown, golden curls cascading down her back that sway with the movement. Her eyes bounce across the hall, her steps purposeful as she maintains a steady pace around the edge of the dancefloor, looking like every shift of her body is being internally analysed to step precisely in a certain order. As she continues to puzzle me, she lifts her head towards the tapestry walls, a frown pulling along her full lips. Her gown had been adorned with all different shades of pink, her hair pinned up neatly with silver pins that accentuate her soft features. Visions of pulling the silver pins out with my bare hands floods my mind, the sharp sting of the metal dropping to the floor layered with our heaving breathing. For a long moment I just stare, I cannot help but watch her endlessly and wonder who she is in the town, and how she received an invitation, I would routinely scour the invite list before each ball, making a note of possible security risks. The palace was open to many visitors this evening, and it was wise to plan for an attack. Just as I sneak another glance her way, she snaps her eyes to mine. Latching onto my eyes as she continues walking, the depth to them locking to my entire being like looking at her was all I was ever made for, what I was born to do. This feeling, raw and new, I hold onto for the precious seconds that tick by. Even now, her gaze feels like she was seeking me out in a crowded room. My feet start moving before I can stop myself, feeling like I recognise her from somewhere. But after I take a few steps, she returns her gaze to the crowd and I feel the loss of her almost instantly. Her body slips into the crowd at the same moment Athena calls over to me, "Evreux! Come, you must try these cakes Miera made, they are absolutely divine."

Where did she go?

I try to follow but Athena steers me away, "I've been meaning to talk to you, I was hoping you could start to train Hale in self-defence?" She says, carefully placing a small slice of frosted chocolate cake in her mouth, "Since his birthday he has a new love for swords and armour, and I'm worried he's going to end up hurting himself" she smiles and shakes her head wistfully, gently wiping at the crumb in the corner of her mouth, "My boy is growing so fast, and Amazu has been so busy with his trade deals, I am not asking as someone who works for the palace, but as his Uncle… if it's too much please say so," grabbing my hand she pleads with her eyes. Those green eyes speak of so much wisdom and promise of a better future, lined with black ink to accentuate the colour.

Raising my closed fist to my chest, I feel a surge of emotion well up inside me. My voice steady but laden with the weight of unspoken loyalty, "It would be my honour." As the words leave my lips, she tilts her head in thanks, her gaze carrying a quiet understanding. In that small gesture, there was grace. There always was with Athena, carrying the weight of ruling Thalor and being a devoted mother all in one. I smile back at her, a shared resolve that needed no further words. At that I bowed at the waist and began a casual stroll around the large room. I took my time assessing the guests, noting their attire and fine jewellery. Men twirled women around the dance floor, and children laughed with their parents. One couple caught my eye, a smile creeping onto my face at the sight. They move together with a harmony that seemed to transcend the moment. Their hands intertwined as their bodies sway in unison, faces lit up with joy so pure it was contagious. Laughter spills from their lips, unbridled and free, as if the world had faded away, leaving only the delight of their shared connections. The way they held each other, arms encircling shoulders and waists, tender yet unshakable, a silent defiance of anyone who might cast judgement. I was delighted in their radiant happiness, seeing the two women lock their gazes and whisper quietly to each other. They were dancing for themselves, and it was beautiful.

My feet land me back to where I started, like some sort of miserable metaphor. My emotions getting the better of me, no matter how far I walk, I always end up in the same place. Standing alone in a room full of joy. A flash of blonde curls catches my attention; the woman I had seen earlier stands alone in the room quietly observing the others as I had. Her eyes look haunted, flickering about the room, and once again I have the overwhelming urge to walk over there and ask her to dance with me. Just one song, a moment I would cherish for the rest of the evening. But before I get the chance, a man who cannot stop staring at her chest takes my place - with clearly more courage than I possess. Maybe I'll get another chance, the night is still young after all.

Chapter 5
Clea

Standing in the *huge* ballroom, the groundsmen clearly took the time to line the walls with bright flowers in lilac, blue, and yellow. Garlands and vines twist up along the walls that seem to move on their own, reaching up high to touch the ceiling, a true mark of spring that never ceases to fascinate me. I don't think I have ever seen this much *green* in years. Each wall is adorned with the hanging banners of the Thalor symbol - a golden background with a simple rose adorning the middle. I had always wondered why a rose kept so much significance to the land, but Athena had smashed her face into the warm pumpkin soup the first time I met her, and speaking with her now seemed like a risky move. Along the edges of the room showcase long tables, sparkling wine carefully placed on every surface perfectly held in small pink glasses that look freshly polished. But that's not what catches my attention, no, it is the fresh roses and paper in the shape of butterflies that are scattered around the table, the paper lifting with an unknown magic as the wings push and float around the table. As soon as I entered the ball, I was overwhelmed by the glamorous bodies covered in fine silk, feeling every step into the room weighed heavily on my mind. Along with dodging any butterflies or prancing feet, I had looked at the walls searching for the diamonds rumoured to have been on the walls, I had overheard that rumour a long time ago and a huge part of me was always curious if it was true.

Unsurprisingly, it wasn't.

I spot Fabian in the crowd, dancing with Sophie, hoping this is the Fabian I have grown to know all of these years. He spins her effortlessly, like he has known her body all of his life, my eyes find the scar on his eyebrow that has my shoulders easing a fraction. He got that seven months ago when our camp was raided, when Evreux was captured by a man that served Caldris - I will never forget the terror I faced in saving him, once again too late, when he had the only memory of his mother ripped from his back. Trying not to fall into the emptiness of that memory to keep the pleased smile on my face, Fabian is just barely keeping his face composed, gripping her so tight. I'm surprised no one else sees the longing and happiness in his gaze being apart from her for so long, or his bandaged arm concealed under his jacket. Looks like the current Fabian in this world had put up a fight. We had discussed prior that Fabian would have attended this ball, and by knocking him out, he could take his place. I forgot to ask him earlier where he ended up putting *himself.* Now, that was a story I'd love to hear, I can just imagine Ev teasing him about being careful not to touch each other and how their fight went. I wonder if he left some water and food for him, after all he knows him as well as he knows himself, and Fabian does *not* like to be tied up. I stand here wondering if all our secrets were spilled to him to keep him quiet when a man who has been staring at my breasts the past seven minutes says to me "Miss, would you like to dance?" a hot hand rests on my lower spine, his arm curving up around me locking me in place.

"Alright," I manage to say, turning towards him as his arm adjusts. He wears a crisp grey suit, and a brass chain that swings along his chest clipped to the jacket. I try to ignore the unease at which his hand presses into me, urging me forward into his body, his footsteps are light as he moves us in sync with the other dancers, and I'm grateful he's a similar height to me so I can peer atop his thinning hair keeping an eye on the room. Even though dancing with a total stranger was not part of the plan, I can't help but get lost in the sensation of moving in tandem to the enchanting music, if only for the distraction it gives my heart and mind, ignoring everything we will face tonight. Smiling to myself, I soak in the radiance of the room filled with the scent of freshly cut roses and beautiful gowns, something I don't think I'll ever get the pleasure of doing again. One step out of line and I'll probably be thrown in the dungeons, or worse, interrogated by my husband.

"The palace is exquisite tonight; wouldn't you agree?" I ask conversationally.

"It does, not as *exquisite* as you, you light up the room. What can I call you? I see no wedding ring, nor a man by your side." My dance partner is persistent, and observant it seems, noticing no ring hidden below my glove.

Silently apologising to Evreux in my head, I smile sweetly and respond, "No, I attend these balls, but alas I never find a suitable man who has the same interests as I do."

"And what might those interests be?" he asks, eyebrow lifting as he keeps my gaze, listening intently to my response.

"I love to read, I long to have a library in my home filled with books. You look like you would enjoy a good story, do you, sir, know any good books?" his eyes crinkle with warmth at that, "I do, my house has a library two stories high. I quite enjoy a mystery book, and a thriller now and then."

Smiling to myself that he took the bait, I push for the information I seek with the mangled book in the library.

"Oh, I love a good mystery myself. I actually came across a book recently… a bit unusual, though, there are a few pages missing. Have you ever come across something like that?" He shakes his head in confusion, "I don't see why anyone would rip pages out of a book, very unusual indeed." As quickly as the dance started the song comes to an end, shifting my body towards the entrance I catch Fabian's view. His eyes deflate for a heart-breaking moment as realisation hits him, his dance with Sophie is over, what must come next will be one of the hardest things he's ever had to do. I tilt my head in acknowledgement and blink twice. *I'm ready.* He excuses her reluctantly, arms lingering on her long sleeves for a few beats until he turns abruptly and strides over towards the direction of the thrones, to Eva.

I spring into action, politely excusing my dance partner with an excuse to powder my nose, internally eye rolling at the final brush of his hand along my ass, and I try to ignore the stare I can feel drilled into my back as I step towards Sophie. My plan is to distract her long enough for Fabian to complete this task, if he's able to gain the information required, we can portal out of here the moment he has those pages. My hand taps on her shoulder, her body instantly whipping around to grab mine as electricity bolts through my body – waves upon waves shooting up my arm and down to my toes. I attempt to rip my arm away, but I'm mesmerised by the storm that brews behind her eyes as her black locks lift from the static.

"I'm sorry! Are you alright? I get jumpy in large crowds and my instincts take over from my army days." she says, profusely apologising as she brushes down her hair, clinging onto the thick strands as if she wishes to keep her hand away.

"I do love that dress on you, you can keep it you know?" From what Fabian has said, her sweet exterior always trips people up and can lower the defenses of those around her, she was gifted with electricity in her blood and learnt her skill at a young age with encouraging and supportive parents, with those foundations she then climbed the ranks quickly and became a close ally to Amazu. Not only was she strong, but she could paralyse a Fae in seconds, a valuable skill indeed. I can't help but look at her in wonder, knowing so much yet so little about this woman. Even those skills are useless now in her eternal prison back home. With the lack of food, water and use of magical cuffs discovered by Laurence, she became immobile and unable to free herself. My gaze drifts to her mate, now talking with Eva, his body vibrates as his fists scrunch together at his sides - barely controlling his rage.

That could be a problem. Eva has been reading body language and facial cues since she could walk.

"You look as bored as I am in this room, please tell me you have some exciting gossip or fun stories you can share? Life in this palace can be so dull…" she waves her hand in the air, a casual gesture, one

I haven't seen in so long. It takes me a second to realise I had been playing the part well, *too well*. Acting bored will not gain me the information I need.

"Do you like to read?" I ask, feeling like an enchanted piano that's stuck on one chord.

"My life is in books, if I'm not in the library - you can find me in the outside training area. Fabian and I were just talking about the boring nature of non-fiction. He's been wanting to get into older books lately, but I'm rambling, what's your favourite genre?"

A small smile flickers on my face, hiding the chuckle that wants to break free. Fabian can scheme rather well, but his questioning is never subtle.

"I like romance," I say timidly.

"Girl, who doesn't?" she says, laughing in her own way that's warm and sharp, a kind of laugh I could bathe myself in or wrap around me like a coat that just fits right. So much so that it makes me pause, an openness that feels like an invitation that begs me to let down my guard, in that moment I could spill everything - to shed the layers of pretence in this conversation. The feeling continues to wrap around me, soft and familiar, but beneath it sparks that part of myself that wants to scream. I miss Bonnie so much it hurts, I miss our days in the library and riding horses, I would do anything to see her once more – away from the torment and cell she's locked into. The fleeting moment digs deep within my heart, and the very reason I volunteered to power through with this plan.

Clearly seeing something in my expression, she frowns, unable to comprehend where my thoughts had gone.

"Have you met my mate Fabian yet? He likes to read too, and I think you would get along. He's not one for crowds though…" The relief I feel in the change in topic is vast but gone in seconds when her head turns to the side searching for him. Needing her distracted, I plaster on my best fake smile and lace my words with so much sugar I fear they would rot and fall out from this facade I have been somewhat keeping up, "I'm feeling rather thirsty, shall we get refreshments?" She tilts her head in confusion as she watches Fabian walk with Eva into the hallway away from the ball.

"Another time, I need to…" her voice drifts off, and cursing internally, I rest my gloved hand on her arm, letting my body sway with the motion.

"I suddenly feel really dizzy, when was the last time I ate?" she snaps her head back to me and instantly holds me upright, her eyes paint a vision of concern I do not deserve.

"You're looking a little pale, come, let's get you some water." We walk towards the refreshment table, and I grin to myself having diverted her attention, then I sway for real this time and blink my eyes to clear the blurriness, when *was* the last time I ate?

A few moments later, I am stuffing my face with cake and sparkling water looking like a savage beast, and not for the first time today Sophie gives me another pitying look. I ignore her stare as the bubbles of sparkling water fizz and swirl upwards in the glass, Laurence had catered for this event once upon a time… wiping the tears that fall to my chin, I correct myself and head to the dance floor, my empty glass tight in my grip.

Feeling slightly better, I begin to sway my hips to the music. Suddenly, a scream cuts through the hall, freezing us all in place, the owner of the high-pitched screech stares wide-eyed at the throne, clutching her necklace. Our eyes snap in her direction, towards Athena holding Eva tenderly, who hunches over clutching her throat, her face a mask of shock and terror.

What the hell?

Two pairs of black boots storm into the room, dragging along something between them. I cast my eyes in horror as they carry Fabian into the room, head bowed with a busted lip.

No. No. No.

Sophie releases a shuddering cry and sprints towards him, clearing a path for me to follow, vines of light sparking along her body. I creep up towards them. The crowd murmur and gasp, accusations are thrown around the room. Words like *traitor* and *murderer* fall from their lips. Fabian crashes to his knees, the guards pushing his shoulders down to keep him there, in front of the thrones. Guests audibly gasp as Amazu and Athena float their way to the thrones amidst the chaos, as soon as they touch the empty seats, the music halts instantly, throwing the room into an echoing quiet. Evreux swiftly joins to motion beside the leaders, his jaw pulsing as he drills his eyes into Fabian. I swear they vowed to never use them, their hands grip the sides quieting the voices around the room as tension thick and suffocation spreads around the ballroom. With all eyes on the leader, and the Fae being held down, Amazu clears his throat and speaks with sharp authority that cuts through the quiet.

"Please tell me why our guards found you with your hands around my sister's throat?" gasps fill the crowd, hands cover open mouths as Fae clutch onto each other. And yet, they lean forward, not caring in the slightest that they are included in a private moment with the royals. Some push to get closer like this is the hottest gossip, and I curse, I too push myself towards the crowd needing to get further not bothering to be polite as I shove my way forward, desperate to get to him. Curling my body tightly, I slip through the crowd. Fabian still hasn't responded, his chest continues to rise and fall, and now up close I could hear the wet sounds of him breathing, it sounds like he's been hit so hard he's punctured a lung and needs a healer soon. My heart beats erratically at the sight, he's too unstable to heal himself, and with the guards with their arms locked around him I cannot get closer with the barrier they have created.

"Fabian, please, tell me this is a big misunderstanding." Athena says, clutching Eva tight with her face set in stone. She's battling something inside, seeing her sister-in-law in so much agony being attacked by a loyal friend within the palace, during her public event of celebration no less. She continues to plead with him with her gaze, the small wince that creeps up on her face tells me she's trying hard to believe what she's seeing – the roughness in which Fabian is being held, and the bruises now layering Eva's neck. I couldn't care less how Eva feels in this moment, I had seen firsthand her act of storming into villages with her infected guards, burning down villages and slaughtering those who opposed her. Even now, a part of me sympathises with her, but it's overwhelmed by the action

Fabian took in attacking her physically. If he were to do so, I believe he would have a valid reason, but the others wouldn't see it that way, and that alone sends chills down my spine at our ridiculous plan now out in the open for everyone to see. There is no more hiding, and Fabian wishes to take the fall.

"Release him immediately, he is not a threat," Amazu orders, with little to no effect as the guards do not move. My stomach drops at the twitching they emit, their entire body battling an inner thought, they feel *wrong*. I know that feeling.

We are too late.

We had gone through the events of these past days over and over, we must have missed something. *Somewhere.* And even though their leader of Thalor had ordered to stand down, their hands tighten around Fabian dismissing Amazu. My fists tighten in outrage, outrage that we were too late to stop this happening – always a step behind Morvath and their plans to infect Thalor. Fingers bite into my palms as hot anger courses through me, no matter what we do, we are always battling the same demon. But why? How are they still powerful now, and furthermore, who set them free? In the book we found, it specified how to kill and entrap Morvath, but who wanted to set the demon free?

"They will not listen to you, brother," Fabian croaks, his head lifting towards the thrones. "This Kingdom has been plagued with evil for far longer than I anticipated, if you need answers, look to your sister," he spits out, not caring who listens, and I wonder if Fabian has had enough of pretending Eva is not a threat. I can only agree with him, but I had hoped in this situation we would be long gone by now, and with the position Fabian is in, it does not bode well with our words. I just have to hope that they would pity him or believe for just a moment for us to escape and plan a better outcome. This has failed spectacularly, and like the crowd, I wait in anticipation as the leaders decide what to do next.

"Did you have too much wine or hit your head this morning? My sister has not done what you are claiming," he turns to Eva and his hands move in intricate patterns to echo his confusion in her language. He finishes his communication by gently placing a hand on her shoulder in comfort, his eyes darkening at the purple hue the size of handprints she now wears as a necklace. A brother concerned for his little sister, the scene turns even more somber as a few Fae in the crowd visibly tear up, clutching their hands to their hearts.

Fabian disregards the act, spitting dark red blood on the floor and his thick brown hair sways with his movements, some strands sticking to his forehead "It's all an act Amazu, please believe me, I'm trying to save you, all of you," his breath turns ragged with each word, pushing a foot to the ground to rise. His statement only spurs more tears to spill on Eva's cheeks, the liquid pooling in her eyes as a sob releases.

I know Eva as a lot of things, but I don't remember her being such a good actress.

Amazu takes a long moment, eyes flickering about the room and towards Eva. He finally releases a breath and stands, eyes locked on Eva as he addresses the crowd.

"Guards, send him to the prison for attempted murder, he will be on trial tomorrow and awaits his crimes."

Crushing dread spears through my heart, the sensation so overwhelming my breaths become heavy and thick as I struggle to breathe. This stupid dress is *too tight.* My breath catches, shallow and unsteady as the weight continues to press on my chest. *How could we be so wrong? This can't possibly be the reality we have worked so hard for.* Then, the sadness settles in as Amazu's pitied stare targets Fabian with a grimace that's layered thick like paint on his face. I feel powerless and adrift, mourning not just what we may have lost, but the person I was when I believed this could be possible.

Taking a few steady breaths to calm my racing heart, my eyes drift to Evreux and a thin layer of hope descends onto me. We have another plan, if we can just survive this evening… but no, if Fabian is captured we will spent longer than necessary here – helpless to stop what's coming. Gripping the glass in my hand so tight, the most idiotic plan comes to mind.

Fabian wrestles in the tight grip, torso jerking to break free as his feet plant on the floor. His voice booms, echoes on the pretty walls, as the crowd turn away in their semblance of sympathy.

"No. Tomorrow is too late, it's *too late."*

Then, in his panic, he says the one thing that stops them in their tracks.

"I am not Fabian, not as you know me," looking at Amazu, his eyes pleading. The room goes still, so unbearably still as we wait for him to continue.

Amazu raises his hand, the movement small but sure. A clear dismissal.

"We can discuss this tomorrow, once the ball has ended."

Ignoring his words, Fabian presses on with his plea, his voice steady despite the tension crackling in the air. Determined and unwavering, he delivers each sentence exactly as we practiced, every word a precise echo of the truth we prepared for this moment. There's a quiet intensity in his tone, each syllable reminding me of every step along the way. Every night building a camp in the woods, each day moving to another location hoping to salvage those still alive. I feel every risk, every big leap we took in those days, each gamble in the air. He knows the weight of what he's saying, to everyone in the room no less, but he pushes forward, word for word, as if the truth itself could be a shield against what's to come.

"Hear my words and hear my truth, I beg of you. I have travelled for great lengths to be here today to right a wrong that has befallen Thalor. A land you have worked so hard to bring peace to. A few months from now, Eva attacks the palace, being possessed by an ancient being, a great evil we never saw coming. I am from the future, where Eva has been responsible for killing thousands of innocent lives. She trapped you all in a prison. The only window is that of a mirror that will hang on the wall for *years* so you can all watch her silent, with no voice, like she has for so long."

Chapter 6
Evreux

With my hand on my sword, I watch as Amazu stands tall assessing the situation, his expression is like a stone wall, impenetrable yet unyielding. But I can sense the turmoil of emotions brewing beneath the surface, desperately trying to break free.

Confusion, anger, and *betrayal*.

I, myself, try to piece together the words that Fabian has claimed about Eva and of all of us. The guards are ones I recognise, but under closer inspection there's a darkness there as they look to us for orders, not us… to *Eva*. My hands curl and I grip the sword strapped to my hip tighter, feeling the air become thick and heavy with a storm that's brewing in this room. My attention focuses on the scene before me, the crowd blurring into the background as I assess the words spoken.

I had met Fabian when Sophie found him in a tavern one night, drunk off wine and slurring his words, but it was love at first sight. He helped her soften those sharp edges I always knew she had and brought out a side to her I had never known myself - heck, at their wedding Fabian and I stood on the balcony talking about how their love restored his own faith in relationships and family. There was a warmth in the way he spoke, genuine emotion brimming at the surface. Ever since then he had become like a brother to me, always trying to show me the wonders of the gift we both inherited at birth. After becoming uncles to Hale, our bond grew stronger - both of us would walk him to and from school and compete over who could get the biggest gift for his birthday. I won with a stuffed dragon. Its wings were the length of my thigh. Hale would run around the room spreading the wings of the stuffed beast pretending to ride it, "Look Evreux, I'm flying just like you!", that toy is still his favourite, even though he has outgrown his toys, he keeps it propped up on the small sofa in his room. One night, after a mission that ended in a devastating suicide, I had crept into his room to check up on him and saw him clutching it tight and sleeping soundly against it.

A flash of pink catches my attention, and in an instant the blonde woman I couldn't stop staring at earlier now stands behind one of the guards holding Fabian down, in one fluid movement she has singlehandedly ripped his throat clean open using a broken drinking glass, the flesh raw and pulses as his blood paints the floor red. She snaps the neck of the second guard before the first drops to the ground. With her arm upraised, the broken glass sharp and dripping with blood extends forward as she shields her body in front of Fabian, standing in a defensive crouch. Her fierce blue eyes locked on us, and with a tilt of her head to Amazu, she sports him a greedy smirk. "Lovely party you're having."

Fabian rises from the ground, avoiding the gushing blood currently spreading across the polished floors in thick gurgles. Amazu casually wipes the drops of blood off his face with trembling fingers, smearing it slightly over his cheek, words stuck in his throat. But it's his wife that speaks.

"Who… who are you? You just killed two innocent men, they had families and lives," the woman just shrugs in response, clearly not caring about the duty of the guard. Feeling my jaw clench, I vow to give these men a funeral they deserve. Their murderer trains her eyes on Athena, weighing the threat they pose to the man she's protecting. Her grip on the glass tightens, threatening to shatter in her reddened gloved hand. The room stills once more, guests instinctively step backwards, the man dancing with her earlier now shaking his head in disgust. Not only did she murder two guards at the palace, but her face also doesn't contain a shred of remorse for the action, if anything her expression looks murderous towards Athena. It was odd to say the least, a villager of Thalor looking at Athena as a threat.

"Fabian was not lying, we are from the future."

We.

So they're both delusional.

"Clea?" Sophie chokes out from the crowd, as she pushes her body forward face slack-jawed at the display, her darkened skin taking a green hue at the sight. Clea? I had thought she looked familiar, this is the same woman hiding as a maid within the kitchens. She was rude enough to ignore my presence earlier, I had assumed she was shy or couldn't hear me with her complete dismissal. But, now I see why. She had a mission to achieve, to infiltrate the palace. Did she sway Fabian with her murderous tendencies, the act of a rebellion brewing within the palace walls has my hackles raising and I feel for the anger inside of me, a weapon I use to my advantage. But this time, I find it empty. In it's place, bewilderment digs deep into my gut, an unknown Fae protecting Fabian from a threat none of us can see. Fabian doesn't shift away from Clea, no, he almost moves towards her clutching his ribs tightly. He's a stranger to me now, claiming to be from the *future*.

My guards attempt to hold Sophie back, in their way of causing the least amount of damage, their eyes clear and assessing the situation. Fabian quietly acknowledges the act, mouth tightening at the corner. She tries to catch his attention, shouting in confusion at him, but he just continues to study the floor, throat bobbing.

"Run while you have the chance, Clea," he whispers softly, accepting defeat.

Clea does not move, her muscles locked tight on her target, desperation lacing her face. Her eyes paint a hauntingly beautiful picture, so much sorrow and pain trapped in her eyes - but all of this could be an act, magic is everywhere in these lands, it can burrow deep into someone's mind. It can alter their perception, and ability to think, to move. I decided at that moment to hear them out, before questioning them later after the ball. I imagine tying ropes around her delicate arms, tightening around her wrists. But where I would see fear, all I can imagine is her lips curving into a smile, the same smile she sported to Fabian. She would be hard to crack, but everyone has their limit if you push hard enough.

The thought makes my cock twitch, and I have to adjust my trousers, now a little tighter than before.

"Five months from now," she finally rasps out, voice not wavering ... "Eva attacks the palace being enthralled by a darker and ancient being. She takes over and slaughters so many... we have been on the run for five years, *five years*, trying to free those captured and bring hope back to the land." Straightening her posture, she stands tall as she spews more lies with such fierce passion on her face.

"She painted the streets red, smiling as she sat on her throne. *That* throne." she says, pointing to the chairs they both sit in, Athena shifting at her accusation.

"If that is true, then why are you here? What was your plan, to infiltrate the palace and murder my sister, a royal to this land who has loyal protectors?" Amazu chuckles without humour, clearly done with this conversation, trying to find any gap or flaw in their plan. I have a hundred other questions swimming in my head, but as I attempt to filter through them, I look out to the crowd listening to this scene unfold - children clutch their parents' gowns, and Fae stand protectively in front of their loved ones. My eyes drift back to Clea, her posture mimicking those in the crowd - protecting Fabian, looking like she has known him personally, and I feel my resolve crack ever so slightly. My chest hurts, and my head is pounding, I rub my chest to relieve the pressure, Clea's eyes leave Athena's for just a moment to scowl at me. The movement is odd, one that looks like she has been perfecting for years.

Feet stomp into the room as more guards arrive, my relief is palpable as I begin to move towards them giving them instructions. We must secure the room, clear the guests and close off all doors. This matter is private, not for prying ears. As they get closer, their faces seem lifeless - similar to the two dead bodies still laying on the floor. Their arms sway with their movements, not in the controlled way I have been training them. They immediately latch onto Clea and Fabian, overpowering the two of them, and they are not kind. "Lewis" I bark out, recognising a soldier I had spoken to just a few weeks ago. He had come to the castle hoping for work, and for refuge. He was a good lad, listened to orders, and I could feel he lacked confidence in his stance. Something I could definitely help with. He ignores my words, not hearing his name. I repeat it louder as his hand grips around Clea, her bare skin pinched so tight. Blood streaks just below his hand, fingernails breaking the surface. She grunts low in pain and shakes her head, at what, I can't tell.

"Stop at once. I would like to hear them out in private, Amazu, dear, let us end this party and get our guests home safely." Her husband nods his head in agreement with cautious eyes. Now looking at me, she whispers softly. "Evreux, please arrange your guards. We must be calm when escorting our guests out. I trust we can gain more information on our new *guests* in private."

Metal slides against metal, the screeching so loud it catches my attention. Amazu gently shifts Athena behind him, hearing something we cannot as the guards unsheathe their swords.

"Stand down," my voice commands.

They do not heed, my mouth parts in shock as a guard beside Lewis raises their sword towards Fabian's head.

"Stand down!" the words roar from my lips in panic, feeling the situation becoming more and more disastrous the longer we stand here. I unsheathe my sword too, stepping forward to intervene. These guards will soon understand the gravity of their mistake, and the harsh retribution that follows. But once again, Clea is quicker, she grabs the sword mid-swing, the metal piercing her flesh - blood ripples into her gloves, staining them an even darker shade of red. With the soldier off balance, she heaves her weight to knock them down, snatching the dagger in his boot she makes quick work of detaining them. I creep closer and catching me off guard - she pushes out her arm and a wave of *something* pushes me back. Falling on my ass, I blink up in shock, not recognising that signature of power.

Her pleading gaze is desperate, but I can only watch as the guards advance on her. Kicking them both down, their knees crash upon the floor, Fabian grunts his annoyance, and his body continues to waver. It dawns on me, his head wound is still pouring blood, and his movements are getting sloppy.

"Fabian, are you alright?" I ask, Amazu chastising me with his eyes only for a second, and I see the uncertainty in his gaze when looking back at Fabian, he needs a healer fast – but each attempt to remove him from the room keep failing. Are they stalling? What do they need exactly, an audience?

"Get off me, you filthy demon," Clea spits at the new unknown guard, shaking her arms behind her back as they detain them with ropes. *Ropes.* Her lips pull back into a sneer that's laced with so much venom it unravels the outrage that tries to seep its way into me.

 Eva finally responds, turning to Amazu, signing, "They're out of control. End their suffering, please. And make it quick."

Words caught in my throat, the disbelief clear in my eyes at her statement, Eva has always been the kind and gentle soul in the palace. Always taking care of others before herself. With all the accusations thrown about the room, with all the chaos, and with all of the current dead bodies at our feet... I had never known her to be so cruel.

One of the guards holds a knife to Clea's throat now, it happens so fast - but I swear the man looks up to Eva waiting for permission. Clearly not in the mood to await orders, Clea once again tries to pull from her binds. His face a mask of fury, the first hint of emotion from a guard here, he moves closer to her face and spits out. "I will cut your throat bitch if you try anything with me, the man you put down was a friend of mine." She smiles sweetly to him, "He did fall rather quickly; I guess you both frequent the bakery down the street?"

She must be a local then.

He digs deeper until a drop of blood pearls on her skin, and I have the sudden urge to intervene. She stares dead in his eyes and says the words that unravel me.

"Harder."

The lights flicker up above, and the candle flames glow brighter, Clea's lips curl into a smile like she was waiting for this exact moment, turning to Fabian who has started to unbind his wrists without them noticing. She whispers something I can't hear, but Amazu responds clearly hearing her, "Who. Is. That."

Clea chuckles low and Fabian swiftly joins in, like a shared joke between them. He mutters, "Our backup, I think you'll like him."

A collective gasp echoes through the room as darkness envelopes us, the candles lining the walls along with the chandelier blinking out in seconds. Panic sets in as a crackling sound erupts from above, a cascade of fire spreads along the decorated walls, the heat swirling around the flammable decorations as it creeps towards us. As the guests look up in fear, screams envelop the room as the heat crashes down on us all. It is not painful, but disorienting, waves of fire angrily crash against each other threatening to consume everything in its path. If this wasn't a life-or-death situation, I might see it as fascinating the way the curls of fire bash into each other with no clear movement. Within the crowd, a shadow emerges, dressed in black. The figure leaps at the guard holding Fabian, just as Clea swings her head backwards to the guard holding her, smashing his nose from the force of it. Fire licks up the walls stronger now, and I raise my arms in front of me on impulse, protecting my face from the wrath of the heat. In my periphery, the unannounced party guest brutally slashes the throats of the guards nearby. More blood spills on the floor, my eyes widen from the brutal scene laid out in front of me as bodies pile up.

Yet, as abruptly as it had begun, the flames flickered and died, leaving behind a thick, choking smoke. The decorative candles, once extinguished, reignited, their eerie glow casting long, dancing shadows. A chill wind swept through the room, a stark contrast to the recent heat. Shivering, I blink away the smoky haze, my vision blurring as I try to focus. Emerging from the swirling darkness, three figures materialise.

One Fae leads the group, hands lifting to remove their hood.

"Mother and Father, am I late to the party?"

Hale.

"Hale," Athena cries, echoing my thoughts.

The boy who is currently tucked up in bed, is standing before us all head to toe in armour, blood smeared up his face, with a wicked smile, and looks older. If I had to guess; five years older. I look at Amazu and Athena, who are slack-jawed and shocked beyond belief. We all realise at that moment; they're telling the truth.

CHAPTER 7
Clea

He does love to make an entrance, I suppose. Taking a glance and seeing the longing in their eyes, it's clear they needed more proof. Eva's eyes sparkle with feigned innocence, but a quick, shadow of malice flickers across her face.

Hale stands between us, clutching the crystal I gave him that allows him to conjure a portal too, "Couldn't wait five seconds for me before you start cutting throats, hmm?" He chastises me as his head bobs towards the various bodies laid out in front of us. It wouldn't be in my best interest to point out he added to the pile only moments before. But that's not important right now. All I can do is shrug, my shoulders aching from the effort. Their lifeless eyes stare up at me, all of the pain pulled from their bodies. They look at peace, with the kiss of death on their lips. However, they are disposable after all. If this master plan that we all concocted works, their sickness and lives will dissipate. Lives were stolen forevermore. Much like we will too. I tell myself I ended their suffering, but I doubt the others in front of me will see it that way.

For an agonising long moment, the fear of the unknown hits me. Where will we go? We will no longer exist after all; would we collapse into death like the guards in front of me? Or will we fade into the void… lost forever. I'd hope for my sanity it's the former. The only wish is in the next life, if I ever get another chance from all of the deaths I inherently caused, I will recognise *him. Them.*

My family.

Whatever the consequence, I would pay the price a thousand times over.

"Reading in the library earlier Eva?" Fabian sneers, signing after for clarity. I scoff, like it would be *that obvious* she took the pages. My eyes find her trembling hands, her face in a mask of confusion. Even now she continues with this charade, which is becoming exceedingly boring. Rolling my eyes for good measure, I follow everyone's gaze to see small cuts tracing along her fingers, the skin dry and cracked. It wouldn't take a genius to figure out she had washed and scratched at her hands to remove the ink stains from the pages. She absently picks at her fingers, either the feeling of dust didn't wash away or she's nervous.

Good.

That explains the scratch marks we found, she must have been mad with rage ripping the pages out. Desperately hiding the one truth behind this all, Morvath has infected and taken ahold of her mind, and one way or another she wanted the pages hidden.

Was she protecting us, or protecting herself?

Her hands move frantically, and I curse myself for the second time today for not learning her communication. Athena chokes out the explanation, my breath hanging on each word.

"Cannot get him out of my head," Athena translates, "Who? Eva, who?" She continues.

Athena pleads with her, kindness lining her features, to which Eva collapses to the ground curling herself into a tight ball. Her shoulders shake with uncontrollable movements as she places her delicately scratched fingers over her face. And for a moment, for the smallest of moments, guilt lines my heart.

Hale turns his head toward me, nodding back in the direction of the crowd, a clear signal for me to clear the crowd of witnesses.

On it.

Within our group of four, Hale has always been the leader. Even though we taught him everything he knows about combat, he grew into his position slowly, recognising the royalty in his blood. We are happy to oblige, seeing as he has the most to gain from our mission - his parents, his title, his future *land*. But more importantly, a better ruler for the future.

My feet pivot towards the crowd, now cowering in smaller groups.

"This ball is over, please return to your homes at your earliest convenience." A few shuffle their feet, the eagerness in their eyes heavily weighing on me - they want to watch this play out, making me feel like a damn circus act. Some Fae had ran out when blood was spilled, the instinct in them clear that running was the only solution. Whereas, the ones standing before me take their sweet time in walking backwards and murmuring to each other.

Even from farther away, Hale's voice rings clear, yet tinged with emotion I can't place. He delves into our past and, more importantly, explains why they must resist the embrace they desire.

In all of my years knowing Hale, I can sense the inner turmoil he is facing. Holding himself back from the true emotions buried under years of suffering and poorly developed adulthood. Although he has this hardened exterior, his eyes scream to be comforted by the arms he has not held in years. He was a child raised in war, ripped from his life, and forced into brutality. Keeping his distance, his voice continues to carry the room "The biggest danger we could encounter with twisting the laws of time, we must keep our distance. Fabian discovered a long-forgotten story of a man who wished to go back in time. He ignored the warning and paid dearly for it."

"What were the consequences? We will pay for it, my son." Amazu says stepping forward. Hale takes a hesitant step back in return, voice cracking ever so slightly. "A few hours after this man went back, he saved his wife from being killed, *let's say… spent a long night together*, then once the timeline was restored, she got sick from the impact and died months later of natural causes. I will not risk your life."

Fabian gave us all gloves for this very reason, if we needed to intervene in any way it stopped the physical touch, and strict instructions on what we can and cannot do while being in this timeline - with this being so new to us, and potentially destructive, we took every caution necessary. Those gloves in question, now covered in blood stains have become annoyingly useless. Why anyone in higher society would wear these is beyond me.

As I continue my approach to the departing crowd, a woman in a short coral dress clutches her child and simply stares at me, mouth agape, and I realise, *fear.*

The stolen dagger in my hand lands on the floor beside me, the fear in their faces enough to stop me in my tracks and loosen my grip on the blade. No matter what they are told, no matter what I say to them, they will forever remember me as the woman who killed the guards at the palace and interrupted the *Spring Ball.*

My knees crack as I crouch down to pick it up, the muscles in my legs groan from my time on the palace floor, the feeling of movement becomes painful. The dagger lifts gently from the ground, and I carefully tuck it into the corset laced in my back. Out of sight from the crowd.

Behind me, Hale managed to explain the appearance of myself and Fabian, a hint of a chuckle with the words "I see you have met my Aunt and Uncle," a strangled cough escapes from one of them.

Movement flicks my attention to the confectionery table, the tablecloth askew as a few dead paper butterflies lay scattered along the floor. But just behind it is a small girl, with her arms wrapped around her body tucked so neatly underneath it. Her brown pigtails sway from her movements. *Has she been hurt? Did I hurt her? She must be traumatised if she saw all of that happen.*

I tentatively walk over and slowly squat down to her level, "Hey, are you alright?" I say softly, her eyes flicker to mine and widen at the blood now drying on my outstretched hand. She moves further back and lets out a small whimper. Deciding to change my approach, I reach into my hair, wincing at the movement, and slowly pull out one of the silver pins Sophie gave me with pink petals adorning it. I noticed she spotted my hair piece when I was dancing with the man who seemed overly interested in my gown, well what was underneath it.

"I have something that may help, this hair pin is magical." I coo and awe, showing her the pin in my hand.

"How is it magical?" she says looking unsure.

"This pin always protects me whenever I wear it, and gives me bravery and strength to battle those who hurt me. I bought it from a magical rabbit where I am from," I smile reassuringly.

"If you come out from under the table, then it's yours." She snatches up the pin and smiles, her small body moving out from under the table. Realising that giving a small child a potential pointy weapon is definitely a bad decision; I stretch my arm out to assist.

"Can I?" carefully, without touching her skin, I push the pin in her soft brown hair.

"It looks great! It suits you."

She grins so wide as she stands, her blue gown shimmering in the dim light, standing straight.

"Come on, let's find your guardian." She follows me into the crowd still making their way out of the door, as slowly as they possibly can. I'd happily slaughter some more guards if it meant they would move even a little faster, time creeps along faster than one might think, but I would hate to scare this girl more than she already is.

"Laia! Oh thank goodness you're here, I have been looking for you everyw..." stopping abruptly, her arms snatch the child into her embrace, venom spits from her mouth as she addresses me.

"Stay away from us, you *monster*!"

In all of my years on the run, fighting for those I love, just a few words can shatter me entirely. My head drops to the floor, not wanting to meet her gaze. She turns her back abruptly, pushing the girl in front as she protests with her mother at being parted with me. Taking a few deep breaths, I attempt to wash those words from my soul. As the last guest leaves the room, I push the doors closed and make my way back to… my eyes immediately search for him, Evreux, he always knows how to pull me from my bad thoughts. His eyes are soft, even now. My thoughts shift back to my Evreux, currently in the future. We had all agreed to split our group, we went back hoping to erase the future, and if that didn't work, they were to break into the prison to free those captured; Amazu, Athena, Sophie, and Bonnie. Evreux should have infiltrated the prison if the wards were broken as Laurence promised. As a tiger shifter, with a newly found fascination with explosives from alcohol, he found a way to infuse both Evreux and Fabian's 'witch gifts' into an explosive that was powerful enough to break the magical wards on the prison. The prisoners were so deep inside that the explosion would not harm them, but it would alert all sixty-eight guards in the area. It sounded too easy, but we trusted him, he was desperate too.

With my task finished, I take my place next to Hale as he continues to speak with Amazu. My gaze slips to Evreux again without my permission. His wings tucked in tight, catching the light in such a beautiful hue. One of our favourite things to do was fly in the sky together. Back then, wings would burst from my back using my Sang gifts, they would lift me up into the sky so high. Soaring up in the clouds, the wind caressing my face, feeling free and unchained. But due to the nature of my *ability*, these wings would materialise as sharp spears. A dangerous risk when flying close to anyone. His wings, however, would always remain soft and inviting. Sometimes, I would cheat and sculpt my Sang wings to be bigger than his, he would chuckle and mutter "Size doesn't matter" with a wink that would pulse straight to my core. Afterwards, we would lay together with our clothes quickly discarded. He would hold me with such tenderness, so at odds with his temperament. If I close my eyes, I could feel his feathers lightly brushing my exposed back. Each night the sensation would soothe and wipe away my physical and emotional scars. I hated him at first, but as the years went by, he became my lifeline, my love, and everything in between.

Evreux's wings twitch, noticing my staring, and I pull myself from those memories, ones that will fade and echo into the deep void. I snap my attention back to the conversation, clearing my throat in the process, just as the wall to my right explodes, and a massive beast crashes into the ballroom.

Chunks of stone shatter and crash mixing with the flower arrangements and long green garlands that break like twigs, jagged debris erupts into the room scattering in every direction. Dust fills the air in a choking cloud, coupled with the sharp scent of dirt and rust from the offending beast. The chaos is immediate, shouts and gasps rise as fragments rain down, clattering against the floor and upending the fragile calm that had settled moments before.

Instinctively, I throw my arms up high to create a protection barrier around us all. The larger pieces bounce off and scatter along the floor in unrelenting waves. I whip my head around and a sigh of relief escapes me seeing Ev unharmed, eyes locked on me. He nods his head in gratitude which is quickly replaced with horror at the gaping mouth of the dragon now making its way into the room.

Where the fuck did that come from?

Its massive, leathery wings beat with a force that sends both Hale and I flying backward like a pair of ragdolls. We hit the ground unceremoniously, he recovers quickly, jumping up and yanking me upright to stand with him.

Hale's face looks grim, his skin smeared with dust from the debris. A small gash on his head oozes crimson, and without thinking, I reached to brush the thick hair from his face. He winces slightly at my touch, his eyes briefly betraying a flicker of fear before the expression vanishes, replaced by his usual stoic mask. I couldn't help but wonder if the wall wasn't the only thing that had cracked today.

Then I do something I know they will hate me for, something I would hate myself for. I raise my arms towards Evreux and the Fae standing nearby, creating a clear barrier. They cannot interfere or fight, their lives and their futures depend on it. Fabian, Hale and I stand on the other side of the barrier, preparing to attack this beast that is currently swiping its ghastly claws along the exposed wall.

Its eyes seem to burn with a feral, predatory intent, a glowing amber light searching in the room for its next meal. As it lets out an ear-splitting roar, flames lick the edges of its jagged teeth as both of its legs finally land in the ballroom, the floor vibrating with the impact. My nose scrunches up as the air crackles with the scent of sulphur that thickens in the room. Grimacing at the scene, this once beautiful palace, for all its sturdy stone and mortar, was crumbling under the weight of it.

"Fabian, take out the legs. Clea, can you clip the wings?" Hale barks at us, eyes not moving from the large target in front of us.

"Time to dance," Fabian quips, seeming more like himself. I roll my eyes absently, on instinct with his bad jokes. His smile causes me to laugh, it's quick, but warranted for the situation we have found ourselves in.

The others pound their fists on my shield, shouting at us, shouting *for us*. More soldiers pour into the hall, and unfortunately for us, they're not on our side. My gaze drifts to Eva for a moment, and a slow, deliberate smile spreads across her face as she tilts her head ever so slightly. Her eyes dance with a sharp malice, the pupils expanding to look otherworldly.

Flashes of kneeling in that field come back to me at that smile, seeing countless villages torn apart by the sickness, and being ripped away from the home I had come to love. She must have triggered some mental alarm to warn Morvath, who has unleashed their beasts to do their bidding. We were careless, too distracted with clearing the crowd and the arrival of Hale to notice.

"I don't suppose you brought any backup," I say jokingly to Hale, knowing it's impossible as I only created one portal crystal for him to come through after we did, "Of course I did, look behind you. They've been patiently waiting for the fun to arrive."

Behind me a group of Fae I trained and ate bread with over campfires run towards us and I smile, I smile so fucking wide. Hale managed to bring an army that matched the teeth and claws, I sprint towards the tiger shifter leading the fight, wearing silver-plated armour, and a fierce glint in his eye. Laughing, I grab the side of the saddle and jump on, feeling the wind whipping in my hair at the speed. The ballroom becomes a blur, as I balance myself on his back. As we move, I finally understand all of those months Laurence had been away, refusing communication, he had stated he had his own plans - looking around at the other soldiers charging forward they wear thick furs around their shoulders. Soldiers from Baskith. Laurence brought them here, in the name of their lost queen Athena.

Gripping onto the saddle, Laurence crouches and launches us up into the air towards the winged beast, my stomach drops at the force as my hands grip tighter. In the background, the night sky displays as a beautiful backdrop to this disastrous night. The sharp bite of Laurence's claws latch onto it, using the jump as leverage I leap off into the empty space, flicking my hands, I wield two new blades using my Sang and slash along the back of its neck. The flesh parts easily under my blades, the muscle exposed and raw.

The beast roars, shaking its massive head back and forth, my feet losing the purchase. I desperately grab one of the large spikes protruding out of its back. The spikes are hard as stone, the texture wet and sticky, my hands slip from wearing these stupid gloves. Above me, snarls bounce around the room as Laurence continues his assault on the beast's face, it screams so loud I cover my ears with my free hand. The beast settles for a moment and seizing the opportunity I launch myself along its neck, my dress transforms - I weave pink armour along my legs and latch my power onto the dress, destroying it entirely. With my legs free, I leap up into the air the same moment the beast reaches for me, its talons adorned with sharp claws that I narrowly avoid. Falling, I raise my arms overhead, and with strength I didn't realise I still had, I slice into the right wing with gravity pulling me down, and following orders, I slice the wing clean off.

My feet slam to the floor, and I duck low just as the wing falls with a loud thud behind me. The weight of it pushes dust into the air, making me cough as the room descends in a thick grey cloud. Soft paws hit the ground as Laurence joins me shortly after. He brushes his large shoulder against mine, a huge, powerful tiger acting like an oversized house cat, his fur brushes against my arm as he nudges me with his head. A low, protective purr escapes him, and I can almost see his familiar grin hidden behind those bright eyes, needing comfort as much as I do in this mess. We have been friends for so long that I laugh at the way he has always been so protective of me - a big soft kitty cat at heart. He shifts, revealing a warrior in silver armour with long red hair tied back, his freckles prominent on his sun-kissed nose. We look towards the fight, and side-by-side we slaughter our way through the crowd. I lose count of all of the arms, legs, and heads I slice clean off. We work quickly, in tandem with each other's movements, as his sword swings in the air with the most delightful sound.

"Get off me you ugly beast."

Fabian.

He shouts across the room and Sophie continues her assault on the barrier keeping them safe. Now sending jolts of electricity to it. The power pulses into my bones, screaming at me to bring it down. My feet waver, and my head pounds. It feels as if my brain is being split apart into two, and I shake my head to clear it, feeling in my periphery metal swinging for my exposed neck. I just avoid the blow, ducking low. More shouting fills my head from far away, my mind locked on thickening the barrier.

I need to keep them safe, keep *him* safe.

My body collapses to the floor, the perfectly waxed floor cooling my heated cheek, I steal a last look at Evreux, and in that moment, I realise I cannot stop the sword coming for me. I push my body to my left, just as the blade digs into my arm. It goes clean through and pierces the floor. Screaming, my voice becoming hoarse, and the helpless sensation pushes into me as I'm pinned to the floor unable to get up - my limbs growing heavy as my eyelids threaten to close. My power quickly fades as my blood spills and mixes with the other dead bodies around me.

All of a sudden, the blade is ripped from my arm as Hale tackles the soldier to the ground, smashing his head with his boot. He reaches for me, pulling me upright, concern laced in his eyes. He exposes his wrist in question, the veins in his arms pulsing with the vibrant red liquid I need, but I shake my head noticing him wavering too.

"Let's find Fabian and end this." I pant, as Laurence rushes to my side, holding me upright, his arm clenched so tight to my waist.

Feeling my shield barely hanging on, my brain pounds into my skull pushing my power to its limit.

"Clea," Laurence says urgently, noticing my discomfort, I have to replenish my blood reserves, but I… I do not want them to see the monster within, to see me as a threat to their home. With regret, I grab a half-dead soldier on the floor, "I'm so sorry," I whisper, and sink my teeth into his neck.

Chapter 8
Clea

My blood pounds as I drink deeply from the half-alive bodies lying limp on the ground, the thick metallic taste lingering on my tongue as it flows down my throat, I am so thirsty.

So so thirsty.

It has been such a long time since I allowed myself to divulge myself in blood, and I feel greedy taking more than I need. I unlatch my teeth from the sad soul below me, their skin still warm from their dying corpse. My eyes snap to another who dares to draw their blade at me, their blood tastes sweeter, and I consume *more*.

I yank off the useless gloves, soaked through with dead blood and dust, with them off I get better purchase on my new blades. The metal swords I picked up earlier had slipped slightly and that will not do. The pulsing light of my swords now glow brighter and stronger than before, the flame-like ripple flowing from pommel to tip. Whipping my new swords in a few circles, they sing in the air weightless, like an extension of my arm.

I slaughter them all. These infected things drop like flies as they draw their last breath. I delight in the crunch their skulls make under my boots, the squelch loud for all to hear.

Smoke hits my nose as Hale continues his fire battle with the dragon, to return the favour he gifted me earlier, I place my palms flat on the floor summoning the Sang deep in my veins. It calls to me like a long-forgotten song, and I embrace the warmth of the power that flows through me, dragging me further and further down. Why don't I do this more often?

With one final push, a wave of Sang flows through the floor, a spiderweb of crystals pulse and grow towards the beast and erupts just underneath its feet. Large spikes of fuchsia spear upwards piercing the beast and locking it in place. It shrieks again on the assault, Hale using the leverage to push more fire into its exposed belly.

I spread my attack to my left, towards more guards entering through a side door they managed to open. They scream as spikes twice the size of their body spear from the ground blocking the entrance, their useless bodies hanging off at weird angles. With my arm no longer stinging, the wounds healing themselves, I stab and slice my way through them all, chest heaving. My muscles scream at me to slow down, but I have a mission to achieve, and I will not *run* this time.

I feed in small intervals, enjoying the power it gives me as I slaughter more and more of them. My smile fades, spotting only three left standing. Arms raised in front of them, eyes soulless and faces lacking emotion, they fight well - I'll give them that. Morvath left their fighting ability rooted in their brain, clearly not caring about the other bits and pieces. Their bodies sway as they walk, feet moving like puppets on a string. The one at the front steps forward, looking like one of the men who held me down earlier that Evreux had labelled *Lewis*. Clearly sensing some sort of preservation when Hale so valiantly entered the hall. His pale skin pulses with sickening green veins. I wait a moment, if only because Evreux knew him by name.

He strikes anyway.

Using his body weight, I dive to the left and push my strength into disarming him, his sword still clutched to his arm now lying on the ground. Lewis' head follows swiftly after, along with the two others.

I release the spikes, and I hear the sickening crunch of bodies falling to the floor in piles, followed by a *much louder* one - looks like the beast finally gave up. I follow my gaze to the sound; flames lick up Hale's arms and the smell of burning flesh hits my nose as the dragon was not just slain - but *burnt* alive. Nervous laughter escapes me, remembering that Hale once told me he used to have a big fixation with dragons.

Laurence stands before me with his hands raised. Waves of fuchsia and peach swirl around me, and I blink the feeling away, collapsing into his arms in exhaustion.

He strokes my hair, "It's alright, it's over," he chants to me. His shirt growing wet from the tears that I couldn't stop leaking from my treacherous eyes. I force my eyes to look upon the destruction, fragments of torn flesh are scattered amongst the rubble, as the remnants of multiple guards lay mutilated and sliced apart. Pushing myself further, I scan the room to count all of the bodies, to recall what their faces looked like, what horrific deaths they must have endured from my stained hands. Even as the sight was truly horrifying, I couldn't stop staring at their lifeless faces, limbs torn apart and lying askew, separated by their bodies. I push my face further into Laurence, inhaling the scent of woodfire and smoke, as his presence grounds me in this moment. What have I done? Not only have I wiped out most of the guards, but I have singlehandedly shown my hand to the leaders of Thalor – showing them exactly what I am capable of. If I had been seen as a threat before, I definitely will be now, my brain attempts to pull together all of the scenarios in the future where this could jeopardise the future events I unknowingly caused for myself. Did these Fae have families? Did they have loved ones waiting for their return? I pull at the sliver of hope within me that these guards will no longer exist with our mission complete, the echo of remorse drilling into me as I couldn't seem to stop myself.

But these were infected Fae, I recall their swaying bodies now as I scour my eyes over their clothing. We have battled beasts like these before, only beheading or a slice to the throat will fully put them down. A rather tame death compared to the gruesome scene in front of me, the memory flickers in my periphery of a long time ago in the earlier days. I had pierced my sword through a soldier who hadn't stopped advancing, they just kept going with the sword stuck in their gut. Only for Evreux to slash the head off did that *thing* finally collapse to the ground and stop moving. We found that the beasts lurking in the hidden parts of the darkness would drop the same way too, although fire also became a good deterrent, much to Hale's delight.

My body shudders as Laurence grips me tighter, locking his arms around me as I breathe in and out, counting to fifty and then backwards in my head. This power within me, it terrifies me. This was the very reason I shove it down, the power bred within me by birth overwhelmes me in ways I don't understand. I had tried once to remove it by creating a shape as large as a horse, expending my entire Sang – but I quickly passed out, the blood used within my body ran dry and my face met the ground. Once fully conscious, I still felt it, burrowing under my skin and begging to be released. Caldris hadn't known, how could he? I was one of many he tried to force this power into. My life with his alone could move mountains, but with my combined brash nature? I couldn't imagine the destruction that would make. If Caldris somehow knew the power of Morvath, he would be unstoppable.

Pulling out from Laurence's embrace, I peek my head over his large shoulder, seeing Eva on the ground writhing, a sticky black substance dripping from her open mouth. It pools onto the floor in waves, her body jerking from the movement. Her eyes blink a few times, like a child waking up from an endless nightmare. Just beneath her, lines of chalk have been painted in intricate designs. They're ones I recognise, from the book I held onto for so long. She continues to look bewildered, as her mind races to catch up with itself. Fabian stands beside her, a large chunk of black chalk in his palm that stains his hands, he just stares at her wearing the same bewildered expression.

My heart swells with pride, Fabian had been uncertain the markings would work with the inability to fully test them on someone like Eva. Although she became the second puppet master in Morvath's games, she was never plagued by the zombie-like state of her soldiers. My gaze pivots to Hale too, making his way over to Fabian and slapping him on the back, nodding towards him in admiration. He too, was terrified of his flames when they emerged shortly after the attack years ago. The overwhelming urge to high-five them both creeps in, but I restrain as Eva gyrates on the floor once more.

Subdued, she cracks her eyes open and looks at Hale in confusion, he moves his hands communicating with her at a steady pace. She flicks her wrists in delicate and gentle positions, her arms looking like they weigh a ton with effort. Hale crashes to his knees and for the first time in years, he looks *relieved.*

I drop the barrier, and Athena immediately rushes to her. Bundling her up in her arms, embracing her only like a mother would with a sick child and presses soft kisses to her head.

For a long minute, I count the specks of blood on the floor.

Giving them a moment to reunite, I turn, Hale would want me to clean up the mess we made. And this room has too many dead bodies to be classed as a ballroom anymore.

I spot him instantly, a man lying under a dead body hiding himself. My eyes widen, and Laurence sighs, seeing my target too. Waving goodbye to him, I at least attempt to wipe the smile off of my face. I send a special thanks to anyone listening in this damned world for this special gift, this man is a sneaky motherfucker. It seems Malik tried to hide when the crowd left, and joining the fight, this spineless prick wanted to watch for information. He was a spy after all, and if he reported back to his master, these years kept hidden would be for nothing, and Thalor would be seen as weak. Weak enough in Caldris' eyes to launch an attack he so desperately craved. So here Malik is, lying under a rotting body, trying to pretend we can't see him.

Pathetic.

Damn the consequences of the future, this asshole is dying.

A somewhat believable sob escapes my throat, "Oh! My lord, what are you doing here!" The shock on my face is partially real, he furrows his brows in response, "Who are you?"

I'm getting sick of hearing that. It's a good thing he doesn't recognise me.

My face hardens, "I am a loyal guard, Sir, how did you get in here? I will protect you, come, let's get you to safety," the asshole sighs in relief, looking to me as a saviour. The stupidity of this man astounds me, he clearly is used to people working for him, not questioning why - just too interested in barking orders and retrieving gifts for Caldris.

I walk closer to him with my strides light and casual. He begins to crawl out from under the dead body and pushes her beside like a sack of potatoes, the dead woman collapses to the floor, jaw broken in a grotesque position. Malik rises and dusts himself off, clearly believing the lies slipping from my lips. "Here, take this sword I found, to protect yourself" I withdraw the sword I retrieved earlier from a fallen soldier, just in case my power drained too much.

Spotting the blade, his smile is grateful and demanding as he raises his arm to collect his prize. His hands reach for the blade, the same hands that caused us so much pain for *years*. I had witnessed Malik delighting in the slaughter of innocents when Thalor turned to shit, wanting Drakharrow to have even more of a higher standing in Virelith.

Those hands…they are also the ones responsible for taking Evreux's wings.

Taking his hand in mine, I swing my right arm up straight to the ceiling with the sword, slicing through muscle and bone. His arm falls to the floor with a loud smack, blood gushing from the open wound. The bastard clutches the stump on his arm hopelessly trying to stop the flow of blood, it spurts out in thick streams painting his hand a delicious red and he backs away from me in a desperate panic. His face white as a sheet.

Laughter bubbles up inside me as I have unofficially won the *'Best gift of the year'* a game Evreux and I started to give us something to do on our long hikes through the woods. The trees would always look the same, so we started it simply by who could get the best-looking rock and manifested to who could give the better orgasm. I enjoyed those competitions more than the rest.

"Stay BACK you demon!" He shouts at me, I roll my eyes *like that will stop me.*

"Come on Malik, let me have the other arm and I'll leave you alone." I tease, his eyes growing larger at my words.

"What? Afraid of me? You don't know me yet, not really, I'm doing this for someone I care very much for, but… also because this is going to feel so, so good. Don't recognise me, buddy?"

The bastard walks backwards, sexist and filthy words leaving his mouth as he desperately screams for others to help. Tripping on the fallen woman he had hidden under, his body slams to the ground in a sickening type of karma. His body squirms like the pathetic worm he is, and using the momentum to shift himself backwards, my steps follow effortlessly. Deciding I was done with toying with him, I carefully placed the sword on the floor and built a weapon of my own in my hand. Wanting, no, *needing* to feel him suffer under the same ability he aided in forcing into me.

Karma's a bitch.

The axe swings in my hand, perfectly balanced as I wedge it between his shoulder blades. I swing with little pressure, prolonging this moment and imprinting it in my brain. It takes a few whacks to detach. Dissolving the Sang axe, and feeling smug, I kick him in the balls for good measure.

Hale steps up next to me, shoulders lifting in indifference, clearly not bothered by my display. He reaches down, avoiding the vomit that leaves Malik's lips and brings fire to his hands cauterising the wounds. Keeping him alive. "Thank you, Hale," I beam at him, deciding to leave him here.

We work for what feels like hours, to clean up the bodies and mess of the room. The walls are smeared in thick layers of drying blood. Laurence works beside me, huffing every few breaths and tapping his foot.

"Why are we still here? We did our part, why have we not returned?" I place my hand on his upper arm, gripping it tightly, and closing my eyes. I attempt to at least try to sort out my inner thoughts, but he's right, we had removed the sickness from Eva and by the looks of it, slaughtered all of the infected guards. We should have corrected the past by eliminating it all today, my gaze snags on the golden tapestries now hanging half limply with deep gashes from the beast's claws. What are we missing?

My only guess haunts me, seeping existential dread through my very being - Evreux and that team could be in danger, by the actions of what we have done, and we could very well have altered the future indefinitely. Sickness creeps up my neck as I stand here feeling utterly useless.

Worrying about worst-case scenarios being my trademark, I smile wistfully, "Do you remember the night before your wedding? I expected Bonnie to be nervous, heck I was nervous for her… marrying someone like you," half of a laugh sits in his mouth, and he punches my arm lightly "Not helping" he grunts out. He had been on his own for most of the years we were left stranded, needing his own space. I had not realised he had ventured so far East to Baskith, the warriors there had always agreed to stay out of any wars or conflict. But somehow, Laurence convinced them to finally join the fight.

"Well… she was just so… happy. I had never seen her so content, and hopeful for the future. She barely slept, but when she did - she clutched that stupid blanket you gave her. It was tattered, and definitely needed new stitching, but she would hold onto it with all her might, and I just know that wherever she is, she is holding onto something, anything to remind her of you, she never gave up. And neither will we" his shoulder leans against mine and we take a moment to breathe, "We can be patient for them, as they have been patient with us," I finish. He wraps his arm around me, nodding to himself, and without a word starts lifting bodies over his shoulder to continue clearing up the hall. He proceeds to lift multiple men over his shoulder, and I chuckle, even now he's been a strong brute showing off his strength. It pulls at my memory, and I get a quick flash of the same stance he'd use when carrying his merchandise, shirtless in all seasons as he lifted the heavy crates of wine and beer. By sheer coincidence, he'd always ask the servants to set up tea and sandwiches outside whenever shipments arrived. Right when he'd stroll out shirtless to carry everything into the cellar for inspection. He'd catch Bonnie's eye and give her a wink, fully aware that she couldn't look away. She would blush bright red every time, and one day, she even spat out her tea all over her dress at the display.

Smiling to myself, I continue to pick up discarded body parts, I shout over to him "I'm surprised you have your shirt on this time," he shakes his head, smile cracking, "In your dreams, Clea."

Chapter 9
Evreux

What the fuck.

Of all my years training in the Thalor army, getting hired in the palace, and working as the enforcer for multiple years would never have prepared me for the events of today. Feeling mesmerized and horrified at the same time, I can't help but stare out into the room from the catastrophe that was the last hour in the ballroom. It's torture, to watch them fight and clear up this mess we clearly did not see, an evil plaguing the castle we did not notice. And yet, I can't look away. My eyes latch onto the six-foot-nine warrior of a man, Laurence.

Laurence.

It's clear he and Clea have some type of connection, and rubbing my chest feeling a tightness there, I long to speak to her, and I curse internally at my hesitation to dance with her earlier. To know who she is, and why her eyes flick to mine each time pain lines her face. Her name is one I have been repeating over and over in my head. I am completely and utterly transfixed by her, she has clearly been trained, and the scars illuminated on her arms paint a thousand stories I yearn to know where they originate from. In the hopes that she gives me the immense pleasure of killing every piece of shit that ever inflicted pain on her. But it's not always physical pain, I hadn't forgotten the shadow of pain that crossed over her eyes as the child's mother called her a monster - my hands twitch, a ghost of a feeling of what it would be like to comfort her, erasing all of the harsh words thrown at her and replacing them with sweeter ones, if that's what she would wish.

I bet Laurence does that. Asshole.

Amazu paces in a small circle he created on our side of the room, his mind working a hundred miles a minute trying to piece together all of this chaos. His footsteps echo in the ballroom, his usually regal bearing now replaced by a restless energy. Hands clench and unclench by his sides, his calm eyes were now darting about, a storm brewing in his head I cannot begin to piece together. The future of Virelith had changed today, Thalor being under attack, one we had not anticipated, from within no less.

Athena continues to hold Eva and rocks her gently, her face etched in pain as Amazu continues his assault on the floor.

"We must speak with them, to gain more information. Keeping our distance of course…" he speaks to himself, then looking in my direction, "Evreux, can I trust you to gather your men. Those that are still *alive*, to be ready for another attack."

I nod my head in agreement, words becoming stuck in my throat. My gaze finds Hale talking to Athena from a distance, he stands tall even after facing everything that was thrown at him today, pride swells up in my chest at that. The orders he gave earlier today sounded so much like his parents, considering that at a young age he was thrown from his family and his life. Regardless, he battled through it all and became the leader he was born to be. But underneath, a spear of resentment strikes true in my gut, knowing I couldn't have been there to help him grow up, to train him the way Athena and I had planned to.

But no, Fabian and Clea were there. And *Laurence*. They saved us after all. Carefully avoiding bodies and debris, my footsteps land me next to Fabian, making sure to adhere to their warnings of keeping my distance. He eyes me immediately and looks like the man I used to know, although a layer of grief and weariness weighs heavy on his shoulders. He continues his work of removing the armour from a dead body, and I raise my eyebrow in question.

"No matter the situation, armour and metal are precious, these men and women fought for what they believed was right. Plus, it's a good material," he says, thumb rubbing on the chest plate, tracing the ridges of the design.

"You have lived quite an exciting life it seems," I respond, a casual sentence to dispel the unease I feel. It's uncomfortable looking at a man I have known for so many years and not recognise why his face grimaces when he looks at Eva, or the brotherly love he feels for Clea.

His jaw clenches, a muscle in his cheek twitching as he struggles to contain his rage. His eyes, usually relaxed with mirth, now flash with a dangerous intensity. Each breath he takes is shallow and ragged, a stark contrast to his usual demeanour.

"Exciting? You would call the last few years *exciting?*" shaking his head he continues his verbal lashing towards me, "We fought for our lives every damned day. Never knowing who would die next, or if we would see our loved ones again" choking on the last part I begin to apologise, swiftly cut off.

"Don't. It's just been…hard. But I didn't do it alone."

I follow his gaze over to Clea as she continues to talk to Laurence. His anger dissipates as he lets out a small smile, "They brought me out of my darkness, and I'm sure after this is all over, there will finally be peace." He breathes deep and continues his work, dismissing me.

His eyes flicker to the now-blocked door we use to enter the ballroom from our side of the palace. In the midst of the battle, Sophie had stopped her assault on the barrier and snapped her gaze to the door. "I have to find him!" she shouted.

"Who?" I yelled back to her, but she was already making her way to the open door. Her golden gown swirled and danced around her as she ran, a shimmering trail that continued even after she left. Her feet carried her forward, as her hair whipped behind her to match her frantic running. Always the smart one, Sophie.

If Fabian from the past was here, where was he now?

Ever since Hale introduced Fabian and Clea as his 'Uncle and Aunty' I have been turning those words over and over. All the theories turn in my head, wondering if in the future Laurence became even closer to Fabian, connecting Hale to Clea. They were on their own for five years after all. And standing here, feeling useless, I wonder what happened to me. Did I fall like the others did as they claimed, slayed by this Morvath, defending the leaders and the throne with my last breath? That would explain the longing and desperation in Clea's beautiful aqua eyes each time she looks my way; did she witness the brutal killing of those close to Hale and Fabian?

For a hopeful moment I cling to the thought that in the future, that glorious woman could love someone like me. My fantasies are quickly interrupted by the man coughing up blood, who definitely soiled his pants to my right, cutting off his arms in such a brutal way was shocking - a move I did not see coming. But… the savagery in her eyes when she saw his arms fall to the ground was imprinted in my brain, something I know my face shifts into when I pry information out of my subjects. My mind swirls and aches from all this confusion, my fists curl painfully at the helplessness I feel. My job is to protect those that I love, and I couldn't even do that.

Athena still holds Eva tight, her body exhausted and spent. Black liquid drying up on her chin and dress. Her arms wrapped tightly as if to shield her from the world's harshness. Her shoulders shake with silent sobs, and she rests her chin gently on the top of her head, fingers tracing comforting circles along her back. Athena doesn't say a word, sensing that nothing she could say would soothe her pain. The moment gets interrupted as Eva sits abruptly, looking around the room in panic. Athena uncoils her arms, as she looks towards that odd black liquid now pulsing and shifting in the moonlight.

We all turn towards it, ever so slowly, to see that *thing* moving on its own and growing in size. Athena places her hand gently on her arm, encouraging her behind Amazu who has crept closer too.

"Fabian, tell me what this is," Hale barks, Fabian hearing the command carefully places the armour he was inspecting and rushes over to his side.

"Did you find anything useful in the book you found earlier? Is this Morvath's doing?" Hale asks, and Fabian visibly deflates, "No, it seems the pages we wanted were already removed," looking towards Eva, Hale signs with kindness in his eyes, "Please help us, do you have those pages?"

She looks up, eyes red and puffy from her tears. Her hands tremble as she reaches into a hidden pocket within her gown and pulls out a handful of torn book pages. The edges were ragged and uneven, a testament to the force with which they had been ripped out. She extends the stolen item, her fingers shaking with a mixture of shame that lined her golden eyes. A flush creeps up her cheeks as she darts her eyes back to the black substance, pushing her hands further this time. Hale gently takes them, and I feel the room collectively hold their breaths when he all at once crashes into her to embrace her fully, arms wrapped so tight. She chokes out a semblance of broken words, that sound like an apology, the voice weak to my ears as she tries to speak. The words mangled and broken. More tears spill down her cheeks, as she returns his embrace not seeming to care about the warning they bestowed. Yet I have the feeling that Hale had longed to hold her like this for years.

Hale swiftly stands, and strides over towards the now clean floor, Clea and Laurence quicken their pace to follow. Crouching low, the warriors all crouch around the floor covered in tattered pages, looking deep in thought. Soldiers wearing thick furs, that I recognise from Baskith have stationed themselves to the side, a few are wounded, but they don't seem to mind.

"Maybe we can…"

"What if we?" they mutter amongst themselves, I watch with rapt attention at all of them together. Standing on the other side, I take a long look at the group. This was the group of survivors. Their bond forges in the shared hardship and violence they were all thrown into. Their glances, quick and knowing, spoke volumes of their time together. A language of unspoken understanding, as they argue and agree in rapid spoken words. But it was their eyes that I couldn't look away from, the fierce determination coiled its way around the room.

"Son, let us help. What are in those pages?" Amazu half shouts across the room beside me. "We need to let them do this, Amazu" my voice a whisper of calm as I address him. He turns to me, doubt and fear written on his face so clear it is like reading pages from a book. In this light, I notice the frown lines creasing his face, his expression shadowed with worry and a hint of anger. Every instinct he has rooted within him is to *command*, to step in and take action on any danger that may befall his people. He glances around, searching for something, *anything*, he could do to help. But like me, he is left powerless.

Athena reaches for her husband, her face pale as her eyes swim with worry and uncertainty. She leans into him, clutching his arm so tight as if she is drawing strength from his warmth and solidity. He wraps an arm around her shoulders, pulling her close, his gaze betraying his confident posture. But together, they stand silent, watching their son be put in a situation none of us were even remotely comfortable with.

Rising quickly, determination set in their faces, Hale turns to us, "Clear the area, this is going to be messy," stepping backwards, Amazu grabs my hand with his free one. All three of us stand as one, waiting for the inevitable to happen, Eva slowly stands too coming towards us and I hold her around the shoulders, needing the connection of another soul in this moment. Her body trembles still, the fear never leaving her gaze. Whatever that thing on the floor is… it came out of her. From what we have heard today, she had indirectly been the cause of Thalor's collapse. All I can do is stand with my family, helpless, and watch them solve the issues of our future.

Clea closes her eyes, and with her arms outstretched, I instantly recognise the shimmer of the barrier she forms. I am utterly transfixed by the concentration in her gaze as she finishes her thick wall around the black mass. Leaving a small opening at the front, Hale steps forward, the others standing behind him. Laurence grabs Clea's hand and squeezes, all thoughts of jealousy gone as I notice the way Clea closes her eyes in contempt.

All at once, Hale raises his arms in front of him, his palms ignited with a fierce, blinding flame, the heat radiating outward in strong waves. The fire flows with an intense, and unmeasurable force, almost unnaturally white and blue. Unlike the fire he used today. His face morphs into a contorted grimace of pain, and finally, he thrusts his hands forward, unleashing the fire in a powerful blast. The flames roared to life, the white light crashing into the creature, illuminating the room with an otherworldly light. The black thing recoils, the form trying to battle the flames licking up the sides. It pushes back, trying to dim the flames, but Hale pushes harder.

And he screams, he screams so loud Amazu latches his arms around Athena who launches herself forward.

"Trust him, Athena," Amazu says reassuringly, as she struggles against his grip, determined to save him. A few seconds later, Clea and Fabian both put their hands on his shoulders, for comfort or strength I can't tell.

Clea moans from the force, "It's working!"

With one final pulse a blazing white light, it pierces the room, the colour shifting to a bright cerulean sparkling with energy as it crashes into us all. Feeling as though a gust of wind hit us, the sheer force knocking us all off our feet, and sending us tumbling to the ground. Eva's body collides with mine, my arms grabbing her instinctively to protect her fall. Lifting my head, I feel the pounding of drums inside my skull as groans echo the room from the other Fae. I manage to rise from the ground with shaky legs, my hand outstretched to help Eva to her feet as Athena does the same for Amazu.

Just when I think this hellish night is over, a bright light shines on the ballroom doors like it's pulsing and growing with every second. I watch in awe as the white glow shimmers and the sturdy doors of the room are melted away, replaced by towering trees and lush undergrowth, a mystical forest replacing the entrance to the room. Leaves rustle softly as the new landscape stretches into the room.

What happens next shocks me beyond belief as a single figure steps through, my heart stops dead as my oldest friend, withered and bruised, stands within the forest landscape.

Amazu steps into the ballroom, ripped and torn clothes stick to his skin as he breathes heavily, swaying with the motion. I look over to his son, Hale's face lights up - eyes wide like a child with a mix of wonder and relief like he was seeing something he'd only dreamed of. For a heartbeat, they just looked at each other, a fragile connection stretching across the room. Then, as if a dam had broken, Hale launches into a full sprint, his legs carrying him across the barren space, kicking up debris and dead flowers in his wake. Gone was the emotionless husk, with sharp words and scars etched along his heart. His father stood waiting for him, arms outstretched, and as they crashed into each other, Hale's body shook as he cried.

Chapter 10
Clea

The light blinds me for a moment, and my feet move.

We won.

I am sprinting at full speed, my half-broken shoes clipping against the dance floor as I see Amazu, Sophie, and Bonnie stumble through the doorway encased in light.

Bonnie.

I fall into her arms, the smell of her hitting me instantly, a sob wrenching from my throat as I wrap my arms around her. My grip is light, with her body feeling so frail, so small and withered from imprisonment. I pull away after a few blissful moments, her face red and splotchy too from her tears as we stare into each other without needing to speak words. We tilt into one another as more tears stain my cheeks, my heart splitting open completely and shattering all around me as she wavers slightly but stands strong with me. Her tears mixed with the grey dust and grime on her face, a testament to her time in prison, beautiful tears washing away the past.

"Are you alright? You're safe. You're safe," I chant to her as her cries grow louder in response. I turn to shout for Laurence, who immediately whips us up into the air, his arms bands of steel as he hugs us almost painfully. A laugh escapes me as we're spun around in a circle, gripping on tight as the room spins in a blur. Our feet hit the floor, neither of us remove our grip in the small bubble we created. My fingers tighten into fabric as more desperate sobs leave me, never wanting to let go, as though we are making up for the years spent apart. The last time we had been together like this would have been at Laurence's home, the home we spent most of our time laughing and reading the nights away. In just this embrace, the love I have for these two Fae crashes into me in relentless waves, a full force of the emotion that fills me with so much happiness I feel like I'm floating. Laurence pulls us closer, allowing us to lean our weight onto him as he strokes our back gently, this moment just for us to enjoy. He has always been there for us, no matter what, the link to the chain I didn't realise we needed. His large hands clutch at our waists, fingers gripping the tattered fabric as if afraid that letting go we may vanish. Bonnie tucks her head into his chest, eyes squeezed shut in contempt as her chest expands in heavy pants, all three of us savouring the presence of being together.

Eventually, I force myself to pull from their embrace and step away allowing them a moment alone. The second Laurence flicks his eyes to her, his face battered and bruised from our battle, the sweetest of smiles graces his face as he kisses her like a man starved. Her arms gripping his stained shirt, not caring where the blood came from, the fabric bunching up in her withered hands. He simply reaches up, and gently caresses her cheek with his hand, eyes locked to hers "I found you, my fire."

"*Laurence,*" her voice cracks out, sounding like she hasn't spoken in months, voice cracked from misuse. The scene reminds me of when they first realised they were mates, in the dense forest and after one of the most terrifying nights we had together, they shared a deep love between them that nothing in this world could ever tear them apart. Even after five years, their eyes still sparkled with the love that was once sickening to watch, and I could only watch in awe at their reunion.

My gaze turns to Fabian stumbling over to Amazu and Hale, eyes wide, he simply pulls him into their hug, slapping his back with pride. Looking my way, Fabian' face cracks ever so slightly "We did it," he cries, extending his arm wide in invitation, and without needing anything else I crash in their embrace too. Hale pulls me tightly at the side, the harshness of his face I had always seen since he matured had been wiped away from a single hug from his father and he winks at me coupled with rare vulnerable smile, looking like the boy I had first met, with a cheeky grin and a saltshaker in hand.

"Where… where is Sophie?" Fabian asks, head raising and moving in alarm. My gaze flicks about the room, looking for the woman who gave me this now ruined dress. I doubt she'd want this back, or offer me more in the future. But he looks to Amazu, still holding his arm, a fierce glint in his eye. Of course, his Sophie should be with those who came through. Where is she?

"*Where is she?*" he repeats louder now, echoing my thoughts, head pushing to the side around Amazu towards the ballroom doors still flickering in the moonlight.

"I need help," Athena's cracked voice booms into the room, as she carries a small woman in her grasp. Her grim face shocks me, the same feeling I felt when gazing upon Amazu when he walked through the portal. I had only known them to wear finery, and never show weakness in front of others, but Athena just huddled in barely hanging on herself as she gripped the bundle of Fae draped in tattered golden clothing. A thin arm hangs out of the bundled mess, smearing with blood and dirt. Sophie's arm has been ripped open, long gashes mark her dark-skinned arms. Her collar bone protrudes her frame, starved and battered. I spring into action helping her to the floor, "We were attacked on the way, Evreux saved her, saved us." Athena explains, her body swaying slightly.

Fabian crashes to his knees, holding her limp body to his chest as he strokes her limp hair with gentle movements and begins to chant words unknown to me. Old ancient words, most likely a healing spell to heal her open wounds. We all hold our breath, and even though I barely know the dying woman in front of me, I grasp her hand in front of me somehow knowing she needs every bit of comfort I can give her at this moment. The difference of this Sophie to the past one is shocking, her face holds so much pain and misery, her body bleak and lifeless. But to our surprise, her eyes spring open, wide and wild, darting around the room as if searching for something to anchor her back to reality. Her chest heaves as she gasps for air, each breath shaky and uneven, caught somewhere between a sob and a pant. Beads of sweat glisten on her forehead, and as she starts to come back to this world her hand grips me back, squeezing so hard it's like she is attempting to ground herself to this moment. Her face is tense, etched with lingering fear and her mouth seems perched between a grimace and an attempt to steady her breathing. For a moment, she seems frozen, caught in the liminal space between the nightmare and the new world around her, her mind racing to catch up to the safety of the present. When her eyes find Fabians, they shift into wonder and gut-wrenching love and sorrow.

"Am I dead?" she whispers, barely audible with her throat seemingly raw.

"Not yet, sugar, you can't escape me that easily," he chokes out, tears lining his eyes. Her eyes devour the scene in front of her, they bounce around the room as shock begins to take route with the palace ballroom being left in ruin and the not-so-subtle pile of dead bodies in the corner of the room. She laughs, actually *laughs,* "What the hell happened here?" Fabian joins in with the laughter, wiping the tears from his face with his dirt-lined fingers. She doesn't seem to care, not at all as she clutches his hand to hers, keeping it locked on her face. Helping her to stand, Sophie finally rises from the ground, her gown lifting. Yellow bruises spread along her legs, along with spots of darker ones, fresher ones by the look of it. Fabian's gaze darkens, ready to burn the world down for her in a single moment, she steals the moment by uttering curse words and a sharp "Took you long enough", Fabian's laugh booms in the room as he winks to her, her returning laugh seems to dissolve all the sadness that poured from his body in waves just hours before. Years of torment and relentless nothing boiled down to this moment.

And I cry, I cry for all of them, for the beauty and the love shared within the room. Warmth spreads throughout my body as I glance at the gravity of the situation. Feeling part of a family.

I stand alone as I watch Fabian rock Sophie softly in his arms and whisper a very shortened version of what happened. Sophie listens with rapt attention; her gaze slips to Eva from across the room - eyes hard as hate echoes her stance.

"Please tell me what you say is true, because all I have known is to hate that woman for what she did to us. She... did so many awful things Fabian," she pleads. He simply kisses her head, holding her tighter.

Amazu strides by me, his voice calm and unrestrained, "He's on the way. You helped to save us all, you are forever in our debt. Oh, and I hope to get a *proper* wedding invite soon." His hand gently pats my arm and strides towards his past self as if he is eager to share the information of the past few years. Excitement lines my gut, my fingers twitching awaiting his presence. My eyes flicker to the golden glow still illuminating over the ballroom doors, even as the confusion brews to how this all came to fruition. But that can come later, as I feel him before I see him, his soul finding mine, and I turn just as his arms find me. Wrapping my arms around his broad shoulders covered in thick leather armour, he smells of cinnamon, charcoal and *home*. "We did it," I breath in his ear, Evreux pulls back and presses his forehead to mine "We did it" he repeats my words and gives me one of those breathtaking smiles. His hands cup my face, stroking my cheek with his soft fingers as his eyes find mine. His black eyes search deep within me, worry lines his face, but softens when I return his smile. We stand there breathing in each other like the world finally feels right again. My gaze lingers and I feel the unspoken words between us, time is short in this life, and we will savour what we can with each other.

His lips crash against mine, his hand curling in my hair, the other wrapping around my waist pulling me closer. The entire world fades away as his body pushes flush against mine, I can feel his urgency and relief in the kiss, and the overwhelming joy of the fight finally being over. Still holding my face, he pulls back to look at me, "We got them out, it was tough, but Laurence's makeshift *bomb* worked. The prison, it was worse than I had thought, so much worse." Eyes closing and lips tight, I lift my arms and smooth away the worry lines on his face, "We did all that we could, this is not your fault, Ev. Just look at how happy they are." I tilt my head to the others, in similar positions we are in, Laurence looking like he wants to throw Bonnie over his shoulder and run them to the nearest bedroom, Bonnie too cannot stop giving him heated stares with her legs wrapped around his waist, practically grinding him in front of everyone.

Chuckling, Evreux nods his head in agreement, "It was truly strange, when we got them out, all of us ran as fast as we could. We passed the black gates, wondering where to go next. They needed water and shelter quickly, but then this huge white light appeared in the trees," looking bewildered, he continues, "Amazu just had this urgency to go through it, and I was so terrified as he disappeared through it, but I heard your voice and I knew everything would be alright, that they made it home." He wipes a tear falling down my cheek, his eyes sparkling too. My eyebrows furrow at his words, would we be okay?

Will future me recognise Evreux, recognise *anyone*? Did we kill a guard that potentially saves Ev in the future, or start an uprising in the village from the chaos?

"Whatever happens, wherever you and I end up, I will find you," He lifts my chin with a crooked finger, his gaze intense and unrelenting, his black eyes penetrating my soul and finding purchase in my cracking heart.

"I will not stop searching for you, my heart knows yours. We will find each other again, in this lifetime and the next." His words wrap around me, and I feel a fierce warmth spreading through my chest. My face begins to relax, my lips curling into a smile that creeps up within me. Butterflies nest and swarm in my stomach at his stare, the feeling makes me want to laugh or even dance right here in this fucked up ballroom.

He pulls me into the crook of his arm, my head resting on his chest, his heartbeat a steady rhythm keeping me grounded. My palms find his back, and I stroke his upper back lovingly, tracing my thumb over the scars and raised bumps where his wings used to be. He shudders and tightens his grip on me. "I have a gift for you," I say sweetly, tilting my head in anticipation of his response. "Do you now?" he says, voice darkening in that delicious sound I love so much, feeling like a thousand kisses down my spine. A guttural moan sounds behind him, and he snaps his neck to see Malik on the floor, now sitting up and somehow, still alive. Rage and destruction coils in his eyes, as his body tenses. He stalks over, clenching his jaw.

"Please, you've got to help me - this bitch cut off my arms and left me here to die!"

Wrong side buddy.

Evreux locks eyes with him, with lethal calm he responds, "What did you just call my wife?"

Eternal Threads of Time

CHAPTER 11
Evreux

Wife.

He, I, called her his wife.

I watch their reunion with rapt attention, my legs locked in place, muscles bunching and yearning to learn everything. *Anything.* My face contorts painfully, my heart beating in my chest. I breathe in and out, listening to their words. But my eyes no longer linger on Clea, they are firmly on his wingless back. His torso is layered in strong armour, a similar pattern I myself wear, but scars on his arms paint a thousand stories of another life. It's his flat back that causes me to let out a soft whimper, his wings weren't cut off gently, no, they look ripped off. Healed badly from the raised bumps. Clea's actions make more sense to me now. A lover seeking vengeance on a past act. The force behind her swing was hauntingly beautiful. And I now understand she was fighting for retribution, but for this man to understand the force of what he did. He had it easy, a quick disarming from her sharp blades. My body turns hot with anger, the situation I must have been put into to be captured and tortured by this man, those wings look *ripped* off. I shift my wings behind me, feeling the strong muscle and bone attached to my back.

"My master is going to rain hell upon all of you. He will slaughter you all and happily march on these palace grounds to claim this land. He has wanted to for as long as I can remember, and maybe now he can while your defences are weak. Trust me, when he wants something, he does not give up." Malik spits out, head straining from the position he is in.

Clea visibly flinches at his words, but before I can comprehend what that means, my future self responds clearly, "Send him my regards from hell." Kicking him down to the ground, with one large swing he raises his sword to plunge it into the man's skull. He makes quick work of wiping the blood onto his leg, and promptly sheathing the sword to his hip. His arm finds Clea again like they were always meant to be there, I feel the phantom touch and comforting presence just watching, wondering what that could feel like. "That man surely has a way with words... looks like you won our game," he winks at her, and I visibly notice her legs tighten together at his tone.

Looks like my hard-on is back. My dick is as confused as I am.

"So, what's my prize for winning?" Clea responds, her tone low and soft, almost velvety. Each word lingered just a little longer than usual, her voice dripping with desire. He moves towards her, gaze not moving, and whispers in her ear, turning her face hot red. The back of his hand stroking against the curve in her spine, her back arches into his touch and their eyes lock once more. I feel her breath hitch, even from over here, lips parting and chest heaving.

Fuck.

I cough to announce my lingering, needing answers, but my brain falls short on everything I want to ask. They turn to me smiling wistfully, and I get the odd sense of intruding in their private moment, like a secret I am not meant to bear witness to. Maybe it is, maybe seeing the woman who I eventually fall in love with will cause me to spiral and seek her out if not anyone else. She's well versed in the local knowledge, and her friendship with Fabian suggests she'll visit the palace soon, exactly where our story could begin.

I greedily store away each look, each word spoken. I find myself feeling excited to hunt her down, wherever she currently is. If she would allow me, I would find Clea in the present and tell her everything I have seen today, hoping not to seem too mad.

Doubtful.

"I.." I start, but my words are cut off by a soft glow appearing on Clea's arm. She raises it in front of her face, caught in a whirlwind of conflicting emotions. Her shoulders sag slightly as if a weight has been lifted. The others wear matching expressions too, their eyes reflect some kind of inner conflict, eyes wide and alert with the touch of lingering fear. Just underneath it, there's peace to their stance as they hold their loved ones close. My chest tightens, and I get the overwhelming sense of dread as all of this could come to an end, and I don't know what to think about that. When Fabian had been captured from almost killing Eva earlier tonight, it had seemed almost impossible for the night to continue. The thought of that happening throughout the ball in itself was an act of pure insanity that if anyone had described what transpired today, I don't think they could capture the depth of which the vast amount of emotions had been splashed around. I would have laughed in their faces, deemed them insane, and they'd be ordered to rot in a prison cell. But here they stand, quietly accepting their reality coming to an end.

Their soft whispers drift about the room, as lovers cling to one another as if for the last time, and Hale wistfully smiles as he drifts into the embrace of his parents. The Fae in front of me have gone through hell, five years of living within a shadow with so much hate in their gut, that they bright from within. Their bodies continue to blur and contort in the night, their skin becoming almost translucent.

"See you all soon, to a better world!" Laurence yells, his fist pumps in the air accompanied with a maniacal laugh, sounding light and free as he holds a brown-haired woman close to his side.

A gasp catches my attention as light spreads up Clea's arm, pieces of her skin from her body flake off in a shimmering light as if drifting off into the moonlight. My future self doesn't panic and does not leave her gaze as he places the gentlest of kisses on her lips, holding her face in his hands. And after a few heavy breaths, he finally shifts his head, tilting it at an angle to meet my eyes, and simply nods his departure.

I step towards them, needing answers, needing to know who she is, where she is - to touch her, consequences be damned. She whispers goodbye to him and smiles at the others nodding in acceptance. She turns to me for the last time and speaks the words that will break me, simple words like a command my body has to follow.

"Find me in the future, Evreux."

Consumed by a light so bright, I shield my eyes with my arm, outlines blurring and then vanishing in front of me as if they were never there. The once vibrant room descends into a quiet, cold and lifeless as the echoes of their laughter drift off into the night, now replaced by a silence that weighs heavy on my heart.

Find me in the future.

I will find you Clea, until my last breath, *I promise I will find you.*

CHAPTER 12
Clea

The ground beneath my feet falls away, gravity forcing my body down until all I can see is darkness, my screams swallowed by the silence around me. The ballroom disappears and Evreux is ripped from my outstretched arms. My head turns left and right, finding something to hold on to in this void.

Where am I?

There was no up or down here, no end in sight - only an infinite blackness stretching endlessly in every direction. My legs extend into the void, vanishing into the abyss as though consumed by its emptiness. The darkness is overwhelming as it wraps itself around me like a thick blanket, seeping into my pores and erasing myself entirely. I feel weightless yet adrift, as though gravity is both everywhere and nowhere, pulling at me from all sides without mercy. The air rushes past, cold and biting, its invisible currents pressing against me as if dragging me deeper into nothingness. There's no sound to anchor me - no wind, no echoes, and no clue as to where I'm headed. My breath comes in shallow, panicked bursts, the only noise breaking the crushing silence. Desperately, I reach out, my arms flailing for something solid, something real - but all I grasp is emptiness, the vast nothingness slipping through my fingers like smoke.

Just when I think I will be falling forever, a voice whispers in the darkness as if they are standing right beside me.

"My dear, Clea, you have been so brave," a woman's voice croaks to me, sounding ancient and young at the same time, a soft feminine voice trying to sound comforting.

"Who are you? Where am I?" I cry, not recognising the void I feel trapped in, forever falling in. I fall for what feels like days, the non-existent wind biting my skin to the point of pain.

Suddenly it all gets ripped away as I land in a small dark room. The rough walls echo and bounces as her voice drifts about, the thick stone marred with deep gashes and smaller scratches. A narrow slit sits high up near the ceiling, cascading a weak light, barely enough to break the thick shadows that cling to the deepest corners. The air feels stale and damp, with a faint sound of dripping water echoing in the quiet. There is no sky, no clouds, or birds. Only light shines through. A solid iron door is to my left, the bolt frozen over and hissing like a snake.

Movement in the corner catches my attention, and an old woman shifts her weight noticing my confusion. As my eyes adjust to the dark, I spot her hunched frame - grey gown, matted dark hair that hasn't been brushed through in months. Bones protrude out of her skin, looking malnourished and sickly. In the dark, I can just make out her gnarled fingers holding a key of some kind. Her black, beady eyes fixated on mine, unblinking, with a sharp intensity that feels like it's boring straight into my soul. The corners of her lips curl upward, but it's not a smile of warmth or joy - it's something far darker, something wrong. Her teeth, crooked and lined with thick layers of dirt glint faintly in the dim light as her smile spreads unnaturally wide, stretching her face into a grotesque expression that makes my stomach churn. It's the kind of smile that doesn't belong to a living person, and every instinct in my body screams at me to run.

But I can't move. I'm frozen under her gaze, her eyes locking me in a place like twin black voids, empty yet somehow filled with a quiet malice that prickles my skin. A low, almost imperceptible sound escapes her lips - a faint, breathy chuckle that barely qualifies as laughter, yet sends an icy spike of dread through my chest. The air around her feels heavier, colder like it's pressing down on me, suffocating. My legs tremble, but they won't obey my desperate urge to run. I can feel my heart pounding in my chest, the sound of my pulse deafening in my ears as her awful, unnatural smile burns itself into my mind.

"You are everywhere, and nowhere," her voice croaks out, clearer now than before. I blink up to her, needing answers, "Am I dead?" I hear my voice squeak out.

"Don't worry, my child. You are very much alive, but I brought you here to warn you." She responds, turning the key over in her hand.

"Warn me from what?" Confusion dragging out each syllable.

She laughs, humourless and knowing, like a mother would to her child sensing the lack of knowledge. I can feel that whatever she is about to say will destroy Kingdoms, the weight of her words heavy in her heart.

"I could feel you travel back, you know? Those portals you used are unheard of in this universe. Something we have not seen and can have cascading effects. Time always has a price, but don't worry, you will not be the only one burdened with it." She rises, muscles tense, close to snapping. She stretches to her full height, dress dropping down to breeze against her legs. The fabric looks scratchy and rough, and as she closes her hands in front of her a hardness sets onto her face that reminds me of someone I can't place.

Feeling like a child, I repeat my questions needing more answers, "What price must we pay?" She pauses for a moment, seeming to collect her thoughts "You will find out, soon enough, time has a consequence. We do not even know what may occur from this abomination of a gift."

Abomination.

Whatever we did clearly angered some ancient being or a pissed-off witch. We understood that the spell we used was not recommended by any means, it became our only solution to stop the spread of plague in our land, if we were not there - it could have spread to the entire Kingdom of Virelith or possibly other worlds. From what I saw, Eva was close to poisoning Drakharrow too. Once both lands were taken over, Virelith as we knew it would no longer exist.

I look around this room again, looking like a prison cell I very much want to get out of, but there is no bed or chains marking the floor.

"Will I remember any of this?" I ask, tightening my fists as they shake from the bite of the cold that descends the room.

She releases a harsh and punishing laugh, "So many questions." With those words, a large hand seeps into the room, ripping me away.

The room fades away, growing smaller and smaller in my vision. Into the void again. My body begins to fade away as I claw at the invisible hand gripping me so tight. I can't *breathe*, my rib cage tightening from the grip, the sense of dying hits me with clarity as my vision blurs. My eyes begin to close, heartbeat slowing, and a single tear drips down my face, Evreux's name the last word on my lips.

Chapter 13
Clea

My feet touch down on the soft, wet grass. Patches of deep green moss cover the towering trees and losing my footing, I stretch my arms out in front of myself to stop my face from smashing into the mud. Birds chirp high in the skies, while tiny insects scurry across the ground near my face.

Now covered in mud, I push my arms against the grass to lift myself up to sitting, the pressure stings and I absently flip over my hands, rough lines of new cuts adorn my palms that tingle like tiny pinpricks that travel up to my elbow.

"Hey, are you alright?" a feminine voice lightly chuckles behind me, I gingerly shift my body to not slip further into the mud as a delicate awaiting hand lays outstretched towards me, the sun blinding me ever so slightly. I'm wondering where I landed when Bonnie grabs my hand and pulls me upright. My brain swims around in my skull from the motion as I blink away the sensation, as I adjust my footing.

"Thanks," I murmur. There's something I need to tell her, but it slips my mind, it's probably that I ate the last of our bread last night - I got hungry in the middle of the night, restlessly turning in my bed roll.

"Of course, you of all people trip over nothing. Come on, Asshole number one is probably waiting for us. It's 'Bring your wife to the bar' night," she says, tilting her head in disdain. It was something Hobbs, our boss, started a few weeks ago, and makes me cringe. It works rather well, but the men often leave less tips for us which he docks our pay for, hence the name.

"Oh shit, it's a Tuesday, I completely forgot! My mind feels a little hazy, I didn't sleep well last night," rubbing my head, something feels off, but I can't place what.

Laughing, she nudges my arm playfully, "Probably because you were chewing on our stale bread all night, like a little squirrel," she says, twitching up her nose as she mimics the noise of a squirrel chewing on a nut. I dip my head in apology, a laugh bubbling in my throat. Guess I wasn't as sneaky as I thought.

We pass a small river, and I take the time to remove my mud ridden boots to wash my legs and hands, the thick mud washing away in clumps – then splashing some over my boot, careful not to spray Bonnie, she'll be pissed at me if I get her best dress wet - she wears it claiming she gets better tips, like a 'Lucky dress'. Considering she keeps getting groped in it, I no longer joke about it being *lucky*. Various hands have grabbed her from behind in that green dress that I hate to admit, I note their faces each time if I ever need to replenish my magic. Although I haven't needed it for a while, and since I'm in hiding, it would be a pretty stupid thing for me to do regardless. Kneeling further into the water, I dip my hands in, the cool water wrapping around my fingers like a gentle embrace. I cup my hands, bringing the crisp water along my face and neck, and I instantly feel better. A refreshed sensation crawls over me, washing away the sleepless night, and feeling more like myself.

As we clear the trees, I straighten my dress as we approach The Sapphire Swan, a small tavern on the outskirts of the main town. It's a quaint tavern; vines crawl up the sides and crows land on the wooden benches outside, releasing a caw as they assess the area for food. Their black wings beat frantically in the morning air, the feathers sweeping leaves and dust into the air that looks almost angelic. With the location of the tavern, Bonnie and I are able to slip away after our shift to sleep. It's not a comfortable life, but it's the only semblance of freedom we have, a fact I grapple onto for as long as I can. It is also the fourth tavern we have worked in these past few years. We had met at the first one, she helped me get the job after all.

Bonnie has big dreams of opening her own tavern one day, like her parents. Despite the pretty picture of a tavern as a family heirloom, they were truly awful to her from what I saw, like making her do the grunt work for little pay while they sat around drinking all of their inventory. She desperately needed to find her own footing without their presence, to be given the opportunity to grow within a business she could call her own, I just knew she'd excel at whatever run down building we could purchase with our little money. She was incredibly brilliant at winning people over, patient and kind with every waking breath. It was what Virelith needed. We promised each other we would try to stay here for a few years, to give her the experience she craves, but I just wished our boss wasn't a snivelling weasel.

"You're five minutes late," Hobbs sneers as we step inside, "Sorry sir, Charlotte and I won't do it again," she says sheepishly, using my alias. I ignore them both, immediately stepping behind the bar to serve the customers waiting there.

I get lost in the rhythm of the day, pouring beers in large wooden cups trying to avoid the drunken buzzards sloshing their drinks dangerously close to me. Bonnie works the floor, she prefers the liveliness of the crowd, the ability to join and leave conversations effortlessly. Gliding along the tavern floor, she balances various empty cups and bowls on a tray whilst dodging the customers walking past her. I take a moment to take in her beauty, long lashes line the russet brown in her eyes. Somehow, her hair always looked glossy no matter where we slept. Now it's tied up in an array of interwoven patterns to shift her hair out of her face, with a thin piece of leather keeping it in place. She smiles shyly at a group in the far corner, three young men call her over, one of them sits quietly holding a dagger with a nasty cut along his cheek. I hide my grimace at their lingering stare, thick and wandering on her swaying hips. Holding the tray in front of her like a sort of barrier, she quickly dismisses them exclaiming the windows need cleaning. Their eyes glance to the windows, eyebrows raised seeing the thick layer of grime on them, clearly never touched in years. Hobbs says it adds to the 'charm' of the place, I on the other hand believe it's to dim the outside light, betraying customers' sense of time - it always seems later than you would think. The perfect setting to line their stomachs with more alcohol.

Later that evening, patrons drift in and out, some accompanied by their wives. Much to our relief the men finally stopped hitting on us every time we poured their drinks. Sweeping a wet rag along the counter, Hobbs stumbles his way over to me, his breath stinking of whiskey and smoke. His eyes are hazy, red-rimmed and wandering. "Come on darlin, just one dance," he says swaying closer to me, no music is playing, but it's clear to see he's drunk off his ass and he has some type of melody playing in his head.

"No, thank you, I'm trying to work," I respond, my voice betraying the calm I pretend to feel. He doesn't like it when I lace my words with anger. Unfortunately for us, we need this job, and more importantly for me, the customers do not ask questions. Turning a blind eye to whatever happens here. It's the perfect spot. Even Caldris wouldn't be caught dead seen in a tavern like this. The town folk shout over each other, their chatter a melody in itself, a noise I can block out whilst here.

Hobbs stepped forward again. His long limbs stretch wide as he continues to move towards me. One meaty arm in particular lifts up and knocks over a cup sloshing with beer. It falls to the floor rapidly as the piss-coloured foamy liquid pours all over the already sticky floor.

I need this job.

"You gonna clean that up, girl?" Sneering at me, the danger in his eyes makes me involuntarily shiver from the feeling, knowing the moment I bend down, he'll have me where he wants me. I've been here before, it's better to just not react, and be quiet. His stare makes me feel like I am covered in thick moss, spiders crawling up my arms. My inner thoughts scream at him as I bend down with the same rag I used for the counter. Hobbs is too cheap to buy more than one, not that the customers know that.

I need this job.

Noticing the bucket to my left, covered in stains that I never ask where they came from, I reach to bring it over. In an instant my hand is yanked upright, Hobbs now right up in my face, breathing down my neck. His stench rots my nose; it would be a miracle if I ever smelled again.

I firmly state my objection again, "Please remove your hand, you're hurting me." He laughs in my face, his spit spraying along my cheek and neck.

We need this job.

I continue to chant the mantra to myself in my head as I imagine myself transported into a luscious bath filled with roses and feathers to wash away the filth on my face, I can't let Bonnie down. A customer calls his name that has his head swinging to the side, he spots the voice in the crowd and adjusting his trousers he plasters on a lop-sided grin and pushes his body away from me.

"Such a prude, you're no fun. Clean this up or you're fired." He growls, flicking his hand towards the floor, nearly slipping into the puddle of beer he carelessly made. He's too drunk to notice, and as soon as his body retreats into the crowd, I can finally breathe.

Half an hour passes by, and the floor is no longer wet, still sticky, *just no longer wet.* My knees strain as I stand upright, absently I look for Bonnie, who is nowhere to be seen.

"Two beers please mi'lady," a man with short brown hair says to me, his arms are crossed with a soft smile, the muscle in his arms shift to reveal dark tattoos that wind and curve along his arm. His eyes wander about the room, and I'd bet all the coins in my purse that he's here to steal something.

Ignoring that itching feeling, I find only one cup behind the bar that's clean and frown, normally Bonnie would have brought some back here.

"Excuse me, I'll be right back," I murmur to him, holding my purse for comfort as I pass. I dip into the kitchen, closing the door behind me. My body freezes, locks into place as a green dress has been left discarded on the worktop.

My legs move, and I grab the dress in my hand, the material cold and scratchy as it hangs from my grip. The upper part of the dress is ripped, buttons popped open at the seams, seemingly removed in a rush. Bonnie doesn't have a lover that I know of, the laces look torn off, and not lovingly undone.

I'm shoving through the crowd now, my movements frantic, each step fueled by desperation. Faces blur around me as I push past with force, my breath coming in sharp, uneven gasps. My heart pounds in my chest as my eyes continue the search around the room. Each second feels heavier, suffocating, as doubt sneaks in, whispering that she was taken and lost to me forever. The overwhelming sensation of being watched seeps into me as I step outside, the wall of fresh air hitting me as my eyes adjust to focus. It's dark, the dim lights of the tavern illuminate along the ground, muffled voices now growing distant the further I walk from the drunken customers. A cat screeches beside me, a pair of green eyes blinking up at me in the night. A black cat brushes up against me, the soft purr vibrating up my leg as it releases a tiny meow. I must steal some sliced salami before we end our shift, Bonnie and I will feed this *adorable* cat and head back to our camp. Just as soon as I know she's safe. She could have been getting changed from having a drink knocked onto her, it's happened before, and I'm probably overthinking this entire situation. I huff a long breath, and point my body back towards the entrance, but there… a bare porcelain leg peeks out the back of the tavern. I pick up my footsteps, getting closer to the scene around the back of the building. Bonnie lies against the back wall as she stares at nothing, her muscles locked tight as she squeezes the flesh of her legs that wrap around her curled up knees. No dress covers her body, as she shivers from the elements. My mouth parts open in shock, and crouching low, she flinches as I get closer. Seeing her like this, vulnerable and broken, sends a pang of helplessness through me. Why hadn't I noticed her gone before? Her face paints a thousand words I have only seen once before. Rage boils within me and I snap my gaze up to the sound of metal. Hobbs adjusts the leather belt of his trousers, fumbling and cursing from his slow movements. An angry exhale leaves my mouth, a large puff of smoke like a dragon exhaling its wrath, violence seeps into my bones at the sight of him – he must feel the shift as his eyes wander over to me, not really seeing me in his drunken haze.

I do not hesitate. My fist connects with his face, then his stomach. Bones crush as teeth cracks and splinter, knocking to the ground from the impact. I hit again, and again, and *again*. His meaty hands raise up to block my attack, ripping at my sleeves to pull my curling fist away from his bruised jaw. But he's weak from the alcohol, and I had the upper hand of the attack. Something he clearly took advantage of earlier. Vile curse words mumble and mix inside his blood-filled mouth, only spurring me on further as my temper rises and fogs in my head, my movements gaining faster as I ignore the dull ache in my upper back.

How dare he take something that is not his?

How dare he.

My knuckles split open on his remaining rancid teeth, red tinges my vision as his face begins to blur and morph into another one that I recognise. Caldris stares back at me, face angry and impatient as he tries once more to subdue my raging temper.

The body beneath me stops resisting, going limp as the head lulls against the stones. I blink my eyes a few times to clear the vision, as Hobbs lies crumpled on the ground. I jolt upright and rush over to Bonnie, still staring out into the night sky.

"Hey, I'm here, you're safe," I plead desperately, her eyes grow distant, unfocused, as if her very soul has slipped away and no longer wishes to return. Her once pale skin now appears almost bluish, and goosebumps spread along her exposed arms and legs. Bruises and thin scratch marks littered along her arm.

"Did he hurt you?" a nod.

"Can I touch you?" a nod.

I carefully wrap my arms around her, her body like a block of ice. I find the discarded dress near Hobbs, not remembering when I had dropped it, it's soaked in his blood. Not finding any other material around me, I whisper a silent apology to her as I sweep the fabric over her arms. Now covered, I carefully pull her icy arms towards me, feeling the dead weight around my shoulders and guide her into the woods. Her movements are choppy and broken as her body sways, my heart crashing inside my chest as she stumbles beside me. I can only hazard a guess as to what happened, my skin itches to continue fighting for retribution, but I must stay beside her and get her somewhere safe.

Others say the woods are the most dangerous place to be, where beasts roam. But those same men never realise, it is never the beast that would rape a woman.

The shadow of the tall trees swallow our figures as we make our way into the comfort of the woods, hiding us from others. Steering our bodies away from the normal larger path, I am careful to avoid larger rocks and debris. Through each step, I guide her movements as her feet step in front of one another. Walking through a new pathway, my hushed voice continues to warn her of anything sharp, her eyes still blurry as her face is set in a mask of shock. Warm liquid seeps into my hand as I adjust my grip on her, the dress had soaked up too much blood from when I carelessly threw it on the ground. But it's all we have until we reach our camp for extra clothing. A tendril of relief hits me as the woodland around us grows thicker, large tree trunks and winding bushes give us complete cover of the night.

My eyes sweep along the area for us to take rest, until a flicker of a fire glows in the distance, the smoke curling up into the starless sky. My movements pause, the decision weighing heavily on me. A fire means another Fae could be out here, but it is small, the likelihood of it being only one person is strong. Bonnie whimpers at the fire, sensing the warmth it will give us as she continues to shiver beside me. Her eyes finally find mine in the dim light, and with a small nod, we trudge forward, deciding the fire will at least melt our muscles and fill our stomachs with a hot meal she desperately needs.

"Bonnie, I'm sorry, come back please!" Hobbs' voice croaks out behind us, his voice laced with malice, no hint of apology in his tone. Immediately, cold fingers grip me harder, squeezing me so tight as Bonnie's eyes widen in panic. Crouching low, we bend our knees to lower ourselves to the ground, hoping he will get bored and give up his search. He's got a tavern to run after all and will need to hire more staff.

Twigs snap, the sound so loud and unsettling, getting too close for comfort. We tuck our bodies behind a tree, our breaths heavy as my heart thumps inside my chest. Bonnie's hand lifts up to press against the tree as her body heaves, retching on the forest floor, wiping the blood-stained sleeve from her dress that smears on her chin. She stares deep into my eyes now, the light behind them flickering and lifeless as I hold her gaze. Words stick in my throat, knowing nothing I could say in the moment would take the pain away, all I can do is lean into her as our laboured breaths drift into the air. It's all I can do until a twig snaps to our side and she's ripped from my grasp, an ear-splitting scream leaving her throat. In that moment I feel a terror so fierce as Hobbs holds a knife to her ribs, gripping her hair in the other. Her head yanks upright as her hair wraps around his fist, teasing more screams from her he has no right to hear. His toothy grin stark in the moonlight, as blood oozes onto his lips. And I wonder what it would feel like to cut off his ears, eliciting screams from him this time, the echoes of the skin tearing and slapping against the stone floor drift into my mind as I imagine him tied up in a small dim room. But I'm not alone, Bonnie stands tall beside me, as we decide what to do with him. A dark shadow looms in the corner of the room, watching us – silent and patient, begging with their black eyes for us to continue. Before I can comprehend what that means, my eyes pierce into Hobbs as I sneer with venom dripping into my words, "Put her down you piece of shit." He digs the knife in slightly, drawing a blood-curdling scream from her throat that cuts through my soul like a thousand pieces of glass shredding me from the inside.

"We're going to have a little *chat*. Both of you whores need to keep your mouths shut if you still want your jobs," he sneers, and pauses to release a wet cough as more blood oozes from him. The helpless weight crashes into me, as I stand here unable to do anything while he keeps her hostage in the cage he made, one wrong word or movement could cause him to put pressure into the knife. Her life lost to a piece of shit who didn't deserve to breathe the same air as her. Her round face now drenched in tears, pleads with me to run, to save myself. My arms shake and tremble at the resolve in her eyes, accepting her fate. At that moment, I vow to do whatever it takes to protect her and to destroy anyone who dares to threaten her. I haven't consumed Fae blood for years, actively avoiding the sensation that could put her in danger, and I have a feeling that his blood would taste rotten, it usually carries the flavour of the host. For Bonnie, this asshole should and will be torn limb from limb.

"Please...run," she chokes out, as a mangled moan leaves her lips, her back arching trying to keep purchase. Swallowing, I raise my hands above my head and crouch to the ground spotting a pretty rock that would look even better smeared with his blood.

Before I can decide how to maneuver this, the silence is shattered by a low, menacing growl.

I freeze. Definitely not Fae.

From the underbrush, a glowing set of amber eyes flash towards us, I lift my head up to the monstrosity as it pushes its front legs out from the cover of shadow. It's golden fur gleaming with an intensity so eerie I do not move, do not breathe as it's growl deepens into a savage snarl – huge white fangs poking out from underneath it's long whiskers. Even if I were standing at my full height, this beast would be larger than me. A small breeze floats around me, the chill seeping into my bones as I wonder how long it'll take for the tiger to rip us apart and chew on our decaying bodies. Our chewed bones would be forever kept in a cave or scattered into the wind. My pulse continues to spike as its body tenses, claws as thick as my fingers digging into the dirt as it places another paw in front of the other, a predator awaiting its next move. But this monster cannot see me, doesn't even look my way, or see me as a threat. No, his eyes are locked on Hobbs, and the knife he is digging into Bonnie's torso.

Hobbs' eyes widen with terror as panic has him shaking his head back and forth. His eyes bounce around the forest, uncertain until he locks his on mine, the bastard simply smirks as cold calculation flickers behind his beady eyes. His hands instantly pull away from Bonnie, so fast it's like he's been burnt with the motion as he pushes her towards the path of the cat-like predator.

"Take her!" he shouts, pivoting his feet and leaving us to this beast like the coward he is, she falls forward as her body curls inwards towards the ground, the sound of quickly retreating footsteps rustle in the dense forest behind her. In the commotion the tiger advances a step, a growl slipping out, without needing a pause I jump in front of her. Staring up at this beast and attempting to bring forward the courage I do not possess.

"Get back!" pushing Bonnie behind me gently, she grips my hand, no matter what - we will get through this together. But if I were given the choice, I would gladly give my life for her. With my eyes locked on it, I crouch low and swipe the rock I spotted earlier, I raise the jagged rock as a pathetic attempt to fight it off. The tiger does not look at me though, but keeps its head directed towards Bonnie, tilting its head slightly and I swear I can hear a soft purr escape its large jaw.

A few agonising seconds pass, and the beast releases a low menacing growl as its eyes snap to our right, leaping into the dense forest as it barely grazes my body diving towards its next target. The ginormous tiger catches up to Hobbs effortlessly, leaping into the air with arms outstretched – lethal bone-white claws extended. It takes under five seconds for the tiger to latch onto his back, jaws stretched wide as it ferociously rips his head from his shoulder. Hobbs' head now rolling on the forest floor as his body slumps to the ground.

With the beast distracted, Bonnie and I gingerly step backwards aiming for the roaring fire in the distance. Our breaths mingle and mist in front of us as our feet pound onto the moss and twigs scattered about, pushing leaves and branches out of our faces in desperation as we launch ourselves towards the safety of the fire. I'm certain we can make it within a minute if we keep up our pace, only a Fae could make a fire like that and a weapon would be handy right about now if the tiger decides we are next.

"We're almost there," I whisper urgently, encouraging our movements, her hand firmly in mine as my legs burn from the effort. We reach the small nest of space, our knees crash into the campfire – a few metal tins sit beside the fire, with a clean and crisp tent that was set up but never slept in. More importantly it's empty, allowing us space to breathe, I rummage my way through the small leather bag thrown to the side looking for anything metal or sharp as Bonnie sits closely by the flames, the flickering fire reflecting on her eyes as she extends her hands towards it, kissing the fingertips with the flames.

She must be freezing.

Our sanctuary is shortly lived as a soft rustling catches our attention, both our heads snapping to the giant paw once again stepping into our space, Bonnie's trembling hand rattling against mine. To our relief, it appeared on the other side of the fire, we could kick at the woodfire – but even that distraction wouldn't be enough time to run. The option to use my Sang gifts glints in my periphery, but it has been too long, and I have not practiced my combat skills for *years*. Let alone ever trained to slay a beast this size. It's head peeks through, but their movements are sloppy like it's been wounded, eyes downcast to the floor. My eyebrows bunch up on my forehead at the display, but as it's body shifts into our space that's when I truly see it – a severed hand grappled in its jaw. Did Hobbs wear an enchanted bracelet to protect him from beasts? That's incredibly insane and too much preparation I would give him credit for, the now deceased man could never remember to lock the tavern door most nights and had forgotten his wife's anniversary twice in a row. His wedding ring still clung to him, saliva dripping onto it that mixed with the trickle of blood running along his palm. Bonnie gasps spotting it, her hand smacked to her gaped mouth as she releases a cry of fear. My hand grazes the floor once again for anything that can be used as a weapon, panic tearing through me once again tonight, but the beast doesn't seem to care. It just stands there, severed arm dripping blood onto the leaves. Back legs slump to the floor as it lowers its head, jaws opening slightly to release the prize caught. Large thumping appears behind the creature and shifting my head reveals a large tail thumping in *delight*. Before I can comprehend its actions, a bright white light shines from the centre of its chest – so bright I squeeze my eyes shut, but when I open them a large Fae male stands where the creature previously was. Thankfully for the sanity of us both he shifted with clothes, half-crouched on the floor as his eyes flick to ours.

"Are you alright?" the tiger-man says, his voice cautious and kind.

All I can do is stare, mouth wide as Bonnie sits stiffly beside me – her grip on me now relaxing. I try to look for a response, but I find nothing, my tongue thick and heavy in my mouth.

"The name's Laurence, are you women hungry?" flashing his teeth he moves to the fire and folds himself to the floor, legs outstretched without a care in the world.

Chapter 14
Bonnie

"So you trade in alcohol?" Clea asks Laurence, hesitance laces her sharp words as we sit about the campfire. Laurence just sits there, arms folded over his bent knees as he picks at leaves, rolling them with the pad of his thumb. His calm stance is off-putting, a stark contrast to his earlier appearance. I still can't comprehend the mechanics of how he shifted, and I keep half expecting the tiger to pounce from the woods any minute. But I can't deny what I saw, what I feel in his presence. He sits opposite me, his broad shoulders and powerful physique tower over the fire by leaps and bounds. Despite his imposing size, the gentleness creeps up in his movements, he's trying not to act intimidating and just wishes to sit by the fire he most likely built earlier. Is he cold? His deep-set hazel eyes hold mine whenever I get the courage to look into them, and each time I do it feels like he can see past the surface of my being – deep into my soul like it's painted on my face. Red hair shifts in the breeze, lose strands that fell out of the bundle of hair atop his head sway with his movements. He's beautiful… a soft smile lingers on his lips each time he tilts his head toward me, a smile I could stare into forever. I can't seem to look away, and I don't want to. There's something about him that makes me feel at ease, safe even. I don't think I've felt this way before, other than with Clea, who hasn't kept her eyes off of his movements since he sat down.

The tiger has put away his claws and no longer wishes to spend the night alone.

He had saved us after all. Maybe the beast wanted company, he doesn't ask us what happened for… *him* to be chasing us, and we don't ask how he can turn skin to fur in a matter of seconds. Fae shifters are not rare, but not common either in Thalor. I had heard rumours whispered in taverns of great beasts that turn into men, but I had not believed them until tonight.

The floor is uncomfortable, but I think even if I were comfortable - sleep may not find me. The exposed brick in the tavern rubs against my skin even now, the roughness scratching my chest as I was pressed against it. The weight of it presses into me as I feel myself falling into the soil, wishing to dig under the moss and leaves to cover my exposed skin and soothe the aching. Shifting my weight off a sharp rock that had been digging into my leg, the dress I'm wearing hangs off my shoulders, just barely hiding my skin. The cotton now filthy and rough in the night air, red splotches adorn the sides that are now dried and crusted, it looks sickening. The dress no longer resembles the pear-green colour I loved so much, but even then looking at it draped along my body feels *wrong*. The overwhelming need to scrub the dirt and grime from the material rises to the surface, but burning the dress seems like a better fit. But that's not what I need, what I crave. The fire comes back into view, and I wonder for a moment what would happen if I were to stand in the centre of it. Would it remove the ache I feel all over my skin, burning away my body like I need it to? My body was a vessel after all, thrown away once used.

His body shouldn't be burned, no, he doesn't deserve that. He deserves to be left scattered into a thousand pieces around the woods, for the crows and bugs to feast on.

He had tried before, why was tonight different? Did he argue with his wife, or was my dress too revealing this time? Tempting his hands to take and take and take.

The flames are comforting though, they weave and build all the way to the top and then smoke rises - releasing into the night. What I would do to burn up and fade into the night, never to be seen again. I reach my hand out to the flame, the outer edge caressing my open palm. The fire cracks and spits towards me, beckoning me into its warm embrace, the fire burns away memories. Fire can cleanse. It stings for a moment, the pain grounding me to the world. I smile, feeling something other than terror or fear.

"Please do not hurt yourself," a man's voice says across from me, his crooked nose littered with freckles.

"Are you alright, Bon... um Bonwin," Clea stutters, she had found a sharp stick earlier that she keeps in her palm. It didn't escape my notice that she has kept herself between us, a Fae shield in her own way. But all I can think of is relief knowing my name wasn't uttered around the fire, the name sacred as it spills into the void of endless forest.

Words fail to escape me, but each time I go to speak, all I can feel is a hand pressing against my mouth. Stopping me from speaking, from screaming, feeling like I couldn't breathe. I can't get that taste out of my mouth, of dirty coins and beer, maybe the fire will solve that - to burn away all traces of him.

"No." A single word, the only word I tried to scream for so long until Clea found me. It is all I can think; all I can say with the world pressing down on me in violent waves. I grip the fabric of my dress and pull it down to cover more of my calves, it doesn't feel like enough. And I do not think it ever will.

"Don't touch her," Clea snaps beside me, and it's then I realise Laurence has shifted closer, concerned or longing in his gaze - I can't tell.

"I want to make sure she's alright," He sneers back to her, voice rising. I flinch at the sound, as they continue to talk like I'm not here. And maybe for a long moment, I don't want to be.

"That is none of your concern, *Laurence*," Clea says standing, holding the stick so tight it looks close to snapping, said stick points towards him in every word. She has always been brash and impulsive, my longest friend for so long. Her fierce protectiveness of me warms my pulsing heart, in the face of everything she always stays beside me. On my worst days, when I snap at her for getting my dress dirty, heck, even dealing with my parents. She doesn't leave, following me through anything that gets chucked towards us. When we first met, I had thought she stayed to remain hidden, but over the years I grew to realise it was me that needed her.

"You're in no danger with me," Laurence starts, arms open wide, "or in my debt like you keep accusing me of. I was nearby and heard screams, an honourable man would not walk by and let that happen. That excuse for a man signed his death warrant when he pushed *Bonwin* to the ground." He pronounces each word precisely, a gleam in his eyes as he addresses me. Resting his elbows on his bent knees, he almost looks sad.

His easy posture is jolting, whereas Clea has remained standing with a stiff spine looking seconds away from attacking the Fae and bolting.

"So you trade in alcohol?" I say, echoing Clea's past question. Both of their eyes snap at me. I wish they would stop the pissing contest they put themselves in. He did save us after all, even if he had honourable intentions, he hasn't ripped us apart with his teeth or shoved us into the cold night. I can't explain why, but I have a feeling he never would, his presence radiates a safety I can feel from this side of the fire.

Clea clearly not convinced, keeps her make-shift weapon in hand but slowly sits down in resignation. Her eyes are hard and unforgiving but soften when she looks my way. I hate the look in her eyes, but I know it's from a place of love, never pity.

"I do, I own all of the distilleries and wineries in Thalor. I was handed the trade from my father who passed away last year." His eyes take on a faraway look, and I want to comfort him. My feet move without my permission, seeking the comfort he craves. He shifts slightly at my approach, scratching the back of his neck and then tucking his hands together that rest gently on his lap.

"Tell me about him," I prompt, genuinely curious.

"He was a good man, a hard worker that took pride in his craft. He trained me as a boy to identify all the flavours of wines - the process of harvesting and the key to getting the fermentation just right," he replies, smiling wistfully.

"Fermentation?" I ask, my mouth twists in a grimace not understanding that word.

"Imagine you have a big bowl of cut grapes, you crush them to extract the juices. When we want to make it into wine, we add yeast, this eats up the sugars in the grape juice. Resulting in bubbles forming to turn it into alcohol. It's like magic, I was fascinated as a kid, entranced by variety of wine we could make." He explains.

Staring at his lips, I consume each word with rapt attention. I had never thought about the complexities of alcohol, my mind solely on the selling aspect of the trade. To have a tavern filled with happy customers, staff who enjoy coming to work, and most of all… a place I can call my own with Clea beside me.

Clea coughs, her fisted hand in front of her as her eyes urge an explanation. Confused, my face focuses back to Laurence as his face had crept closer. No, I had moved forward, entranced by his storytelling. I snap back, uttering an apology. I wait for the nausea to hit, but notice there is none, feeling a wholeness being near him I cannot explain. My body yearns to be closer to him again, but I resist, feeling the need to set boundaries.

"How kind of you, to spill your secrets and let us warm by your fire," rolling her eyes, Clea doesn't feel the same pull as I do, and I wonder if he has a sort of tiger sense to pull people in. His magic is unknown to me, the perplexed sensation causing my mouth to scrunch up.

Without thinking, I mutter the words I had been thinking, "You're beautiful." His head tilts towards me in fascination, warmth spreads through my heart at his smile.

"I am nothing compared to the amazing woman sitting in front of me," he drawls. My skin is covered in goosebumps and feels so hot, even on this chilled night I can feel the redness creeping up my neck. He notices the movement and audibly swallows. His eyes sharply find the floor, muttering a quick apology.

"I'm sorry, that was quite forward of me," he brushes his hair back with his hand, the veins in his muscles pulsing, making his shirt tighten along his upper arm. I have the sudden urge to run my fingers through his hair, wanting to know what it would feel like between my tainted fingers.

"You're damn right it was too forward, she is amazing, yes, but…"

"Come home with me," he interrupts Clea, looking at me with such intensity and safety. His tone like we are deer caught in a trap; hand outstretched with palms wide.

"The hell we are, you think you can just swoop in at the last minute like a goddamn saviour." She shakes her head, but I see the hope behind her hard eyes. She is hesitant, always being cautious. I can almost feel the cogs turning in her head, thinking of all the ways this could go badly, but for some unknown reason, I trust him.

"Okay." One word leaves my lips, and Laurence smiles, an infectious warmth spreads through my body once more, and I almost feel weightless from the feeling.

"Okay," he responds, smile growing.

"I think we should get some sleep while the fire is still burning, I can take the first watch." Laurence offers, nodding to us in confirmation.

"I'll take the first watch, I'm not that tired." stubborn as always, Clea pushes herself up and as featherlight as a cat, she swiftly finds a thick tree branch to rest atop. She swings with one graceful movement, kicking her leg up as she settles into her seat – perching on the solid branch. Her head tilts towards the forest, the jagged stick in hand as it flips and twirls in her fingers.

"Alright," Laurence replies, unconvinced as I am seeing the dark shadows under her eyes. We both lower our backs to the ground, keeping a large gap in between us. He reaches into a brown leather saddle tucked neatly within the tent and without a moment of hesitation he tosses a thick soft bundle of cotton towards me. A hand-knitted blanket made from luscious wool rests in my hands, heavy and warm. He watches me as I bundle it up tight and tuck it under my head, and curling my body up tight I can't help but inhale deeply at the intoxicating scent of pine and woodsmoke that lingers on it.

With my nose stuffed into it like an addict, I drift my gaze over to Laurence as he rolls onto his back, one arm behind his head and the other lazily draped over his stomach. His eyes are closed as his breaths turn deeper, a carefree close-lipped smile on his perfect face.

Sleep tugs at my mind as I slowly drift asleep, the calming effect of the scent pulling at me as I succumb to it.

Opening my eyes, feeling more rested than I have in years, large fluffy clouds drift over us in the sky in soft whispers. My arms push into the ground, as I focus on sitting upright. My eyes immediately latch onto him, Laurence sits with his legs outstretched and arms perched behind him, a quiet smile pulls at his lips again, one that feels like it's just for me. It's quickly replaced with darkness as his gaze flickers to my exposed arms, his body turning rigid at what he sees. Now in the light, the bruises and scratches I bear cannot be hidden. But through all of that, I can't help but return his earlier smile.

Clea's snoring can be heard for miles, something I would hate to tell her knowing she'd probably obsess over it for months. Despite the comfortable camping area we built for ourselves, I truly never felt rested with the night creeping in, so I never wake her. She's still leaning against the tree, her leg swinging off a branch, drool dripping down her chin as she sleeps. Laurence turns his head following my gaze, the instant his eyes leave me I feel a chill descent - even though the sun still shines on my bare skin. He barks a laugh seeing her, probably noticing the same thing I do - the fierce woman who would cut throats and raise hell in towns, drooling like a child, face etched with contempt.

She wakes abruptly, blinking the sleep from her eyes, and frantically looks around for the noise, locking her eyes on Laurence, she huffs and wipes her face with the back of her hand. Standing, she winces as she stretches her arms and legs, the guilt eating at me knowing she tried to stay awake for us.

"How did you sleep, my fire?" Laurence asks, tilting my head in the confusion of the name, realising he is talking to me.

"Fine," I respond, silently cursing myself for the lack of vocabulary I clearly do not have around him.

Clea stalks to us, cracking her neck. "We need to retrieve our camp and find water. Plus, I desperately need to bathe." Speaking to me, blatantly ignoring Laurence's presence, I look down at my hands covered in dirt and grimace, sniffing myself makes me feel even worse. I stink worse than a wet dog, and I wonder if Laurence cleans himself like a tiger would, the thought causes a chuckle to slip from my lips.

Laurence chuckles with mirth, his lip curling up deliciously, seemingly holding himself back for some unknown reason. He adjusts his shirt, brushing away the fallen leaves, "Now I need to know what went on in that pretty head of yours to make such lovely sounds," he breathes, and my body tingles at his words. A current of fireworks works its way through my legs, to my upper thighs, and I fight my impulse to look away and to hold his gaze.

"I was wondering how you bathed, in your Fae form, or groomed yourself like a cat," I mutter.

Laurence barks a laugh, while Clea raises an eyebrow, holding back her own smile. "I can do either, but a bath is my preferred method, my tongue does clean rather well." He winks, it's devilish, and I cough to hide the blush that threatens to creep up my face.

Dirty thoughts run through my head, but I shake it away, he is still a stranger to us after all.

"Graphic. Come on let's get moving, how long of a walk is it to your home?" Clea asks him, "Only a few hours' walk, if we leave now, we will make it back for a late lunch." My stomach growls at those words, loudly announcing my hunger, we didn't eat last night - too exhausted from the day. We can never go back, not that I ever wish to, but our lives working at that tavern are over. We have no place of work, no money, and could face prison time if Hobbs' murder leads back to us, the Thalor dungeon is not kind. I shiver with nerves, trying to feel optimistic about our new companion. Lifting the blanket in my hands, the woven threads brushing my fingers, and now able to see it in full in the daylight – a teal colour spreads through it with white thread winding around the edges, littered with small sticks and leaves that I instantly brush off. I fold it neatly, making sure it's tucked up correctly. Finally smoothing over the front, I walk over to Laurence and hand the bundle of cotton to him, his eyes linger on the blanket for a few heartbeats.

"You can keep it, it suits you," he says, placing his hand on the fabric, his finger moving an inch towards me heart wrenchingly slow as it grazes mine. Sparks fly in my vision, his touch instantly warming me. He closes his eyes in contempt, my hand pulling back abruptly not understanding that feeling. But I know in my gut, I want to do it again.

CHAPTER 15
Clea

As we approach our camp, my relief is noticeable, finding all of our belongings still intact. With our tents pitched close to The Sapphire Swan, it didn't take long to navigate our way to them, Laurence had been able to direct us with his sense of smell – that was what he told us anyway, his easy movements and casual stance had my guard up the entire way we weaved through the brushes. I would be a fool to trust him this easily, there was no denying the looks he kept giving Bonnie, an unsettling feeling festered in my gut at that look as I couldn't figure out his motives. Unsurprisingly, he moved like a cat, with light footsteps and a keen eye for spotting woodland creatures before they were visible. His heightened sense of smell and hearing paired with the teeth and claws? Lethal. And yet, his boyish laugh combined with arms swinging lose at his sides betrayed the power within him, a stark contrast from his tiger form, a big bungle of orange fur growling at us only hours ago.

"We'll just be a moment," Bonnie declares to our new companion, walking into her tent.

"Take your time, I'll be by the river," Laurence replies, his body turns away from us as he strolls over towards the riverbank we used yesterday. How was that just yesterday? Bonnie motions over towards her tent, quickly stuffing old coats and books into the bags we have that are filled with holes. She carefully avoids the larger bag set by the tree, they had been the home to a nest of hedgehogs that pitched their tent when we arrived here, the little creatures snuggled their way into our bags, and we even gave them names. Even after they moved on a week later, I didn't have the heart to move their nest, the idea that something could deem our camp as a safe haven was a reminder I needed to keep for myself when the nightmares of my childhood crept in.

    Bonnie starts to deconstruct her tent, pulling out the metal pins from the ground. I've got to know how she's feeling with our new situation, it's all too much for just one day and going to another Fae's house? It seems a little too coincidental, his appearance in our hour of need. We would need to move on regardless of our new companion, I'm sure we could find a place somewhere else, I've heard Baskith isn't too bad once you overlook the cold weather and brutish nature of the villagers. I had thought it over and over last night, my legs swinging on that tree branch as my mind played through all of the scenarios of today. He could be lying, his promise of a better life could be like a beartrap. We'd walk forward, but unbeknownst to us, there's a solid metal contraption just hiding underneath the layer of safety we reside in, ready to snatch us up and trap us. I'm always cautious to trust a man who would openly say "trust me", like it's a verbal contract they must spew out to lure the other into a false sense of security. But I cannot deny that odd scratching sensation in the back of my skull when I saw him sleeping by the fire, curled up on his side without any bedding or protection for his head. It had seemed so familiar, to be out sleeping in the woods with him, an inner voice telling me that I should trust him. Bonnie seems to echo my feelings, with the way her body moved towards his on our way here, I don't think she even realised it, like some type of magic was pulling them together. Maybe I should be more optimistic, the path in front of us is wide open and who knows what could happen in the future? If she says no, we run and we don't look back. Keeping my tone low and confident, a layer of caution weaves into my words as I address her.

"Do you really want to go with him? We just met him, he could be a psychopath."

She considers my words for a few heartbeats as her eyes roam around what we called home for the last few months. "I truly want to go. He seems nice, and he has spare rooms. Imagine sleeping in a bed with an actual roof! Plus, I want to know more about his business, I think he could help me, maybe give us a job." She blushes, quickly turning her head to conceal it.

"Oh my days, you have a crush on him!" I giggle, a childlike noise coming out at the realisation. She blushes deeper, confirming my suspicions.

"I do *not!*" she replies, joining me in my hilarity. She carefully places the blanket she was gifted, choosing a place on the ground where there is the least debris. Pulling my own tent spikes out of the ground, I shake off the fallen leaves and begin to fold the makeshift tent into the satchel I left here. We have no real belongings, just our bedding, and a metal pot to heat over the fire. We would sneak vegetables from the kitchen in the tavern, one day we managed to get a bundle of cheese, and I have fond memories of us breaking up smaller pieces for Tiny and Bron – the hedgehogs - and savouring the last mouthful. Nibbling at the edges with our bread, the flavours swirling in my mouth. I decided then that cheese was my favourite food, to which Bonnie called me a mouse for it.

"I trust your judgement, if you want to go then we will. If anything seems off…we run." She nods her agreement, seemingly happy with my acceptance.

Coincidentally, as soon as we finish packing, Laurence appears. His movements are choppy, kicking up leaves with his boots in a careless action, and *whistling*. And I wonder if he's making himself known on purpose as to not scare us, scare her.

He clearly saw the same haunted look in Bonnie's eyes that I noticed last night. As we talked, she did not move, eyes cast towards the fire. My heart nearly leapt out of my chest when she stroked the fire in a loving gesture as if it was the answer to all of her problems, I made a mental note to keep her away from any larger fires.

"Are you both ready to go?" Laurence says, I lift the satchel and bedding into my arms, and Bonnie does the same. He walks up to her and huffs, stretching out his arm palm facing up – his head tilts towards her stuff. "It's alright, I can carry it," she squeaks out.

"I know you can, Bonwin, but I would like to carry it for you."

This guy is laying it on thick.

"Okay, thank you," Bonnie says handing over her gear, he loads it up on his shoulder and steps towards me in the same gesture. The grip on my bag tightens, these trinkets mean little to nothing to me but the idea of him carrying everything that belongs to us puts me on edge.

My feet move towards the pathway as I turn to Laurence, "Which way, oh mighty saviour?" I ask, eyebrows raised. He smiles in response, "Follow me."

We walk in the woods all morning, the sun close to being over our heads, marking it as midday. A few birds sweep into view, pecking at the berries close to rotting on the floor. The view of the forest has always fascinated me, the endless depths in them. The feeling of getting lost in the trees, birds flying high up in the skies as they move from one place to another fills my soul, and I don't think I could ever express into words how peaceful it makes me. All around me, the leaves turned orange and brown as they break away and drift to the floor. This was always my favourite season, not only was my birthday coming up, but as a child, I would watch the leaves fall from my cell and count them all. It became something to look forward to, counting each leaf that fell each day. I would kick and scream when the guards would come in to take me to see Caldris, his conversations were dull, and the training was intense, but I was just annoyed that I couldn't watch the leaves fall.

Laurence and Bonnie chat ahead of me, and my arms have begun to ache from the trek, the muscles in my shoulder scream to be released of the weight. But I would rather die than let him carry my stuff too or ask for a break, we're too exposed, and Laurence knows his way around these woods – he never stops to look about, just continues walking with the casual ease of someone who was born in this land.

A snap sounds ahead of me, and Bonnie raises her foot noticing she stepped on a rather large twig. A mass of swirling black crows leap into the sky at the sound, their wings flapping so beautifully, soaring into the sky as one. I know I can create wings, it's something Caldris tried and failed to do with me, but I wish I had tried harder because looking up and seeing those birds soar as one group makes me feel free and adrift, as if I could join them too. Bonnie yelps, her body jumping backwards as her foot catches on a thick long to her left. Her arms flail out to her sides, I drop my belongings unceremoniously on the floor, leaping forward the same moment Laurence does. Unfortunately for me, he's faster, gracefully catching her in his arms. She latches on almost instantly, her body curled tight around his. He holds her in an embrace, arms locked around her. Their faces so close to each other, breaths heavy in a sort of embrace they're locked into. All I can do is stare at them, needing to interject and scream at him to get his filthy paws off of her, but words catch in my throat as Laurence strokes her back almost tenderly. Bonnie blinks up at him, eyes wide and soft as they crinkle in contempt.

"I knew it," He breathes, as he stares deep into her eyes. Her breath hitches, moving closer at the roughness of his voice. A blush creeps up on her exposed neck, and I move forward in the entrance too. My foot steps on a bundle of dried leaves, just as Laurence snaps his head to me, all kindness gone from his face. I watch in horror as he pulls her upright, pushing her behind his bulking frame, his arm still locked tight around her. His head tilts forward, his eyes darkening as a growl escapes his throat. Recognising the stance, I lift my hands up – palm facing his in a placating gesture.

"What?" I say, breathless, looking around in confusion.

Bonnie continues to look on wide-eyed and dazed from the interaction, but her hands remain on his upper arm as they squeeze tight – her eyes now flicking about behind me for any danger. He continues to hold her in a tight grip, almost primal, but Bonnie doesn't look in fear – she just holds on, as though letting go would be more painful than falling from a great height. Laurence's body remains curled around her as if sheltering her from an unseeable threat, a living shield against a storm close to crashing into them. And that's when I notice it, every muscle in his powerful body was taut as he assessed me, his eyes weighing the threat I would pose to the woman in his arms.

Bonnie did not look plagued in pain. No, she looked back at him with *love* in her eyes.

"How much further?" I ask, needing to break the unsettling development between these two. Bonnie, hesitating, removes her grip on him slowly. Seeming reluctant to do so.

Her gaze drifts to her hand as it flexes, "I can feel you, in here," she says as she places her hand on her heart and squeezes the tattered fabric, eyebrows scrunching.

His body shifts to face her, and in the same movement, his hand lifts up gently to caress her face. A lover's embrace.

"So can I, my fire, my mate."

My mind goes blank, a ringing in my ears that pounds into my head. *Mate.* A name that chains you to someone, that's unforgiving and unbreaking. A soul bond you cannot escape from, a death sentence. In all my years of running, that one word can bring me to my knees. Bonnie has been through so much and does not deserve this wicked fate. A mate bond can trick your body into wanting things, needing things you cannot want. My eyes widen in horror as she leans in towards his embrace, inhaling his scent like it's an answer to all of her prayers.

"I just forgot, Bonnie, we need to retrieve our clothes from the tavern. With Hobbs dead, people will notice our absence and grow suspicious." My words come out sharp, lies spilling out like coins out of a purse. My eyes stare into her, pleading to her, to understand the spell she's under. I curse internally at her real name spilling from my lips too, my desperation making my tongue loosen. Once we reach the tavern, we'll use the crowd as a disguise and make a run for it. She will never have to know the pain and suffering a mate can inflict on her, I will not allow the same control to befall her.

"It will be alright, I want to go home with Laurence," she responds, her tone clear and unrelenting. Her eyes paint another picture, of trust, and eager to start a new life. It makes my stomach churn, my insides turning inside out as my instincts scream at me to grab her and run. But… she has made her decision known, and if he ever raises his hands against her, they will be promptly removed from his body. I reckon I could swipe a knife or two from their kitchen, that's if I make it there alive, Laurence is giving me a warning look dripping with anger and hatred so thick it chokes me, I scoff in return, my eyes tightening in malice.

"I promise no harm will come to her, or you. I know it seems quick, but I had this overwhelming urge to run in the woods last night." He speaks clearly, gazes turning to Bonnie's awaiting eyes in a softness so intense I fight to keep my eyes locked on his. "I couldn't sleep, I was tossing and turning for so long. My head pounded, and I had this feeling I was missing something, and I had to find it. As soon as I hit the woods, my headache disappeared, my body pulled me forward for miles. When I heard screaming, my feet pushed me towards it. Every part of me coiled with the darkest of thoughts, I wanted to rip that motherfucker for holding a woman the way no man should. When he pushed..." he stops, gathering his thoughts, fists curling, "pushed you down, I noticed the spark in your eyes, what I had been looking for. Unlocking all the answers to all the questions I have been asking myself, and I wanted, no, needed to know who you were," taking her hands in his, "I killed him for you, I enjoyed every slice of my claws, wanting him to feel powerless and defeated. My face was the last thing he saw, Bonnie. If I had more time... I would have made it last."

My hands fidget restlessly, rubbing together as I stand here frozen amongst the dead leaves, a silent witness to the scene playing out before me. Her face glows with a radiance that seems to brighten with every word he speaks, a warmth I can almost feel from where I stand. I take a step back, unable to ignore how perfectly they seem to fit together, how effortlessly complete and whole they seem in this moment, side by side.

The lingering glances they exchanged, were filled with unspoken understanding, and the soft words they shared were too quiet for me to hear but loud enough to echo in my chest. Something about it hooked into my heart and tugged painfully, like I too were missing that connection. I felt helpless to the feeling, my world tilting as if I were being thrown upside down, arm outstretched for someone to catch me. Bonnie's smile tilts just so, as Laurence mirrors the action, two souls lost that were coming together. His declaration had been so breathtakingly honest that I could feel the bond already forming between them, the beautiful stillness of the woods around us seemed to take ahold of the situation as the wind drifted and swayed around their bodies. It felt like the rest of the world had fallen away, leaving only the quiet hum of their shared breaths and unbreakable strength of their bond.

I huff, "Fine, you can hold my stuff. How much further?" I repeat, ready to get out of these woods. This bastard can hold my stuff to stop his wandering hands for the remainder of our trip.

Bonnie chuckles, hand covering her mouth in delight.

"Do you have food at your home?" she asks him.

"For you, I have enough food to feed an army, or your friend here," he winks to me, I flip him off and hand over my things to his outstretched arm. He holds it all effortlessly, giving her a panty-dropping smile as he continues to walk towards his home.

CHAPTER 16
Bonnie

The air is crisp, sharp with the bite of winter nipping at my cheeks as I pull the blanket around me tighter on the back porch. Steam rises from the hot tea in my gloved hands, caressing my face in a warm embrace, it swirls up to warm my fingers as I hold it close. The bitterness of the tea warms my insides, my lips perched on the rim of the cup, careful not to burn myself.

My eyes wander to the forest in the distance, where the trees stand bare and tall, their branches stretching towards the pale sky like delicate, skeletal fingers. Icicles pepper the needles of the tree, hanging off in the morning sun as they warm and drip to the ground. The back of Laurence's estate is truly my favourite place within his land, I had found the perfect spot to enjoy the breathtaking view of the landscape and conveniently it is also within the new 'training arena' that Laurence built. Clea swings her training sword at Laurence, her movements quick and light, her body has been wrapped in training armour - an exact copy of Laurence's, just a little smaller. Their mouths release small puffs of air, white clouds spill out on the exhale, showcasing the chill they both adhere to when training. From the looks of it, they're boiling, their faces dripping sweat from the exercise. Their swords sing in the air as they swipe at each other, my eyes focusing on his muscles rippling in his tight black shirt. He is tall, towering over Clea and uses brute strength for most of his attacks, whereas Clea waits for the best moments to strike, eyes focusing on his every move.

The blade whistles through the air, each movement a dance they both know so well. I have watched them train for weeks now, after being at his home for just two months. The first time I watched Clea wield a blade was *incredible*, I had known her mate trained her as a child, but I never truly understood the depths of it. She never flinches, body confident and strong, matching all of Laurence's strikes with her own. I pitied anyone who would go up against them, as their movements moved with each other. I can see them both side-by-side in battle, swords singing at the front lines, an unstoppable force.

Laurence steps forward, then lunges, thrusting his sword with force. Clea parries with a quick flick of her wrist, the sharp noise of metal ringing out. She strikes back in attack, his foot stepping back just in time, chuckling at the challenge. Her eyebrow arches, a smirk tugging at the corner of her mouth before she lets out a snort that sounds suspiciously like she's trying to stifle a laugh - and failing miserably. She's challenging him to continue, taunting him with her movements.

I prefer these kinds of fights to the verbal ones. She had struck him with so many harsh words when we first settled here, so guarded and careful with everything he offered. It took time for us both to adjust, Clea more so, Laurence provided us with lockable and cozy bedrooms with our own sense of freedom as we roamed the place as we pleased. Her resolve cracked each night, especially when he would lay out platters of food and wine for us. Being on the run hadn't left us with many food choices, but I'll never forget the look on her face when she was given a platter of cheese and meat. She devoured it like a starving animal. Laurence teased her about drooling, and she shoved him playfully in return. At that moment, I knew the three of us would be okay.

They continue to circle each other, hands outstretched awaiting each other's moves. Clea looks healthier, happier even, to have a place to call home in the safety of these walls. We have both filled out, the only clothes I had no longer fit from the weight gained. As we were eating properly, clothes seemed to wrap around my curves, allowing me to enjoy the sight I see back in the mirror. Laurence hasn't asked for his blanket back, and I'm glad he hasn't. The only gift I was given, became my most prized possession and I decided that he would have to pull it out of my dying hands if he wanted it back.

"Boss, shipment is here," shouts one of his workers, I think his name is Adam, he has so many workers it astounds me how big of a business he runs. Maybe-Adam is lanky looking, he waves over to me, he has become a friend to me too - always keeping his distance, he once tried to hug me as a kind gesture and Laurence almost snapped his head off in warning. Walking over to me he plops down next to me; the movement urges me to shift away but I stay rooted in place.

"Who's winning?" he asks.

"I'm not sure, Clea managed to swipe his arm earlier and drew blood," I responded with pride, she's so damn strong. Maybe-Adam whistles in delight, "What a woman," he remarks. It's no secret that he has a little crush on her, heck, all of the workers do - men and women linger around when they fight. And I can see why, her powerful thrusts match his, from whispers, no one else has been able to keep up with him. Not only does Clea enjoy using her built-up energy on him, but he would wake up earlier on their training days, handing her the safety vest like a dog holding a lead wanting to be walked. His eyes would sparkle with delight each time she agreed, following along with excited steps.

They end their session, and Laurence swaggers over to me, his hand reaching out as I take it without thinking, needing to be closer to him. His hair is tied back with a piece of tattered leather, the sweat beading down his neck in thick droplets, his frame towering over me in the morning sun blocking out any light. He is truly breathtaking, and it takes monumental effort to pull my gaze from his frame as he growls in my ear.

"You are a sight to behold. I have matters to attend to, but I will return later this evening. I have a gift for you." Guiding me inside, I jump up on the kitchen counter, my legs swinging off the table. I grip the bench looking up at him playfully, "And what is that?" I ask, he stands a few inches from me, his fingers grazing my knee as he keeps his distance. His eyes burn into mine, the heat from the gaze illuminating a haze around me.

"If it's a dead mouse I wouldn't be too happy with that," Clea says walking in, with Maybe-Adam hot on her heels offering to clean her blade.

"Don't you have somewhere to be?" Laurence snaps back at her with mirth in his eyes.

"Yeah, yeah, I'm coming. Or is that your line?" She says to me, and I giggle, tucking my head down hiding my reddening face from view. His body radiates heat, the scent of his sweat is intoxicatingly sweet.

"I must be leaving, but I restocked the library with some newer books, more to your *tastes*" he chuckles, and I smile as he had been listening to my endless rambles of the romance books Clea and I had been devouring since coming here. We had almost run out, and we definitely weren't bored enough to pick up the historical texts.

"Don't be too long," I whisper, and his lips lightly touch against mine. If my feet weren't hanging mid-air, I know my knees would go weak and they'd collapse from the feel of it. The sensation crawls along my spine, feeling butterflies in my stomach with every touch he gives me. He is always gentle, his body reacting to mine in such delicious ways. I feel safe in his arms, it was hard at first being close to him, but he has always been patient and kind with me, realising I wasn't ready for anything too much too soon. The fire in my veins makes me feel alive. He makes me feel alive.

Reluctantly, he pulls away, pulling my dress to cover my bare thighs and snarls behind him at another worker who lingers at the doorway impatiently. The man rests against the doorway, arms crossed, and from Laurence's look he quickly straightens himself and coughs, "We must leave now sir," he says urgently.

Hopping down from the counter, I say my goodbyes to him and find Clea changing into her usual armour. Her clothing is fitted with leather straps crossing along her torso, securing a few daggers she says her farewells to me and follows Laurence out of the house. Something I didn't see coming was Laurence offering her a job as a guard. They were training for the first time, and after landing a blow to his torso, with wooden swords no less, he had offered her the job on the spot. She had thought he was joking, my heart swelling with pride at the offer, she had looked at me for a long moment before shaking his hand in agreement.

Once their horses drift from view, I stand in the entrance hall and spin on my heel towards the library. Laurence's home is truly magical, the large wooden cabin is a haven of warmth, and I don't know if I ever want to leave. It's nestled amongst a dense forest of towering green trees; the large windows allow the warmth of the sun to breach through the thick glass. As I walk, my toes feel the seeping warmth of the floorboards, it confused me at first - but Laurence explained the large water pipes that run underneath that allow the heat to rise to keep the house warm.

The house is made mostly from large carved pieces of wood, the living room is a large open space within the front, warm green sofas fill the space – with plush cushions that I love to sink myself in on the evenings with Laurence. The kitchen is next, nestled by the back door, with an incredible view of the stretching forest and training area - a huge area for his workers to prepare the meals, the kitchen staff is quiet, and they usually keep to themselves. I'm yet to have a full conversation with them as they whirl and glide along the floor to begin preparing the evening meal upon their return - the smell seeps into the house, buttered chicken and steamed vegetables is on the menu it seems as I see Glinda chopping and peeling the vegetables, with her daughter by her side preparing a freshly caught chicken. I wave to them in greeting as I continue my walk towards the library. Turning right, I open the grand doors to the library. It is used primarily for meetings and to store business documents, but Clea and I have found this area to be a favourite of ours as we continue to add more books here, the dark leather-bound business volumes sit in stark contrast to the colourful spines of the romance novels we love. The collection is slowly growing - much to our excitement, making this room feel even more like ours too.

    I nestle myself into the large worn-in red corner sofa that has so many cushions my body feels swallowed by it and open the book I was reading. I wrap myself tight in my blanket kicking my feet and enjoying the moment. The library smells of wax candles and a thousand stories, a warm hue descends into the room as I hold my book between my hands, feeling content to sit here. Looking out of the window, I spot a lone deer standing motionless in the woodland, its delicate frame outlined by the shadows of the midday sun. It lowers its head and chews on a patch of dead grass, the brittle blades offering little nourishment in the barren chill of winter. Each exhale sends small clouds of mist curling in front of its face, the vapor quickly dissipating into the air. Its wide, dark eyes dart around nervously, scanning for dangers, its body tense and posed to flee - a feeling I can attest to. I shift slightly, leaning closer to the glass to get a better view. The faint creak of the sofa beneath me must have carried outside, for the deer's ears swivel sharply towards the sound. Its head jerks up, the half-chewed grass dropping from its mouth. For a moment, it freezes, its lean body rigid as it stares in my direction, sensing something but unable to see me through the frost-lined pane. With a sudden burst of energy, it leaps away, its slender legs propelling it through the trees in powerful bounds. Its white tail flashes like a ghostly beacon before disappearing entirely, leaving only the quiet of the forest behind.

Trying to focus back on the book, I read without concentrating on the words, my mind elsewhere. Laurence and Clea have been quite a while, and the sun will begin to set in about an hour. I reach a spicy part of the book and slam it shut immediately. I can't be reading that right now, I look out the window again for any witnesses, and I shrink down into the sofa, my eyes glued to the page. The author explains some tricky scenarios that don't seem possible, and I begin to feel a pulse between my thighs, a sensation that feels foreign to me now. My skin feels so hot, clothes sticking to my skin, and my mind drifts to Laurence as I trace my hand down my body. Feeling a little reckless, my body immediately relaxes at the attention I give myself, moving further down to finally touch that spot that would unravel me, here in the library.

A loud bang jolts me from the vision of his face between my thighs, and I jump up, book discarded.

"Hello, is anyone there?" I ask carefully, walking softly to the door and gripping the handle. The cold metal bites my hand, shouldn't the house be heated? I hadn't noticed in my private moment, my cheeks heat when I glance back at the romance book lying still on the sofa. With my hand on the door handle, I apply a little pressure to peek my head into the corridor. Feet scuffle around, my heart beating at the same pace. I creep out of the library, following the sounds of chatter in the living room.

"You're back early!" I chuckle lightly and round the hallway, my feet stop at the entrance hall to three strangers in Laurence's home helping themselves to his cabinet full of the different flavours of wines he keeps stocked up in the living room. Words fail me as my feet take a step back, eyes flickering about the room trying to note anyone I recognise.

One man is sitting on the sofa, his beady brown eyes locked onto me from his position on the sofa, his wandering eyes smile at me, the sensation feeling like nails on a chalkboard. I eye the front door, it wouldn't take much time to run for it, the guards at the front gate should alert Laurence and give me the protection I need. As I take a moment to gather my thoughts, I didn't notice the kitchen was no longer lit up by candles - descended into darkness as did the rest of the house.

I do not feel safe, and that makes bile rise to my throat.

"Don't run off now, Bonnie, is it?" The short man sitting says, my hands curl on instinct at the use of my name. Another man is sitting on the sofa beside him, on a single armchair with his legs swinging over the edge, hands twirling a dagger in between his hands as he focuses on the pressure of the tip pushing against his fingertips. Swallowing hard, I step back again, and at that the third man by the window pushes off the window ledge and walks towards me, feet heavy. He doesn't speak, only flicks his head towards the sofa beside the man who spoke earlier.

"Sit down," the man sitting says to me, impatience clear in his tone.

My hands shake from the feeling, but my feet move forwards, and I sit down on the chair closest to the wall with all three of them in my view.

"Laurence will be home any minute," I mutter, my voice hitching, betraying the power behind the words I try desperately to push.

The man smiles, definitely the leader as he leans forward to clasp his hands together.

"It's not him we need to talk to, you must know why we're here, don't you?"

"I…I don't know what you're talking about. What do you want from me?" I say, trying to keep my voice steady, but the quiver of fear betrays my calm composure.

"Cut the act. We're not here to play games," the man with the knife says, head raising to lock eyes with me. The scar on his cheek looks sickening, barely healed, and poorly made stitches line up the side. The leader chuckles and takes a sip of the wine from Laurence's cabinet directly from the bottle. The wine jostles in his grip, his throat bobbing as he drinks deeply and a sour feeling creeps in as he lazily helps himself to Laurence's special blend now tainted with his hands.

"At least we'll have refreshments," he growls, his voice dripping with malice. As he speaks, he drags the sleeve of his arm across his mouth, the motion slow and deliberate, a gesture that makes my stomach churn. The faint scrape of the fabric against his skin is the only sound in this suffocating silence.

I feel trapped, caged in my own home, the walls closing in like the bars of a prison. My eyes dart around the room, searching for an escape that doesn't exist. Their presence fills the space, heavy and oppressive. My pulse thrums loudly in my ears, drowning out my scattered thoughts, and bile rises in my throat as panic tightens its grip. I try to avoid their gaze, but those piercing, unrelenting eyes feel like knives, cutting through every feeble attempt to shield myself.

As their words hang in the air, cold and menacing, a suffocating dread washes over me - I might die in this room.

Chapter 17
Bonnie

"You've got answers. Answers we need. And you're going to give them to us, one way or another." I swallow hard, these men are clearly after something. The man standing hasn't spoken yet, his eyes dart around the room, observing every detail and finery the house has like a wolf. His presence is heavy, guarding the door if I run for it.

"You're shaking," the leader observes, tucking my hands under my legs to hide the trembling, my thighs tightening on impulse. A nervous laugh bubbles inside me, trying to buy time, "I'm not sure what you think I know. But I don't know who you are, and I would like to kindly ask for you to leave," I say, my voice becoming more assertive. This is not just Laurence's home, Clea and I have made this our own too, and I plan to defend it with the only resource I have, time.

"Enough," the leader barks, his voice cutting the air like a blade, leaning forward his eyes demanding answers and *soon*.

"You think we're here because we enjoy the view? This fancy house is nice and all, but we've got better things to do," the other man says, rolling his eyes, seeming uninterested at the scene.

"Maybe if you told me what you're looking for, I could help you. I don't want any trouble," I continue, effortlessly trying to dispel the suffocating feel of the room.

The man standing, quiet as a mouse fidgets, his clothes are loose on him as he watches the leader talk with rapt attention. A guard dog awaiting his master's orders.

"You were there, weren't you? That night everything went sideways, and we didn't get our payment. Why else did you and your friend run off." The leader continues, lips curling into a smile as his eyes assess my reaction.

"I...What night? I don't go out much..." my heart pounds in my ears, they've got to be talking about Hobbs and his disappearance. We hadn't thought of the repercussions of giving a cover story, and we must have been noticed somehow. I didn't know running from one monster would lead three others to our door.

"Look. You can cooperate, or you can make this difficult. You think we came here without getting your description and name? We just want to hear it from you. Make this simple for yourself and tell us where Hobbs went," he continues to push.

"Who?" I ask, my voice hitching ever so slightly.

"The owner of The Sapphire Swan, your former boss." The man with the knife says, almost bored. My voice stumbles, words catching in my throat like glass shredding me apart from the inside.

"Spit it out," the leader snaps, voice almost growling.

As the night falls, the shadows in the room deepen, stretching long and sinister across the walls. The absence of staff in the house becomes painfully clear, their usual loud bustle replaced by an unsettling silence. The figures before me seem to blur within the shadows of the descending night, their presence amplified by the quiet as if the room itself conspires with them.

"We're not leaving until we get what we came for," the man says with a sing-song voice, his tone remaining unnervingly calm as he pushes harder with this knife, skin splitting ever so slightly.

"I don't know who you are referring to, I work here," I say, trying to deflect.

"Don't *lie* to us Bonnie," he spits out, head tilting as his eyes squint noticing my trembling, my body telling him all of the secrets my lips try to hide.

"I'm not. I promise," my voice squeaks out, and I finally curse myself for not training myself in self-defence or working on sharpening my tongue like Clea can. If only she were here, she'd know what to do. The knife spins in his hand, as he wipes it on his shirt. The overwhelming fear of him using that on me makes my mouth tremble, the thought of Laurence and Clea coming back home to see me bloody and dying on their carpet… I couldn't do that to them. They're all I have in this world, the two most important people to me. Maybe if I tell these men what they need to hear they will leave, I could lie and say Hobbs ran away with the money they're owed but I already lied about not knowing him. The inner conflict makes my head pound, and my vision goes blurry as a few tears spill down my cheek at the feeling.

"Tie her up," the leader says, as the larger man standing creeps towards me.

"Wait, please, I don't know who you're talking about. Please, don't touch me." More tears spill as a sob leaves my lips. I feel helpless, again, a red-hot feeling overwhelms me as anger takes over.

"Don't touch me!" my voice rising now, spitting in his face as the quiet one grabs my arm roughly, his other hand holds thick lines of rope with dark stains on them that definitely does not look like red wine.

His round eyes look at me for a moment, and his hands hesitate for a split-second sensing something in mine just as a flaming pink blade shoots into his skull. It pierces against the back wall as his body falls against it with a loud thud, his arms hanging limply at his sides. His jaw unhinges and relaxes, a scream pierces my throat at the sight.

"You have overstayed your welcome, Barnaby, take your other goons and leave before more blood gets spilled." Laurence spits, his voice dark and thick in the room as a whimper releases from me seeing him here. The sound is like a growl that speaks to my bones to submit, his commanding tone keeping me rooted to the floor.

The bright fuchsia dagger flickers in the dark, flames seem to dance on the edges of the jagged blade, the only light in this grim room.

The man holding the dagger sneaks up to me and holds it to my throat in warning. A snarl leaves my lips, surprising me, the anger boiling over as I find myself in this situation *again*.

"If you don't remove your hands from her this instant you will lose yours," Clea snaps to him, warning in her eyes, her mouth pinching in anger. The man holding me chuckles "I'd like to see you try. The moment you do, this little lamb will be spilling all her insides over this pretty floor of yours" he says, and I wince, feeling caged and trapped.

"If you cause even one mark on her body you will regret it, it looks like you also made a mess in my home. Leave now before we slaughter you like you did my staff." Laurence snaps back, eyes hardening at those words, gaze trained on the man who captured me. My mind races to catch up to me at his words, *the staff...*

Barnaby stands, wiping his hands from his trousers in a casual stance. "This woman was responsible for killing a man who owed us a large debt in coins. Therefore, it is their responsibility to pay it. We are not leaving until we receive that payment, her and the blonde would settle the bill I think." he says, his grin laced with thick tar making my blood run cold.

"You're mistaken in your assumption that we would give you anything after you broke into our home. Leave this instant or you will be carried out, in pieces." Laurence threatens again, gaze never leaving the man who holds me tight.

The man laughs and draws out a dagger, movement scuffs behind Laurence, he spins and takes a hit to the gut from a fist he didn't see coming.

The room descends into chaos, swords and daggers start flaring. The only light in this room is Clea's bright sword as it slashes through the air. Now I can see it clearly, the vivid glow pulses with energy, and colours of fuchsia and deep crimson paint the air with streaks of colour as it arcs and twirls in graceful, fluid motions. Each swing leaves a fleeting trail of light, a dazzling display that lingers for a heartbeat before fading into the darkness.

The man drops me, his feet rushing forwards, but I don't see where - as I immediately duck to the ground and curl to hide behind the sofa, my hands covering my ears at the sounds within the room. The material of the sofa keeps me grounded as I press my back to it, my knees curling up as I tuck my body in tight.

"Told you," Clea sweetly says, at who, I don't know. Large thuds hit the floor along with metal slicing bone, my heart pounding in my chest drums out the sounds behind me. A few moments later, what feels like hours, and the fire roars to life in the room. Someone is screaming, it's so loud I squeeze my hands over my ears tighter.

"Bonnie. *Bonnie*," someone says to me, touching my shoulder. Their voice is muffled, but the movement makes me jolt and I turn in fear and scramble away from the noise. Terror blinds me for a moment. The room comes back into view, just as Clea crouches low in front of me and whispers to me, shushing me and comforting me with tender words as reality comes crashing back to me. I launch into her arms, gripping tight.

"Close your eyes," she says, and I follow her instructions immediately.

"Laurence is coming, just keep your eyes closed, okay?" she continues, rubbing my back with her palm as it calms my racing heart. My breaths come in quick pants, and I notice the screaming has stopped, my throat raw from the sensation as the sound stops coming from my own body. My shoulders shake coming in sobs as

I breathe in her scent, and take solace in her embrace, feeling better now she's here and safe.

He approaches softly, my eyes peeling open to see him, "Are you both alright?" panting, he sweeps his eyes over my body checking for bruises or marks, a question in his eyes. I put my hand on his arm in response, giving him my permission, and he crashes his body into me - wrapping around so tenderly, my body hugging him back just as fiercely.

I peek my head over his shoulder out of the window spotting Clea running into the woods, pink flames illuminating her body. Laurence notices and without a word winds his arm around my waist and hooks my legs under his other arm as he carries me out of the room. My eyes close on instinct and I bury my head into his chest, ignoring the wetness I feel there.

"She wants to do a perimeter check. We had been discussing a trade deal with a tavern close to the one you worked in and overheard whispers of the hunt for you both. They saw you in the gardens and planned to attack with us distracted. We ran as quickly as we could," he admits, head bowed.

"I'm so sorry, we let you down, left you here with no protection," forehead resting on mine, voice breaking, "I can't lose you, my fire." Seeing vulnerability in him splits my heart apart, and needing that look to leave his face I ask, "I have visions of her riding in your tiger form, storming ahead and charging into battle." His lips curl up into a smile, a hint of amusement in his eyes.

"She gripped so hard, I'm not surprised if I see my fur scattered along the woods," he responds chuckling, feeling my mood lighten.

"She did ride you!" I choke out, trying to hide my laughter at the image.

"I would do anything to get us back, and I wasn't leaving her there. She's a good fighter and a better friend," he admits. My heart grew three times the size at his comment.

We step throughout the house, his body instantly stills "Close your eyes again, Bonnie" he instructs. I close them without hesitation, as he slowly walks me upstairs laying me on the bed in my clothes urging me to rest. I do not ask or make a sound when he leaves the room. As I felt the large steps he took being held in his arms, the vibrations in his growls every time he would lift his leg pierced my heart. I pull the duvet over me; head resting on my pillow as I hear the sound of large glass cabinets breaking downstairs.

CHAPTER 18
Clea

"Again," I command, voice raising to match the sounds of crates jostling.

"How many more today?" Bonnie moans, her hands bracing in front of her face, fists upraised. We had found an old soft barrel that Laurence was planning to throw away, it had grown mouldy and seen better days. But it was better than the bale of hale we had tried using for a few weeks, the barrel was placed on top of wine crates to give the perfect height of a body.

She drops her arms, wiping the sweat off of her forehead as her panting echoes in the stables in the early morning sun. I pick up the water canister and hand it to her "Drink" I instruct.

"You're being so bossy today, what's up with you?" Bonnie accuses, I respond with mock outrage, "You're still not done, stop trying to distract me," laughing, I lift her hands upright again. Her hands are wrapped in thick cloth as she curls them into a fist and punches the barrel, the wood shifting with each movement. I hold it steady on the other side, arms gripping the side to take the brunt of her hits. She finds a good rhythm, and I whisper words of encouragement as her pace gets faster. Her brown hair is tied back, and she fitted herself with the same clothes we wear for training,

Laurence almost dragged her into their bedroom at the sight of her - no longer wearing pretty dresses, but in tight gear. I had to convince him for a whole eight minutes we needed the daylight for her training, dragging her away as her resolve started to crack too.

One, two, one, two. Her movements are quick and fast, she's getting better the more time goes on and I try to imagine I do not see the flicker of emotion in her eyes. It's clear she doesn't see me standing opposite her, no, she sees Hobbs and those men who held her hostage in her own house a few months ago, her mouth always sets in a frown and her face gets lost in a haze I know all too well. All I can do is hold the crate, against her attack, trying not to remember the darker times. My heart splinters each time her blow lands, the pain in her eyes evident.

I look up to the sound of footsteps, Adam, Laurence's second comes to a halt in our make-shift training room. "Hey ladies, Mr. Laurence has asked for your company, he would like to go to the market and would like to know if you want to join?" he looks in awe at Bonnie, noting her improvement. Her face lights up, "A market! I haven't been to one in ages! What do you say, girls trip?" she asks me, eyebrow raised, and my own smile lifts to my face.

"Yeah, let's do it."

"I will let Mr. Laurence know," Adam says, turning to leave.

"Oh Adam, tell *Mr. Laurence* he can ask us himself next time," I tell him, he flusters and blushes just a little on the cheeks looking embarrassed. "Are you coming?" I ask for conversation, he's a nice guy, a little shy and definitely needs to come out of his shell. I'll admit that he's handsome, blonde curls adorning his head that sway with his movements and he's well spoken, I think another version of me would go for someone like him. I just know Bonnie would combust with excitement if I did, double dates… heck, double weddings. Adam becomes another reminder of how lonely I truly am; I have never laid with a man since leaving Caldris. In fear, he would find out and hurt them. They would never understand. I do not have a choice while Caldris is still breathing.

"Yes, Miss, I will be accompanying you all. I also have errands to run," Adam replies with a smile on his lips, his eyes linger on my face as they always do. It would be so easy to give in, either a one-night stand or maybe falling in love… it's better this way. I tell myself that each day, but I know in my heart that loneliness creeps in as I watch Bonnie and Laurence embrace with love and contentment in their eyes or the sounds they make in their room - I swiftly make my way to the library on those *occasions*. It never bothers me; I just feel happy knowing Bonnie is healing… in whichever way she needs to.

"We have to change though, I smell so bad," Bonnie says sniffing herself, she scrunches her nose, and not for the first time does she remind me of a deer - her doe-eyed look, small nose and full lips. She unwraps her hands, as I place the barrel down no longer balancing and stretch my arms too. I have been so overwhelmingly proud of her, after the arrival of the unwanted guests in the house she begged me to train her in self-defence. Once we covered the basics she was hooked, wanting to learn more, especially how to punch someone enough to knock them out cold. I could definitely use the help protecting this place.

My home.

A smile lingers on my lips at the thought, I had been working with Laurence since he offered. Feeling the need to fill the void of doing nothing but sitting around and reading. I needed to feel needed, have a purpose to keep my mind distracted, keep the bad thoughts at bay. The pay was good too, better than working at a tavern. But over time, the work became more than a paycheck and an activity to dispel the boredom, feeling the belonging rooted in my soul - the urge to protect the house, along with Laurence and Bonnie. I had that feeling for so long that when the intruders slaughtered some of the staff in the house I snapped, their deaths were quick and painful. Once the three men were taken care of, we found a few lingering about the house. I hadn't thought, I just swept the area and ran into the woods needing to secure the house. It felt more like pest control, killing all but one. I even found a pencil and pad in one of their pockets, I had written a message and stuffed it in the hands of the last man standing, with the instructions to never come back or speak of the occurrence or I would find him. The note read:

There is a target on anyone's back who would work with a rapist.

Laurence sat in the living room waiting for us after we bathed and changed. His eyes take on a faraway look, closely watching the red liquid in his glass tilt and flow with his movements. His face visibly brightens as Bonnie enters the room. The living room had been rearranged, new brown furniture dotting the area. It had been the first task after cleaning the area and arranging a funeral for those lost to us that night. Their lives were stolen from them too soon, Laurence had spared no expense in their burials and gave their families enough money to live off of for their entire lives. It would never ease the loss of death, but it would make their lives one out of poverty they would face without the income of working at the house.

"Your carriage awaits," Laurence teases, rising from the sofa and guiding us out of the front door. He opens his arms wide, showcasing the four horses saddled and ready to head out. Walking up to my horse, its large, kind eyes meet mine. I reach out my hand gently, feeling its head lean into my touch, the black mane silky and thick under my touch, flowing through my fingers like waves of soft velvet. Time seems to slow as the horse closes its eyes in trust, I run my hands along the leather saddle - Laurence and Adam make quick work of latching the cart to the back of our horses and he swaggers over to lift Bonnie up onto her horse, hands lingering at each touch. I can feel Adam shift beside me, and in one big swoop I latch my left foot into the straps and swing my other foot over. I must keep my distance. My body comes alive as the horse starts to move, my muscles shift to the movement of the horse and I have the overwhelming urge to take off into a full sprint. The feeling of sitting on this large beast brings me back to the day Laurence had let me hang on when we raced to reach Bonnie during the attack, and if it wasn't an intense situation I would have enjoyed the feel of the wind in my hair and speed in which he ran, I was close to vomiting when I jumped off his back, the apple and cheese I had for breakfast sat uncomfortable in my stomach as I relieved them of theirs. The horses trot into a line, as we move out of the housing estate, its feet clicking on the stones. We move past the worker houses, and outbuildings, the gates passing us by moments after. Bonnie sways with the movement too, her body adjusting to the movement, but it's her eyes that I can't look away from - they light up from the sensation and my smile grows wider seeing her enjoy this as much as I do. Guess we found a new activity. Clearing the gates, large fields spread wide in front of us, Bonnie squeaks in delight as the sunlight splashes on her face, and with a small jolt to her horse she grips the saddle tighter. Securing her stance, her back adjusts to the new sensation. A laugh slips out of me at the complete contrast in Laurence's stance, the exact opposite in front of me with one hand resting on his thigh as he leans back in his saddle to talk with her. We fall into easy conversation, Bonnie talking animatedly about the things she wants to buy for the house, Laurence hanging off every single word in utter adoration.

Looking down, I notice silver flashing on the side of the saddle I hadn't spotted before.

"Evreux?"

"That's the name of the horse Miss," Adam informs me.

"Where did the name come from?" I ask in wonder, reaching over to see Bonnie is riding 'Fabian', another name I do not recognise.

"Ah yes, these horses were rescued from the war zones, they decided to give them the names of the soldiers who helped save them from the battlefields," Laurence explains.

"Let me guess, you're riding Amazu?" I ask him.

"Who else?" He confirms, shrugging nonchalantly.

Of course, Laurence had chosen one of two leaders of Thalor, I had never met them but spotted their faces from afar when hosting gatherings in the town announcing their latest news of the town and being present for new shop openings. They seemed kind, taking time to speak to their townspeople. I hadn't had the urge to speak with them, like the others would, being crowded by villagers vying for their attention. Sometimes it made me sick, their faces splitting into sickly-sweet smiles and laughing at all of their bad jokes. They were just people, after all, born into their lineage, and I had the feeling that staying away was something they appreciated.

Arriving at the dedicated horse stalls just outside of the market, I dismount my horse and use the rope to secure him to the post. My hand brushes along his mane, the sensation like soft black feathers that float in the wind. The others dismount too, guiding their horses in the same fashion and checking the fresh water and hay is available to them.

My legs are so stiff, inner thighs burning from all the clenching from riding Evreux. The market hums with life in early spring, a riot of colour and scent filling the entire street. The air is fresh and sweet, the aroma of ripening fruit and the delicate perfume of blossoms hit my nose. Sunlight pours through the open stalls, showcasing the jewellery and glass stands. Walking to the fruit stand, Laurence greets the owner like they're old friends, chatting animatedly about the grapes and apple shipment he has for him. Bonnie and I scour the market table, piled high with vibrant fruits in every shade. Strawberries, peaches, and apples are piled high in triangle shapes. She tugs on my arm, moving us to the next stall with freshly picked flowers. Lavender bunches sway slightly in the breeze, and I take a moment to breathe in the intoxicating sweetness of them. I spot pink tulips, immediately falling in love with them, Bonnie and I purchase a few handfuls, my grin widening as I imagine the bunch I purchased sitting on the windowsill of my bedroom.

The vendors' voices catch my attention from the other side, and my attention is once again on the jewellery laid out on pretty little ceramic dishes. I have never wanted fancy things, but looking at the prices and feeling the weight in my purse gives me such a warm feeling, I purchased a bracelet and a small silver necklace, something about it just called to me. Bonnie buys some for herself too after looking through the jewellery, and we help each other put them on as we walk to the cheese stand, and unsurprisingly I buy a few rounds of cheddar, brie, and blue cheese.

We start to walk back the way we came, the crowd whispering about an exclusive upcoming ball in the palace. Ladies gossip and spread elaborate stories. A comforting warmth fills my heart as I take in this place, the simple act of shopping for food stirring a longing within me to feel like just another person going about their day. It gives me a glimmer of hope - a taste of the normal life I've yearned for so deeply and for so long.

"The walls are covered in flowers and diamonds; one brick could buy you a new carriage."

"I heard they have a live string quartet, and they fly above the dancers playing their instruments."

"We are going, my husband secured us tickets, it will be Laia's first ball. As long as she behaves."

Bonnie yanks me from the crowd, "It's so loud, shall we go find Laurence and Adam?" we are in a small alley, and Bonnie visibly relaxes at the quiet, the loud sense of the market continues in the pocket of quiet we found.

"Yeah, my feet are a little tired anyway," I lie. Even though I love it here, I'd much rather we leave and return another day if it would help her feel better.

My eyes flick to the other side of the alley, it's a long tunnel of old grey cobblestones. A tall woman walks down the centre, her dark skin illuminating the afternoon sun, wearing a simple yellow-ish dress.

"Ah, I see him! Come on," Bonnie says to me, but as I turn, I catch a man walking by - too close to her. He's clearly been following her, he's hiding his face each turn, she stops to look up at the building and looks to make a mental note of something up high. Bonnie tugs my arm, the same moment the man attacks, he swipes by her, pushing her forward and sprinting off in the same direction.

"Hey!" she shouts and tries to run, her legs catching on her tight dress as she stumbles.

"We've got to help her," I say to Bonnie, already walking towards the other woman.

"Who?" she replies, keeping her pace beside me, as we reach her quickly.

"Are you alright? I saw the entire thing, I didn't catch his face, I'm sorry," I speak to the woman, she blinks back at me in shock. "I'm okay, thanks, the bastard took my bracelet," she rubs her wrist, and I swear I see sparks lighting up her fingers at the motion.

"He had brown hair and brown eyes. He looked to have been following you for quite some time, if he stole a bracelet then he'll probably look to sell it nearby." I inform her, trying to get as much information as I have for her.

She laughs, it's low and menacing, "Oh we will know who took it, but thanks, it was charmed by my family to curse anyone who took it..." she grins, her face falling a moment later.

"....It was kind of you to check on me, my name's Sophie," she says, and I smile back, "I'm... um, Charlotte."

"Nice to meet you Charlotte, and...?" she says, eyes flicking to Bonnie standing beside me.

"Bonnie," she bows low to Sophie, the movement is odd until I note the stance of the woman and the very fine gown she is wearing. She comes from wealth, if I had to guess, she was royalty or close to one.

"I see you've met Sophie," Laurence comes bounding over slinging an arm over Bonnie's shoulders, and smiles in greeting.

"Hey Laurence," Sophie rolls her eyes, mirth lacing them. But behind Laurence is a rugged man who greets Sophie in a way only a lover would. He kisses her cheek, strapping his arm around her waist. He's a tall man, with shaggy brown hair lacing his emerald eyes, like the others he doesn't dress up in finery but wears open-top buttons, his easy smile reminds me of someone but it's gone instantly at the flicker of metal that dangles from an earlobe. The tiny dark sword swings with his casual movements, on others in the village it would look rather odd, but his black eyeliner completes the look making his eyes even brighter.

"Laurence was just giving me the latest details on the order for the ball, he has enough of that sparkling wine you like - it will be delivered in four days," the man smiles, nodding to Laurence.

She visibly brightens, smiling wide, "You're a great man, Laurence." Sophie quickly explains how we met and raises her bare arm noticing the lack of a bracelet adorning it.

"We'll get Ev on it, Soph," the man promises, eyebrows furrowing in annoyance. He holds her arm in his and slowly strokes her arm in comfort.

Laurence claps his hand on the man's shoulder and widens his arms, pointing towards us. "Fabian, I'd like to introduce you to my newest companions. Bonnie, my mate, and …"

"Charlotte!" I burst out, I'm sure I sound like a crazy person, but sharing my name out in the street with people I just met is not a wise move to keep hidden.

Laurence coughs, quickly wiping the confusion off his face from the pleading look I give him.

"Fabian, like the horse, right?" Bonnie says proudly, Fabian rubs his jaw with his hand chuckling, "Ah, I see you took the horses here, how was the ride?" he winks playfully, and as Laurence laughs, we swiftly join, unsure how close they both are. Fabian smirks, folding his arms in a casual pose. I smile, enjoying being part of a group of just normal Fae laughing and chatting at the market.

I realise now I look *normal*, I guess you could call this hiding in plain sight.

"We'd best be going, I will see you two later tonight," Laurence says, hugging them both, kissing Sophie on the cheek in farewell.

"It'll just be me, kitty cat, Sophie had last-minute plans to help with the ball setup. And I guess, now needs Evreux's help to find the scum who took her bracelet." He scoffs.

With that, Fabian and Sophie pivot to turn back the way she came, my gaze following them towards the palace. I couldn't take my eyes off of the towering structure, the palace climbed towards the sky in large blocks of grey stone and sharp points along the top reaching so high. The windows sparkled in the sunlight, and the entrance held the most beautiful artwork of flowers and crystals, something rolled through my heart like a long-distant memory I cannot recall.

CHAPTER 19
Clea

"So...Charlotte?" Laurence asks as we all flop onto the sofa and high-backed chairs, exhausted from the day. Beams of soft light spill into the living room, casting a glow over the new furniture, the afternoon sun is setting as Fae settle in for the night. I reach for a clean wine glass on the central wooden table that a server had brought through, grabbing the red wine next, I squeeze my finger and thumb over the cork as I not so carefully pull it out. Laurence grabs two glasses now, placing them in front of me as I pour the deep amber liquid in generous waves. I add an extra thumb measurement to mine, knowing that this conversation will be a difficult one. Handing her the glass, I flick my eyes to Bonnie, she places the wine beside her with a nod in thanks. Her eyes hold mine for a moment longer, and with a small nod, her eyes sparkle from her smile, one I have seen before, trust and encouragement.

"I wanted to use a fake name," I shrug as I take a sip of the wine, the tang of cherry and spice hits my tongue, swallowing it down, I feel it burn my throat, and it instantly warms my bones. I settle into my seat in contentment.

"Are you both planning to go to the *Spring Ball*?" I ask them out of curiosity, with Laurence knowing someone in the palace. I wouldn't be surprised if he got an invitation, and Bonnie too. I bet it would be a great location for Laurence to propose, the bulge in his jacket has been so annoyingly obvious I'm surprised Bonnie hadn't noticed. He went to the market to buy a ring after all. I spotted him watching us picking out jewellery earlier today, I had pointed out rings to Bonnie for her opinion without her even realising she was picking out her own engagement ring.

"Yes, we did get the *royal* invitation. Don't dodge the question Clea, why Charlotte?" Laurence persists, he sits opposite me, Bonnie curled into his side. His arms rest casually on his knees in his own way of showing trust, and his eyes crinkle with his lazy smile – he's patient, and ever so kind. I would expect him to laugh or crack a joke, but he just sits there waiting for me. Not quite an interrogation, but I can sense he is trying to understand me, listening without judgement.

All I can do is stare, Bonnie listened when I cracked so long ago - we had run into Malik in one of the taverns we had been working in, it was a *no questions asked* kind of favour, I bolted so fast but she just ran with me in silence until I was ready to explain, we found a job at The Sapphire Swan swiftly after.

I look over to Bonnie, her eyes now closed as she breathes deeply in sleep nestled beside Laurence. Her head is perched on his arm, face completely relaxed and content, her head lolls a little in front and without a word, Laurence carefully lifts her up to lay across his lap, his head leaning against the chair's back. I grab a thick burgundy blanket from the other chair and wrap it around her. He smiles at me, and as I settle back into my seat, a deep sense of brotherly safety and love washes over me. I trust Laurence, he has stood by us both no matter what and kept me around like a third wheel, or some would say a stray cat. He never treated me any differently, and I am beyond grateful to him.

I exhale slowly and polish off the last of my red wine.

"It is quite a long story. I'm sure Bonnie has told you?" I say to him, my tone low as to not wake Bonnie, his eyes remain locked with mine as he shakes his head, *No*. A warm feeling spreads across my chest, Bonnie kept my secret as she always promised, and my love for her grows tenfold for that act of kindness.

"Alright, I'm overdue to share my story with you, I'm surprised you hadn't asked sooner when I materialised my *gift* earlier." I chuckle, it's light and open. It's true he hadn't asked, but I had the feeling there were more pressing issues from that night and I had been rather volatile - my emotions needing the outlet those men gave me, I had shut myself away for quite some time afterwards needing to calm down from my rage. He nods, agreeing with the unspoken statement, clearly thinking the same as I had.

"I was originally born in Drakharrow, my birth mother had died during childbirth. It was a dangerous birth, one that Caldris had orchestrated."

"The leader of Drakharrow?" Laurence asks, recognising his name.

"Yes. Twenty-two years ago, he received a prophecy, one from an elder known for having the gift of sensing mate bonds with two Fae. A year prior, a large event had taken place to celebrate Caldris and his lineage. It was an event that happened every ten years when the Sanguinara crystals were at their most powerful. I never understood why, but those parties were quite scandalous. Guests didn't wear clothes, and participated in *activities*." I grimace, those parties were rumoured to be large orgies all in the large palace. Caldris had abstained due to feeling ill but had most likely been witness to my conception. The thought never fails to make my stomach churn.

"Because of this *party*, many women became pregnant that year. The prophecy read that his mate was due to be born, with the mother already pregnant. He did not wish to wait. He was an impatient man and one with many resources. Caldris sent an order to his guards to gather all of the pregnant women in his land, and he... he imprisoned them all."

I pause at Laurence's raised eyebrows, shock registering on his face. He nods his head once, a silent urge to continue, concern laced in his eyes.

"There were around sixteen women who were caught, I found out later that some did not survive the capture. Once he had them in his grasp, he decided that if his mate were to be born...she should have wondrous powers to meet his own." It was no rumour that Caldris was a powerful leader, Drakharrow had ancient ties to its land along with the crystal's powers.

"Caldris had the power of the Sanguinara crystals through his lineage, through his blood. He wanted his mate to have that same power 'an unstoppable force against Thalor' - he said. That's why no one can defeat him." I lower my head, I hate running from him, I have tried to fight back but he wins *every damn time*. I turn my palms upright and a pink glow illuminates my fingertips, it doesn't require much effort, but I cannot keep it for long in this state. Laurence's eyes grow wide in awe, watching the fire-like substance dance along my palms.

"The crystals were a natural phenomenon, large pink chunks of rock formed in the land. They were quite beautiful, they would light up the town and were rumoured to bring good luck. If even a drop of blood dripped onto it, it would grow in size and grant you a wish. It was stronger than glass but would always shrink back to its original size. Caldris decided to take samples of one and tried infusing his magic into them. It took a few tries, but he was able to replicate his power in a mirrored sense, but it was dangerous and required replenishing. With his first *experiment*, he implanted that new magic into a newborn baby that was born in the dungeon just days after being captured. The baby… did not make it, so he tried a different approach. And injected it into the pregnant women. He believed if he could weave the power into the very bones of the children then they would have a better chance of surviving."

"How many children survived?" Laurence rasps, remorse in his eyes.

"Eight, five girls and three boys," I replied, my voice void of any emotion. I look at Bonnie again, sleeping soundly, seeing her so content and happy gives me the strength to continue my story.

"He slaughtered the boys…" I wince, "As you may know, a mate can only recognise the other once they mature into an adult. We were safe until we turned 16. We would train each day, instead of hearing bedtime stories and drinking hot chocolate, we would go to bed with broken bones and bruises. Growing up with four other 'sisters' was all I ever knew. Blood and violence was woven into my very being at a young age." And as much as I try to squash it, sometimes my temper has a way of coming to the surface more often than I would like. But Laurence knows that about me.

I pause to refill my glass, giving my hands something to do.

"Is your father still alive?" He asks me.

"No, I had heard later on that my father had been one of many who fought against the capture and didn't make it," I said, tears threatening to fall. My parents had owned a farm and were honest, good people. Before I escaped, I had visited his and my mother's graves, well *the grave*. It was a mass grave, the large, covered pit was horrifying - I would sit by it some days, giving me some sort of connection to my parents. It also never failed to fuel my rage.

"And your 'sisters'?" Laurence asks.

"When our birthdays arrived, and the bond did not form, a girl would have the chance to be granted freedom. But to do so, she had to prove her strength against us all in a fight. None of them left alive," choking those words out, I can still see the desperation in their eyes each time we would have to fight each other to the death, the challenge was a death sentence. Even if we could disarm our siblings, Caldris would not allow that type of power to roam free. Long forgotten memories resurface now, the ghost of a long-healed scar in my heart pulses painfully as I see their faces in my mind. I miss them all dearly, especially Charlotte, she was the one who truly taught me how to control my powers. She was brilliant, mastered all of the challenges Caldris had orchestrated and was painfully shy around him, but so was I at the start. She even showed me how to create small animals in my palm. She favoured small rabbits the most.

"I'm so sorry," he says, head bowing. "How did you escape?"

"I was the youngest, so when I officially matured into a woman, I had no one to battle, but Caldris recognised the mate bond instantly. On the night of my birthday, he… claimed the mate bond." I swallow audibly, determined to get my story out, but I could not stop the tear that escapes as a sob burst out "I lay bleeding in his bed as he left to attend to his duties, Magpie, a soldier of his found me. With Caldris occupied, he gave me clothes and showed me the underground tunnels to escape. Long story short, I went through the tunnels, but not before finding his experimentation room and destroying everything - all of the Sang crystals he tampered with."

"And then you came here?" He asks.

"Yes," I smile at the memory, and chuckle at the coincidence, "I had hidden myself in a crate full of wine, called *'Paws & Pints Brewing'* wanting a better life, and hoping Thalor could be a new start."

"See even then I was looking out for ya," he chuckles lightly, now currently the owner of that business and continues. "What a crazy coincidence, that was before Drakharrow closed its border of trade, I haven't been able to sell to them for *years.*"

"What will they do without your watered-down wine?" I joke, and he simply growls playfully at me.

"There is another part of this, curse, whatever you could call my gift. It requires replenishing, and drinking blood is the only way to materialise larger forms." I say, head bowing. He had seen me bite one of the men in the house during the chaos of the attack, and he had tip-toed around the subject ever since.

He nods, considering my words. "That explains a lot of things… thank you for sharing your story. It truly means a lot to me that you would trust me with the vulnerable parts of your life. It's something I don't take lightly," he says, the words lifting my spirits as he continues, "That also explains why you were sleeping in the woods and working at that seedy tavern. I thought you were in love with Bonnie this entire time."

I spit out the wine I was sipping, "Maybe I am," I joke.

He smirks, then his face becomes serious "I'm very glad to have you in my life, Clea. I am eternally grateful you have been such a great friend to Bonnie. You have and will always protect her no matter the battle, something I would do for you too." Tears lining my eyes, I process his words. I cannot remember the last time I truly felt safe being in the presence of, let alone living with another man. He stormed into our lives on one of the worst nights of Bonnie's life and has wormed his way into my heart. I actually care about the bastard; he has given us so much without ever wanting anything in return.

Clearing my throat, I pronounce my words with as much gratitude as I can muster.

"I am very grateful we met you, Laurence, you oversized housecat."

He nods his thanks and blinks softly.

"I invited Fabian for drinks this evening as you may have heard earlier, I can cancel if you would like your privacy. This is your home too." Laurence says, my heart swelling with emotion at the statement.

"Thanks for thinking of me, but I'd like to see him again - to socialise more, I mean. As long as you don't tell the same clearly fake story again of you saving that kid from drowning." I chuckle, wiping the tears from my cheeks.

"It happened!" He exclaims, and Bonnie blinks awake just as we hear a knock on the door.

"Good evening," I say to her as Laurence gets up to answer the door, she stretches like a cat, and yawning she says, "I must have fallen asleep, did I miss Fabian?"

"Unfortunately not, my dear, I just arrived," Fabian says strolling in, his trousers are loose fitting, kept held up with a leather belt that has a skull on it. His shirt is open once again, revealing black chest hair and golden chains adorning his neck, he rolls his sleeves up to showcase the row of tattoos that weave up his arm. He comes in and takes our hands in his and kisses them in greeting, a gentleman laced with an agenda. He gives me the feeling that he would leave each house he arrives in with his pockets full of stolen trinkets, the gleam in his eye as he roams the fully furnished room says it all. I roll up my dress sleeves, showing off the new golden bracelet adorned with red rubies that I had bought earlier with a silver feather necklace. His eyes flicker to it for just a moment, and I wonder how long it'll take for me to notice once it's gone.

He sits down to my left, and the other two take their seats. All four of us sit in a square pattern with the table in the centre, Laurence excuses himself and comes back retrieving a stack of cards.

Shit, I never learnt how to play. With Bonnie out on the tavern floor most nights, she observed the customers playing variations of the same game with the flat pieces of cards, each with the Thalor symbol on them in complex styles and colours to symbolise their worth. I hadn't paid much attention, nor wanted to participate in the chatter. Conversations in the tavern usually drifted towards hatred, a few beers in would further loosen their tongue. Thalor didn't keep the blatant hatred of Drakharrow a secret, each time it would dig up old memories of what could have been, lies and rumours would circulate as no villagers from here have actually crossed that side in years. Even though I would rather listen to another one of Amazu's dull speeches than go back to Drakharrow, I still think of them on my birthday, my parents who fought for me with every dying breath. Laurence starts to flick through the cards, turning them the right way up as he mixes them up in a random order, fingers smoothing over the soft edges as he goes. It reminds me of when I managed to steal a pack for Bonnie one night, she tried explaining the card game to me, but she spoke so fast with excitement of us being able to play on our own that I didn't catch any of the words.

"Let's split into teams, Bon…"

"I take Bonnie!" I shout, wanting to be on the winning side "women vs men" I say shrugging my shoulders in challenge, pinning two genders against each other is always a fun way to get the men riled up - each gender tries to prove something by winning, and therefore receives bragging rights. Laurence chuckles, and Fabian smirks nodding to him. "You're on," Laurence says, taking another sip of wine, he starts to deal the cards between us.

"So I was carrying twelve new bottles of our Red collection into the tavern by the lake," Laurence drawls.

"The Fishing Boat?" Fabian replies, taking a sip of wine.

"Yes! That's the one," Laurence continues, their voices zone out in my head. I've heard this story so many times now, but it's Bonnie's favourite. Even now, she listens to him like she has never heard the story before, completely in awe at his words. Noticing my glass is empty, along with the two bottles on the table, I push my legs upright to find some more.

"In the kitchen, the brown cupboard to the left of the stove," Laurence slurs to me, he's drunk the majority of the wine - it usually takes him quite a few to feel the effects, but with his bulking frame and tiger shifting abilities, he burns off the alcohol easily. Stepping into the kitchen and finding the cupboard Laurence mentioned, I open it to find two unopened bottles of wine and a bottle containing a weird blue liquid. It's labelled with his company logo, so I reach for it too, trying to avoid the spider's web weaving in the corner.

Proudly walking back with my treasures, I also grabbed some snacks from the countertop that the kitchen staff had prepared for us. Little cubes of cheeses calling to me in delicious voices I couldn't say no. I placed the heavy bottles and tray of food onto the table, now cleared as they saw me approach. Fabian takes a red bottle, and quickly opens the top, pouring himself another. His shirt has opened more as the night has gone on, and his shoulders seem more relaxed as time goes along. He strikes me as the kind of person who wouldn't just be loyal to the grave for the ones he loves - he'd move heaven and Virelith to protect them. He had casually mentioned stealing trinkets for money when he was younger to feed himself, openly admitting to his crimes. I don't think there are any lines he wouldn't cross for others. And I find myself warming up to him even more, finding the similarities in my story. The glint in his eye tells me that he not only enjoys stealing but that he might actually *crave it.*

"I see you found my first attempt at making a new beverage," Laurence chuckles, picking up the bottle in his hand. The bottle swishes, the glass catching the light of the candles and making a gentle slosh sound from the movement. He taps on the glass with his finger, looking at it wistfully.

"You worked on a new recipe?" Bonnie asks in awe; she's swaying slightly but hasn't had nearly enough the amount the other two have. Her cheeks are a little rosy from the wine, her body is relaxed within the newly bought chair she's in.

"I did, after we lost the contract with Drakharrow, I was desperate to prove myself to my father. We needed more business, and I had been experimenting with a flower grown in our garden."

He pauses, his mind lost in the memory.

"It tasted awful and took *weeks* to ferment, it's highly flammable and could definitely be dangerous if mixed with other chemicals," a cheeky grin pokes on his face at that omission, I hadn't realised Laurence had a thing for explosives "My father passed when I was able to finish the recipe. I had forgotten all about this."

Words stuck in my throat. I look over to the painting on the top of the mantlepiece, thankfully it was one of the few pieces of furniture that survived the attack. It was crafted when Laurence was just a young Fae, he had told us he just shifted and his father was immensely proud of him, you could see it in his everlasting sense of pride now painted on the canvas evermore. Laurence stands tall in the portrait, posture perfectly aligned, exuding effortless confidence. He is dressed in finery, clutching his waistcoat with poise wearing a proud smile.

Fabian lifts his glass in warm regard, "He would be proud of the man you became with your business, and the love you share with your fiancé."

Laurence snaps his head to him, eyes wide - just as Bonnie squeaks "Fiancé?"

Oh shit.

Wanting to retract my kind statement of Fabian earlier, I look at him in annoyance, he quickly wipes his face with his hand and stumbles out a half-apology.

"I think you should drink the unknown liquid to make up for it," I joke, a wave of excitement bursts into Laurence as he quickly agrees, chuckling at the face Fabian pulls at the suggestion.

"I'm not touching that stuff, no offence Laurence, but it's been sitting in your cupboard for who knows how long and there's weird black bits floating on the top," he says, grimacing at the bottle.

"It's unlike you to back down from a challenge, Fabian," Laurence teases, staring him down in challenge.

Fabian looking unsure and a little pale gazes at the bottle again. "You don't have to if you don't want to," Bonnie says as he reaches to pull it towards himself. Her tone becoming urgent and worrisome.

Fabian grabs it regardless, wiping the dust from the top and as soon as the cork is popped off, we all cough and gag, the *smell*.

"Smells like a dead skunk in there!" Bonnie exclaims, and giggles covering her face.

"Smells like vengeance, don't worry brother, it won't kill you," Laurence says, now lifting his glass in the same gesture as earlier.

We all laugh as Fabian pours the liquid into his mouth, drinking it down.

As his throat moves, the liquid sloshes and spurs in the bottle, his face grimacing as he continues to drink. The smell alone has me wanting to block my nose, a very strong smell of Rose and Lavender - reminding me of cleaning supplies.

Laurence quickly stops him after a few gulps, "Steady! Anymore and I would have Sophie to deal with if you passed out and died on my sofa."

Bonnie bursts out into laughter, making us all turn to her. The feeling is like a burst of light breaking through a cloudy sky. Genuine joy spills from her that feels almost foreign, yet whimsical all at once. I can't remember the last time she laughed this hard, so unguarded and content. It's the kind of laugh that's contagious, making me smile just witnessing it, the two men matching my expression watching in rapt attention at her joy.

"Lovely to know the thought of my death has you this entertained," Fabian chokes out, coughing as he clears his throat and reaching for some food to wash down the taste.

"It's not that," she starts, clutching her belly in laughter, "Laurence said 'Steady' to the horse" she rasps out. At her words, Laurence chuckles too and turns to our confused expressions, "Bon Bon over here rode the horse named after you earlier."

"I did," she giggles, pointing to me as she speaks to Fabian, "Clea rode Evreux! Do you know him?"

"I do, he's like a brother to me." Fabian remarks

"What's he like?" I ask, the question slipping out of me before I can stop myself. Fabian turns his head towards me, brushing off the crumbs that formed on his chest.

"He trained with Sophie and Amazu for years growing up. He's a bit of a loner, married to his job sort of thing." Fabian remarks, shrugging his shoulders. My mind tries to imagine what he looks like but all I can see is the horse, black fur gleaming with the daylight sun, standing alone in a field - gaze locked to mine. My mind imagines him with wings, the horse leaping up into the air and flying away until all I can see is a small speck of darkness on the horizon.

CHAPTER 20
Bonnie

The night stretches on, the sun now a distant memory as I sip my second glass of sparkling wine. The effervescent bubbles rise within me, warming me more deeply than the fire ever could. Laurence is engrossed in conversation with Fabian, and it's clear their bond runs deeper and longer than I had imagined. Their easy rapport warms my heart, drawing a smile to my lips as I watch their closeness. Their voices rise in an animated discussion about the upcoming *Spring Ball*, the details of Sophie's elaborate plans filling the air - fancy liquor, gleaming glassware, and flowers adorning every surface. It took me longer than I expected to realise that Laurence was providing the alcohol for such a grand event. The business he inherited from his father was larger than I initially understood, but the changes he's made over the years are clear. Watching him grow and refine the craft his father cherished fills me with pride. I drink more of the fizzy wine, enjoying this moment and committing it to memory, Laurence is so carefree and happy. His hand reaches out and closes with mine, sensing my fidgeting "Bonnie, you remember Mr Maddox? The one who ordered ten times the amount by mistake." Laurence says to me, bringing me back into the conversation, Fabian looks to me awaiting my response like I am to answer an ongoing debate.

"I do, the order form had an extra zero on it, he was so angry," I laugh in response, remembering that day. Mr. Maddox needed a type of red wine that was especially crafted from an expensive berry Laurence had found with his father years ago. It was especially hard to make and took longer to ferment. Laurence worked day and night to complete the order, whistling as he worked - I had perched myself in his workshop and read almost all of a new book I picked up that day. He never wavered, taking small breaks, his strong arms lifting the equipment as he worked. When Mr. Maddox came to pick up his order, Laurence had rushed out with the thirty bottles of wine. The man had started sweating from the volume of it all and paid for it all anyway not realising his mistake.

"He loved it so much he passed it around for every birthday and celebration, his wife was so pleased with all of the praise they got, to this day I don't think he admitted his mistake." Laurence said, now sipping the mysterious liquor, he grimaces but continues to drink. Fabian, unconvinced, continues on "I don't buy it, how can Mr. Maddox find thirty people to give bottles of wine to? The man is unbearable!" chuckling, Laurence follows up with "Apparently now he is a favourite in the town."

Fabian nods his agreement, swaying slightly, he pats his knee loudly causing me to flinch from the sound, as he stands abruptly. "Well, it's been a great night catching up, but I must get back home. Bonnie, it was wonderful meeting you properly," he slurs and starts to walk over opening his arms for a hug which I avoid, the smell of alcohol stinging my nose. Laurence slaps him on the arm slowly pushing him to the door, holding onto his bulking frame, he almost bumps into Clea who has been sleeping on the sofa for the past hour clutching an empty bottle of wine.

"Sorry Charrrrrrrlotte," Fabian giggles, *actually giggles*. She readjusts her posture and continues her snoring, her head cradled by her arm. I reach for the blanket draped over the chair where Fabian had been sitting, their voices murmuring farewells in the background. Carefully, I spread the blanket over her, ensuring it covers her arms. With a soft touch, I take the bottle from her loose grip, setting it quietly on the table to avoid any harsh noises. She stirs slightly, tucking herself in instinctively and nestling deeper into the cushions, her breathing steady as she drifts further into a peaceful sleep.

Laurence gently steps back into the room, soft feet pressing on the floorboards, his presence drawing me in before he even reaches me. His hand reaches up to graze my cheek, soft and warm - a tender touch I had been yearning for. Slowly, his fingers drift down my arm, his touch light yet grounding, until he takes my hand in his. He lifts it to his lips, kissing my knuckles with a lingering warmth that sends a shiver through me. His hazel eyes meet mine, locking me in place as butterflies take flight in my stomach. There's something profound in his gaze, a depth that speaks directly to my soul. The warm browns and fiery oranges in his eyes swirl together like beautiful melodies, filling me with a sense of belonging. I remember the first time I saw him in his tiger form - the raw fear and the inexplicable pull to let myself be consumed by the beast. At that moment, I thought surrendering might free me from my suffering. But now, those same eyes ensnare me not in fear, but in the overwhelming sense of him, of us. His lips press another kiss to my knuckles, then trail slowly up my arm, each featherlight touch igniting goosebumps that ripple across my skin. Heat blooms within me, pooling low in my stomach, and I feel the flush of it rise to my cheeks. Cupping his chin with my hand, I guide his lips to mine. He kisses me softly, unhurried and tender, our mouths moving together as though they've always been meant to meet. His arms wrap around me, drawing me closer, encasing me in his warmth. I pull back just slightly, needing to take him in. In the glow of candlelight, the stubble on his jaw casts a shadow that scratches lightly against my palm. His smile spreads, filled with longing, and I feel myself fall further into him.

He gazes at me with a quiet question in his eyes, his gaze drifting softly across my face as if searching for an answer. After a moment he whispers to me "It's late" softly swiping my lips with his fingers.

"...And I taste my fine wine on your lips, let us get some rest, my fire," he says gently.

At that, we both glance at Clea, snoring like a beast in eternal slumber. My gaze flicks back to him, the way he sees her warms my heart, someone other than me that she can trust and depend on. More importantly, a friend and ally in this cruel world. I hungrily trace the lines of his face with my eyes, and feeling the pulse of heat slowly growing, I know that tonight… sleep will not quench the thirst I have for him. My mate, and my everything.

He looks back at me, his eyes darkening at my stance and in an instant, my feet are swept from under me as he carries me upstairs. My feet dangle and brush against the wall in his haste, and I press my hand to my mouth to muffle the sound of my giggling.

Laurence's smile could stop wars, relight all candles in the land. It's that bright. Feeling mischievous, I creep up onto the bed as soon as my feet land on the floor, I sit there facing him as he readjusts his trousers. We have laid together before but tonight feels different. Tonight, I met those closest to him and felt myself slowly opening to the quiet joy of being part of a family - a warmth that holds me close and fills my heart with love.

My hands graze the bedding behind me, the fabric soft and welcoming beneath my fingers. The intricate threads of the duvet catch my eye, their orange and black stitching forming a pattern that almost resembles a tiger leaping gracefully into the woods. I see it in his eyes, the beast lurking underneath - and the thought only makes my pulse quicken. He just stands there, the heat in his gaze penetrating me. His hands rise as he slowly starts to unbutton his shirt, lifting it up over his head and laying it gently on the chair beside him.

The room feels hot and thick. His eyes never leave mine, hungry, yet restrained. I have always felt him holding back for me, being gentle and kind but that's not what I want tonight, and by the way he stalks towards me tingles in my chest, the sensation apparent in my gown. His gaze tracks the movement, my dress doing little to hide my arousal.

His knees crash to the floor in front of me, in front of the bed. Without looking away, his lips kiss my right knee, his thick lashes blinking in the moonlight. His hands close around my shoes, and ever so gently he slowly removes the straps and places them on the floor. He takes his time, hands braced on my calf as he looks at me in prayer, as if I hold all the answers to the questions he has been asking his entire life. Finally, he lifts his head to me, the motion causing his hair to shift gently - soft strands sway with the movement. A few errant locks of fiery red hair escape their binding, framing his beautiful face. I reach up to stroke his hair, and ever so slowly I pull the leather bind out of his locks. Running my fingers through them, my hand getting lost in the sensation of it all, soft purrs emanate from his chest as his eyes softly close leaning into my touch. His finger trails up my calf, lifting my dress up tenderly, my bare knee now exposed - he kisses the bare skin. His lips are hot and wet, each kiss sends a jolt of fire up to my inner thigh. My breaths come in and out as my chest expands in yearning, his hand continues his exploration up my legs, slowly parting the material until I'm completely bare to him. The corner of his lip tilts up deliciously, noticing the lack of undergarments I am wearing, and I bite my lip nervously at his stare. The midnight air kisses my exposed skin, and the moonlight filtering through the window casts a beautiful hue into the room. As he moves, he never explores further, enjoying the moment as much as I do. In that moment, I just knew that if I were to say *No* or walk out of the room for any reason - he would not follow, and allow me the space I needed in this vulnerable moment alone between us. It had taken me a while to open up about what happened at The Sapphire Swan, a wound I will wear for the rest of my life, but Laurence… he washes that vicious memory away. The first time we had been intimate together, he had seen something in my eyes, because he refused to continue regardless of my asking. I am glad he did, the overwhelming rush of being mated took control of my senses sometimes... and I am forever grateful for his patience and kindness with me.

His hair brushes against my bare thigh, a featherlight touch - I reach up and thread my fingers into it. My grip reaches his head as I push ever so slightly, and at that, he becomes unleashed - head diving between my legs. He lets out a moan that sounds like a growl as he descends on my wet heat, grabbing my legs with both arms to gain better access. Guttural moans leave my throat at the sensation. His tongue laps at my core, finding that bundle of nerves that desperately throb with need. His fingers dig into my flesh, pushing wider, and I whimper "More" in a breathy tone, needing more of him near me. His grin is feral as he removes a hand from my thigh and slowly pushes in two fingers. The sensation has my toes curling and a moan releases from my lips, louder this time, from the onslaught of his mouth and fingers. His pace quickens as I feel stars' shine in my vision as I come undone from touching that perfect spot within me. My core tightens so beautifully as my heart races, desperate for release. The fabric of my dress sticks to my skin from the sweat forming on my back, my head kicks back as his hands roam upwards to cup my breasts and grab my waist. Feeling the peak arise, a guttural moan leaves my lips.

"More," I squeak out again pleading in my voice, needing more of him near me. At my words, he leans towards me, lips glistening with my wetness.

"Do you want my cock or hand, Bonnie?" he asks, his guttural voice laced with desire as his face shifts closer to mine.

"Feel how sweet you taste," he says just as his thumb swipes along my lips. The taste is indeed sweet; the musky scent fills the room as his nostrils flare enjoying the smell. His bare chest glistens with sweat that I long to run my tongue along, the hard lines of his chest like a sweet melody only played for me. My hand reaches out to touch it, his beating heart pumping wildly under my palm, my hand drifts lower - eyes latching on the bulge in his trousers.

"Use your words," asking again, I look back up to him as he awaits my decision.

"I need you, all of you," biting my lip as he follows my gaze. He kisses my lips again, sweetly, before wrapping his arms around my waist and lifting me further up the bed, trailing kisses up my stomach and relishing in the softness of my skin. He reaches up to lift my leg up around his waist, lips latching onto mine, tasting so sweet. My hands fist his hair, and I pull him closer, causing a sensual moan from him. His bulge presses into me, and my wetness pulses with the closeness of him wanting him closer.

I reach down, driven by an aching need for him to fill the void inside me, to quench the fire within. He lets out a soft chuckle, his smile radiating love and tenderness that makes my heart ache. With deliberate care, he removes the final barrier between us, and in one fluid motion, he thrusts into me, my insides stretching so lovingly as he pushes deeper. A whimper leaves my lips at the sense of fullness. Hooking my other leg around him, I push my heel into him urging him deeper, he complies, a rough grunt escaping him along with his heavy breathing. He moves slowly and continues peppering kisses on my cheeks. I push further wanting more, "Greedy" he moans in my ear, biting the flesh softly.

With one last thrust, his hands push under my legs and in one fell swoop I land on top of his bent knees, able to seat myself fully. My legs hover over his, as he grips my waist. He slowly guides me down further, lips brushing my neck. I yelp in pain, the feeling stretching me so much my head spins, the sensation still foreign from the sure size of him. His movements stop abruptly; his face comes into view as he tilts my chin up searching into my eyes. In response, I softly blink into his gaze, and my legs push me down deeper - taking him greedily. Once I adjust, my hips begin to rock gently, the sensation hitting a deeper spot inside of me that I hadn't realised I had. A moan slips from my lips again, wanting to take him in completely. My lips crash against his, my arms winding up around his shoulders for better purchase, and he smiles against me in appraisal, his arms wind around my waist and one trails down further down my belly. His fingers softly circle the bundle of nerves that aches painfully.

"You are so beautiful," his voice filling the sound of our bodies colliding. His hips move faster, the pace quickening and pushing deeper within me and my vision explodes with fire and stars as a wave of climax hits me. The feeling continues for a long minute as I chase the full high, my mouth stretching in a soundless scream as Laurence continues his pace within me. I collapse into his arms, as I wipe the sweat from my brow. Coming down slowly from my high, my breath quickly catches up with me as the room comes back into view. Laurence nuzzles his head against mine, as his hands grip my waist, inhaling the scent of me. My hips begin to rock again, enjoying the sensation of being connected to him, and ever so slowly the pace quickens once more. His forehead presses against mine as he stills for a few moments, following in his own climax as his arms wind tighter around me.

Like bands of steel, his arms guide us down to lie side by side. Grabbing a small towel from a bedside table, he begins to wipe the remnants of our pleasure from my thighs. He works quickly, softly moving the material to clean my body and then his. The pillow gently cradles my head as I wait for him to move closer, a contented smile spreads across my face. I feel safe, cocooned in this moment, as a pleasant ache hums through my body. And in my bliss, a memory resurfaces from tonight.

"Ask me to marry you," I breathe out, his lips parting for a second.

"Marry me," he breathes out and not missing a beat I respond "Yes."

The moonlight continues to spill into the room, as my eyelids grow heavy. My cheeks ache from smiling, the echoes of our lovemaking still lingering in the air. With a tender touch, Laurence reaches for the duvet, his movements unhurried and careful, as if preserving the fragile beauty of this moment. He drapes it over me, tucking it gently around my shoulders, enveloping me in its comforting warmth. His hazel eyes linger on me for a heartbeat longer, and I can feel the care in his every action, a silent promise of love and protection as the night deepens.

"I was wondering what Fabian had meant earlier," I say, wistfully remembering his slip-up earlier.

"Please, my love, do not say his name to me whilst we are in bed, naked," he chuckles and I smile too, loving the warmth of this moment. "But yes, I had planned to ask soon," he admits, looking sheepish.

I take his hand in mine and press it against my chest, "I think I would have hated something elaborate, this seems perfect," my hands stroke his hand linked with mine.

"Really?" he asks, seeming a little guilty.

"Really." I assure him, the words so confident and assuring spilling from my lips. Sleep pulls at me again and my eyes begin to close, blissfully happy and wrapped up in his warmth.

Chapter 21
Evreux

The tea scolds my hands, my knuckles had barely healed from the beating I gave Andreas, now a distant memory - feeling like it had been months as opposed to days since the events of the *Spring Ball*. The morning sun seeps through into the sitting room, shining a light on the empty grey sofa opposite me. Sophie patched up Fabian quite well, seeing as he had a concussion from his future self who had knocked his ass out. I watch him with a heavy heart, his brown hair frames his face - usually full of cheer and mischief, now shadowed by furrowed brows as he nurses his coffee.

Amazu had instructed us all to gather in our private sitting quarters, to discuss the strategy for the upcoming council meeting, to find a way to spin the events that had caused the palace to be in so much ruin. My mind was spinning from all the unknowns we had faced, trying to figure out what had happened for our world to have turned to shit so fast for the only solution to be for them, *us*, to go back in time to defeat the evil that took route. The confusion churns within me, a living thing in my stomach that burns and tightens with relentless energy.

Not only was the palace infiltrated, but the rug was also pulled out beneath us, a large shimmering portal had spread into the ballroom that I had been in thousands of times - only to disappear moments later with these intruders. My hands itch to continue training, to take Hale out to our battle arena and train him in combat and skill to be ready for anything else that could befall us. He was only a young Fae, all he should care about was his studies, facial hair growing and having crushes at school, not thrown into war with weapons and the fear of death.

We were all on edge, not only did we not see an evil descending in our home, but another group of Fae fought in our place, and I know for certain that I never want to feel that helpless again.

"Ev, your hand is burning," Sophie softly says to me, placing her cold hand on mine. I unclasp my hand over the tea I was holding and place it down not realising how hot it was, my mind adrift and wandering. It did not help that I haven't been able to sleep ever since that evening, her piercing blue eyes the only thing I see when I close mine.

The tea sloshes onto the table with a thud, and I grasp my hands together tightly, my palms red and sore, trying to ignore the pounding in my head from the relentless questions blurring through my mind. Sophie takes her seat again, concern in her gaze laced with a storm that's brewing behind her eyes - I can see she is struggling as I am, trying to understand what had happened between us all, in between seeing Fabian from the future and tending to the injured one to my right all in one day was something I hadn't thought was possible.

I hadn't thought time travel was possible.

But we are alive, and I know who we can thank for that.

The huge grey doors crack open and Amazu and Athena walk through with arms linked by their sides, their faces set in determination, and I consider adding something stronger to my tea in anticipation of the upcoming conversation we are to have. Dressed in their finest attire, they had clearly taken the time to cleanse themselves of the past, scrubbing away the memories and presenting a polished stance, ready to start anew. In stark contrast, Eva has been curled up on a single armchair by the window, a shadow of herself. She hasn't eaten or bathed since the event, her hollow, haunting eyes tell stories of sleepless nights and unspoken horrors. Her once lively form was now gaunt and fragile, curled into a tight ball as though she could physically shield herself from the weight of her thoughts. She was utterly silent, motionless, a mere whisper of presence that pierces my heart. If not for the nervous habit of biting her nails every few minutes - a small, compulsive action breaking the stillness - I might have thought she was asleep. Yet even that small motion felt desperate, like a lifeline tethering her to the reality she seemed ready to slip away from.

Amazu had adorned a light blue jacket, gold threads woven around the cuffs fitting perfectly to his body. He moves to sit on the empty sofa with a tight grip on Athena who is dressed in similar clothes, their way of presenting a solid front.

"Thank you for gathering here, we wish to discuss the events that happened at the Ball, what to tell the other leaders, and how exactly we will address our people. It is of the upmost importance to continue the peace and strength my husband and I have built." Athena starts, which has us all nodding in agreement, Eva watches her lips to read the words and continues to shuffle - burrowing herself further into the soft cushions.

"Amazu and I have been speaking about the specific words spoken during that day, some of it is not quite clear to us yet, but there seems to be powers of being we do not understand ourselves," she finishes, mouth in a tight line. A server comes in with a new tray of hot teapots, two empty cups, and another filled with perfectly shaped sugar cubes. The sugar knocks against each other once placed down, and I can't help but imagine the time it took to make those silly shapes, something I still find a novelty - something to make food pretty and easier to digest. All the fancy stuff goes right over my head, growing up I would be thankful for bread without specs of mould or it being charred and burnt, I wipe the sneer on my face I can feel, knowing it will anger Athena who unlike me had grown up with the finer things in life.

Amazu pours Athena and then himself some tea, "Fabian, let's start from the very beginning. Could you walk us through how you came to be unconscious? I understand you were struck rather severely to maintain their deception at the ball?"

I sit up straighter feeling the need to defend them. I was part of that group after all, the bitter words sinking to my stomach like the sugar cubes Athena drops into her cup.

"Yes, I had just collected my jacket from the tailor and was laying it on the bed, I had thought Sophie came in but next thing I knew - I was hit around the head with what seemed to be a candlestick." Fabian says, eyes wide and unbelieving. "My hands fell onto the bed, and grabbing the nearest thing to me, a god-damned pillow, I tried to defend myself... only to see my own face staring back at me with green hair no less. I had thought the hit to my head was playing tricks on me, or a witch had placed a curse on me, but he just stood there holding the weapon. His face was... haunted. We fought for a little while, he met me blow for blow, knowing all of my tricks and got the upper hand." Letting out a long breath he continues, "Next thing I knew, I woke up in a broom closet, with Sophie shaking me, she looked so panicked I could sense something big had happened."

"It's not your fault," Sophie says to him reassuringly, sensing the inner turmoil inside himself, a feeling we all felt, being defeated in our own palace, being ambushed and forced to watch.

"Did he say anything to you at all?" Amazu pushes.

"Not at first, only a mumbled 'Sorry' before everything went black," he responded, rubbing his head absently, the bandage doing great work of healing his head wound. We were lucky to have healers in the palace, they were paid well, enough not to spread rumours. I had promised Athena when they worked on healing those of us injured that we would keep the secret between us, if this secret got out before we could, Thalor could fall.

Fabian shakes his head in anger, "That bastard took my place, and danced with Sophie, inserting himself in all of it. I heard Laurence made an appearance when those beasts started arriving, is that true?"

Athena nods her head in wonder, "He came in at the right moment it seemed. This future Fabian and a woman named Clea had been battling with Hale against our own guards. Laurence had led the charge with Baskith soldiers, it was truly breathtaking, seeing them all fight together. We cannot deny the connection they had with Hale, they risked their lives for each other and for us." It was truly remarkable, not only had connections and bonds formed those five years, but Laurence had somehow convinced the Baskith people to fight for us - something they are not known for. They were a closed-off village in the snowy mountains in the East of Thalor, we had attended just one event there with it being Athena's original birthplace, even she seemed grateful to leave that place or from experience, her overbearing parents. The soldiers had seemed enraged, fighting in her honour. That realisation alone could move mountains, the weight of their loyalty undeniably strong in the face of danger.

Athena pauses, collecting her thoughts before continuing her recollection, "I cannot comprehend how we walked through that bright light. I didn't recognise Amazu at first, he had looked…" She stops herself, a single tear running along her cheek as her mind transforms back to that moment. It truly was grotesque, a testament to the years enslaved. She stirs the tea quickly, bringing the cup to her lips.

"It was strange to see us defeated." Amazu continues, placing a hand on her knee "But we rose from the ashes, as we always do. We will find out what spell was used to remove the sickness within the ball. We recovered the book, Fabian, do you think you could look at it to give us the answers we seek?" Amazu asks.

"What spell book?" Fabian queries, interest peaked.

"A collection of pages was retrieved that seemed to weave an intricate spell. It seemed to require a lot of fire to activate and burn it away. Hale…" his resolve cracks for just a moment, as he blinks to return his train of thought "He'll grow up to be a fine leader." Amazu's eyes shine with the memory and Athena places down her mug to hold his hand in hers, my heart squeezing at the motion.

Clea.

"It breaks my heart to have seen him left alone, without his parents. At least in this future, Evreux had been there to train him," Athena says, turning to me, her voice laced with pride. A small smile stretched on her painted lips as she nodded to herself. A quiet satisfaction lit up her face, a nod that spoke of relief and validation, as if the words she just uttered were exactly all she needed to continue living with the thought that her son had grown up without his mother. A comfort seemed to glow within her at that.

"He wasn't alone," I state, thinking of Fabian and Clea who had stood together with him, fighting for and with him the entire time.

"He was not. Somehow, he got corrupted by the events. Something must have happened for the hatred to have taken such a deep route in him, to all of them, for Fabian to have wanted to kill Eva. We must find out who this Clea is, maybe she knows or had an influence on the others." Amazu says, looking at Eva, as we all took a moment to process those words. Strangers had broken into the palace to kill someone dear to us, we were all blindsided. My mind was stuck in an endless loop seeing Clea standing there in her blood-soaked gown, arm raised in a protective stance.

Clea.

"Did anyone speak to her?" Fabian said.

Sophie nodded her head at that "Yes, I found her in my room looking through my things, she had said she was a maid. But now I wonder if that was all a lie to get close to me and snoop through my room. I had helped her into the ball, giving her a gown and everything." She snaps the final part, looking down at her hands in frustration. We could all feel the sense of betrayal she felt, clearly feeling something for this woman who crashed into our lives. Clea had connected to her immediately, latching onto her for the reason she needed, nothing was stolen as we had found, but why else was she going through our rooms? A spark of longing etched through me knowing she was right there, getting dressed with Sophie before the ball, I had been with Sophie only moments before. I should have stayed, if only to see her for a few precious moments.

"It seems she may have used her connection to Fabian to understand you better, maybe even manipulated you in that moment," Amazu considered, "But she meant well. She clearly will have a connection to us all," his eyes flicker to mine for a gut-wrenching moment, "and I cannot deny her trained ability in battle, we need her on our side wherever she is. Did she say anything about where she was going or who she was?" Amazu says, eyes locked on mine, all heads turned to me seeking answers, the very question I had been asking myself.

Feeling my jaw tense, I shake my head, I had more questions than answers, and I was itching to go out of the palace in search of her. "No, the last words she spoke to me were to find her in the future. She did not give me any specifics. Although she clung to

Laurence quite closely, maybe he knows her somehow?" I say hopefully.

My gaze looks to our leaders, Amazu pauses for a moment and declares, "Laurence has been invited to the council meeting, he visits the taverns often with his trade and could be valuable in spreading the right information. These guests will hopefully influence those to not spread false claims. Caldris has also accepted."

"He's coming here?" Sophie gasps, only Amazu has met the Fae - his powers unparalleled to ours, a threat he had always posed to the safety of the people here, from what I have heard he would knowingly do anything to gain power. If he were to find the true nature of the evil that took route, it could have catastrophic events, maybe even what sparked Morvath in the first place. It seems Amazu was rather shaken by this attack, for the need of Caldris is one to show security and strength.

Amazu nods slowly, the motion heavy with reluctance, even now he is dreading his arrival.

"Indeed, all mention of Morvath must be strictly between us, Caldris would gain even more power than he currently possesses if this information were to fall into his hands, if it hasn't done so already." He looks back at me, lips pressing in a thin line. "We can ask Laurence if he may know who Clea is, but we need to be careful, she could be dangerous, her powers are unlike anything I have seen and although she was on our side this time, she may not be an ally to us now." The words hit me like a blow to the heart, in a way I can't fully grasp - my future self loves this woman I have yet to meet, a stranger who stirs both fierce protectiveness and searing anger within me.

And that thought, the conflict, is slowly tearing me apart.

"She wouldn't hurt us. I... I just know it, I can travel to his house tonight to ask him," I announce, heart pounding at the hope that he may know *something*.

"I don't think that is a wise decision, we must focus on keeping this as a secret for now. Evreux, I empathise with your need to find her, but I kindly ask you to speak to your men first. We must find out what we can, and quietly." Athena interjects, squashing my plans entirely. My heart deflates, knowing I have to wait another week before getting the answers I seek.

Sophie speaks up, hand resting on her chin "Fabian, who was Laurence with at the market? We bumped into two women, right? Charlotte and another who he introduced as his mate?"

"Who?" I spat out, my tone unrelenting and demanding. Did Clea love him? Had I lost my chance at meeting her properly, and Laurence came in at the right moment? My legs bounced in annoyance, glancing out the window feeling like every second was being wasted as I just sat here and drank tea.

"Calm it, Ev," Fabian whispers to me, sensing my agitation, "I went to his house just last week," he said swiping his hand over his face, like the memory just resurfaced thinking about it now, "He invited me round for drinks, and I met Bonnie his fiancé, well... she would have been if I didn't mess up his proposal. She had brown hair and was rather quiet. Charlotte on the other hand was loud, seeming reckless and abrasive, and she seemed to watch my every move. They had an unshakable bond, and for the first time in Laurence's home, I felt like an *outsider*. It is their home as much as it is his." he finished.

"Laurence and Bonnie are close to being engaged?" Amazu asks, his face scrunched sensing something. His mind piecing together the puzzle.

"He was planning to propose at the ball, but their plans *changed*," Fabian's mouth quirks to the side, a telltale expression that says it all - somehow, he had managed to worm his way into the proposal plan and failed spectacularly.

"Yes, Bonnie, that's right," Amazu states, nodding to himself. "Before the others had returned, and they were cleaning up the debris, I heard Laurence and Clea speak of a wedding between the two. They shared fond memories of staying at their house. Maybe this Charlotte, is Clea with a hidden name?" he says, hand rubbing his jaw recognising the connections and my head snaps to him in shock, she could be at his house right now. I picture her curled up on a large sofa, wrapped in a blanket with a book in her hands. Her head, full of beautiful golden curls, turned toward the window as if waiting for something.

"We must also discuss this 'Morvath', they had warned us about the evil power this being possessed. We must spend our time researching, to gain as much information as we can. We must scour through the library, and the texts found on that day." he states, then nodding to himself he looks to me and Sophie, "Report any murmurs of Morvath to me immediately, we cannot have that word spread around like myth." We both grunt our acknowledgement and soon the room begins to descend into more chatter about the events, their voices muffled by the spinning inside of my head. Eva had turned her gaze to watch the birds dancing along the window ledge, not wishing to learn more, and I do not blame her.

"Let me go to the house, I need to know if she is there. *Please*," I say, my tone pleading.

"We have made our decision to wait, there could be cascading effects meddling with their lives. We must use this time to research before the meeting." Amazu says, dismissing me.

All at once red-hot rage boils inside of me, and I stand, not wanting to hear any more of this and need to burn off the energy burning inside of me.

"Okay, boss," I spit, storming out of the room and slamming the door. My boots thud against the floor, a steady rhythm that drowns out the pulsing of my heart, not wanting to hear any more accusations of Clea being manipulative or dangerous to us. She saved us all, only asking for one thing when she left, for me to find her.

And I intend to keep that promise.

Walking to the nearest balcony, the beautiful landscape of cascading mountains and trees calls to me like a long-forgotten melody. Shifting my back, I stretch my wings to their full height embracing the wind caressing each feather as I close my eyes, the feeling calming my racing heart. In one fell swoop, I leap into the sky, my wings cut through the air as the palace below me becomes smaller. The air becomes thinner the further I go, the wind strong and crisp, the smell of freshly cut flowers disappearing and replaced with the soft song of the skies. Once I can no longer see Fae walking about below me, a scream rips from my throat. I scream in frustration and agony, laced with excruciating confusion and anger. The town has begun to wake up for the day, as the sun rises in the morning sky, taverns unlock their doors and children wake up for school. Normal life begins anew, and I stay stagnant, never moving, always a step behind. My wings guide me towards those snowy mountains in the far distance, I fly for a few minutes gaining a vast amount of distance, finding peace in the open air. My body jolts to a stop as I notice the estate in the distance, a large wooden house stands tall amongst the trees. I can't be sure, as I have never visited myself, but Fabian's description did not do the estate the justice it deserves. But I was given orders from my leaders, and with a heavy weight in my heart, I turn my body back, back towards the palace and away from Laurence's home.

CHAPTER 22
Evreux

"Welcome Caldris," the words leave my lips as I greet the seven-foot warrior standing in front of me. Caldris, the leader of Drakharrow and our biggest threat to Thalor. He is dressed in the deepest of black, sharp thorns protrude out of his crown that weave within his long silver hair. His face is set in a scowl, from the time he entered the palace gates to enter the meeting room I don't think I have ever seen the man smile, and something tells me if he did his entire face would crack like dried paint. He scoffs in response, barely looking at me as his eyes search for Amazu. He strides along the council room, a servant trailing behind him looks to me in apology, this must be Magpie, his highest-ranking soldier and closest advisor. He's also the one who organises all of his travels and does the dirty work. I nod my head to him in acknowledgement, knowing that the job doesn't have much gratitude in it. The room had been dressed up with large golden tapestries, the windows and doors freshly cleaned. The servants had taken all day yesterday to make this room as presentable as it could be, and we made sure our guests took a different route, bypassing the ballroom entirely that was still in repairs. Whispers of the castle's ruin had been spread about the town in gossip, which Sophie and I had been trying hard to alter, spreading other rumours to soften the blow. My feet move to greet the next couple of Fae who arrive - Tristan and Lexi Farmborough. The two owners of the largest farming organisation within Thalor, they single-handedly keep the farming trade alive - putting fresh meat and vegetables on all of the tables in Thalor. Their eyes flicker about the room, they had attended the ball and seemed nervous to be on the castle grounds again. Both dressed in their finest of gowns, looking similar to the ones worn at the *Spring Ball.* Farming in Thalor earns good money, but it had been speculated that their wealth was declining due to a horrible disease that befell some of their prized animals. Some had theorised it was due to the 'Runners', an old ancient myth of small beasts would tunnel under the crops and steal the food. It was an innocent scary bedtime story read to children to warn them off of property, but even I grew weary when I'd hear the telltale scratchy noises late at night. I greet them kindly, their eyes crinkling in genuine warmth as they note my presence. Last year, I had sent fifty newly trained guards to their farms for work - my soldiers needed to learn more discipline, and these two farmers needed workers. The union had sparked hope back into their eyes, as did the soldiers when they truly understood the labour of hard work. I, myself, had worked there for a short period too - my wings had been very helpful in transporting livestock around the field.

"Fabian, I see you have recovered from drinking half of my inventory," a loud voice booms, as Laurence embraces Fabian in what seems to be a bone-crushing hug. Laughing in response, Fabian guides the new guest into the room, my eyes trained into his skull seeking the answers I need. Amazu wants to address this cautiously, and I had promised to stand back, noticing my staring, Laurence walks in my direction and shakes my hand with a warm smile in place. "You must be Evreux, Fabian has told me a lot about you. Your wings are… huge dude, how does your back cope with that?" He asks, catching me off guard. I don't think anyone has ever asked me that before, as there are other Fae in our Kingdom who possess this ability, and all I can do is half-smile at the balls of this guy, knowing getting on his good side could land me an invite into his home. He raises his eyebrow awaiting my response, his smirk still in place, his eyes warm and inviting. "It took a lot of getting used to, and you are?" I say casually, if I were to announce his name it could come off as suspicious, and I must play this carefully.

"The name's Laurence, I'm guessing this bastard," Laurence gestures to Fabian with his thumb "has not mentioned me. I supply the alcohol for the palace, I'm guessing he's too drunk to mention who supplies all the good stuff," he says chuckling, and I find myself smiling back, his presence comforting and warm. If Clea is with him, I can feel why, he has a non-threatening stance in his posture and a smile that could warm anyone's heart. I tilt my head, noticing his fancy clothes and tied-back hair, looking smart for the occasion clearly in his business element. Did he have breakfast with Clea this morning? Did they say goodbye to each other, did she do his hair?

He touches his hair noticing my staring "I got quite lucky in the genetics, want any tips?" He says winking at me, and I fight the blush that creeps up on my face and stroke my shaved head nervously. "That's alright thank you, I prefer it short." I chuckle back, awkwardness stills in the air and a thousand conversation starters flutter about in my head to keep this going but I am helpless in my alcohol knowledge and I can't bond with this guy over his hair routine.

He shifts on his feet for a moment before looking around the room. "Alright, looks like I need to take my seat, I will see you later," he says in dismissal and saunters over to a spare seat at the table, the others following his lead.

Amazu catches my gaze from across the room sporting me a curt nod, clearly hearing the conversation.

Bat ears.

He joins the remaining guests, pulling out the chair for Athena and finally sits beside her. Caldris coughs catching his attention "Shouldn't the women be attending your boy?" he says to Amazu, gaze not even acknowledging Athena or even Lexi who had also travelled for this meeting. My hackles rise at the tone, clearly dismissing the women in the room as just women who tend as wives and mothers, and I feel Amazu shift his posture slightly fighting an inner battle. His hand holds onto his wife, and he says in a tone that leaves no room for discussion.

"No."

Caldris picks up his wine at the same moment sneering at the liquid as it sloshes about in his glass, either annoyed at the response or the refreshments, I cannot tell. Looking at Laurence, I can see him bristling too at the comment and lack of manners of the room, his eyes locked onto Caldris in a warning stance - a storm that's brewing in them, his stance looks ready to pounce, as if he wishes to leap onto the Fae to tear him apart with teeth and claws.

Interesting.

With all of the guests seated, my eyes trail to the empty chair placed beside Fabian, it had been allocated to a notorious gang leader Barnaby - he had deep roots inside the underground gang within Thalor and would never miss an opportunity to gain information. I take a mental note to speak with him directly afterwards, he is tricky to find but always visits those who owe him money.

Athena stands and addresses each of us with her words, eyes softly latching onto each guest warmly, "Thank you all for joining us today, under normal circumstances we would have given more notice. However, there was a new development that we must discuss. A group of Fae infiltrated the castle, befalling a few of our own guards. The matter has been taken care of, and the group has been executed." My fingers bite into my palm, the anger trying to seep its way out of my skin. This was the plan that was decided last night, we had agreed to spin it in such a way that would not make the palace look weak, but strong about our defences.

"And the dragon?" Caldris asks Amazu, once again ignoring Athena and smirking like a cat for knowing that small piece of information. I look around at the soldiers who stand with us and wonder if any one of these men had leaked that part of the information, as I am damn sure there were no witnesses at that time. But who knows, maybe a villager had been gazing up into the palace at the right moment and saw the huge black beast break in. Hell, the noise of the stone breaking was ear-splitting. I curse myself for not investigating those rumours in the town. Looks like I need to have a word with an advisor of mine, a bricklayer who can do magical things to the stone walls without help from otherworldly gifts.

"Disposed of, we needed to remodel the ballroom anyway," Athena responds, gaze fixed on him that flicks to mine to confirm she had the same thoughts, and I dip my chin in response.

"A dragon?" Laurence booms, his eyes lighting up in delight and a laugh escapes from Fabian, we had gone through the events since our meeting over and over and Fabian's favourite part was Laurence leaping up on the beast with claws outstretched. Noticing Caldris staring at us, I school my features to neutral, the bewilderment clear on Fabian's face at remembering that this Laurence technically was not even there at the time, so, of course, he would be surprised.

There goes my sliver of hope that they'd remember. That she might remember.

"Now you all know the events; we must discuss the next steps in informing the public. Athena and I have chosen to host a public speech in the town square, there will be no invitations or announcement of our arrival. We will stand with our people as one, to deliver the news. The most important part is that it was resolved quickly, and the palace has been secured from those who betrayed us." Each of his words stings, a pinprick to my heart. Such brave warriors fixing a mistake we had not seen, now painted as the villains in the story. Looking at Amazu, he is either a good liar or actually believes the story. My gut twists, feeling guilty for continuing this story, heroes going unnoticed in the face of such pain they endured.

"Did these terrorists steal anything? How did they get into the palace?" Tristan asks from the table; he has been snacking on the small plates of cheese and olives ever since taking his seat along with drinking some of the wine. Although the food gets stuck in his beard, the sight is grizzly. Meanwhile, others eye it like it's poisonous, and I can't help but feel there's a lot of damage control still ahead.

"I would like to know how they got past the guards." Caldris smirks, our defences have always been strong and something I just know he is dying to break into. Even now, I can see him glancing towards my soldiers by the door and noting them all. Most likely wondering how much blood he could spill to breach our defences. It has been a long agreement with the leader of Drakharrow that we do not spill blood on each other's land, if he were to do so would be an act of war. I tighten my grip on my sword, ready to make a move if necessary.

"We are still assessing the situation, they acted alone without help, and my head guard assures me they are no longer a threat." Athena states, looking to me for confirmation.

I had known for the past week that I would never see them again, my soul wrenching for the lost lives. They won but lost their futures and stories that will never be told. I swallow hard fighting back the tears I know will fall, I only knew them a short while, and yet I feel like I had known them my entire life.

Clea.

"That is good to hear, I would hate for all of your efforts in guarding this place to go to waste" Caldris remarks, he smiles knowingly, and Amazu returns his matching one that doesn't reach his eyes. But it's not Caldris that catches my attention, but for only a moment, so quick I may not have caught it - Magpie clenches his fists under the table, clearly distressed about their defences. Caldris is brutal, yes, but in my reports, it has been said it is almost impossible to escape his clutches, the only way out is death. It was common knowledge that a girl had once tried but was quickly silenced before reaching the border never to be seen again.

"And where is your son, Hale, he is slowly approaching adulthood. Correct? He was always such a *fiery* child." Caldris remarks, his lips curve into a smile as he continues to nurse his drink.

"He is out with friends, these meetings bore him." Amazu casually shrugs, hiding the tension in his jaw. It is clamped so tight I'm surprised he hasn't broken any teeth.

They fall into tense chatter, trade agreements and shipments are quickly confirmed as functioning, a weight looking to lift from some of the guests here who had wanted to know if their trade was still operational. Unlike the leaders, some of the townspeople needed to keep their businesses going, to feed the people like nothing had happened. Sometimes I envy vendors in the town, making and selling art to villagers for their coin, but my artwork isn't pretty, it's destructive and I doubt I could sell carved-up traitors from my blade for any source of income.

As a break descends on the room, the servers come in wielding more trays of fresh grapes, cheese and some type of chutney. The smell is mouthwatering, I had skipped breakfast this morning, my gut churning with the thought of seeing Laurence, but as I stand here, feet unwavering - my gaze follows the tray of sweet and salty treats. Fabian wastes no time and plucks a tray for himself and places it in front of him, Laurence goes to take a piece all for Fabian to smack his hand away, in retort he smacks him at the back of his head and finally takes a cube of cheese from the tray. It looks like mouldy cheese, a delicate cheese paired nicely with wine. I'm sure he knows all about that though so that's a conversation I can't start there. I sigh, feeling utterly useless once again and my hands itch to break bones and slice throats - not stand guard and watch rich folk eat fancy cheeses and talk about the weather. To cure my sense of boredom, I stroll across the room to get a better view of the guests and stop by my leaders, completely bypassing Caldris whose gaze penetrates the back of my head, a face I wish to never see again if I can help it.

"Try some," Athena urges, pushing the plate towards me, the grapes look appealing, but the cheese emits an aroma that makes me gag, my insides curling up inside. I smile and thank her for the generosity before quickly moving on and coughing to disguise the sounds made in my stomach.

"It seems all matters are resolved unless there is anything else you wish to discuss?" Caldris asks Amazu, popping a grape into his mouth, the juices exploding in his mouth. The room stills at his tone, as he chews, I get the feeling the way he eats is always intentional. Crushing a small piece of fruit between his teeth with so much force it seems like a threat.

"That is all, but I see there is something on your mind. Care to share with us?" Amazu responds casually linking his hands together, mouth set in a hard line and eyes focused on him.

"Indeed, there is," he starts, mouth curving up at the side, clearly amused at taking control of the room as other voices quiet. We had declined all meetings at his palace, not wanting to step through and see all of the destruction, we had considered it before but knowing we could not do anything about his prisoners or slaves was an area we knew we could handle much better in meeting rooms as opposed to swords and forced entry.

"You see, I was not planning on attending today. But the funniest thing happened to me the other evening, the night of your fancy *Spring Ball*, I was lounging in my throne room and the book I was reading mysteriously disappeared. I had thought I was going mad," he continues, enjoying the retelling. I lean forward, seemingly intrigued by this story, "At first, I had thought it was a mere act of stupidity of my servers' misplacing items, but it happened again later that night at dinner. My wine glass and entire food display just disappeared. A vast black void just opened right in the dining room, consuming the food and wine in sight to just vanish." Flicking his wrist for emphasis, gasps flood the room, and I force myself to do the same, it was no mere coincidence that the same night portals were wielded here could appear elsewhere. The horror evident on our faces continues the ruse we are upholding, Amazu looks straight ahead at him considering his words and I envy that brain of his, you can almost hear the clicking of a plan forming in his head.

"Disappeared? Can you describe how, exactly?" Athena prods, question in her gaze, and Caldris finally flicks his eyes to her and after a few moments of nothing, "She asked you a question," Amazu spits out, clearly angry at the continued lack of politeness given to our female leader. By all counts, all three leaders rule with the same level of authority, a fact Caldris still cannot fathom. It might be why he's struggled to find a female companion all of these years, if he ever found love or god forbid a mate, they would be severely disappointed.

He chuckles, deep and low, no hint of humour in his tone, "My dining table can hold fifteen men, I had been dining on my own, a feast befitting a king no less. Turkey on a silver platter, with roasted tomatoes that the chef does the way I like. Oh, and don't forget the Broccoli was steamed with rich butter imported from the farms on *my* side of the wall," Caldris says, explaining the meal in detail as Amazu's face turns to stone, enraged at the response to drag this conversation on. Lexi seems to bristle too at the jab from her side of the table.

"Spit it out," Amazu barks, anger lacing his tone we all feel.

"Very well. I had just started to eat my delicious meal, and darkness descended onto the table - a large circle appeared underneath the banquette, and everything was consumed by it". Murmurs and shocked expressions flood the meeting room, Amazu tilts his head in thought, and Magpie stills beside him, seeming very interested in his fingernails. Another puzzle piece it seems. Could this be a ruse to hide his actual motive? The power Morvath used was relinquished that day, who's to say it did not travel elsewhere.

"Do you have any information on what could have caused it?" Amazu asks, genuinely curious as we all are. Adding another point of information to the list of unknown events we are tirelessly trying to solve.

"If I did, I would have sorted it already," he responds, rolling his eyes in disdain. "Do you know of anyone with the ability to wield such power?" Caldris asks, his fists curling at his sides. Only two known causes drift to my mind, one that Morvath has some connection to Drakharrow and the other being the light that had drifted into the room when the Fae dissolved - light cast over this side and darkness on another, a poetic mystery of events happening the same day. But even so, looking at Amazu, my heart beats uncomfortably in my chest - if he wanted to, he could give away the exact location of one woman who could have a connection to this event. From what we have gleaned, Clea could be with Laurence and by the way he keeps shifting in his seat, I'm almost certain of it.

"I do not," Amazu speaks with clarity, and my muscles relax, my legs no longer coiled in anticipation. "If we do find anyone of the sort, we will let you know, and please inform us if you have any more *disappearing food,*" Amazu pronounces with mirth, which enrages Caldris ever so slightly - but it's laced with caution as he holds back whatever retort he wishes to spill.

Clea is safe for now, but it seems their interference with time has cascading effects. I rub my chest absently, my heart aching with the overwhelming feeling of helplessness. Each time we get ahead of one problem, another one rises. Another day of completing tasks and never feeling satisfied with the outcome.

CHAPTER 23
Clea

Laurence left just a mere hour ago, the cooks had prepared a lavish spread for us - piles of fruit and juices filling the table. My fingers pull apart the croissant on my plate as I huff in boredom that creeps up in me, with Laurence gone there's no work to be done. I had almost begged him for me to go with him, as his guard, but he concluded that it was not necessary and going in place of Bonnie felt strange. My eyes drift to the new staff now departing the room to their houses on the estate, Glinda who now sports a large scar on her throat waves goodbye to me. It was a miracle one staff member survived, but shadows continue to haunt her at the loss of her daughter.

The pastry crumbles in my hand, each piece breaking apart easily. The soft, buttery scent drifts up to my nose. I'd already eaten four of these and now feel stuffed, my stomach aching from the excess. Though we've adjusted to this new lifestyle, I still struggle to leave food uneaten. Hopefully, the kitchen staff can wrap it all up to save for later.

Bonnie chews loudly across from me, shoving fruit into her mouth, looking as stuffed as I feel. I laugh, both of us overwhelmed and bored by the sheer amount of food filling the morning. Laurence had arranged everything for the entire day, not knowing when he'd return, and it's almost insulting to think he clearly believes we can't handle food - or ourselves. There have been more guards this morning, Laurence exclaiming he wishes for more protection. And although I agree with him, the weight of their stares bores into me and I get the sense of feeling trapped.

"I don't think I could eat another bite, my stomach is so full." I groan, fantasising about going up to my room and curling under the duvet for the rest of the day. My half-read book sitting on my side table calling my name. I had finished last night on a toe-curling steamy sex scene, and I purse my lips thinking about it, once again reminded of my lack of companionship.

"Me too… Fancy a trip into the Market again today?" Bonnie casually asks me, pushing the fruit around her plate in boredom. "Sure, what for?" I ask, the dream of reading in my soft bed drifting away, maybe I could squeeze some in later before dinner.

"I was hoping to get Laurence a gift, he has been so generous, and I want to thank him for helping out with the wedding plans. I had not expected a man to be so *involved*." She chuckles, "He's got so much on his plate right now, and the meeting he's attending today seemed serious, I was hoping to surprise him with something," her eyes light up thinking of ideas.

"Your plate is also full of plans, and too much melon it seems," I smirk at her, and she lifts her head up to me and quick as a fox she picks up a cube of melon and throws it at my face. The wet lump of fruit slaps my cheek, leaving a gooey residue that I quickly wipe away laughing and pop the melon in my mouth instantly regretting putting more food in my body.

On cue, Adam walks into the room and idly stands about, casually looking out of the kitchen window. He attempts to act like he hasn't seen the view a hundred times, the view is nice, but his eyes are locked on the table we're sitting on. Laurence had clearly asked him to stay in the house all day looking over us. He's paranoid, after Bonnie said yes to their engagement, he has been like a hovering mother hen, not giving her any space so we have to be sneaky. Adam would tell him immediately of our plans, and it would ruin the surprise, plus I have the feeling that Bonnie could really benefit from a day away from the house. Not only that, but the magnitude of everything Laurence has done for us weighs heavily on me sometimes, a clean bed, clothes on my back, and fresh food each day… my skin inches to repay him in a small way. Even if it's to be a reason for Bonnie to smile or a fun story we can tell him later.

"Meet you at the front in ten?" I whisper, coughing to cover it as I attempt to walk out of the kitchen in a casual stance, my arms swinging by my sides as I sigh in boredom.

She nods her agreement quickly, giggling up the stairs, Adam looks at us questionably - his golden blonde hair looking styled today, and I note his sword looks freshly polished too, something he doesn't often do, and I wonder if there's a reason he took longer to get ready today. He stands by the window, the morning glow casting a beautiful shade on his face. He watches me, and I watch back - I imagine walking over to him and peeling off his clothes, taking him upstairs to play out every fantasy I want, his calloused hands rough but gentle. A cough brings me back to reality, and I blink a few times to clear the vision. I move abruptly, excusing myself upstairs to get dressed.

"Any plans for the day?" Adam asks me as I walk past him, my shoulder brushing his. "A smutty book and my bed, care to join?" A blush creeps up his neck in response and he looks into my eyes for a quick moment and then crashes to the floor in dismissal. I bound up the stairs two at a time, anticipation coursing through me. I hope to catch Adam off guard enough that he'll avoid me for the rest of the day, just like he usually does. Duty comes before pleasure with that man, maybe once he's off the clock he could accept my offer.

I make quick work of getting ready and listen for Adam's footsteps outside, he strolls to the barn checking on the horses and on time he does his usual perimeter walk.

Now's our chance.

I bolt downstairs, seeing Bonnie casually reading a book on the sofa and I grin a wicked smile, *all clear.* I grab her hand, and we creep out to the barn, Adam will be twenty minutes top, and we just need to clear the gates in that time, easy work. We approach the barn, hiding from the gardeners who tend to the rose garden outside, making clippings to keep the spring season in bloom. The floral scent is thick in the air as we reach the horses, my heart pounding in my chest at being caught. We had been training with Laurence for weeks in the barn learning how to mount the horses on our own in case of an emergency, and it paid off as we work fast, a wonderful warmth spreading through me at how quickly we were able to get on the horses. With a final check of our bearings, we lightly kick the horses into gear and storm out of the barns. My hair whips around my face, dirt kicks up as we speed faster towards the gates. I was riding Amazu this time, the easier horse to choose in the stalls as the one I had ridden before was lazily drinking and didn't seem to want to be disturbed. A strange feeling washes over me at that, riding another horse feels *weird*. The beast under me is strong, powerful and without the pleasure of meeting the leader myself, I can feel this horse was selected to be Amazu. His strides command presence, and leaps ahead with authority, a stark contrast to Evreux who was sleek and fast. Adrenaline pumps through my veins as we clear the gates, at the exact moment the guards had been taking a break and left it open for trade - whether it was fate or correctly timed I will never know.

The horse surges faster beneath me as Bonnie races by my side on Fabian, her laughter mingling with the pounding of hooves. As we clear the estate, a smile spreads across my face at the sheer joy of riding together, feeling utterly free and unburdened. The path ahead is smooth, lined with grass that grows tall, brushing against my boots - a sign of the growing wild season.

The wind rushes past, whipping through my long blonde hair and sending my gown billowing behind me, the fabric caressing my skin as the fresh air fills my lungs. Streams flash by, the water glinting in the sunlight, while deer pause in the meadows and birds sing overhead as if they're singing just for us. Reckless and powerful, we ride with abandon, weaving in and out, the rhythm of the horses beneath us mirroring our shared exhilaration. It's euphoric - pure, unfiltered joy - binding us to this untamed moment of freedom.

The morning sun casts a golden glow as we ride closer towards the market, the stalls coming into view, the towering village rising majestically ahead. The tall buildings pierce the sky, nothing like the towering embrace of the palace, but it holds the vibrancy of Fae fluttering about the beautifully weathered stone buildings, looking like vines are holding up the crumbling structures. The energy of the crowd fills me with delight as we dismount our horses, the smell of the market calling to me so vividly.

Once complete, Bonnie takes my arm as we walk together towards the crowd of Fae.

"You really thought you could sneak by me," a loud voice booms behind us, as Adam comes barrelling in riding Evreux looking pissed as hell and covered in mud it seems. He's out of breath, waving us down to stop. Feeling a little guilty about being caught, we walk up to him, "We're just going on a secret shopping trip," I say shyly, shrugging my shoulders to ease the tension in his.

"That is quite alright, but let me escort you, Mr. Laurence will have my neck if I let you out of my sight. It is my duty to keep you safe," he slips out.

"I didn't realise you were our bodyguard." Bonnie snips, not overly happy about the lack of freedom.

"Please allow me to rephrase, I promised him I would look out for you both while he is away, heaven knows you don't need my protection." He looks at me with admiration, laced with something else I cannot place. He quickly dismounts, patting himself off and removing some of the dried mud and grass he picked up on the way. "Poor Evreux over here is exhausted, you two are rather fast," he chuckles, and even he seems lighter - maybe he needs this trip as much as we do.

"Please may I escort you both?" he asks, and we hook our arms around him - pulling him towards the market.

It's exactly as I remember. I tug Bonnie towards a wood carving table, where the vendor expertly wields a knife, shaping a hawk perched on a branch. The detail is breathtaking, the emotion in the hawk's face so vivid that I nearly decide to buy it on the spot, even as my eyes wander to the other intricate designs on the table.

"Do you have any tigers?" Bonnie asks excitedly, gripping her purse in anticipation and I look at her with the same smile just knowing that it would be the perfect gift for him.

"No, ma'am, but I do have a lion?" She says, furrowing her brows in concentration as she picks out the lion she crafted, it truly is breathtaking, Bonnie's face visibly deflates at the difference in animal craft. She hums to herself looking at the other items.

"I could carve one for ya, if that's what you're after. Takes me four working days, and I can send it to your home for a price," the vendor continues, her black hair woven into a tight knot on her head as she asks Bonnie hopefully, clearly loving the craft. They fall into easy chatter about the shape and size, my brain internally sniggering at the girth and length of the body Bonnie is describing.

"Can you do the claws too? Like it's leaping in the air!" She continues, opening her purse looking like she'll spend everything she has just to make something Laurence would like, her engagement ring glinting on her hand. My eyes wander around us, this town would be the perfect place for thieves. The last time we were here, a bracelet was stolen after all, with the noise of the crowd it's the perfect disguise. For some, stealing a small trinket could mean feeding themselves for a week, something I know I can relate to. My gaze follows to find Adam now casually leaning against an evening wear stand, and I raise my eyebrows in question gesturing to his choice of spot and he immediately recoils in horror, stalking our way in embarrassment "Found any silk slips you like?" I tease as Adam runs his hand through his hair shaking his head "I hadn't noticed." Laughing, I cross my arms "Maybe you could buy one for a woman in your life?" I prompt, trying to gain information from him, he's as blank as a piece of paper sometimes and making him blush is my favourite pastime. He doesn't wear a wedding ring, and his lingering looks tell me he's into women, but there's more to him that I honestly want to uncover.

"That would be inappropriate, ma'am," he says back to me, his face in a blank mask not cracking one bit. I sigh in resignation and stroll over to the clothing stand as Adam follows behind me. The gowns are displayed in a variety of colours, the fabric silk and satin and smooth, the beading beautiful in the design and I'm astounded at the amount of work taken to make these in so many colours and sizes. A yellow gown catches in my periphery, and I wonder who in my life would wear a colour so strong, the woman on Fabian's arm seemed to like the colour but her name slips my mind. I pick up a light pink nightgown, the hem covered in white fluffy balls that do not look comfy at all to sleep in, but I guess that's not what it's for. But who would I wear it for? I would say myself, but my sex life has always been non-existent. If I were to invite anyone to my bed, it would get complicated and potentially at risk - making it difficult to keep lovers. My mind drifts back to the man standing next to me, a one-night stand would be nice, I absently look his way as his eyes latch onto mine with so much heat my pulse quickens. That look tells me it would never just be for one night; he'd take his time and enjoy every second of it. I drop the gown quickly feeling my body heating and loop my arm through his quickly strolling away from the shop, needing to clear my head from the way my mind had drifted. We both look as one to find Bonnie still with the woodcarver, looking like she has already started to sketch the idea. The tiger stretches upwards, claws outstretched with a gaping jaw. It hits me that this is the moment we met him, when he chased after Hobbs with such huge claws and teeth, this moment being so important to her that I feel my eyes water slightly at the thoughtfulness of the gesture. My gaze locks to Adam again, and I stifle my laugh at both of us in the same stance, protectors at heart. My eyes linger for a few moments on his face, he clears his throat as it bobs, both of us in a secret moment within the bubble we have created. He moves us forward, my eyes unable to stop looking at the dimple on his cheek that formed with his sweet smile that was shining bright in the sun.

"Looks like the council meeting is over, we should head back to the house before Mr. Laurence does," Adam says sternly, our private moment over, his words bringing me back to the market in front of us. My head swings forward the same moment a sword gets plunged into Adam's gut. Blood spurts out of his mouth, as he slowly looks down at the sword, eyes unseeing. All I can do is stare, body locked up tight as a scream rips from my throat, my head snaps to the Fae holding the sword.

Caldris.

Chapter 24
Laurence

My skin itches to shift, my ass becoming numb in this wooden chair. I sat through the endless council meeting, watching the same conversations loop around in circles, each ruler trying to outmaneuver the other without ever actually saying anything of substance. It struck me as a tedious game - like a dog chasing its tail.

Then it dawned on me.

I was the one sitting here, watching grown men chase their own words in circles. And worse, I was growing fascinated by it.

My back leans against the chair, glad to just sit back and watch. I have been trying so damn hard not to act strangely, no one in this room but me knows Clea is staying with me, and I intend to keep it that way. She has been so strong, facing so much death and pain in her life. Ripped away from her parents, imprisoned, and becoming a plaything for Caldris makes me sick to my stomach. Anger coils in my gut each time my gaze would find his, or even worse when words leave his lips, if he weren't so highly regarded and important to the Kingdom, he wouldn't have stepped into this room alive.

Thankfully for me, he left a little while ago and the effect was instant, everyone visibly relaxed and Amazu's posture returned to the casual one I had known for many years. Even Fabian seems in a lighter mood, but there's an edge to him I do not understand, something he is holding back from me and the looks he keeps giving Evreux makes my skin itch.

"It has been a…"

Wonderful? No. Interesting? Definitely not.

"…insightful day." I speak to Fabian, careful with my words with Amazu hearing everything I can with his super hearing. A gift I don't think I could handle, hearing people getting freaky in the palace or even their bowel movements, it's surprising he hasn't gone insane with the feeling. I make a move to stand, just as Evreux appears blocking my path to the exit with an edge to his eyes, his face gaunt as it was earlier. The man clearly has not been sleeping, the palace being breached really got to him, huh.

My feet move towards the hosts "It was wonderful seeing you, Amazu and Athena. Please send my thanks to your chef. Your order will be here in a few days; I have been a little preoccupied with my new fiancé," I say.

"Thank you for being here, you're welcome anytime. Give Bonnie my warm wishes," Amazu responds, delight in his face, my hackles rising ever so slightly at the use of her name - Fabian has been chatting about me it seems, that man can't hold anything back.

Walking to the exit with Evreux lingering like a bad cold that I cannot shake. His eyes are piercing, the black pools of them deep and demanding, I raise my eyebrow in question as I see the others leave the room saying their goodbyes to the leaders also.

"If it's alright, I would like to speak with you privately?" Evreux says, seeming like he rehearsed that question a hundred times. I glance at the clock on the wall, I had told Bonnie and Clea I would be back within a few hours, a conversation wouldn't hurt.

"Sure, anything for a long friend of mine," my eyes search for Fabian only to see him walking out with Amazu and Athena, Evreux extends out his arm forward to guide me in the same direction as the others, his other hand clutching on his sword. A faithful guard it seems, not happy with intruders.

"An advisor of mine would like to place an order with you but is occupied currently, could I arrange to collect it myself?" he asks, a nervous tilt to his features.

Scratching my head at the soft tone in his words, it's a strange request, usually my orders are placed with local taverns and we would only allow collection on rare occasions I would agree to beforehand. I would never allow strangers to my home, even now with Bonnie and Clea, it's an intrusion with risks associated. "That is an option, but I would recommend our delivery service, what tavern do they frequent…"

Our movements are slow as we reach the end of the hallway when booming footsteps come our way cutting off my words, a panicked guard comes racing around the corner. She comes to a complete stop and addresses Amazu and Athena directly.

"There has been an attack in the market, the villagers are in panic," eyes flicking about in distress, Amazu pivots to her demanding more information, his face tense and tired. "What happened, Carol?" he asks.

"Reports say Caldris and his men have killed a few villagers in the town, one of them was known to work for Laurence," my head snaps to her at that declaration.

"Who?" I bark, all thoughts of conversations gone.

"*Who*," Amazu asks at the same time with lethal calm, a storm brewing in his eyes with his people being in distress.

The messenger woman looks to the both of us mouth agape, sadness in her eyes she answers his question first. "A few villagers who were at the market, a man had bled out and a few women were hurt." She cries, tears blurring in her eyes which find their way to me as she unravels a piece of paper with blood smudges on.

I know that piece of paper, each of my workers holds them that has the contact information of all of my taverns and alcohol distribution locations. Each piece has their name at the bottom, a new initiative I started to make each worker feel like their name mattered, not just numbers to me.

My hands shake as I snatch the paper from her hands and uncurl the worn paper. It has clearly been folded and touched many times, as the edges are frayed and worn. One word appears at the bottom next to blood smudges that cause my heart to break into a thousand pieces.

Adam.

One of my closest workers, a close friend of mine, he was loyal, and duty-bound through and through. I had instructed him to look after Bonnie and Clea.

"Who else was hurt?" I bark out, a growl ripping through my throat.

"Just a few women who had been selling their fruits, sir. There are reports Caldris had ordered his men to find something, two women were reported to be sprinting through the street."

"Are they alive?" I ask, my whole world collapsing inside of me. Knowing the next word to come out of this woman's mouth would completely destroy me.

"I am not sure, sir."

I clutch the paper to my chest, thinking of ways to avenge his death and put Adam to rest. The paper cuts into my palm from the pressure. My eyes drift to the window as the rest of the room disperse to wherever - I couldn't care less. The window holds the display of the village in Thalor as my eyes strain from the moisture gathering. I trust Clea to get them home safely, but the relentless energy in my bones screams at me to get home to check on them. If anything were to happen to them…

"I'm sorry for your loss." Evreux says behind me, he startles me for a moment as I had thought I was alone, his voice tinged with annoyance and I'm guessing he's getting rather agitated at my lack of conversation. He wanted to speak to me about an order but my business brain has long gone with the new threat to those dear to me, a grunt leaves my lips, and I snarl at him as I stride past the door.

"I have more important things to tend to, I hope you understand," the words come out in a growl, my hands curl up wanting the claws to extend, to tear at anyone who caused my family harm and to rip Caldris to shreds. Maybe he would wander into the forest, and I could spin an epic tale of a bear that crossed his path. The Kingdom would be in chaos, but they would rejoice to not have that piece of shit as a leader anymore. I shake my head at the thought, it would be bad for business and I'm acting out of anger, and more importantly the women need me right now. They most likely watched the whole thing and are traumatised by it. If Caldris found her in the market, there's no telling what he would do, and with blood slain, Thalor is under attack.

"Charlotte is Clea, right?" Evreux says behind me, longing seeps from his bones confusing me for a long moment. Does he work for Caldris? Did he have anything to do with the attack, wanting to hold me back for long enough?

I snap my shoulder around ignoring his question as I continue to walk. He follows, his footsteps quick as he tries to keep up with my long strides.

"I don't know who you're talking about," I retort, dismissing the situation and wanting to get the fuck out of this room before I say anything further. Today has been a mess, my arms yearn to comfort Bonnie from today and check in with Clea, they have witnessed so much death today and I must hire more guards and by the looks of it - adding a pay bump of salaries to our house staff house to keep our secret.

Stepping past the doorway, boots scuff on the floor behind me and in a blur - a solid whack cracks against my skull, the floor rushes to my face, and my vision goes black.

I wake in a room that smells strongly of piss, my arms bound in chains to the side of me, they feel heavy against my skin and my pulse spikes when I cannot feel the beast within me. It's sleeping somehow, and I turn my wrist over at the sensation not understanding why I am unable to shift.

Boots scuffle in front of me, a man seems to be pacing around muttering to himself and pulling at his non-existent hair.

Evreux. This asshole knocked me out.

I rattle the chains to get his attention, my jaw clenched at the aggravation I feel deep within me.

His head snaps to me as his feet pause, his eyes wild and unseeing as he focuses back on me, looking like he just remembered I was in the room with him. It's then I look around and find myself chained to the floor in what looks like to be his torture chamber, sweat beads on my brow and chest as I take deep breaths which I immediately regret from the stench of this place.

"Fabian!" I shout, hoping he's somewhere nearby to let me out of these chains. This man has clearly gone mad, his wings droop against the floor, his shoulders look so haggard, he blinks manically and grabs a chair from the corner to sit in front of me. The dim light casts a light on his face, showing him completely to me. I have the feeling that if I do not give him the answers he seeks, weapons will be used. My eyes drift to the tools laid out next to me uncleaned and my swallow is audible.

"I'm sorry," he starts, bowing his head and clasping his hands together on the back of the chair that rests between us, "I haven't been myself lately. You see, I was given a task by someone who is lost to me, and I need to know the answers I seek." His tone is pleading, desperate.

"Do you know a woman named Clea? Blonde hair, blue eyes, with a power to wield a sword at will," he asks, face straight, and icy terror rips into me as I fully understand the scope of this situation. This is an interrogation room. Evreux is commonly known as the ruthless one in the palace, extracting information for Amazu and Athena by any means necessary. His skill is unmatched, and strong going by his ability to drag my body to this room. I wonder for a long moment if he is working alone or for his leaders, they must know I am here after all - unless the attack in the market is keeping them busy. Hopefully, for my sake it's the former, and I can bargain with them to get out of here.

"I don't know who you're talking about," I repeat the same words I had spoken earlier, was it a few minutes ago or hours? There are no windows in this room, distorting my sense of time. Clea had not known the name Evreux, questioning it when we rode our horses late last year, had they met since then?

"Why is Caldris searching for her?" Evreux prompts, switching his angle of questioning.

I scoff, shaking my head.

"Why ask me, ask him yourself. Now, unchain me, you crazy bastard!" I say, voice rising and I wince at the pressure in my head from the movement. The bastard knocked me out pretty good, the blood feels sticky in my hair but it's no longer dripping down my neck which is a good sign.

"What do you mean by that?" he asks, tilting his head in confusion and a hint of anger seeps into the words.

I sigh, annoyed at this conversation, "You're a close ally, you could sell information for anything. Amazu and Athena are good people, but they are strong leaders, and I wouldn't trust my life with their decisions when it comes to the safety of many." My gaze locks to his, meaning every single word. I have known them for many years, I'm grateful to not attend their balls or spend much time with them as I never feel certain in their presence. Fabian and Sophie are the only exception.

Evreux stutters, his face masked in horror.

"I would never trade her, not for anything in this world. She is the most important thing to me now. You have more of a bargaining chip though, trade stopped with Drakharrow when your father passed - with Clea in tow, he would give you anything you wanted."

My lips part in shock, a lot to unpack there. I realise I don't care about his fantasies as he clearly needs a few days' sleep and food, he's not making much sense.

"I'd never betray her, she's become family to me and Bonnie," I confirm. If this man is indeed enthralled by her, he'll hopefully appreciate the protectiveness I feel over Clea.

"I was right, she has been here this whole time!" he shouts, a smile breaking on his face in relief.

Relief?

"Why do you care? She has enough shit to deal with, leave her alone." I respond, Clea has been running all of her life and has finally found somewhere she feels safe. It's in the small things, like how when she arrived, she would lock her bedroom door and sleep only once I had retired to my rooms. She'd sneak out at night to train too, I'd find sword marks along the trees out the back, far away from the house. But now, she feels safe enough to fall asleep in the living room and trains with me and Bonnie. We have become a family, and I'll be damned if the man before me rips her away. She doesn't need another man chasing her.

"She's living with you, isn't she?" He continues, ignoring my warning. I snarl, low and menacing. The tiger within me breaching the surface of my eyes, itching to break free, and casting a warning to him. His face breaks, his gaze turning to the floor as something is clearly eating him up from the inside. From what I heard from Fabian he's a good friend and a good soldier - they had named a horse after him, after all. I relax my tone a little, shifting my approach.

"Why do you care?" I utter, my thumb tracing the handcuffs trying to find a latch somewhere.

He pauses for a moment, weighing up his response, and scratching the back of his head.

"She's everything to me…can you, introduce me?"

Words get stuck in my throat, a big fat '*Hell no*' the only thing on my mind. But I cannot anger him further, I need to have this conversation work out in my favour, or these four walls could be the last thing I see.

"Release me first, then we will talk," the words leave my mouth in regret, if he goes anywhere near her, I'll snap his pretty wings off before he gets the chance. I continue sweetening the deal "You can come by the house tomorrow morning, but please release me so I can check on them, they could be hurt." His eyes light up at the invitation and he bounces on his seat, wringing his hands together in anticipation.

A knock sounds at the door, and Evreux actually skips to the door like a crazy person. The door swings wide as Fabian stands there slack-jawed from the display. I give him a loaded stare, urging him with my eyes to get me the hell out of here.

"Not cool, Ev," he says, walking in and making quick work to undo my chains, my gaze locked on Evreux the entire time. His face is set in a grimace, regret lines his eyes, as he watches Fabian's frantic movements. Once the chains break free from my wrists the sensation is instant, the tiger creeping up to the surface of my skin screaming at me to let it out. I attack, claws rip from my skin as I grab onto Evreux's shoulders and push him against the wall. My breath now thick and heavy as my head pounds, but he just looks at me with a blank expression, nothing in those black eyes of his.

I push him once against the wall for good measure and head for the door to get home.

"Laurence, we got intel on Charlotte and Bonnie." Fabian says to me, placing a hand on my arm.

I look to him to continue, "They jumped on a horse and ran away in a hurry, Caldris is putting all of his soldiers on it. Why is she important to him?" He asks, confusion lining his face.

"I don't know," I lie, panic consuming me as my movements quicken.

"Why would they run?" I heard behind me, both men following with rapt attention seeking answers from me. But at this moment all I care about is their safety, and making sure Caldris keeps his claws out of her. Evreux is fast, he gains on me quickly, but he does not touch me this time.

We run towards the exit; the afternoon sun is swallowed by the clouds in the sky. I need to shift to be faster, with regret, I turn to the winged Fae.

"If you care about her like you say you do, she may need you, and those wings of yours can carry you faster than I can run in this state." I wince, feeling the pounding in my head becoming harsher as I feel the tiger ripping free. "Please protect them both." I finish, my skin ripping apart to allow the fur to transform all over my body, my bones stretch and pull my muscles, my throat burning from the force of the vomit that threatens to leave me.

Evreux rips off his shirt, seeming for better access, but a part of me wonders if that's on purpose to showcase his rippling muscles. "Where would she go?" he asks, and I almost don't reply, wondering if telling him would be worse. But nothing is worse than Caldris. Shifting my large head towards Fabian, I nod to him to speak for me, my mouth not able to form words.

Fabian speaks for me, "She would probably head back to the house, she would make sure Bonnie gets there safe."

Evreux takes a deep breath, his arms twitching and head clearing. I see him smile, a real smile that's not manic or hell-bent. I'll have to ask Clea later about this *development*, not understanding their dynamic in the slightest.

"Thank you," he breathes out, and takes a huge leap into the skies, flying straight towards my home at speeds I had not realised was possible.

My paws pound on the pavement as I take a different route, needing to avoid the crowds. The people of Thalor have been through enough today, as have Bonnie and Clea. Their faces blur in my vision as I move as fast as I can, entrusting the psychopath who chained me up with their safety wasn't something I hadn't thought would be a good idea… but I could sense the genuine emotion in him, if anything, he would protect them before I got there.

CHAPTER 25
Clea

"Run," Adam chokes out as Caldris pulls out his sword in one swift motion, his body sways as he keeps his grip on me, the warmth draining from his body as he goes limp, falling to the ground. Panicked sobs threaten to spill from me as Adam's eyes find mine for the last time, the bright essence of him flickering out.

Screams fill the air as Fae are shoved into each other, not caring about anyone else around them as they scramble their way out of the scene that plays out in front of me. My body is locked frozen as I stare at Caldris, I haven't moved an inch, and my muscles are coiled up so tight I can't breathe. His bright mauve eyes penetrate my soul as he stares at me with enough fury that my legs wobble, the mate bond pulling at me to submit. His lips curl in delight as he assesses me, his prize from years of searching that just happened to fall into his lap. My head pounds as I push against the mate bond, nausea tugs at my stomach too as I resist the call of it. I lift my feet, now weighing a ton, and step backwards. *No.* My pulse thuds so loud in my ears, my erratic heartbeat drowning out the screams around me. How could I be so careless? Coming to a populated area multiple times was a mistake I should have seen coming, and it cost Adam his life. His lifeless body leaks blood, the sticky red substance pooling under his stomach. It stains along the market floor, creeping up to his beautiful hair as it sticks to it in thick clumps, his face stuck in a perpetual shocked grimace.

Reaching my arm out, I pull the wooden crate of apples from the fruit stand towards me at the same moment his hand snaps out towards my neck. I heave the heavy weight for the contents to crash in between us, red and green apples bounce and roll along the floor as Caldris had missed me by mere inches. The fruit vendor attempts to shout at me, but my feet are running, I run so fast that my vision turns white from panic – the edges of my periphery blurring and shaking. I frantically push past villagers, as more screams sound behind me. His booming voice drifting away as I move, the harsh syllables sounding like a hammer to my skull as flashes of my childhood come back to haunt me. Metal swings and slices behind me, and Fae cry out for loved ones slain in my name. A sob wrentches from my throat at the innocent blood being spilt, but if he catches me… I am all he needs to overpower Thalor. It was what I was built for, made for. An unstoppable force against Thalor and everyone inside of it. Long ago, Magpie had whispered plans to me about his plan of attack, with me as his weapon there's nothing he couldn't do. I cannot allow that.

I spot her hair, Bonnie is crouching low with the wooden vendor and bolts upright to run with me, her coins flying and spilling against the vendor's table. We gain distance, she runs by my side most likely sensing the wildness in my eyes. She has run with me these past few years after all, running side by side reminds me of the time we had spotted Malik - but this time… she can't come with me, her life is here with Laurence. Tears prick my eyes as I realise this will be the last time I visit this place - the last time I wake up in the comfort of a safe home, filled with food, happiness, and cherished memories with those that I love.

I had let down my guard for one day, *one day*, and I had ruined everything. My biggest worry today was Laurence finding we had slipped out, or even not liking the gift we purchased for him. I had been fantasising about Adam and thinking about pretty books in a pretty house.

I was a fool.

"Clea," Bonnie urges.

"*Clea,*" she says, repeating my damn name again.

I pull harder, weaving us in and out of the crowd as we duck towards a side street, to my left ten guards power through the streets in their hunt for me. I need to get her home, away from this mess.

We reach the stables, two men stand with their arms crossed - a casual stance, but I note the blue and silver material that flashes on their arms. With the adrenaline pumping through my body, I run straight into the bigger one on the left, using my shoulder to knock them down, their head smashing against a wooden beam knocking them unconscious. I recover quickly and jump towards the other, but his body is slack as he's now lying on the ground - stomach squashing a huge lump of horse excrement, as his arms go limp. I swing my head to Bonnie, whose grip is tightly on a metal horse bit as it dangles in her hand. A smile cracks my face at her resourcefulness and bravery in the situation, it's all I can do just as we leap onto Evreux without hesitation. My arm reaches out as Bonnie takes it to leap up behind me, her arms close around mine and I shout to urge Evreux forward. I need her close, her arms keeping me grounded as my mind screams in turmoil. He bolts out at full speed. Our heads whip from the force and my grip on the reins tightens so painfully it bites into my hands, my legs burning from the effort of holding on.

"Faster," I urge the horse, and without words we lean forward granting us more distance. As we ride, the echoes of screams and moaning become quieter, I scrunch my eyes closed as my heart thumps in my empty chest. All around us, the wonderful glow of the sun becomes shrouded in thick clouds that merge and cover the beautiful sky, then, as if the sky were screaming for us - the clouds ripped apart as the sky cracked open. The rain comes down in a torrential downpour, each drop landing on my head feeling like drops of ice seeping into my bones. The rain soaks my dress, and I latch my hand around Bonnie's that squeezes tighter as she shivers from the onslaught of the cold rain. She clings to me, as I latch onto Evreux, his hooves pounding against the drenched pathway. It was as if the sky were mirroring this day, clouds weeping at the sight of it all.

We made it back twice as fast, covered in mud and dead bugs from the force of the final sprint. The horse nearly collapses as we reach the gates, guards swing them wide at our fast approach, their faces in a mask of confusion as we bolt through the estate. The stables were dry as we jumped off the horse, Bonnie's hand tightly clutches mine as we run into the house as one, my hands immediately moving to lock the doors.

"You're bleeding!" Bonnie says, panic in her tone as our breaths attempt to recover from the journey here. I follow her gaze to my outfit, once beautiful and bright cloth now covered in dirt and grime – Adam's blood splashed and smudged along my side. My knees crash to the floor as my head grows fuzzy, his face all I see when I see my clothes. Hands pressed into the green rug, I blink away the vision. It's all my fault. Sweat drips down my forehead as Bonnie throws more questions at me, her voice becoming more urgent as I do not answer, a towel is draped over me at some point. But all I can focus on is the dripping of rainwater from my nose onto the plush rug, and the feeling of loss. Bonnie orders all of the staff home, I lift my head to her posture now commanding and authoritative and the smallest of smiles pokes its way onto my face seeing her like this. Maybe she doesn't need me anymore. I'm putting her in danger just being here, he's seen me now, and I can't try faking my death – he would know if I died.

Why is he here? Did he come to the council meeting too? There must have been such a huge event for him to grace his presence here. What could have happened?

I thought I had more time.

"Caldris killed him," I whisper, the words feeling like wet grass stuffed in my mouth.

"What? Caldris is here? Who did he kill?" her voice but a whisper now as she visibly shakes with fear. Arms clutch my sides, as she holds me on the floor. But she cannot be down here with me, she deserves to be up high like she was just moments ago - this is all my fault, and he'll come for her next.

"Adam," I squeak out his name, the thick rug blurring in my vision as salty tears track down my face mixing with the rainwater.

"No. No. No," Bonnie chants out, now sitting against the wall with her head in her hands, her once beautiful brown hair matted and soaking from the harsh winds of our ride here. I grimace at her expression, noticing her face tinged red with the cold.

"He was at the market, Adam died protecting me," I bow my head as the words come spilling out of my cracked lips. My breaths become heavy as reality crashes down on me, knowing I have to leave.

"It will be alright," she says wrapping her arms around mine again, forcing me to look at her. "We can get more guards for the house" she continues, her voice confident and assertive. Her voice does nothing to calm my racing heart, he cannot find me here, Bonnie and Laurence's dead body comes into view. Now he knows I'm in the area, there is no stopping him. He has been hunting for me my entire life.

"He will never stop; he rarely leaves his land. Something big must have happened for him to attend the palace, attend the meeting." I mutter, and as realisation hits me, I gasp in shock, "Laurence was at the meeting," Bonnie's face goes as white as a ghost, as she looks at me. Without missing a beat, I stand abruptly, head feeling dizzy as I sprint up the stairs. The candles haven't been lit, and with the absence of workers around the estate, the entire house feels dead. The dark wood that covered my bedroom once gave me comfort but now suffocates me, my body rotting from the inside out, my footsteps leak water as it drips and taints the once-clean floorboards I had spent so much time in. Looking at the bag beside my bed I know what I must do.

I pack quickly, shoving as much as I can in there as I run back downstairs not touching any food to take with me. They have fed me more than I deserve, and I have signed their deaths by being here.

A hand grabs my arm "Stop, please." Bonnie cries and her eyes dip in concern looking at my expression. I have to get out, lay low for a little while, and once he's gone, I could come back in a few years. I have lived alone in the woods before, and as much as it pains me, I could do it again.

"Thank you for being my friend, someone I can fight for, someone worthy of fighting for. I will find you again, I promise," I say, a single tear falling as I say my goodbyes. She shakes her head in disagreement, urging me with her face to stay.

"Please, don't go, we will work this out!" she screams at me, tears falling too. And I'm selfish, I stay for a few long seconds trying to remember the way she feels - the way her long lashes frame those beautiful wide eyes of hers and the cute button nose she always has. I take the glass bottle out of my bag, the thick red liquid sloshing around as I tip it back choking on the feel of it. Thankfully last night Laurence had caught a fresh deer which I helped to skin, keeping the blood for myself. The blood spills down my throat, and I wipe the remnants from my face. I wave my hand in a circle motion and turn out the door, Bonnie's hand pounds on the shield I made to keep her inside, I hate to lock her in, the shield will work for as long as I can keep it - and I intend to leave it there once I'm gone. Tears continue to fall as I hear the muffled scream of her voice calling my name, as my feet take me into the forest.

Chapter 26
Evreux

My wings soar through the skies, the wind biting at my face as I urge my body faster. I know this route, I had taken it a mere week ago, and my pulse thrums with the excitement of finally seeing her - seeing those sparkling blue eyes up close once more. The scenery is breathtaking, with fields of grass sprinkled with a riot of wildflowers, the sky continues to crack and rumble - splitting open above me as the rain pours along my wings making the flight near impossible. Maybe once I find her, I could take her high up into the skies on a sunnier day, show her the wonders of being this high up and the beauty you can find in it. If she doesn't remember me, I'll find a way into her life, even if it's just as a friend. Would I tell her the whole story of how we know each other? She could be furious if she found out that I kept the truth from her. So many uncertainties, but we'd figure it out together. She may not even like me, maybe the future version of me is better in ways I cannot be, I did knock out and tie up a close friend of hers. An oversight on my part. How could I compare with another version of myself I do not know? Memories and stories were lost to me forever.

Clea, I'm coming.

The large wooden house comes into view, the black fences curling around it for protection. The guards huddle underneath a wooden structure, a small outbuilding to the side of the gate, their backs instantly straighten at my approach, not recognising friend from foe. I land in front of them, the gate blocking my way in.

"I have come for Laurence, who is on his way, I have come to check on Bonnie and Clea." My voice is certain, even though I'm trembling with excitement, my eyes flick about the windows looking for a head of blonde hair peeking out. What would I look like to her? First impressions matter in the way of love, should I change my clothes?

My thoughts are interrupted as a small woman runs from the front door, rushing down to meet me. My hopes are shattered as her brown hair comes into view, but I do not dwell on those feelings as I look upon her face. Her eyes are puffy, tears racing down her cheeks as she stumbles over, her dress is soaking wet, and even in the spring air she must be freezing cold.

"Is Laurence okay? Is he hurt?" she mumbles, lip wobbling as her voice cracks out in silent sobs. I wince, knowing I was the reason he was kept back from my own selfishness, but I relax my face as to not alarm her.

"He is on the way," I breathe out, the flight exhausting my lungs. The guards do not open the gate, and Bonnie makes no move to open them. Seeming mistrustful, and rightly so after the chaos they escaped.

"Is Clea alright?" I ask hopefully.

"I don't know who that is," she lies, looking away and biting her lip.

"Please, just tell me she's alright," I plead, and she must see something in my eyes, the desperation and longing I feel as she blinks at me for a moment.

"Who is she to you?" She asks, feeling aggravated being asked that question over and over, a burden I feel I will be placed with for the rest of my miserable life without her, *without them* to explain. Maybe I am going mad like Laurence said. There is not enough time to explain, feeling a shift in her mood, the sky continues to pour relentlessly on me, and I fear I am too late. Taking a long breath, I respond with strong conviction in my tone "I am a friend of Fabian, my name is Evreux, and he wishes to know if *Charlotte* is okay," she looks at me in confusion, and a hint of recognition, using her fake name to prove my ability to keep the secret. She sniffles, wiping her face with the back of her hand. Her face reminds me of the villagers who had been running and screaming in the market, I had been flying over whilst mourning some of their deaths. Crashing realisation hits me.

I shouldn't be here.

Caldris has just declared war on Thalor by spilling blood, the reasoning unclear to me, and I need to be back home to keep the people safe, *our people safe*. Amazu and Athena need me to lead the guards and to secure the villagers' safety, and I would only cause more confusion and pain for Clea to know she had another life, friends and family she built only to be ripped away from the fragment of time. With Caldris declaring portals opening up in his home, there's a solid connection there that may only spread more issues if I interfere. My feet take me in the opposite direction with a muttered goodbye to Bonnie. My feet feel as heavy as my heart in resignation. Maybe once this calms down, Laurence could be true to his word and invite me over with Fabian, and we could start again.

"She's planning to leave." Bonnie blurts out behind me, moving forwards as her hands grip the gate in desperation, her hand wrapped around the bars as rainwater drips down onto them. "I don't know you that well, but there's something unsaid and odd about this situation, and I have this weird feeling that you could help her somehow," I immediately press forward, my mind spinning at this new revelation. "She took her things with her, and I fear she won't come back. Please, you have to help her, Caldris... he, he can't have her, not again. *Not ever.*"

My gaze flicks to the tree line behind the house, more questions swim through my brain at that sliver of information. But right now, I have an order, her permission to keep fighting, "I will not let harm come to her, you have my word" and with that, I jump into the skies in search of her.

The sky cracks and moans above me, the rain pouring down in relentless sheets of water that continue to drag me down, smearing the world into a blur of grey and brown. Flowers wilt, and trees sway from the wind forcing me to beat faster. My lungs burn with each inhale as I battle against the storm, my feathers drenched in the tears from the sky, each beat echoing my desperation and ache in my chest. Somewhere up ahead I spot a figure weaving her way through the dense trees, my heart beating faster as I fly overhead in search. I call her name, her real one, the name I scream in my dreams that is etched into my soul. By the tenth time, my voice cracks, swallowed by the wind and the rain. Coming into view, she doesn't stop, her jacket flaring out behind her in a mad rush, she pivots, hearing a barrage of men pounding their swords in a circular arrangement. They each wear a patch of blue on their shields, the Drakharrow symbol. She sees it too and pivots her path away from them, feet pumping wildly as her arms propel her forward, I swerve to catch up and decide in that moment that I would start any war, I would slaughter all of these men if it meant she was free. I descend down, aiming for the soldiers instead, and release the full power of my strength on these men. There's twenty in total and I land in front of them with my wings dripping rainwater down my back. I pull out the sword attached to my hip, and I swing.

I raise my sword for the woman who saved my life just a few weeks ago, fighting for me not for any sort of reward or recognition, but to save those she cared for, for the prospect of a better future. A true martyr who deserves freedom. My sword swings through the air striking men down, three men surround me as I spin in circles and entrap them with my blade. I crack bones and slice stomachs to bring them down. I do not need to kill, so I strike their legs and feet bringing them to the ground. The rain pounds on their metal armour and drags them into the mud below our feet, the smell of rain and metal thick and heavy in the air. My foot catches on a patch of mud as I lose my balance, and in my distraction, two men escape my clutches and run towards the path she created. Screams catch my attention as a great orange beast powers in, and slices the two that had escaped, one consumed by the jaws of Laurence and the other thrown against a tree like a ragdoll. He joins me to continue fighting those here, and we work in tandem to immobilise the rest. A sort of comradery descends on us both as we attack and swing at the soldiers, I cut them down and Laurence sinks his teeth in them, blood spraying on our bodies as we continue. My body aches, a slice lands on my arm as my body feels worn down, pinpricks of pain flutter along my back as I assess the wounds I had not realised I gained during my fury in the fight. Fighting with emotion is dangerous, and reckless, but I power ahead. My wings now rendered useless are caked in mud, weighing down the muscles I had trained to maintain. I push my feet faster, my sword slicing through muscle and bone and a sigh of relief leaves me as the last soldier falls. My gaze immediately looks for her, my eyes scanning the trees amongst the rain and bodies lying about. It's not a pretty sight, definitely not the best introduction I would have liked, but I saw her capacity to love someone like me. A twig snaps to my right, but instead of the incredible woman I have been searching for, Laurence stands tall in his beast form. His head is locked on something behind me and I turn, my body pivots as we spot Clea now standing at the top of a hill across the field. Her figure now small in the distance, my feet move instantly, stepping over the fallen soldiers, just as a bright pinkish circle appears beside her.

Not again.

She raises an arm, waving goodbye, her other arm nestled on her heart as her body shakes. My dead heart splits apart, breaking apart from the inside at the scene. A roar sounds to my side, a tiger screaming in agony and protest.

We both go to move, Laurence attempting to run as he slips in the mud from the field - his claws sinking into the ground beneath us as a growl releases from his mouth, his paws limping. The lumps of feathered flesh on my back do not move, I push them desperately, normally instruments of freedom, now heavy and useless as they weigh me down by the clinging mud. As I move, it churns up more mud, burying deeper into the ground. Feeling trapped and helpless, I push myself to my feet, my legs digging into the muddy floor as my wings drag along with me, my body gives in as I collapse to the ground, my arms outstretched to reach her just once, to hold and touch her *once*. My head raises in time to watch her retreating form step through the portal as she disappears. A scream pierces the sky, my throat raw and aching as the sound relentlessly escapes from my body, a giant head pushes my body, pushing me upright, his black eyes searching. And I look up at the tiger, pity lines the beast's eyes as Laurence stares down at me, telling me exactly what has transpired here today. She is lost, to us, to everyone, and no one knows where she has gone.

Chapter 27
Bonnie

I stand with my forehead pressed against the large glass pane as the rainwater drips from my body onto the waxed floor, my eyes searching relentlessly in the woods for anyone to come home. I selfishly hope that Laurence finds her, or even Evreux, and brings Clea home. Back to our house, and back to me. I was furious when she blocked me out, the tattered brown bag she used for so many years before I met her clutched in her arm, she planned to run - to live by herself again. As soon as the barrier around me disappeared, I ran outside to nothing but the cold bite of the wind and rain. I was just glad Evreux had turned up, he had looked truly awful, and without knowing him at all I trusted him - the haunted look in his eyes cracked my heart open in ways I did not understand. Once he left, it gave me the strength to go too - my feet carried me upstairs to our room as I grabbed some supplies and a sword for protection. The sounds of the forest grew so loud, soldiers stormed outside wielding strong armour and fire torches, and with regret in my heart, I remained inside. I had caused Clea to be in such dangerous situations, getting caught or killed would just add to her pain, and she needs her time to be free. I just know she'll come back, she always does, this is her home. She belongs with us, no matter what. Even now, my heart yearns to go outside, she has been gone for an hour now - the rain has stopped its relentless pour, now a soft mist in the air.

I slam the doors open as Laurence finally emerges from the forest covered in black feathers. My feet pick up the pace as I run to him. Laurence limps slightly, eyes downcast as he moves. His dazed face lifts to mine as my feet slap against the wet grass, determination pierces his features as he sees me, body moving quicker to reach me faster as urgency takes route, despite the pain. Relief slams into me at his face, he's alright, and he's home. As I get closer, I notice the half-awake Fae man draped around his shoulders, he is being semi-carried around the arm, with his beautiful black wings caressing Laurence within. In one big movement, Evreux slowly lets go and crashes his knees to the ground as I rush up to Laurence. My arms latch around his shoulders, my face pressing tight into his shirt as his arms wind around me. He nestles his face into my hair, inhaling deeply, the mate bond calming now I'm in his arms. His shirt soaks into me, his hair dripping a mixture of blood and mud onto my arms but I don't care, being held tight by him is my safe haven and the only place I want to be right now.

"Please tell me you found her." I whisper to Laurence, my tone pleading. He finally lifts his head from my shoulders, his haunted eyes filled with remorse.

"She's gone, Bonnie." A choked sob escapes me at his words, his arms grip me tighter as his large palm wraps around my waist.

"I'm so sorry. She escaped at the last moment, there was a chance, but she left. She did it to keep us safe. We will see her again, I'm sure of it." He reassures me, rubbing my back in small motions.

An agonising moan sounds to my left, as Evreux sinks even further to the floor, the fallen angel looking like his entire existence was ripped away.

"Please come in, you both look like you need a bath and a hot tea." I pronounce, seeing them shivering in the cold, covered head to toe in scratches and mud.

"Are you alright?" Laurence asks me, and I shake my head, not wanting to discuss this in front of our new guest.

"I will be better once you're both inside, clean, and warm." The two Fae men exchange looks at my words. Laurence tilts his head to Evreux, inviting him in and then wraps my arm around his shoulder, looking in a similar fashion to how he carried Evreux, and I wonder for a moment why that is until my feet give out and I answer the call of sleep that had been dragging me down.

I wake to the sound of a crackling fire, in fresh bed sheets that smell of rose petals. I roll over to see Laurence sitting in the chair in the corner of our room, his face cast in a glow from the moonlight. He has bathed and changed into new clothes. His eyes look far away as he nurses a glass of dark amber liquid. Ever so slowly, I sit up, rubbing my tired eyes noting I had dozed off for long enough for it to be the middle of the night. My arm stings, I look down to spot a new clean bandage that winds up my arm, I didn't realise I was injured. Frowning at the bandage, I touch the wound and wince, peeling back the cloth to see the bruise in a deep purple looking like handprints. Laurence tracks the movement, his eyes darkening.

"I'm relieved you made it here alive, I heard the guards were pretty rough," he breathes out.

"Clea held onto me tight, I didn't realise how tight," I say, twisting my arm around. I had known of her strength all of these years, her hand clamped onto mine so tight it felt like iron. She had pushed through the crowd like a mad woman, the air thick with the mingling scents of spices, sweat and fear. All of a sudden, the market had descended into chaos of screaming and panicked shouting. She never stopped to explain, her frantic pace just kept moving, the terror in her eyes the only reasoning as I followed her. The villagers had blurred as we past them and until now I hadn't realised how hard she was pulling me. Despite the pain I feel, it is nothing compared to her absence even now. She has always been my anchor, all I could do was follow and trust in her as I always have. She is so relentlessly brave, and I fear it will get her hurt or even *killed* one day.

"Caldris and his men tried to take you from me." His voice becomes gruff as he takes a long drink from his glass.

"And Clea?" I ask, it is stupid to ask, but a small part of me hoped she would find her way once the guards gave up their search.

Laurence sighs, shaking his head, his eyes are shadowed with worry - looking like he hasn't slept at all. "I did a perimeter check, she chose to run. She knew the risks, and she still chose to run."

"She's all alone Laurence," my voice breaks, she could be anywhere - if she had run East, she could be on her way to Baskith, with no one and nothing. It's freezing over there at night, even the spring warmth doesn't last long over there.

"We could find her and help. She needs us," I persist, pushing myself out of bed as my feet touch the cold wooden floor.

Laurence stands and softly sits by my side, grasping my hand in his own. His voice is a gentle whisper filling the void of the bleakness in the situation "I have a feeling it's safer for her to be on her own, she will make her way back. She knows this is her home."

I wish she didn't lock me out, to convince her that it's safe here. But even that is a lie, the house was breached once already and there's no telling what Caldris will do once he finds her here. My body sinks into the mattress, the weight of defeat pressing down on me like an invisible force. I can feel it in my chest, the dull ache that refuses to subside, a silent acknowledgement of a truth I can't ignore. As much as every fibre of my being wants to reach out; to bring her back to me, I know deep in my heart that this is for the best. Laurence seems to be battling that same exhaustion in his eyes as he looks at me in resignation. It's safer if she stays hidden, keeping a low profile for just a little while longer - wherever she is. But still, I cling to the hope that this separation is temporary, the longing to see her, and hear her laugh is rooted in my soul. The exhilarating feeling of us riding our horses now just a fleeting memory. Laurence had done as much as he could with the resources he had, he even managed to send a winged male from the palace.

"What about the other Fae? Evreux?" I ask, my curiosity peaked. He desperately needed a healer, and fast, his wings had looked raw and bleeding, caked on with mud.

Laurence's eyes harden for just a moment at the name, he clenches his jaw and growls out, "I sent him away," my mouth parts open in shock, and at that, he closes his eyes and continues.

"I made sure he got cleaned up first, he refused leftover food or a bed to sleep in. It was strange, his entire being shifted... all he seemed to want was to be inside the house. From the events of Clea leaving, he only wished to get home. I granted him a horse to borrow, his wings were in pretty bad shape." He grimaces, I'm not versed in the species of winged men to understand the healing time. From what I had heard, some Fae were born with it, but others could weave a powerful dark spell to retrieve wings of their own, only they would know how long it would take for those delicate muscles to stitch back together again.

"Did he tell you why he was after her?" I ask curiosity spiking within me, his wild eyes swimming in my vision from last night.

"Sort of... I don't truly understand his motives, they're brash and reckless, but he's hurting. He seems to believe he's in love with her, and was desperate to find her," he says, bewildered with the memory. My fingers trace the nightgown I'm wearing, feeling the threading that loops around the edges of the material.

"Clea never mentioned him to me," I say, my brows furrowing in confusion.

He brushes an arm through his hair and blows out a big breath seeming to be as confused as I am by it all.

"I don't think *she* even knew, there's missing pieces to his story. I promise I will do all I can to find out." He says, nodding to himself. He pauses for a moment; thoughts spiral through his head as if he is piecing stories together. "At the meeting, Fabian had been acting strange, he's holding something back. We had only spoken to him a week ago, how could so much have changed?"

My head bounces in acknowledgement, the curls in my hair bouncing with the movement as I consider the words.

"My head hurts," a small, shaky laugh escapes my mouth, unbidden and fragile. But even as the sound leaves me, it cracks, unravelling the broken feeling within me. Tears begin to slip down my face, the treacherous liquid hot and relentless, blurring my vision. The laugh breaks into a sob as a deep uncontrollable ache shakes my chest and steals my breath. Laurence shifts to move closer, placing his arm around my waist and encouraging me to lie down. I lean my head against his shoulder, hand tracing lines around his scarred chest, just as it feels like my entire world is crumbling beneath me. We lie here until the sky bleeds from the dark sky to a lighter hue, he holds me for so long that I hear the soft purring sounds escaping him as he drifts off into sleep. Brushing his hair back to see his face, I frown at the scratch mark now showing on his cheek. His face relaxes as sleep consumes him, and I keep my hold on him as strong as I can just as sleep pulls at me too.

Chapter 28
Evreux

I walk down to breakfast with stiff movements. Athena and the healers had spent hours tending to the deep wounds on my back, their hands pinning me down against the plush carpet of my room. The sharp scent of chamomile and peppermint filled the air, stinging my nose and making my head swim. Those strong herbs, renowned for their ability to soothe inflamed and irritated skin - worked alongside their careful hands, bandages, and salves to stitch the ragged gashes on my back and wings. They had worked tirelessly, their focus unbroken, stopping the infection that had begun to take hold. From dragging myself through the mud to half-slumping over the saddle on the ride home, it felt like a miracle that I was still upright. As I leaned against the doorway for a moment to steady myself, I briefly wondered if they had any spells or potions that could mend wounds deeper than the skin. But those, I knew, weren't so easily healed. Sophie had reminded me time and time again that for those kinds of wounds, only time could truly help. She would say it with a patience that was both comforting and frustrating, her steady presence grounding me after every gruelling return to the palace. I could only hope she was right this time.

I was thankful that the fight could be explained by defending the townspeople from the barrage of Caldris' men, although the location was misplaced, I had raised my sword to save the people of Thalor - an order I would have been given regardless, if Athena only knew the truth of why I was marred with these wounds...

The smell of freshly baked bread calls to me as my stomach protests in hunger, my footsteps heavy and cautious. So much has happened in the last twenty-four hours - enough heartbreak and chaos to fill a lifetime. The weight of it presses heavily on my chest, threatening to crush me and drive me to my knees in anguish. But I keep moving. Each step feels like defiance, a refusal to let the despair swallow me whole, even as it claws at the edges of my resolve.

Alas, I shuffle my feet towards the breakfast table, knowing that if I don't, I don't think I'll ever leave the confines of my bedroom.

Athena, Amazu, and Sophie are already seated, tucking into their food and coffee. The smell hits me into a daze as I sit beside Sophie, she quietly places food on my plate and pours me coffee, I smile at her in thanks, words not forming in my throat like I want them to. Lifting the piece of toast into my mouth I chew on the buttery bread, swallowing it down with hot coffee. The coffee burns down my throat, the caffeine buzzing through my system as I had longed for.

Athena and Amazu discuss the events of yesterday casually, carefully skirting around the larger issue at hand. Caldris had drawn blood, causing the treaty to break and a part of me is grateful to have one morning without something crashing down on us. Talks of war and politics aside, I bask in the blissful moment of just eating toasted bread with butter and drinking my bitter coffee.

My eyes flicker across from me, Athena sits nursing her own bowl of fruit with her eyes fixed on me with a steady, unyielding gaze. She had been the one to hold me down last night, her soft hands stroking my arm as she spoke to me the entire time. Even now, her presence is firm and comforting, her posture one of quiet strength as her eyes bore into mine. "How are you?" She asks, her voice low and full of concern, carrying an edge that requires an answer. The bloody battle with Laurence drifts into my mind, as I can see the command in her eyes - she's concerned, yes, but she's also prying for information on last night.

"I have been worse," I lie, a smile pushes on my face as I pretend that I am anything but alright. I can't shake the feeling that opening up to her would only deepen the ache, knowing all too well that their decision about searching for Clea was final.

But even now she is gone, Laurence had looked as lost as I did with answers of where she had gone. As we reached the house, he gently cradled Bonnie upstairs and aggressively pushed me towards resting at his house. My resolve had cracked as I declined, knowing that if I spent one more second in that empty house, with reminders of her everywhere - it would have torn my shredded heart apart even further. So, I sit here, staring into my coffee cup that is almost empty as the tears threaten to fall. I do not regret my choice in the slightest - cutting down the men chasing her, that is, interrogating Laurence was a fault in hindsight. The act itself is so uncharacteristic that it's a glaring reminder - I need time to process everything, to clear my head of the shadows that claw at me in the dead of night, screaming at me to take action.

To do something.

All I can hope is that when I find her again, I won't lose control and act like a manic asshole.

Childish laughter spills from the hallway connecting the room, as our heads turn to watch Hale come bursting in, Fabian hot on his heels. They're both holding fake wooden swords as they swing at each other.

"No swords at the breakfast table" Amazu chastises them, laughter bubbling up in his throat as they heed his warning.

Hale swings his sword at Fabian, his floppy brown hair catching in his eyes as he moves. Hale takes an easy shot of hitting his leg which was obviously exposed, and Fabian crashes to the ground in mock pain, grasping his leg.

"Ah! I've been hit!" he cries, his hands gripping his fake wound. Hale stops his movements, mouth parting in an O shape and pauses to reach out his arm. We all watch as Fabian lifts his head, smirking, and grabs his hand pulling him down with him. They both crash together as Fabian tickles him relentlessly; giggles echo around the hall and I close my eyes at the sound. His laughter sounding so pure and full of joy, that it seemed to light up the entire room. It touches something deep within me, the deep ache that relentlessly sticks in my gut, lifting my spirit so high I feel like I could soar from the warmth of it.

Sophie shakes her head beside me, the corner of her mouth lifting at the display. Her eyes water at the scene as she places a hand on her belly, and it's then I take note of the herbal tea she sips instead of coffee, a drink she swears by every morning. Joking about the gross-tasting green tea, her words were something like 'Grass floating in hot water tasting like dirt'. It's moments like these I cling to, surrounded by my family. Sophie spots me staring and flashes her sharp eyes at me in warning, I mockingly seal my lips like a lock and key as she stuffs bread into her mouth.

"Not the croissants!" Athena cries, just as Amazu throws a chocolate croissant at Fabian's head, the pastry exploding on contact, Fabian grabs the pieces and playfully smudges them in Hale's hair.

"Uncle Evreux, help me!" Hale shouts at me, and I gingerly jump up grabbing bread rolls and continue to throw them at Fabian in battle. He lifts his hands in defence, and I take the moment to tackle him to the ground myself, Hale jumping on us both as we all descend in laughter so hard my stomach hurts. We all lay there on the floor, and I grab Hale shaking him playfully as he shrieks in mock outrage, I continue my onslaught of tickling, my hand shaking his floppy hair that scatters pastry crumbs around him. His small hands reach beside me, towards the bread rolls scattered on the floor, I quickly grab his feet and pull him back. He grunts, reaching for those soft rolls as a weapon against me. He's strong, I'll give him that, as he's just close to being an adult, his muscles have strengthened over time. All at once, we hear a sizzling in the air, burnt food drifts into the air and my head whips up looking for what had caught fire. Amazu turns his head searching for the answers we cannot hear.

"Ouch!" Hale screams, I let go of him immediately as he nurses his hands to his chest.

"Let me see," I urge, Hale simply uncurls his hands to reveal blisters barely forming. It is then I turn to see the bread roll black and burnt, the smell assaulting my nose. Not just that, the carpet around us appears black and dead. Athena rushes over and gently assesses his wound and excuses herself with him in tow, muttering sweet words about getting patched up at the healers as she kisses his blistered palm.

"How?" Fabian muttered in shock, that small piece of detail we had already forgotten.

Hale had fire powers during the battle, he mastered them of course by then, but I hadn't thought… they must have started to manifest when he was in a heightened situation.

"He truly does have these gifts from birth," Amazu considers in wonder, as we all look to each other for confirmation.

"Can someone tell me what the hell is going on?" Fabian urges, and we quickly explain the events of the ball and how truly powerful Hale could be. And how dangerous, if he was able to burn himself.

CHAPTER 29
Laurence

3 months later…

    The spring season goes by fast, shipments come and go in a blur. The business is as busy as ever, and I haven't stopped working since Clea and Adam were lost to us. Their lives left a void in our hearts; shortly after his death, I hosted a service at the estate. He had wished to be buried alongside his mother atop the mountains in the dense forest, his final resting place alongside those he loved. Fabian had assisted me in carrying his casket up the hill, it was a long path we both took on foot, my feet were raw and bleeding afterwards. A necessary pain to keep myself routed to, even now my feet itch from the healing wounds - a stark reminder of my failure to protect those under my care. His funeral was short, only a few had attended with having no living relatives, we were his family until the last day. Bonnie had constructed a beautiful garland of lavender bushes and tulips to place atop the freshly overturned soil, and I used a wooden crate carved with his name and title to complete his honour in the scene. He was a loyal soldier, and a good friend, his last duty to protect Clea and Bonnie - doing just that. His life just disappeared, his role was filled, easily replaced, a fact that makes me want to retch. Life keeps moving forward without him, the first few weeks were hard, the months became easier over time. The only good news I received was Caldris seizing his attack and returning to his home, but I could feel something coming, we all could.

Now, the flowers are in full bloom, and the blistering heat melts the bones of those lost to us. Bonnie has barely left our room, wedding arrangements no longer being discussed and although I have tried, nothing seems to help her get out of bed. I help to bathe her daily, and talk to her about my day, new contracts and a new flavour range I have been experimenting with, but nothing can fill the gap that was ripped open in our lives. Sometimes, on her good days, she looks out the window but as soon as any large vehicles arrive, and I head outside she quickly disperses. I was unsure why at first, until I remembered that once Adam had walked in on Bonnie and Clea drinking iced tea on the porch outside to watch the deliveries, they would pretend to speak as if the workers outside were saying something different, speaking in silly voices and pretending other stories existed in that space. Adam had deemed it harmless, when he reencountered it, Clea would say the most outlandish things turning Bonnie into a fit of laughter. Adam had been holding back his own laughter when telling me and had asked to stand outside their door to 'guard' on those days, I had agreed knowing it was the highlight of his day too.

Clea was the glue we all didn't realise we needed, and with Adam no longer drifting about, the house feels lifeless and empty. Old wounds seem to split open each time I try to discuss her, the same story and words leaving me. Clea is not coming back, and neither is Adam. This is our new normal, and I don't know how I can deal with that.

I finish my drink, the amber liquid scorching my throat as the sun reaches its peak in the sky, casting the front garden in hues of bright yellow and orange. Right on cue, Evreux appears in the sky, he visits each week, purchasing a bottle of red wine each time. It is always the same bottle, as he carries the exact amount of coins too. I had insisted we could add his order to the regular one at the palace, but he had refused, the excuse of 'stretching his wings' I had bought the first time. But after the second time, his eyes had lingered on the house for a few moments longer than anyone would deem normal. He gently touches his feet just outside of the gates as I grab the bottle and head outdoors. Nodding to the guards at the door, triple the amount since the attack in the market, and the gates groan open. They catch slightly on the grass, being overgrown and thick with the growth of summer. Evreux walks in, as usual he looks up to Bonnie's window and smiles slightly in greeting, knowing she watches his arrival too. A strange sort of agreement has befallen us all, the three of us clinging to the hope Clea will return and skirting around the issue with each conversation. It's amazing how much of an impact a woman can make on everyone's lives. The relationship Evreux has with her still confuses the hell out of me, even after I plied him with alcohol, he refuses to elaborate.

I extend the bottle to him, the glass warming in the sun as he takes the bottle and carefully places it in his bag. He is draped in an all-black ensemble, his usual attire for his job at the palace. It's summer, and the poor guy has thick leather trousers and straps around his torso. I hope for his sake the air up in the sky cools his body down, he must be roasting in this heat. Sweat pools slightly on his brows, his breath remaining steady even after the flight he took to get here. The brown satchel hangs from his shoulder, looking more practical than the rest of his outfit. The heat has him glistening with sweat, which doesn't exactly help sell the whole 'mysterious' vibe he's clearly going for. His black wings unfurl gently, stretching out from the usage. I wonder for a moment if they would ever burn in the sun, even now I can hear Bonnie scolding me for staying out in the sun for too long. But his wings, though once damaged, now bear no visible scars, standing as a symbol of his healing journey and renewed strength. I just wonder if he has worked on his internal ones, and the way he stands there looking at me confirms that he has lost that sense of crazy he once sported. I still overcharge the bastard by a small amount, my small victory of revenge for him tying me up. But even then, I couldn't hold that against him, clearly going through some mental break. I had forgiven him the second he swung his sword to cut down the men that chased after Clea.

He reaches into his bag to extract the same brown envelope that contains the money for the wine.

"Any word?" He asks.

"No," I respond, my voice steady, though tinged with the sadness that inevitably seeps in each time I respond to his repeated question.

His head dips in a nod, the fading sun glinting off his eyebrows as he looks up to me.

"See you next week," dismissing him, I turn to signal the guards at the gates. It's almost time for another delivery and having him linger around isn't good for prying ears.

"It may be sooner than that." Evreux hands me a second envelope, unlike the normal one chunky with the coins that cling together in his grip - worn and torn up from multiple uses. This new one, it's clean and crisp, a new envelope with the royal seal on it proudly stamped. Taking it in my hands, the writing on the front is our address.

"You're a post boy now? If you need a job I could do with another transporter, you'd be quicker than my carriages and more handsome." I tease.

A semblance of a smile is his only response as he secures the tie on the bag and turns to leave. I pop open the wax seal quickly, noting the beautiful penmanship of the letter.

Dear Laurence and guests, His Highness Amazu and Her Highness Athena request your attendance in the palace immediately.

"They want us at the palace, why?" I say to his retreating back.

He takes a few steps and pauses, head turning to look over his shoulder, "Items have been going missing, similar to what Caldris spoke of and we were hoping for insiders to that knowledge to help us search for the answers. Fabian suggested it." He says, maintaining his stoic expression, though his hands tighten into fists seemingly frustrated with the words.

"I will speak with Bonnie and send word soon," folding up the letter, the guards close the gates just as Evreux jumps into the sky back the way he came.

"We have to go and help them," the voice hits me as confusion barrels into me, the guards snap their heads away from the house just as I turn to see Bonnie in her nightgown standing by the front door without her shoes on, her grip on the door as her head peeks out.

"Will you be alright with…" *leaving the house, talking to people, talking about Clea.*

"It could be related to her, she's got to be here somewhere and needs our help," her voice croaks, "…I miss her too much to not try." Taking off my jacket, I wrap it around her shoulders walking her inside the house.

After I quietly draw us both a bath, the hot aroma smelling like the first night I met Bonnie - I bought the soap especially for us, closing my eyes I can hear the sway of the trees and crackling flame as I undress and step into the large bath enough to sit five Fae. Bonnie undresses, and I lift my hand up to guide her in the bath to sit opposite me, her body thrumming with energy as she casually picks up the washcloth and for the first time in months, begins to bathe herself. When she reaches her hair, I lift my body over to her and take the soap from her gentle hands, leaning her head back as I massage her temples. Her body relaxes as I massage the soap into her long brown hair, her eyes closing with content and her lips curving up into a smile. I kiss her forehead just before she dunks under the water to rinse herself off, I move back, swirling bubbles all around me. A lot of bubbles. That's when I notice the oils I purchased some time ago had tipped into the bath, bubbles foam and grow as they spill over the edge. I scoop them up, failing to dampen the damage that's causing the wooden flooring as more and more bubbles spill over. That's when laughter rises up in me at the display, and I turn just as Bonnie smears the bubbles into my hair then all over my face. Blowing out a quick breath, causing them to stick to her face too she joins me with a rare tilt of her lips. Her face blooms into one of hope that makes me ignore the rancid taste of soap in my mouth. I return her smile, wiping away the suds from my face. She looks up at me, cheeks pink and lips soft, eyes wide with adoration. My hands dive into her hair as I search into those endless eyes of hers, and ever so slightly, I press a kiss to her soft cheek.

My hand cradles her head, her cheek pressing against my hand as her eyes close ever so softly. "Are you certain?" It's her choice. It always will be.

"Yes," she responds with a soft sigh, her wet lashes sticking together as she looks at me with determination I haven't seen for so long.

"When can we leave?" Her soft lips form the words as my heart flutters.

"As soon as tomorrow morning, I have business to attend to today. But we can pack some clothes and be on our way as soon as you're ready," I confirm. A shipment of fresh and clean glass bottles were arriving today, the order had been cancelled previously and I was in dire need of them to complete the first batch of 'Lavender Spritz' - the new flavour I had perfected. She'll never know it, but since Clea took it out of the kitchen for our night in with Fabian, it had sparked that feeling back into me to try it once more. The liquor had a purplish/pink hue to it, with sparkles that would swirl in it once shaken. I had perfected it for her, for us to open on her return.

"Tomorrow sounds perfect," Bonnie confirms, and as the water turns cold, I guide her out of the bath and wrap her in a fluffy white towel. We both dress in freshly dried clothes as she gingerly lays down in bed, I hold her tight as her breathing becomes heavier, head falling deeper on my shoulder and limbs growing heavy. I listen to her steady breathing, heart beating in a steady rhythm as I consider the weight of tomorrow. So much is unknown, the last time I visited the palace, it did not go well. Not even considering the fact Evreux had chained me to the floor, leaving me with a nasty bruise on my wrists from the cuffs. But that day haunts my dreams, hearing the devastating news of Adam's death and not being able to reach the women as quickly as I wanted. I had failed in my duty to protect them.

Bonnie's arm twitches softly in her sleep, and I gently pull the duvet up to cover her exposed arm. This small woman in my arms is my entire world, the reason I breathe, the reason I push myself so hard every day - to ensure her safety and happiness. I'd do anything for her, give up everything I have, even my very heart, just to see her smile. Her laughter is the melody that keeps me alive, the light that chases away every shadow. She is my everything, and all I can hope is that I'm enough for her. The depth of my feelings terrifies me sometimes, the weight of tomorrow's uncertainties pressing heavy on my chest. But as long as she's by my side, I know we can face anything together. If she asked me to, I'd wait days, weeks, months - years, even - for her. Anything she needed, I'd give without hesitation because loving her is the only thing I've ever known. She will be my wife whenever she is ready, and when that time comes… once she's healed, she will find the key to the tavern I purchased for her, waiting for her warmth and light to change the town forever.

CHAPTER 30
Evreux

I open the grand front doors to the only two people in this world who might hold the answers I seek. I had skipped breakfast this morning, a small sacrifice to ensure everything was ready in time for their arrival. My routine felt almost ceremonial, every step deliberate as I prepared for this moment. Anticipation had taken root in my chest the moment I received Laurence's message late last night from an advisor of mine, passing notes in a tavern a quick way to convey information, confirming they would come. It had been a last-minute acceptance; one I hadn't dared to hope for. I had worried they might decline, given my not-so-warm welcome to him last time, followed by his quick departure. My insistence on visiting their home weekly after the event likely didn't help matters, the only connection I have to Clea clinging on by a thread so tightly bound it's close to snapping. Laurence is a good man, friendly and approachable, and from the way he carries himself you can see the weight of confidence he has on his shoulders from years of trade. I can't shake the interactions he had with Fabian out of my head, the casual ease and booming laugh that would fill a room, the joyous nature enough to fill the emptiness inside someone's heart. Yet underneath that I also noticed the cracks that appeared to the surface these past visits, his guard has been raised significantly – for him to triple the safety of the house and reduce visits, he's limiting outsiders into his home. His loyalty on protecting those he loves so strong it blinds me, Sophie and Fabian come to mind when I imagine those I would protect without the weight of being duty bound to the Kingdom, as I am for Amazu and Athena. To them I am a head guard, managing hundreds of soldiers with force and connections, but even then the lingering thought of being replaced creeps up into me, could it be easy to detach my position and live a violence-free life? No, that's simply not possible, Thalor needs me.

Their help today will be invaluable, and the weight of what they might share is heavy on my mind. As I stood before the grand front doors, the thought crossed my mind again - perhaps today will be the start of something new. Or perhaps not. Either way, I had to try.

"Welcome," my voice comes out in softer tones as my eyes close in greeting.

Laurence huffs at me and storms past looking like he drank a barrel's worth of coffee this morning with his light bouncy steps. In contrast, Bonnie follows quietly behind and greets me sweetly, her apricot gown sweeping by her feet as she enters. My gut twists at the memory of Laurence tied up in my interrogation room, and I wonder if she would look at me the same way once she knew. Maybe she already does, but she must hide it well, it would be hard to ignore the way her eyes glued to his every few moments - their love like two magnets pulling them together.

"Is there a reason the head guard is spending his time drifting about opening doors?" Laurence remarks, arms folded as he watches me carefully. I had been instructed to greet them, along with a tour.

Athena had suggested it would set the right tone, but I just hoped the tour did not result in the kitchens where he would see the countless unopened bottles of red wine amongst the inventories.

After a few moments of silence, clipped footsteps descend the grand staircase, Amazu appears and smiles with warmth at our new guests. His posture is stiff as his eyes search the room for the remaining guest, face tilting in confusion. I had withheld the information of Clea's disappearance, along with my involvement in her escape, and I have a feeling Amazu was looking forward to seeing her again if only to pry her for information. Assess the threat she could pose.

"Laurence, it is wonderful to see you again. And this young woman must be Bonnie," extending his hand in greeting, Laurence takes his hand and shakes firmly. His muscles seem to flex under his blue tunic as he maintains eye contact with Amazu, his tall frame exceeding that of the leader. Bonnie takes his hand next, awe and wonder in her eyes being in close proximity to the highest man regarded in Thalor. In another life they may have been locked side by side, sick of each other's faces as they avoid the rats scuttering about in the prison they were locked in for so long. Amazu clears his throat loudly breaking the image from my mind.

"Likewise. I hadn't expected to be back here so soon." Laurence responds, flickering his gaze at me in distaste. Containing my scowl, we take them on the long grand tour around the estate, where Amazu points out the architecture and relevance of each headstone and paintings adorning the castle. We had ignored the prison cells underground where I avoided as much as necessary, one of the prison guards who I had known all of my life had given us a warm greeting. Llyod was an older gentleman, grey hairs poked through his once dark brown hair, but my eyes couldn't meet his. He was a groundsman now, his role changed some time when I was stationed at the camps with Amazu. Fabian's father, a man weathered by years of hard work, had skin marked by the elements of labouring outdoors. Yet, despite the toll on his body, he had remained in the palace, choosing to stay close to his son.

"May I take your bags to put into your rooms?" A quiet voice of a maid says when we reach the common meeting area, with her arms outstretched.

"That's alright," Bonnie responds, dipping her head in acknowledgement. Laurence places his hand on the small of her back as she clutches the strap of her back in her grasp. I don't miss the shadow that crosses her eyes as she tucks it behind her.

She must not feel comfortable sharing her possessions.

"This is a lovely home, your Highness," Bonnie says, blushing sweetly at the casual stance he sports.

"Enough of the pleasantries. Please, call me Amazu," smooth as always, we continue to walk at a slow pace. My wings drag along the floor now and then. I had taken another perimeter check last night and my back ached, no matter how much I trained, my wings always seemed like a burden when they were meant to be a precious gift. But I couldn't imagine my life without them, the fact is not lost on me that I may lose them someday.

When we stepped into the newly renovated ballroom, I had looked to Laurence to note for even a fraction of recollection, my chest tightening slightly at the blankness that befell his features. Now, he just looks bored, unamused compared to Bonnie's excitement. My smile tilts at her face even now, looking much happier than I had seen her previously. With their connection, I wonder if Clea would give anything to see her like this even after she left. "Have you lived here your entire life? The architecture is stunning," Bonnie asks, her eyes drifting to the high ceilings and intricate carvings along the wall as we exit the ballroom. The walls tell stories of past rulers and wars we have all faced, each carving is done by hand, by a variety of Fae over the years. The latest edition was one Sophie had done, currently hidden by a large topaz curtain, but it depicts a large dragon flying in the air with mighty wings. Along the top is a tiger, claws outstretched, a woman wielding a large sword jumping mid-air to slice the wings, and a tall man casting fire magic towards it. I visited that carving more than the rest.

"I was born in the palace, my parents raised me to take the throne when needed. Don't be fooled, I spent time in the training camps, so I wasn't always sporting a golden spoon in my mouth," he responds, chuckling in the way he always does, in a humble sort of way. A technique he has mastered for years. How to make new people comfortable in his presence. I don't comment that the tent in the training camps he had was larger and far grander than the others, he even had staff collect his meals. I had been grateful to have known him prior, or else I may not have survived the terrible winters we faced with no allies of my own. Even then, with the face of such wealth, Amazu would share his extra food and warmth with those around him. Either to save face, or collect allies, I am never sure.

"It is quite a lovely palace," her voice drifts in the background, soft and warm, Laurence keeping a hold on her back. We step into the library and Bonnie's mouth drops open as her face splits into a smile as big as the sun. She looks alive at this moment, a stark contrast to the dull shadow in her bedroom window. She had yawned at the lengthy stories in the art gallery, giving me the sense that she finds words more poetic than paint strokes. She spins, making her skirt sparkle in the light, taking the entire room in. Laurence wraps his arm around her again, thumb rubbing along her back as he looks at her like she holds the very stars in the skies with her smile.

"This is…." she starts.

"I know right," Fabian finishes, walking over with a book in his hand. He's dressed casually today, top button wide open to display his chest hair and the chunky necklaces he favours so much. His hair is tousled, like he has been running his fingers through it. He sports me a cheeky wink at my staring, and I avoid my gaze, avoiding the creeping blush appearing on my face.

"Fabian, my friend, how are you?" Laurence asks, clapping him on his back in a bone-crushing hug. The tight embrace is reciprocated, and it's not lost on me the everlasting envy I feel from the closeness they both seem to have.

"I'm alright, better than him," his thumb points to me, and I shake my head in mock outrage. I had bathed this morning, but warm water and bubbles could not erase the circles under my eyes.

It is no secret I have been experiencing a recurring nightmare; each time I would blink awake in my room and get up to look in the mirror, my wings would appear to be ripped clean off - a recurring scene that plagues my sleep. Blood ran down my back in gushing waves as my upper back screamed in agony, the feathers of my wings scattered amongst the floor in puddles of my own blood. Each time when I look back at myself in my reflection, I saw her standing there. Clea would reach out of the mirror, her pale arm extended out to reach for me with her face edged in despair, and each night, I would go to touch her outstretched hand only to be ripped away from the dream. I had woken in a pool of sweat each time, Sophie had rushed in the first time, hearing my screaming but... she stopped after the fifth time. Only strong doses of herbal tea seem to quell my bodily reactions, a nighttime elixir to dull my senses enough to get a few hours of rest.

Moving to sit at the table, wooden chairs scrape along the floor. I choose a stool, uncomfortable is an understatement, but it gives my wings room to breathe. The room quiets as we are seated, other guards and maids off-duty stare at the new guests arriving. It takes all but thirty seconds since we sat for Grus, the Librarian, an older gentleman who had worked here before I was born, to stroll over and say hello to us all. With a quick nod from Amazu, Grus walks over to another group and within a few moments, they trickle out of the room, leaving us alone to prying ears. Normally, clearing staff out of this room is uncommon, but the conversation and research we are about to conduct must be done so alone. Grus comes to join us again as Amazu passes him a slip of paper, the list of books we made to start our research, not only is he a brilliant Librarian but he was also gifted with wings – unlike me he was born with them and doesn't remember anything but the weight on his back. His wings flow in a cascade of white feathers that shine with radiance, whereas my black ones usually swallow every glimpse of light – darkness seeping into the room as I enter. He has been a close friend of mine since I was officially hired as a guard, helping me to train and develop my wings naturally. One of my favourite memories was learning to fly without causing too much air to sweep up into the atmosphere from the powerful strides. He had laid out hundreds of pages of paper on each table surface and asked me to touch the ceiling without a page moving an inch. It took days and a lot of pages moving before I got the handle of it. With his age, I have since insisted on helping move heavier tombs to the higher shelves. He had refused at first, his love for books so strong he would be more afraid of their wellbeing than his. But now, I receive his notes to aid in moving books about and sometimes I wonder if he prefers the company, but I answer his call every time, his weathered face one I have come to depend on.

Grus casually collects the books needed, and places them on the large table in front of us, adjusting his wonky glasses as he does so. A weathered smile throws my way, before he departs.

"Thank you both for being here today, as you can see, we need help with research. But first, I would love to hear how you both met," Amazu starts, his tone is inviting, hiding the deception of one of the main reasons why he brought these two here - to pry information out of them about Clea and if the black portals were of any connection to her gifts. She was the only one of us known and potentially able to wield such powers that could trigger larger events.

It was a large assumption, with her power showcasing light pink swirls, but there was no denying the shield she trapped us all in. Morvath was the obvious choice as we had theorised, but with his power diminished by the other Fae we had ruled it out. One theory we had discussed was that Morvath may have already sunk his claws into Drakharrow, maybe even be the resting place of that wicked power and the reasoning to why Caldris had such impacts over his side. But Sophie had countered that Caldris wouldn't show his cards like that, he didn't care for the wellbeing of his people, he most likely cared more about his silverware disappearing.

"I'm not much of a reader, but Bonnie is, do you recognise any of these," Laurence turns to her, Bonnie's eyes greedily looking over the books on the table and memorizing the intricate paintings on the front. They are truly beautiful books, with intricate hand-painted artworks on the front.

"I do not, can I?" she asks, Amazu pushes a book towards her, a red bound large volume covered in white dots on the front. She opens it gingerly and bites her lip, thumbing through the pages.

"Because you asked so nicely…" Laurence sneers at me, and grabbing a book he slams it to the desk in one big motion. The book is old, older than all of us and yet he carelessly grabbed it with his meaty hands. My back stiffens at his disregard for it, needing to reprimand him for Grus' sake. Yet if I do so, Laurence may spill our little visit in my torture room, and I do not need that secret coming out. It would waste the few days I had agreed to Fabian's experiments of potions and witchcraft to hide the secret of what I had done from the leaders, he had been tampering with a few new

that could alter someone's
and headaches some of odd
one potion forced my hair to
was bright fucking blue. He
hair when he saw me, hands
out of breath. I had shaved it
strange colour that spread around
sure. He promised it would wear
time any time removing it straight
been filled with bright blue hair,
grotesque, like I had just captured
critters. I had been grateful my
feathers didn't change, those would have been hard to conceal. So as
Laurence continues to manhandle the books, I keep my mouth shut.

"...She was working at a truly awful tavern with a friend of hers," he swallows, "And I had walked in hoping to get a new business deal with the owner, and it was love at first sight," he finishes.

Lie.

About what, I'm not sure. But he had scratched the back of his neck, a nervous tell I had noticed at the council meeting.

"Which tavern?" I ask casually, already knowing the answer. I had frequented every tavern in the land since the last time I saw Clea, hoping to gain information on Laurence. I had visited The Sapphire Swan out of mere coincidence to catch up with the owner and it had slipped that they had a previous owner who was ripped apart by a sort of bear. The same night, two women fitting their description had gone missing, *Charlotte and Bonnie*, about three months before the *Spring Ball*. The same women Fabian had met, too.

"The Emerald Duck," the liar continues to lie, as Bonnie shifts in her seat.

"I don't think I have heard that one," I snipe, head tilting. Amazu clears his throat, clearly aimed at me.

"That's a sweet story. I can relate to love at first sight of course, my wife, Athena and I married to secure a trade deal with Baskith, but I was head over heels for her when I saw her. I remember agreeing so quickly, she had hated me at first, a fiery woman. I loved her even when she threw insults at my face; she was unlike anyone I had ever met." Bonnie swoons at the story, leaning forward. I had heard this story countless times; hell I had lived in it. They truly were a match made perfectly; Hale's face would light up whenever the storybook would come out - the one Amazu had written for her one birthday of their love story told by him. The book was choppy, but it was filled with all of the letters Amazu had written to her in the early days when he needed to express how he felt to her in any way he could. If he tried telling her in person, she'd just slam the door in his face, not wanting to marry a man she just met.

"So, what shall we look out for?" Bonnie asks.

Amazu takes a moment, scanning the area for anyone in hearing distance and nods his head, confirming our privacy.

"There have been reports of a black void being present in Drakharrow, a few platters of food fell through as Laurence is already aware of. We have tried searching ourselves, but we have come up short; unfortunately, as these mysterious forces have been appearing in our own palace, we are growing desperate. We do not know where it came from, the first report was on the same day the palace was attacked on the *Spring Ball*. We ask you both to be private about the matter and give us information you find on any power that echoes this one or even one that seems out of the ordinary."

Although this was something we needed answers on, his ability to reveal the truth in such a soft way is incredible - he speaks like it is a secret amongst us, a ruse to make the new guests feel like they are accepting special information. The book we had retrieved from that day was burnt, and barely salvageable, it was locked up with Fabian who had been devouring the text in the long hours of the night.

"I don't mean to pry, but what power is this exactly?" Bonnie asks, biting her lip.

Amazu considers her question for a moment, his shoulders seem to relax as he moves forward to spill more half-truths to our new guests. His eyes never waver, as they latch onto Bonnie, giving her his full attention.

"I do not deem it prying, I know we are asking for a lot from the both of you. Please look for anything in relation to a power known to control the mind and spirit, and anything in relation to black pits of abyss. We fear these 'portals' as we have been calling them, may end up growing and result in more items going missing. If they grow or spread to other parts of Thalor, our people will begin to fear living inside their own homes." He links his fingers together, pressing the closed fist against his mouth, seemingly forming the right words.

"This is why it is our top priority, the safety of our people always will be."

Bonnie latches onto the statement immediately, as her face drops the smile she was sporting and furrows her eyebrows in concern.

We all reach for a book each and open it up in front of us. The book I had chosen was newer than the rest, as it did not contain the layer of dust or cobwebs as the others had. I am a few chapters in when staff come in carrying trays of coffee and tarts just as my stomach rolls, the delicacies are placed on a polished silver tray, as they are placed on the table. The sound seems to wake the sleeping tiger as Laurence jolts upright who had been trying to pretend he wasn't sleeping, his fist propped up on his cheek.

"This coffee smells wonderful, thank you," Bonnie reaches for a cup and casually starts grabbing other empty cups and places in front of the others, looking at ease, filling in the role of caretaker. Her life working in a tavern shows so clearly, as does her need to care for others. Lucy's eyebrows shoot to her forehead at the display and smiles in greeting. Bonnie continues, not caring. She was hired for the *Spring Ball*, needing more staff to accommodate more guests, and thankfully was attending to the kitchen when all hell broke loose. She has lingered ever since, always leaning into my space, asking too many questions.

"Hello Evreux," Lucy says to me, her face going beet red as she hands me a cup, hovering around me for a few moments. She is a couple of years younger than me, thick black hair that's pinned up to her head in a tight bun.

"Thank you, Lucy," I say as she pours me the wonderful smelling brown liquid in the cup, at her name leaving my lips, her hands shake causing coffee to spill a little on the table.

"Oh, I'm so sorry! Let me clean that up!" Grabbing a cloth from her dress, she presses on the table, leaning forward. She stays perched there for a long moment, and I avert my eyes back to the book in front of me. The scene I was reading about literature and documents being forged hundreds of years ago, it talks of how to decipher real text from fake. I have reread the same sentence five times, waiting for Lucy to move, when she doesn't, I turn to Fabian beside me.

"When the letter 'A' is written in ancient scripts, some writers had difficulty with connecting the capitalised word with the remaining letters. This difficulty became prevalent with the use of squid ink, as it is notoriously known for not being the best choice to write with." Fabian rests his hand on his mouth, trying to hide his smile, "However, an author by the name of Taheai Aloki was able to solve the problem by redesigning the way it was drafted. Some found this more popular than others, but the style made some conceive it to look like a star being drawn. Some came to theorise it meant it was a sign from the heavens…" I stopped as he burst out in laughter, unable to control it any longer. Finally, looking to my right, Lucy slips out of the doors, and I let out a long breath.

"Dude, she's so into you it's funny," Fabian laughs, returning to his own book. Sipping on my coffee and noting the bitter taste I promptly add sugar and cream.

"She should focus on her job," I respond, feeling eyes drilling into the side of my head. Bonnie's gaze is light, warm even, as she tilts her head looking like she's trying to unpick my brain at my reluctance to converse with other women. Fabian had always said she lingers because of me - but everyone becomes a blur to me now. In another lifetime I probably would ask her to dance, to warm my bed. But times have changed; I have changed. I fear at this rate, if I ever do see Clea again, I might end up strangling her - anything to release me of my torment of her absence. She barely knows me, not even realising she has become the entire focus of my life.

CHAPTER 31
Laurence

Hearing footsteps in our room, I blink my eyes awake from the lovely dream I had of me and Bonnie having a picnic on the back porch. I packed a basket with sandwiches, grapes and small cakes which seemed to melt in the scorching sun - the memory makes my mouth water even thinking about it. I make a mental note to recreate that with Bonnie soon, preferably with less clothes. I reach out for her beside me, but my hand only finds a warm patch where my amazing fiancée should be. Startled, I sit up, my eyes immediately drawn to her. She's standing just a few steps away, wrapped snugly in that luscious blanket she always clings to, her soft eyes meeting mine. She looks irresistibly tempting, the blanket slipping slightly to hint at her bare skin beneath as she moves.

My gaze roams over her, and a shiver runs down my spine as I take in the sight. Tilting my head, I silently plead with her to come back to bed, my eyes doing all the begging. The duvet slides down, exposing my stomach - one of her favourite features - and I can't help but smile suggestively, hoping to entice her back into my arms.

"I've got somewhere to be! Put your muscles away, you beast!" she squeaks at me, throwing the blanket at my face. I pull it away to see her retreating form, my cock standing painfully upright in my undergarments. She had been spending a lot of time with Sophie in the library yesterday, hours of research with their heads in books. I smile wistfully at the memory of her explaining the vast number of books last night that she had found, and the impending fear or needing to buy more books lingers in my mind. With the way she had lit up last night, I was half tempted to send a messenger to the house to ask them to build more shelves on the back wall.

We were given a medium-sized double room to sleep in, and I'm glad we had brought extra clothes with us for this very reason as we were able to sleep after the long day of researching and exploring the palace. It truly feels strange spending time here *socially*, as opposed to talking about business. I rub my eyes, blinking away the sleep that drags me down into the plush cushions and I absently check the clock mounted along the wall. I can just make out the start of the day, dawn just broke if I had to guess by the tinge of orange that sweeps into the room. The water splashes and trickles in the private bathing chamber attached to the room, my heart warming as Bonnie had woken up earlier today to either see Sophie again or to get back to the task at hand. I had tried to read, but each time I did, I could feel my eyelids start to close. There's only so many times a man can take being jabbed in the stomach by Fabian to realise I couldn't take any more words in those damn books. I think the only book I have ever purchased for myself was a thesaurus. Not only is it terrible, it's also terrible. Thankfully Evreux had suggested I spend some time in the training hall this morning before joining them. The need to land a few blows on that pretty face of his was too hard to pass up, so I happily obliged.

She walks back into the room wearing a cozy as fuck green sweater and loose-fitting pants, looking like a goddess.

"I'll see you later in the library?" she asks, placing a bracelet on her wrist.

"Where did you get that?" I ask curiously. It is a beautiful piece of jewellery, definitely not something I had bought her.

"Sophie thought it would look nice on me," she smiles, then sheepishly, "I don't have to keep it."

"It looks good on you," my smile creeps up on my face, enjoying the sight of her playing with the clasp of the bracelet as she bites her lip in absolute concentration. Touching my feet on the plush carpet, I stand to my full height. "I'll come find you later after the training session," I murmur in her ear as my arms wrap around her torso, my arms fitting to her body so beautifully I hum in contempt.

"That sounds perfect. I look forward to hearing all about it," she says, and with a light peck on my cheek she makes her way out of our room with a sweet smile.

Evreux is already at the training grounds when I arrive, sitting on one of the stone benches looking deep in thought, it took me longer than I had expected to find my way here from the tour yesterday that was endlessly long. I ended up asking a guard who was patrolling the area, guiding me to the underground training pit. The room is illuminated by torches, the ceiling open and bare to the elements. Fabian strolls in behind me with a sweet bread roll in his mouth, the icing dripping along his chin as he says some words that resemble something like '*Morning*'.

Evreux just smirks at him, "If you get any food on the training floor, you're eating off of it." And I wonder who had crawled up his ass today to be in such a bad mood. He stands, moving into the light - casting a creepy shadow on his face revealing dark circles under his eyes, it seems the winged male didn't sleep much last night. His eyes harden at whatever he sees on my face, the energy seeming to spread across the room, speaking of violence.

He strides towards me, biting out the words, "You're good in combat. But I was able to attack you from behind," he says, wrapping his hands in cloth, his cropped shirt protruding his muscles.

Feeling the challenge, I take off my shirt and grab the cloth too for my hands, brushing aside the rude comment and deciding to at least get one hit in to satiate my annoyance for this prick. My sandals softly brush against the floor as I move, and moving into the area, soft sand cushions my feet. The grey sand is contained by black obsidian stones, the edges a little jagged at the top and I have the sense those are weapons too, one misstep and you could easily break your neck falling on one of them. Standing in the middle of the arena, Evreux joins me, eyes never leaving mine. His jaw is set, but his eyes... there's nothing but an empty void within them. He clenches his teeth and sets his feet into position. Fabian leans his forearms on the black pillars as he links his hands together, looking almost *excited* to watch this display.

"You ambushed me last time. I will not allow you the same *privilege*," I taunt, pronouncing the last word for extra emphasis as I widen my arms at the palace we stand in, his mouth curves into a grimace but I see the underlying gleam in his eyes as he takes on the challenge.

I advance, both of us circling each other like cats. Throwing my fist forward, he dodges my blow and shifts to the side leveraging his wing for support as he kicks his leg out to my torso. I pull back at the last moment just as he adjusts his stance.

"Can you do any better than that?" he barks out, a half laugh cracking from him.

Grunting as my only response, we dance around each other for a short while. The sand kicks up into the air, the chalkiness adding to the air as it clings to my throat. His movements are loose, almost chaotic, yet purposeful as he moves. I faint left and punch with my right. He catches the movement, but he doesn't see the second one coming as I swing my right arm, hitting him square in his jaw, his head jolting back a fraction.

Oh, he looks pissed as all hell.

A shit-eating grin spreads on my face.

He cracks his neck and shakes out his hands, seeming to contemplate something. A few moments later, he touches his lips, seeing the blood now leaking out of his busted lip. I can't hide my smile at seeing the fucker bleed, he deserves more than that from the hell he put me through. Then he does something I hadn't anticipated, softly brushing his finger against his lips and sticking out his tongue to taste it. His face recentres, and his sleek body charges towards me harder this time. His punches no longer danced around mine. His mind is far away, somewhere I cannot see as I block his punches. The force pushed me back, my hands tingling from the feeling.

"Ev," Fabian says, his tone one of warning.

He keeps punching, not seeing me anymore. I wonder where he is, where his mind went. That thought lasts all but three seconds as he lands a blow in my ribs. The pain is blinding, the feeling rippling through my torso. With me momentarily dazed, another hit of his fist slams into my nose. My head pounds in a fierce rhythm just as a wall of sand hits my body, Evreux swiping his wing against the ground.

Bastard.

I blink, eyes burning from the foreign feeling. The room becomes a blur as I rub my eyes, just as his body comes charging at me. His shoulder connects with my stomach and my entire world flips upside down as I'm thrown up into the air and land on my back. All of the air is expelled out of my lungs as the sand cushions my fall. I grab his ankle and shift my arm slightly - orange fur bursts from my arm as I use my tiger-shifting strength to pull him off his feet. He slams down beside me, face smacked into the sand that now paints his face. He pushes himself upright, the muscles in his back tensing as sweat drips from his face. He stays knelt, arms and knees on the floor. His wings draped on the sand as he bows his head. Both of us pant, our lungs out of breath.

He raises his eyebrow at my arm, still in tiger form, looking weird as fuck attached to my Fae body. He stares at me for a few moments before a soft chuckle leaves his body as he stands.

Fabian walks over, extending his arm to help me up, "Dude that was awesome, I didn't know you could shift only parts of your body. I wonder if..."

"Don't finish that sentence," Evreux quips, lips full of mirth. He hands me a cup of water that I knock back in two gulps, feeling the crisp water slide down my throat. Even water tastes better in the palace.

"Athena has asked me to travel to Baskith with her," Evreux says in the silence. The statement stunned me entirely, not just the crazy topic change but the fact that this seems like he might actually want to have an honest-to-god *normal* conversation involving me.

"Don't they hate outsiders?" Fabian asks.

"Amazu believes it would be a good time to reconnect with them, maybe gain some insight if they are experiencing anything going missing also. Athena insisted she wanted to go visit her parents and requested that I join her." Evreux explains, staring at his hands. Although he does not seem plagued with the decision, if anything he speaks with us like it is final with no discussion to be had. I couldn't say I wasn't intrigued to go myself; my business didn't fare too well over that side. They don't exactly follow the laws of Thalor, but I've heard they're good people. I could easily justify hopping from tavern to tavern, hoping to find Clea working at one. It wouldn't surprise me - bartending is the kind of job you can slip into with ease if you've had experience, disappearing into the crowd when needed.

"Well, make sure to pack heavy, I was almost blown away last time," Fabian chuckles, seeming to remember a memory I had not recollected as he walks into the ring with Evreux.

"You've been to Baskith?" the question leaves my lips before I can stop myself.

"I have," he says, leaning back on the balls of his feet with a wry grin, hands gesturing animatedly as if to emphasise the danger. "Nearly froze my toes off because I packed the wrong shoes - and let's not even talk about the trousers. That was a close call with a part of me I'm very much not ready to part with." he shivered theatrically, his shoulders hunching as if he could still feel the icy bite of the wind.

"You had hovered by the fire so close I was surprised your balls hadn't burnt off," Evreux says, and a bark of a laugh breaks from my lips - as somehow this stone of a man was capable of basic humour.

"My junk still works, at least," Fabian quips, a wink my way as Evreux seems to smile slightly - a memory resurfacing just at the peak of his gaze.

I relax my arm against the cold bite of the stone as they start to parry - their movements are quick, and precise, both matching each other quite well. Where Evreux attacks in quick patterns, reckless and strong, Fabian watches the moves - especially the exposed ones he can take easily.

"Can I come?" I say, the words tumbling from my mouth with all the forethought of a rock rolling downhill. The idea feels completely unhinged even as it leaves my lips.

"No," Evreux replies curtly, his attention fixed on blocking a swing, his body shifting smoothly as he ducks low to avoid a jab.

Fabian straightens up - head tilting in confusion, "Why?"

The question is thrown about the room, and I await his response as I, too would like to know why the hell not. The room falls silent except for the muted shuffle of their movements. Then, Evreux's sharp gaze snaps to me, eyebrow raised in question. Just once, I'd like to talk to him without feeling like I'm trapped in a novel titled *Are You Dumber Than You Look?* My hands twitch, and I rub them together, stopping short of the telltale nervous habit of scratching the back of my neck.

"Business didn't go so well over the mountain, and Bonnie doesn't seem to like the cold enough for us to casually stroll on over," I say.

Fabian smirks, crossing his arms with a cocked brow. "It's not on your list for honeymoon-type destinations then?"

"Not in the slightest," I respond dryly. Evreux's gaze lingers on me, his head tilted slightly as if he's weighing something in his mind. The intensity makes my fingers twitch again, but I hold my ground.

"Who's going to sell me overpriced cheap wine?" Fabian chuckles, his grin broadening.

"I can make arrangements for my absence," I reply, my tone pointed. Though, truthfully, I'm not sure Bonnie would be thrilled about me vanishing for a month. Still, if she understood the real reasons behind it, I think I could get her on board.

"Well, when do you leave?" Fabian asks him, echoing my thoughts exactly.

"In a week or so," Evreux answers, pulling the cloth tighter with a methodical precision. "We plan to be there for a month."

"A *week*?" I blurt out, that's so *soon*.

"A whole *month*?" Fabian exclaims at the same time, his tone teetering between disbelief and amusement.

Evreux sighs, "We cannot go in blind. We must gather supplies and start communication in preparation." His words are matter of fact, aimed at me, clearly confusing my expression.

"Would Bonnie be alright with you being away for a long period?" Fabian asks me; my response is immediate, "I will discuss this with her before it is decided, with me away, she could spend more time at the palace, and I have a feeling she could do with some female companionship." It is not lost on me the hope that builds at the enjoyment Bonnie would find staying here long term. Being outside of the house and having a purpose for getting up each morning is worth more to me than anything. I could easily delegate the business trade to a few workers who had been begging for more responsibility, even Bonnie if she were to want to, and it would be good for me too to outreach to other places.

"Laurence, dude, it's dangerous over there," Fabian says, shaking his head in astonishment.

"Fine" Evreux spits out.

"Really?" my eyes widen at the sliver of hope that rises within me.

"You're both mad." Fabian says, cursing. While he's distracted, Evreux lands a soft blow to his nose, which he quickly recovers by lifting his arms up once again – the sunlight now dancing on his face.

"Athena will have to agree, but I don't see why not," he says, shrugging casually, the motion so unlike him it startles me.

The session seems to end as they exchange their goodbyes, and Evreux stalks out of the pit, hands reaching to unbind the cotton straps. I catch his arm just as he hits the door; his head snaps to me, a warning in his eyes.

"Thanks," I rasp out, the thought of getting appraisal from this man sickens me but it does not escape me that he seemed delighted at my request, even if it has been layered with the pretence of gaining more information out of me - or even my quick demise on this potential suicide mission.

"Don't mention it," he says and rips his arm free from my grip.

He stops and turns to look at the open ceiling. His legs launch him upward into the sky, a layer of sand peppering the air and choking me slightly, the only resemblance of him being in this room.

"Asshole," Fabian mutters, coughing and waving his hand to dispel the dust from the air. I do the same just as Fabian comes closer.

"Hey, I was wondering - didn't Charlotte want to visit the palace?" Fabian's tone is casual, almost idle, but his gaze lingers, searching mine for something more.

I force a light laugh. "Missing her already?" The words slip out before I can stop them, and I instantly regret it. The weight of keeping up the lie and dodging every question about Clea's whereabouts presses heavily on my mind. He chuckles, nodding his head. "Some Fae would dream of an invitation to the palace. Thought it was a no-brainer."

Just when I think I've figured him out, Evreux kept Clea's disappearance to himself then.

"True," I reply smoothly, the lie falling from my lips with practiced ease. "But she wasn't feeling well and decided to stay at the house."

Fabian simply nods again, accepting it without question.

"You, though," he grins, shaking sand from his hair, "You should probably take a bath to wash the sand off. Plus, you stink."

He laughs to himself, and I manage a chuckle, but my mind lingers elsewhere as I imagine what it would feel like travelling to Baskith.

"I've got a better idea," I say, sprinting from the room. I run for the library, grey dust flying off of my body in waves as I head for Bonnie.

CHAPTER 32
Bonnie

My thumb brushes to the next page of the book I'm reading. I had picked up an ancient book describing old mythical beasts. Its cover was cracked and faded with age; the title barely legible: *The Beasts of Forgotten Shadows*. The edges of its pages were frayed, their corners curling as though reluctant to reveal their secrets. As I reach the first section, it reads, 'Herein lies the truth of what lurks beneath.' Beneath that, a sketch of a monstrous figure emerged from the sea, its serpentine body coiled around a crumbling house by a lake. The creature had multiple sets of eyes that glowed even in black and white, and its jagged teeth rippled slightly as if it were dripping with seawater. The eyes seemed to follow me as I turned the page, but the next entry chilled me further, a small multi-limbed beast tunnelling deep beneath the ground. Its claws were gnarled and sharp, capable of slicing through solid rock and Fae flesh. The text described it as a beast of famine, said to emerge from the depths of the ground to devour entire crops, leaving nothing but destruction in its wake. It had been notoriously bad for farmers; some say you would know when it would come from the faint scratching beneath their fields right before their lands turned barren. I shuddered and glanced over my shoulder, half expecting to hear the same scratching sounds beneath my feet but shook my head at the absurdity of it, reminding myself that I'm in the grand palace library and I can't fall prey to what some had deemed childish rumours. Even so, the room was silent except from Sophie's scribbling and my own shallow breathing. She had insisted we write down anything that deemed 'useful'. I couldn't imagine how any of this was connected, but it was on the pile of texts given to us by Amazu so I couldn't complain, I had welcomed the distraction to help in any way that I could. Sophie had been reading a book on magical gifts given by birth, speaking of witchcraft and vampires that roamed the lands - I had tried to peek at her notes, but I wasn't subtle, she would shift the notepad slightly towards her when I tried. Taking a sip from my lukewarm cup of tea, my eyes scan the page for the next entry that I'm sure would keep me awake all night - it was an unfinished sketch, a dark mass swirling in black inky shadows, almost impossible to discern. The outlines of the swirl contained jagged claws, and under closer inspection - I could almost make out a hand holding strings above a small girl. My fingers began to tremble at the name "Morvath - beast not of size but in the mind." The text below warned of possession and dark coercion, making me turn the page quickly, not wanting to read any further.

"Sophie, I think I may have found something," I whisper, remembering the angle towards mind control being what they're looking for. Her head lifts up to mine as she stretches out her arm, requesting the book. I hand the heavy tomb to her, feeling the darkness and weight of those awful stories leave me immediately, happy to get rid of those words that are imprinted in my brain. Her face scrunches in thought as she reads and scribbles down more notes of hers.

"Thank you," she says softly, and I feel immediate relief at those words. I had been enjoying my time here, and feeling somewhat useful to these powerful Fae who look after Thalor gives me a sense of pride, like I am achieving something within the void I find myself slipping into.

The door cracks open, jolting me alert as my racing heart tries to calm down, just as Laurence comes barrelling in peppered in bruises and a layer of grey dust on his body. He had had the foresight to put on a shirt at least, giving respect to the palace. Fear blinds me for a shattering moment until my mind races to catch up with me as I recall his mention of training with Evreux this morning. *That* I didn't see coming. Grateful for the break Laurence is offering me, he sports me a truly wicked grin that I find just downright contagious and *adorable*.

"What the hell happened to you?" Sophie chuckles as she places the pen down on her notes.

"You should see the other guy," he says, a spark of mischief in his eyes. And with him just standing there, tall and confident, sends a surge of pride and warmth straight to my heart.

"You look half mad," I say, a smile creeping up on my face, too. "Need a break?" he asks and needing to know where his thoughts go - to dispel the horrific book I had just read; I nod my head quickly.

"Is that a yes?"

"Yes," and with that, he lifts me out of the seat as my view flips, he lifts me over his shoulder and begins to sprint out of the library doors. Grus waves at us with wide eyes, making my laughter grow even further at the absurdity we have both caused in the library.

"Save some energy for the main event," Sophie's voice booms from the distance, I can't help but laugh louder as he's practically running with me over his shoulder, the absurdity of it all making my stomach flip with excitement. We're tearing through the grand hallway of the palace, the echo of his footsteps bouncing off the marble floors, and I can't help but think how ridiculous it is. Here I am, being carted around like some prize, surrounded by all this elegance and luxury. It's such a crazy contrast - reckless but so much fun that I can't stop grinning. His laughter echoes off of the walls in a beautiful melody and he adjusts my body so I'm cradled in his arms. A few hallways and quick turns later, we reach outside the palace gates just as a large expanse of water cascades in front of us. He looks at me, eyes wild and free, "Fancy a swim, my fire?"

"You're positively mad, but yes!" With those words he leaps, both of us fall for what feels like forever - the water rushes to me quickly as we both plunge into the water. Warm water rushes up around us, my body submerging for a few heartbeats until Laurence guides me upright and I gasp, the thrill of it all surging through me and causing a laugh to bubble in my throat. Panic seeps in for a moment as I stare into the endless depths of the water, thinking earlier of the beasts from mythical legends that had swarmed lakes and dragged Fae down with claws and teeth. But looking at Laurence, the beast within him stirs gently, and I fear for the underwater beasts from his wrath - his teeth and claws are much sharper. I pull my arms up as we swim side by side to a shallow part of the lake, the water turning a shade of grey as his body washes away the sickly shades he had sported earlier. There's something so freeing about being submerged in the water, the world around us fading into the background as we float together weightless. Perching atop a smooth rock, I push the water from my eyes, Laurence doing the same as he emerges from the water. Sunlight glints off the beads of water clinging to his skin, tracing the sharp contours of his chest and arms with a radiant sheen. His intense gaze locks on me while the water trickles through his auburn hair, catching the light like molten copper. He moves with a steady, deliberate grace, each stride exuding raw strength. There's something timeless about him, like he's a god that just stepped out of a mythical book, risen from the depths to walk amongst us. The sight of him, dripping wet and utterly magnificent, steals the breath from my lungs.

"I can't believe we just did that," I gasp, the words tumbling out in uneven chunks as I struggle to catch my breath from the swim and his ability to look perfectly beautiful in any scenario he's pushed into. My eyes drift to the lake, and I'm momentarily stunned by its beauty. The water sparkles under the sun's golden rays, each ripple catching the light like scattered jewels. The soft waves lap gently against the shore, their rhythm soothing even as my heart pounds from the thrill of the jump.

Up above, I frown, seeing how small the drop actually was, thinking it was much higher at that moment and a large part of me longs to jump in again. Absently, I stick my tongue out as the saltwater drips along my upper lip, Laurence tracks the movement - his gaze darkening as he watches the movement. His eyes flicker down to my now soaked jumper, now doing little to hide my breasts as the fabric clings to the contours of my chest.

"You wicked woman, like a temptress to pull me under," he says, flicking my nose playfully. "But I do wish to discuss something important with you, and if I do not, the villagers of Thalor will get a front-row seat to your moans of pleasure," he says, gaze never wavering as he slowly sits beside me. His words send a thrill between my legs, and they open without my permission. The water swims and swirls with the movement, causing a laugh to slip from my lips. Before my thoughts waver to what exactly that would entail, my eyes find his "What is it?"

He takes a few moments to gather his thoughts, the earlier adrenaline of jumping in fades away as his demeanour shifts into a serious stance.

"In the training ring, Evreux had informed me that in a week's time, he plans to travel to Baskith with Athena," Laurence says, his calm voice echoing off the shore.

"Wow, that's a long journey. It's rather cold over there." My shoulders jerk involuntarily as if the chill of the place had reached me just from thinking about it. Laurence had once floated the idea of travelling there in search of Clea, but the thought of the two of us attempting it alone had seemed too dangerous to entertain.

"Wait. Why did you want to be outside the palace grounds to tell me this?" I ask, narrowing my eyes at him.

"I wish to go with them, and I wanted to speak with you first," he replies, his words landing like a stone in my chest. My mind spirals with questions, but only one escapes my lips: "Why?"

He dips his head, his hand pushing his wet hair from his face. "I may have exaggerated the potential for a business deal just a little too much," he admits, his tone laced with guilt. "But honestly, I think it's time we looked for her."

"This is why we're out here and not in the palace," I say, my words more of a statement than a question.

"*His Highness*," Laurence bites out the title as though it burns his tongue, "...could overhear the real intention behind my request." His voice sharpens with a rare flash of anger, an emotion that I wouldn't expect in this situation, but it burns hot in his words. He turns his head slightly, avoiding my gaze, and I catch the tension in the line of his jaw.

"What are you not telling me?" I press, leaning forward, my arms crossing in a gesture of both curiosity and unease as the water swirls around me.

"If I go with them as protection," he begins, his tone softening as he lifts his eyes back to mine, "You could visit the palace as much as you'd like to read in the library, they could even escort you there if needed. If that is what you desired."

My heart flutters for what feels like the hundredth time today just looking at him - this brave, selfless man who seems to do everything for everyone but himself.

"Do you truly wish to go?" I ask, studying him closely. Because deep down, I can't help but feel that this beautiful, selfless man rarely does anything solely for himself.

"It is," he starts, "but... I do not want to push you on this, Bonnie, but I would really love to call you my wife before I go," choking on the last word, I grasp my hand in his as I move to straddle his legs. Perching and semi-floating on his upper thighs, I take his face in my hands, the stubble scratching my thumb as I swipe it along his jaw.

"If this is what you want, we will make it happen. I love you so much Laurence, but I can't help but feel scared. We do not know a lot about their town. What if you get hurt, or never return to me?" tears paint down my face, the tears mixing with the warm saltwater on my face and dissolving into the abyss of the lake. My resolve cracks and a sob releases from my throat, what he plans to do - it strikes so much fear into me that I can't *breathe*.

"If Athena agrees to my request, there will be preparations for the week to plan it all. I promise you will be there every step of the way, and if you ever feel it's too much or you do not feel certain of the plan." he takes a deep breath, and with certainty laced in his hazel eyes, he finishes with "then I will not go, your word is final. You are to be my wife, we will approach these decisions together."

His words settle heavily on my heart, casting a flicker of light into the small shadow that lingers in the depths of my mind. I can feel, with every breath I take, that he's being honest with me. If I were to oppose it, we'd make the decision together. But the unease seeps deep into my bones, relentless and consuming, urging me to scream for him to stay, to return to our home and shut out the world. But I know in my heart that this is something he has to do.

"Okay," is all I can say, as I press my forehead to his, breathing in the scent of him.

"I know it's not the big wedding you had hoped for, all I care about is calling you my wife and spending the rest of our lives together, in whichever way we do," his words hit my soul, the smooth melody of his voice vibrating through my skin.

"I guess the books of scary monsters will have to wait, I have a wedding to plan," and I flick his nose back, a ghost of a shine appears on his eyes as I stare deep into them. Laurence has gone to such great lengths for those he loves, and this step, the ambition that leaks out of his pores is so contagious I cannot help but feel excited too.

"Before you ask, I will take care of the arrangements for my staff to look over the books for the time I am gone. Even then, you will have the final say in anything you don't feel is right. I trust you with every thread of my being."

"I promise to do right by the business, *Merlot about it,*" I say, chuckling to myself that I finally have the right time to use that phrase Clea had once said to me, with it feeling right somehow. The pain in my chest seems to ease the more I talk about her, knowing that wherever she is, I'm sure she's slinging insults at anyone who tries to cross her.

He tips his head back with a booming laugh. "That was painfully good, my fire. But we'd better get out of this saltwater soon - any longer, and the sea monsters are going to think we're pre-seasoned snacks!" he says, gnashing his teeth together near my neck.

I screech, feeling something touching my foot at the same time and hastily agree to get back inside.

"Laurence, how the heck are we going to get out of the water?" I giggle nervously, glancing up at the cliff we had so boldly jumped from earlier. There are no smooth stone steps or a wooden ladder in sight, and the thought of being stranded here forever as fish nibble on my toes sends a shiver down my spine.

Without a word, he turns to me, his expression calm as ever, and crouches slightly. "Climb on," he says, motioning for me to wrap my arms around his neck and my legs around his torso. I do as he says, my fingers now wrinkled from the time in the water, and I cling to him like my life depends on it - which, frankly, it might.

With a deep breath, Laurence launches himself out of the water, gripping the rock face like some kind of spider monkey. I shut my eyes tight, refusing to look down as he scales the cliff with an ease that borders on absurdity. My heart races, but his steady movements somehow keeps my panic at bay.

Before I know it, we're back on the footpath where we started. He hauls us both up, sets me down gently, and then shakes himself off like a drenched dog. Instinctively, I throw my arms up to shield myself, even though I'm already soaked. Without missing a beat, he takes my hand, leading me back toward the palace. My heart feels lighter than ever. With him by my side, I could do anything - even dive into monster-infested waters without a second thought.

As we walk, a wild idea takes root in my mind. I wonder where the nearest lake is to our home, because I already want to do that again. And again. Preferably with less clothes.

Eternal Threads of Time

CHAPTER 33
Amazu

Waiting in a wide-open field by the Thalor border was not how I envisioned today would unfold. I had rearranged a few meetings - reluctantly, but necessarily - for this long-overdue conversation with the leader of Drakharrow. At dawn, I took a horse from the stables and slipped quietly out of the library, careful not to draw attention to myself. It felt important to make an appearance among my subjects before departing, though the act was half-hearted. Athena hadn't noticed my restless glances toward the clock, my fingers drumming against the edge of the desk. By now, nervous impulses were commonplace, as we all lived under the same constant shadow of unease.

The wall of Drakharrow loomed in the distance, rising high into a grey, brooding sky. Its dark, craggy surface was unwelcoming. An ugly scar across the land and a brutalist structure that defied any notion of beauty. Even the clouds seemed dimmer here, as though the wall itself leached light from the heavens. My gaze lingered on the black gates, where weathered blue banners snap in the wind, each emblazoned with the gaping maw of a dragon. The painted beast's glassy wings shimmer faintly, giving the illusion of movement, a trick of the light that never fails to unsettle me.

Those gates were the only way in or out of the land - a stark reminder of both protection and imprisonment. Standing before them, I couldn't shake the prickling sensation at the back of my neck, as though unseen eyes were fixed on me from atop the battlements. The guards remained hidden, but their low voices drifted along the wind, indistinct murmurs that set my teeth on edge.

The silver-haired brute was twenty minutes late and my patience was thinning with each passing second, my boot tapping impatiently against the grass. He kept me waiting - as if his time were more valuable than mine.

Finally, the gates groaned to life, the sound a deep, resonant boom that echoed across the field. The chains rattled and thudded against the stone as the gates creaked open, their movements slow and ponderous, worn down by time and neglect. The metallic clatter carried a sense of foreboding - a tired sound, weary from years of misuse, much like the land itself.

And yet, here I stood, waiting.

And then, there he is, strolling out as if he owns not just this place but every whisper of grass he steps onto. Even now, the tall grass sways in the breeze, the sound carrying his voice - not that I would need that, I could hear his order to open the gates only moments before they did. I had opted to stand quite a bit of a distance from the towering walls to give the sense of privacy, but the thought of Caldris needing to walk an extra distance, as I had to meet him here, filled me with silent delight.

"I didn't think you'd show," Caldris says, his voice sharp and sardonic. He finally reaches me and stands rigid, his broad shoulders squaring as his piercing purple-ish eyes scan me with barely concealed disdain. His hands hung loose at his sides, but there was an edge to his posture, as if ready to strike even without a weapon to hand. I maintain my distance, knowing he could cause so much pain and death with a flick of his wrist.

"I do when it concerns the safety of my land," I reply evenly, my eyes narrowing ever so slightly. My golden robes glinted faintly in the light, a stark contrast to his somber black tunic lined with silver. I tried to maintain the calm expression I had always worn, but the strain of my long journey was beginning to show, betraying the simmering irritation etched across my features.

"And what exactly do you want?" Caldris asks, tilting his head slightly. His voice carrying a mockery I would not accept from anyone else as his jaw tightens, hinting at the effort it takes to keep his temper in check.

"I want peace, as do my people. Resign your act of war so we can be done with it." My tone attempts to remain calm and deliberate, but I cannot stop my hands from squeezing painfully at the notion and destruction this man has caused to my people.

Caldris scoffs as he leans back, the corner of his mouth twitching in a humourless smirk. "I already did. I left, didn't I? And yet, you had to drag me back here." He shifts his weight, his boots stepping on the wet grass, the movement was simple - but seemed deliberate somehow, his stance now displaying guarded irritation.

"My sources have found your men in my town, spying," I shoot back, my voice dropping an octave as the rising anger surfaces within me. Evreux had caught one of them, but he had taken his own life before giving any information. The barbaric nature Caldris drills into his soldiers sickens me to my core, each holding so much information they would rather die than give it up. Alongside that, Caldris had knowingly spilled blood in my home in search of something. For what, I couldn't care less, but the lingering weight of the power that is Morvath still perplexes me. If he had known about the attack, and the reasons for it, he could grasp this power and take it for his own.

"Come now," Caldris drawls, waving a dismissive hand. "I don't care about your pathetic excuse for a town."

"Then why slaughter innocent people and my soldiers whenever you had the chance?" I press, taking a step forward.

"What is it that you want, Amazu?" he asks again, irritation seeping into his tone, the way he addresses me feels mocking - a small lilt in the pronunciation, I keep my eyes hard and set on his face as not to betray the rising anger that comes in relentless waves at being in his proximity.

"Call off your spies," I demand, bringing the full weight of the words to the front of the conversation. If they were to linger any further, information of the *Spring Ball* events may surface, and the name of Morvath would drift about before they were excused, there's no telling how much information had been spilled already.

"That's a tall order," he replies with a slight shrug, his eyes rolling ever so slightly. "I've already paid for them."

"That's not my problem," I counter, my lips pressing into a thin line.

"Well then, let's be done with it," he snaps, gesturing broadly at the empty field. "What a riveting conversation you've pulled me into."

Ignoring the jab, my tone shifts to a colder one. "Please, enlighten me as to why your men linger here."

"There is something here that I had lost," Caldris says, his voice turning softer, almost wistful as his eyes search for something behind me I cannot see.

"Care to elaborate?" I ask, eyebrow hitching up.

"It is none of your concern," he snaps, his tone abruptly harsh once more, hitting a nerve.

"It is when it's *my* people who are being threatened"

"She is not yours!" Caldris barks, his eyes flaring with raw emotion. My lips twitch into a slow, mocking smile as he took the bait I laid out.

"Ah, so this is all for a woman. You should have said so at the beginning. We have plenty of whorehouses if that's what you desire."

"Watch your mouth," he snarls, his fists clenching. I wouldn't be lying if I said that hitting that nerve inside of him didn't bring me a spark of immense joy, he had attacked my people and could do so again if provoked. And yet, I just can't help myself with taunting him further.

"That's it, isn't it? The only reason you grace this part of the Kingdom - the reason for your tantrum in my market," my smile becomes wicked now.

"I didn't realize '*our*' had become '*my*,'" Caldris sneers, his tone dripping venom. "Forget about your precious wife already?" that makes me pause, a dull-witted move I hadn't corrected in time.

"Let us stop this nonsense," I say, exhaling sharply, annoyed by his quick perception. "Unlike you, I actually have a wife to return to."

With those words, I hit my mark as Caldris visibly bristles - his shoulders stiffening as his eyes narrow slightly.

"I will call off my men," he says, his voice dangerously calm, "and even open my gates for trade if you grant me one thing." He finishes, raising a single finger to me.

"And what could your cold, dead heart possibly want?" I ask, my voice dripping with sarcasm. I know exactly why he attacked the market, two women that were associated with Laurence spotted running away from him? It was easy to connect the dots, especially seeing how powerful Clea was at the *Spring Ball*. The only unknown I will admit not comprehending is why *her*, I can admit she's powerful, but is she worth the risk of starting a war? Caldris had spent countless resources to reinforce his barriers and cut off as much communication he could between our lands - it seems Clea is quite a prize he wishes to get. Unfortunately for me, Athena hadn't gained any information from our new guests, my patience wears too thin - but a good leader knows when to bide their time.

"Bring her to me," Caldris says, his gaze darkening with the finality of his words.

"Who?" I ask, feigning ignorance.

"Don't play dumb with me," he growls. "I know she lives within your lands, finding her in your filthy market only confirmed it. Bring Clea to me."

"What is it about this woman that warrants such a high reward?" a small part of me curious if he'll actually spill this secret he's kept locked tight. This woman has single-handedly crashed into our lives and somehow nestled her way into Evreux's mind.

"That is none of your concern," he bites back.

"Then answer me this: why would I willingly hand over an innocent woman who resides under the protection of my land to you?" I ask, my words heavy as I push the protective leader angle. If it were to become known that a villager of my land had been given away for my own personal gain, it could tarnish my reputation.

"I will give you everything you've ever wanted," Caldris says, his tone laced with a dark promise. For a moment I lean in, seeing what the brute could potentially offer for the price of a mere woman.

"Power. Virelith will be yours and yours alone."

"You would give up your land to us for a woman?" I ask in a mocking tilt, my disbelief evident as I feel my eyebrows creep up on my forehead.

Caldris's lips curl into a cold smile. "You misunderstand. I would renounce my throne to you alone. And your dear wife can continue her wifely duties as she sinks to her knees before the new King of Virelith."

"You must be certifiably insane to think I would ever agree to those terms" my voice barks out, a humourless laugh escaping me.

"Everyone has a price," Caldris said smoothly. "And that is mine. All you have to do is bring her to me, and it will all be yours."

CHAPTER 34
Bonnie

I stroll through the halls, my feet heavy, feeling the weight of Laurence's absence. He had left just a week ago with Athena and Evreux, he had refused the furs to wear to bore the harsh biting cold – he has his own after all. I turn over the wedding ring that I now proudly wear on my ring finger - a constant reminder of the love we both share and the commitment I will always have for the man who flipped my world upside down. He has undeniably been the one who has always stood by my side and accepted the parts of me that I could not. As I roam the long hallways, the creeping sensation of homesickness finds its way into my heart. The palace no longer feels as exciting as it once did, and I know in my heart that it was because of Laurence - the light in my life that makes every room a home as long as I am with him. But now, with him away, I find myself longing to step into my own library as opposed to the massive one I have become accustomed to.

Their meetings about the trip had bored me senseless, but Laurence had seemed so overjoyed about the prospect of going to Baskith which grew more and more every day. As much as I longed to go with him, the cold weather aside, I have a good feeling about it. Once preparations were complete, we arranged a meeting with Athena and Amazu - considering they were the Fae responsible for upholding not only the safety but the law within Thalor, getting married to Laurence had seemed so easy it was laughable. If we had arranged the marriage without the help of the palace, we would have had a variety of hoops to jump through to attain a representative. But considering Laurence had offered to join Athena on her quest, she was so thrilled at the idea and as a form of *repayment,* she married us the next day. I can almost imagine the shock that would register on Clea's face once she knew how easy it was for us to get married, and in the palace, no less. Their kindness had warmed my heart, but it didn't stop the barrage of tears that threatened to fall when Laurence and I stood before Athena, my eyes had roamed the room for her blonde hair and wicked smile. A piece of her was with us though, a hidden secret I kept to myself as I had lined my bouquet with bright fuchsia and pinkish flowers peppered into the design. I clutched the floral arrangement so close to my heart as I looked into his eyes and recited the lawful words that bound us together.

    I continue to walk past the guards stationed at every main door. Their expressions are warm, offering me kind smiles as I pass. Sophie had once told me that if you got too close to a guard, they would instinctively back away to maintain distance, their vigilance so strong to the palace wishes for the safety of the leaders and those who reside in it. She had once continued stepping towards a guard in an act of *boredom* and the poor guard ended up in the market square at the end of the palace pathway. The memory makes me chuckle softly, with a layer of unease from the punishing prank, as I continue on my way. The guards open the doors for me in silence, their movements smooth and practiced. My stomach growls, cutting through my thoughts, and I make a quick detour to the kitchens.

There, I snatch up a handful of pastries - some for me and some for Sophie; she's eating for two now. She loves the chocolate ones, while I prefer the sweet cherry candied fruit. I pile them into a small basket, feeling rather sneaky like I'm stealing them from the kitchen.

Athena had reassured us during our first dinner here that we could help ourselves with any food or wine aside from the planned meals, but sneaking these pastries fills me with a rare sense of playful rebellion, a feeling I haven't enjoyed in months.

With my arms full, I lean my back against the heavy library doors, using my weight to push them open. The old wood groans in protest before giving way, revealing the quiet sanctuary within. Sunlight streams through the towering windows, illuminating the empty room in golden light. I slip inside, the basket tucked securely in my grip and shut the doors behind me.

As always, my eyes are drawn to the massive bookcase that dominates the room. Yet, despite the beauty of this place, I can't help but long for the familiarity of my own red sofa back home.

As I step into the room, my eyes wander to a small book left on our table.

That's odd.

I remember Sophie, Fabian and I had taken extra care in putting away all of our books before dinner was served. My gaze roams the room again, confirming there was definitely no one here with me, someone must have come in earlier. Taking a closer look, the book is strange. The front cover is bright green with a smooth cover, the glossy texture is odd - it is not painted or drawn on like the other books I know. The gleaming white pages make it look untouched, unnaturally white in this light; I don't think I have even seen pages so *white* before. I pick it up with my spare hand, noticing the name of the author 'Tracy Hill", as I turn the book over, feeling the weight of it in my hand. Titled *'Temporal Gateways: Exploring the Myth and Theories of Portals and Beings from Outer Space'.* My eyebrows shoot up my forehead, where did this come from? Sophie will be pleased, this seems to be what she was looking for. As I go to place it down, a simple square of paper lies face down on the table that I hadn't noticed. I reach with my hand to turn it over and as I do, my entire world crashes. Pastries are forgotten as the basket of croissants drops and bounces on the table, the flakes crumble and roll to the floor. This page, it looks like a painting, like someone took a still portrait of an exact moment with clear clarity. The painting shows a woman with blonde hair sitting on a long metal structure in a field with snow dotting the chair she is sitting in. Everything about the painting seems otherworldly, the details so thoroughly painted, but the woman in the centre... I will never forget that face. Clea smiles up at me, her hand covering half of her face as she wears a thick jacket with fur adorning the shoulders. I don't need to see it in full to recognise her, the scar on her wrist gives it away. Time seems to freeze, my breath coming in rapid pants as I hold the paper in my hands. She's wearing different clothes, and her hair has been cut shorter. But she's *alive*. My hand clasps over my mouth, the same moment the door creaks open.

"I got us some breakfast!" Sophie announces, seeming to have the same idea as me. I quickly tucked the painting of Clea in my dress. She comes bounding in "Are you alright?" she says, her eyes flickering to the pastry scattered on the floor.

She gasps at the book now haphazardly discarded on the desk, her eyes seem to light up at the title with the same spark of curiosity she gets when writing down notes in her book. Her hands move instinctively, shaking with excitement, like some golden treasure she was waiting for. "This is... incredible. This is what we have been searching for, well parts of it." she says, flickering her gaze to mine for a moment. "This seems too good to be true." Her hands hold the book in an iron grip as she turns to me fully, "I need to bring this to them, as if they just left before we found this," she says, chuckling to herself.

"It just appeared when I came in, I do not understand how," I try to explain, thankful the shock on my face is masked by the book contents. The piece of paper jammed down my chest, feeling hot against my skin. Thankfully with her distracted, she does not see my hands shaking with excitement at the new piece of information I have stored with me. I've got to get home once Laurence returns; this tiny painting could be the information we need. Regardless, the background had been rather strange, it was definitely not one I recognise and cannot be from Drakharrow as she had been smiling slightly. The only other place could be in Baskith, where Laurence is, she had been dressed in warm clothing and snow wasn't common in the larger villages of Thalor. I want to rush home so I can tell him everything I have found, I'm sure that once he sees this - he may know where this was created, maybe he has sat on this very bench and could be so close to her without realising it.

It didn't take long for the others to come find us in the library, I sit at the table - my knee bouncing relentlessly, it would be rather rude to leave without saying goodbye. Amazu seems delighted at the book contents as his eyes greedily soak up the contents of the book, clearly the book contained the information they had been after from the strange magic that had been appearing in their Kingdom. Sophie continues to read a short extract from the book as I take a bite out of the plain croissants she had brought through, the pastry mixing with the butterflies in my stomach. The mangled and broken ones I discarded now cleaned up erasing my earlier moment of inner turmoil.

"So, this person is insane?" Fabian quips at the book, laughing without humour.

"This feels important somehow, and don't use that language, she's clearly mentally disturbed. What is a human, or an alien?" she asks herself - my mind also leaning in that direction, the author seems to use strange words I've never heard of. It seems this is deeper than I had anticipated.

I'm glad I'm on this side of the table at least, too messy.

"This is brilliant, can I ask you to read this cover to cover?" Amazu asks her, he turns to me slowly, arms clasped together as a pleased smile grows on his face.

"I want to express my gratitude for the time you've spent here at the palace. It has been a pleasure getting to know the remarkable woman Laurence has spoken so fondly of. It seems we have gathered the information we sought, and as such, your presence in the library is no longer necessary. You are, of course, welcome to remain in the accommodations provided, though I believe it may be best for you to return home for now. Rest assured, both you and Laurence will always be welcome at the palace, and we look forward to seeing you at future meetings by his side." I can only smile in return, as I had been waiting to speak with him for this very reason. I stand quickly, my hand outstretched as I shake his and say my goodbyes to Amazu along with Fabian and Sophie as I make my way up to the spare room we had been sleeping in, my feet light as I battle the impulse to skip and twirl about. I pack quickly, and sweet talk my way into taking the horse Evreux had used that awful day months ago. Striding on top of the horse, with my bags tightly secured, I lift my face up to the sky and smile as I start my journey home.

Chapter 35
Amazu

I turn to Fabian just as a perimeter soldier informs me of Bonnie's departure. With a subtle nod, I acknowledge the messenger and gesture for Fabian to continue. Between us rests the Verdialith Stone - a deep green artifact bestowed as a wedding gift from Athena's parents, originating from Baskith. But this is no mere trinket; the stone is veiled in legend, its presence carrying the gravity of ancient lore. It is said that those who hold the Verdialith may commune with the dead - beings from a realm beyond mortal comprehension, a place we theorise to be the land of the departed. The stone seems to hum with its own quiet power, its very existence demanding both reverence and caution. It had been locked away for centuries in my personal collection, just waiting for the perfect moment to be used.

Before me lies the newly uncovered book that Sophie and Bonnie discovered, its pristine pages brimming with secrets written in strange, unfamiliar script. I find myself quietly grateful that Bonnie departed soon after the discovery, leaving no room for suspicion. What lies within these pages is ours to uncover - a privilege we now hold.

The text speaks of lands unconquered, places I have never seen nor heard of. The pages themselves are strange, the pale parchment unlike any I've encountered before, and the images within - fixed like paintings frozen in time - seem to belong to a world far removed from our own. It feels as though the book, much like the stone, carries with it whispers of distant realms, waiting to reveal their mysteries to those bold enough to look beyond the veil.

My eyes drift to the book again, reading the first page: *"Gateways seem like voodoo, but stranger things have happened to this fucked up world. What if portals and aliens were real? What would you do if a random woman just appeared in your bedroom, looking as confused as you did with your hand in a box of cereal and the other down your pants."* we all look at each other in bemusement, the words are strange and foreign to me. Clearly another work of fiction.

"I have seen a Portal up close, they can appear in multiple colours and can stretch so wide that a human could walk through. But would they be the same coming back out? The Government have tested on humans before, Area 51 containing Earth's hidden truths from us. Look at the Greada Treaty and reported alien abductions. With the advance in Artificial Intelligence nothing is impossible, it seems...."

The language is crude, laced with a casual indifference toward the mention of other species - beings from a world far removed from our own. The words jolt me, a stark reminder that what lies within this book is both foreign and unsettling. Yet as I read it for the first time, I knew with absolute certainty that the Verdialith Stone, long shrouded in myth, would one day prove its worth. That day, it seems, has finally come.

The atmosphere in the room shifts the moment Fabian approaches the Verdialith Stone, his eyes gleaming with anticipation. His affinity for magic has long been a quiet blessing within the palace walls, from reinforcing protective barriers to uncovering hidden artifacts buried deep within its halls. His contributions, though understated, have been invaluable.

He shakes out his hands, a practiced motion meant to steady his focus, before closing his eyes and taking a steadying breath. His fingers graze the dark surface of the Verdialith, and the stone responds instantly - pulsing under his touch, a faint glow rippling across its surface like a heartbeat. With a slow, deliberate exhale, Fabian gently caresses the stone, muttering Sophie's name. The air in the room seems to tighten around us, anticipation mounting with each passing second. The Verdialith lifts from the table in a fluid motion, its roughness catching the faintest glimmer of light as it begins to spin lazily in the air. The quiet hum of its rotation deepens, growing louder, resonating through the room with an almost living presence.

The energy shifts further - colder, heavier. My breath mists in front of me, the sudden chill creeping into my bones as I watch, transfixed. The stone tilts slightly on its axis, spinning faster, each rotation imbued with purpose. Then, without warning, Sophie's voice breaks through the vibrating silence.

"Hello?"

My gaze snaps to Fabian, and we share a brief glance of confirmation, a flicker of satisfaction passing between us. The stone descends with a resounding thud, settling back onto the table as though exhausted from its task.

It worked.

But the true challenge still lies ahead.

Turning my attention to the book, I study the strange text scrawled across the back cover. A string of numbers followed by peculiar words: "*If you find any strange bumps in the night or find yourself getting probed, get in touch!*" The meaning eludes me, the phrases foreign and perplexing, yet unmistakably an invitation. Beneath the text, the book's origin is printed clearly: York, England.

Fabian rubs his hands together briskly, warming them before reaching for the Verdialith once more. There's no hesitation this time. His movements are purposeful, precise, and his voice rings out with unwavering command as he repeats the ritual.

"Verdialith Stone, please contact Tracy Hill, located in York, England."

The response is immediate.

The stone lifts again, but this time with a startling urgency. It spins faster - far quicker than before – spinning in a blur of motion. The quiet hum grows into a deep, resonant drone, vibrating through the floor beneath my feet.

Then, the room erupts.

Pages of the open book snap to life, flapping furiously as though caught in an unseen tempest. Loose papers lift from the table and spiral into the air, drawn into the stone's chaotic pull. Small objects - ink pots, quills, even the chairs - rattle violently before rising into the whirling storm.

The wind builds, howling through the chamber like a restless spirit, tugging at curtains and battering the walls. The lamps flicker wildly, their flames casting erratic shadows that stretch and distort across the room. The very air feels charged, thick with a strange energy that crackles against my skin, each prickle a reminder of the ancient power we've unleashed.

And then, just as abruptly as it began, the chaos ceases.

The stone pulses in place, a deep, steady rhythm, now throbbing with a vivid green light. It hovers there as though considering - thinking.

Fabian and I exchange a glance, neither daring to speak. We simply watch in silence as the Verdialith lingers in its quiet contemplation, waiting to reveal what lies on the other side of the veil.

"Ouch, what the hell was that?" a soft feminine voice comes through the stone, along with birds chirping in the distance.

"Hello, am I speaking with Tracy Hill?" I ask, my voice remaining calm, even as my pulse thrums with the energy.

"What the fuck is that voice, oh my god, I'm going crazy just like Charlotte said."

"My name is Amazu, ruler of Thalor, I heard you are the author of the book that speaks of portals and time travel?" I say, pronouncing each word as clearly as I can.

"Woah, hold up, is this some weird prank - that place sounds made up. Wait! Are you aliens!" She says, the green light of the stone pulses with each word spoken, showing the frantic nature of her voice.

The connection crackles faintly as the voice on the other end sharpens, cutting through the lingering hum of the Verdialith Stone. I keep my tone measured, my words steady despite the strangeness of what's in front of me.

"I am unfamiliar with the specifics of what you speak," I begin, choosing my words carefully. "But we have encountered events similar to the portals you describe in your writings. Your knowledge could prove invaluable. I would be honoured to invite you to my home for further discussion."

There is a pause, and then her voice returns - sharp, skeptical, and dripping with mistrust.

"I'm not going to your house; you could be a *murderer!* If you even exist at all."

The accusation is biting, though not unexpected. I keep my composure, willing calm into my response.

"I assure you, I am very real," I reply evenly. "There is much we must discuss. However, I do not know your precise location and am therefore unable to send a carriage to retrieve you. Would you be able to travel to the palace in Thalor, within the Kingdom of Virelith?"

The silence that follows stretches uncomfortably, broken only by a burst of incredulous laughter from her end.

"Wait, wait... Kingdom?" She blurts, her disbelief palpable. "This is so strange,"

The deflation in my chest is subtle but undeniable. She sounds utterly unhinged - how someone of her disposition managed to pen a book of such importance is a mystery in itself.

"Right," she continues, voice dripping with sarcasm. "I'll consider it. You know, after I check my brain for worm-like parasites or whatever this is."

Despite the absurdity of her words, I remain composed.

"Thank you," I say, bowing slightly toward the stone. "Please, make your way here at your earliest convenience. Your insight could prove vital."

Her response is hesitant, almost begrudging.

"Uh... okay?" The word hangs in the air, more a question than a confirmation.

Without further warning, the Verdialith descends with a heavy thud, settling back onto the table. Its glow fades slowly, leaving behind a muted pulse that mirrors the strange encounter we've just endured.

For a moment, neither of us speaks. The room feels still, save for the lingering chill left in the stone's wake. Whatever door we've just opened, it's clear there's no closing it now.

Acknowledgements

First off, thank you so much for reading my book! I hope you enjoyed stepping into the world of Virelith as much as I loved writing these scenes. These stories have been living rent-free in my head for years, looping on repeat night and day, and the only way to quiet them was to get them down on paper. With the help and support of my incredible friends and family, I finally managed to string all those words together into a story I'm genuinely proud of.

A huge thank you to my amazing husband, Luke, who's been with me every step of the way. He listened to hours upon hours of my rambling about characters born in the chaotic mess of my brain, nodding along even when I'm pretty sure he had no idea what I was talking about. Your love and patience made this possible - thank you for always cheering me on.

To my brilliant beta readers - Eloise, Carelynn, Kim, and Mairéad - thank you for your sharp eyes, honest feedback, and for telling me (nicely) when something just wasn't working. Your suggestions and insights helped me shape this story into something far better than it started. A big shoutout also goes to my professional mentor, Maria, who not only gave me valuable advice but constantly asked for updates and matched my excitement about this book's release. Your enthusiasm kept me going when I doubted myself.

I also owe a massive thank-you to the incredible writers and readers out there who inspired me to keep going. BookTok, you absolute legends - you gave me more than just endless TBR lists. Your tips, insights, and empowering words helped me step away from the doom-scrolling (okay, mostly) and back to the keyboard, even on the harder days.

A heartfelt thanks to the fantastic team at Authors Solution - you turned my dream into reality and made the publishing process a joy. Working with you has been truly delightful.

This is my first published novel, and I'm already excited to grow my skills and explore where these characters will go in the next installment. If you've made it this far in the

acknowledgements, I applaud your dedication because, let's be real, I usually skip this part too. As a little reward for sticking around, Clea will definitely be back for the next book as her story is far from over. And with that, I'll leave you with a question that's been haunting Evreux every waking moment: Where did she go?

See you in the next one.

Alice

Printed in Great Britain
by Amazon